Rachel L. Schade

Castle of Dusk and Shadows

- A Fae of Brytwilde Novel -

RACHEL L. SCHADE

CASTLE of DUSK and SHADOWS

- A FAE OF BRYTWILDE NOVEL -

DRAGON SHADOW
PUBLISHING

ISBN: 979-8-9876059-0-5

Cover by MoorBooks Design

Map and interior formatting created with Canva

www.rachelschadeauthor.com

For the fatherless daughters:
Yes, we're strong enough.

ALSO BY RACHEL L. SCHADE

Silent Kingdom Series

Silent Kingdom
Forsaken Kingdom
Broken Kingdom

Cursed Empire Series

Empire of Dragons
Empire of Traitors
Empire of Monsters
Empire of Ruins

MAP OF

WILLOWBARK

ASHWOOD

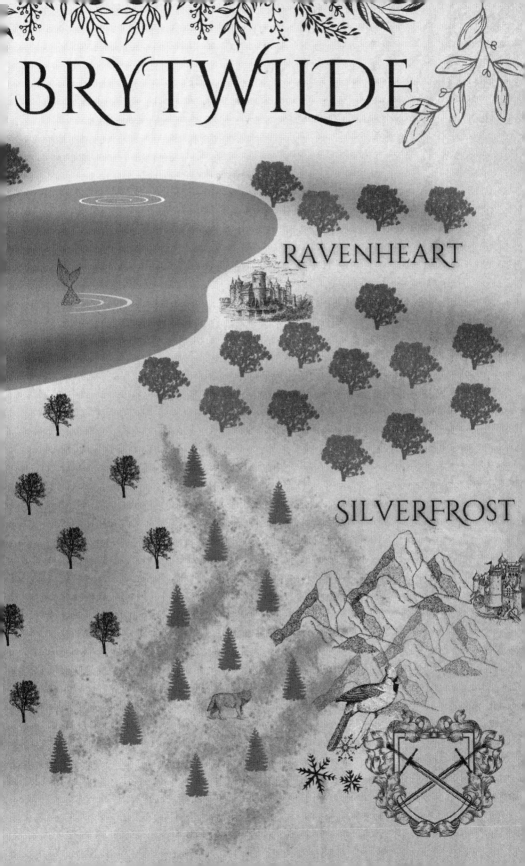

BRYTWILDE

RAVENHEART

SILVERFROST

CHAPTER ONE

Insistent rapping on the front door startled me from a restless sleep. At first, I thought it was the pounding of my own broken heart, reverberating in my head as I tossed and turned through my haunted dreams. But the sound only grew louder, until I cracked open my eyes to find my older sister Grace already sitting up in bed, the silver moonlight pooling through our window framing her golden hair like a halo.

"Elle?" Grace's voice was no more than a rasp in the darkness as she called to me, not realizing I was already awake. As I sat up, she swallowed, voicing the same thought that had flared to life in my mind. "It's time. Isn't it?"

I merely cast her a look, hoping my expression offered comfort. There was nothing to say.

Throwing back the bedcovers, I seized my dressing gown and blearily trailed Grace down the creaking staircase toward the front hall. Several dark forms—two of my sisters and our mother—gathered behind our maid Hannah, who tossed one uncertain glance over her shoulder, her face pale, before yanking open the front door.

"I have a message for Mrs. Blackford and her daughters," a smooth voice on the other side of the entryway announced without preamble. I glimpsed bright clothes and a large envelope with scrolling font before the stranger turned away.

Hannah closed the door and turned to us all, the envelope held aloft in her shaking hands. "M-Mrs. Blackford, ma'am."

Mother stepped forward, lifting her candle to peer at the writing. "He was a fae messenger, wasn't he, Hannah?" she asked, squinting at the envelope with an inscrutable expression.

Speechless, Hannah merely nodded, turning the envelope so we could see the wax seal and its symbol: a wild tree with empty branches covering a full moon.

Mother glanced up at Grace and me, where we were still huddled on the staircase, and then at Isabel and Bridget, who clung to one another in the hallway. "Wake up Maggie, girls, and meet me in the parlor."

My fear melted into anger as I followed Grace back up the steps toward Maggie's room. Out of us five girls, she was the only one who had her very own space, which suited her just fine, as she preferred to keep to herself. "Did they just summon you to your own wedding in the *middle of the night?*" I whispered. "How dare they!"

Grace glanced at me, brow furrowed. "I doubt that is a message about a wedding quite yet. They probably want to meet us all and see how I've turned out. Likely it's a ball invitation."

I gritted my teeth and swallowed back the urge to scoff aloud. "In the middle of the night," I repeated.

Grace shrugged. "We were always told the fae have a flair for the dramatic. I suppose if one is a magical, immortal being, one doesn't need to keep regular hours?" She frowned in thought. "Maybe they don't even sleep at all."

"I don't like it," I said, and Grace sighed, pausing outside of our sister's room to take my hands in hers. I was startled to find that, though her tone was level and her expression calm, her hands were cold and trembling. So she *was* nervous, after all.

For nearly as long as Grace had been alive, she'd been betrothed to the fae queen's son. It was an arrangement that granted us security upon Father's death. As a family of only daughters, all our possessions, including the house, would go to Father's nearest male heir, a cousin we had never met. When Grace married the fae prince, the royal family would give us a home. We would want for nothing—our every need provided for within their grand castle. Or so they claimed.

Grace had turned twenty-one last week, and Father had died only a month ago, after his horse had thrown him. Apparently, word had finally spread to the fae. Honestly, we'd expected Grace to wed the prince on her eighteenth birthday, even with Father still alive, but that milestone had come and gone. But they wanted her now, a wife that could bear their crown prince's heirs.

Now, with her arranged marriage to an unknown fae looming nearer than it ever had, it was, unsurprisingly, Grace who was comforting *me*. And I felt like a fool for it, even as I held back my threatening tears. "I know," my older sister said gently, pulling me into an embrace. "But now we don't need to worry about being thrown out of the house. The fae will give us all a home. You'll all be there at the castle with me."

The proclamation thundered in my ears, more terrible than comforting. We'd grown up on tales about the fae and their greedy, bloodthirsty ways. How could we ever call a place among them our home and truly feel safe?

As my sister and I pulled apart, we studied one another for one long, quiet moment, letting a hundred silent confessions of fear pass between us in the narrowing of our eyes, the set of our jaws. I could read Grace better than anyone. She would never admit it out loud, but she was just as afraid and upset as I was.

But we had also grown up hearing about the fae laws:

Only fae could possess and wield magic, unless a mortal was gifted a portion of their power or a charm; being a mortal woman came at the risk of being chosen as a bride for the fae; and—in everything—there was no denying the fae. We powerless humans were at the mercy of their whims.

For all my twenty years, I had lived securely in the mortal town of Riverton. The edge of the forest was an invisible line I'd known never to cross, one that divided our world from theirs. Of course, there were half-fae who lived in our town, and occasionally fae or their human messengers ventured into our world, but I'd relished a sense of safety. A sense, however misguided, of being untouchable.

Now, with the possibility of having to make our home in their woodland kingdom sooner than later, every rebellious act I'd ever committed weighed on me. If Father were only here...

But even Father had agreed to Grace's betrothal, because he wasn't immortal and knew his limitations. For all the times he'd secretly taught me about magic, for every conversation we'd had about the injustice of the fae lording their wisdom and power over us, he had been bound to them and their laws as surely as the rest of us were. He'd been forced to promise his family to them for our own survival.

At last, I squeezed my eyes shut and nodded, not wanting to fuel my sister's fears even more.

After all, she was the one who had to marry a fae and produce heirs with him. Since fae women were often infertile, the fae frequently relied upon arranged unions like Grace's to continue their lines. Especially when it came to their royalty, who, shockingly, didn't want to rule forever and longed to have offspring to pass on their crowns and responsibilities to.

If the prince's magic ran strongly enough in his blood, most children born from his and Grace's marriage would be fae. Some might be half-fae or fully human, but it was almost guaranteed that my sister would be raising a future ruler of Brytwilde.

I suppressed the urge to cringe. In their world, I might be subjected to the dangerous whims of immortal beings known for their careless attitude toward us humans, but I wouldn't be forced into a loveless marriage. I wouldn't be expected to give birth to fae and raise them to behave like their father. I wouldn't have to smile and pretend. I wouldn't be married to a cruel kingdom as well as its brutal prince. My choices would be my own.

Or so I hoped.

In the parlor, Mother reposed near the flickering hearth while Bridget and Isabel curled up on the couch across from her, whispering and giggling as if this were all a joke to them. I supposed I shouldn't have begrudged them this small portion of happiness, not after these long weeks of mourning. It was the first time I'd heard them laugh since Father's death. But still, it hurt. I hated that they viewed the fae as magical and captivating beings, sometimes brushing aside how dangerous they could be. While Mother had emphasized the fae's dangerous side to Grace, Maggie, and me—as her three oldest children—she'd coddled my two younger sisters, as if hating to instill fear in them. I worried that her choice to diminish the risks of living in Brytwilde would do more harm than good. Sometimes I was convinced Isabel and Bridget merely saw our move as a chance to be swept away into a new world of magic and ballgowns.

Behind me, Maggie sniffed derisively and found an armchair to sink into in the corner, her posture stiff. Ever since her eighteenth birthday, she'd taken on a more formal attitude, as if trying to distance herself from

Bridget and Isabel's girlish ways. But when Isabel had only turned fifteen this past summer, and Bridget was only a year her senior, I found it easy to forgive them. They were perhaps sillier than Grace or Maggie or I had ever been, but they were still quite young.

I joined Grace on the floor between the couch and Mother's seat, too restless to want to sit further away when I wanted to know everything.

"Now that they're here, read it, please!" Bridget begged Mother, clasping her hands dramatically. "Did they invite us to the castle?"

It was almost startling to see Mother in her white nightgown and robe, when all her day clothes were in mourning black. She sat up straighter, lifting a letter opener from the side table and slicing open the thick, creamy envelope. My pulse throbbed in my ears, threatening to drown out all other sounds.

Thankfully, Mother's voice was loud and clear as she read. "Queen Griselda Ashwood, our Illustrious Ruler, requests the presence of the Blackford family at her upcoming Autumnal Feast, to be held at the Ashwood castle on the eve of October second, beginning precisely at sunset."

For a long moment, Mother stared blankly at the letter, her expression inscrutable, her pale blue eyes distant. The fire snapped in the hearth, and my breath seemed to echo loudly in my own ears. Even Bridget and Isabel remained uncharacteristically still, as if the truth of our situation was finally settling over them. At last, my older sister stirred beside me.

"Mother? Is that it?" Grace asked.

Mother stood, crumpling the letter swiftly and tossing it into the fire, watching the edges brown and crisp as it slowly turned to ash. "The rest is only a reminder of your engagement," she said primly.

My throat constricted, and I had the distinct impression that Mother wasn't telling us everything, that she was concealing the fact that the reminder had been more of a carefully veiled threat. Not that we had any other choice. Escaping the betrothal had never been an option for Grace. For any of us.

Her eyes darted to me, a sharp, wordless look that warned me not to speak further on the subject. I could almost hear her warning voice in my ears. *Don't argue, Ellie.* It was the one topic I'd constantly disagreed with Mother on, always insisting there must be another way. But I was younger and more hopeful then, refusing to accept the inevitable.

It was clear now that all my fanciful dreams of escape were just that—dreams. We had no other family who could take us in. Though Mother had spent the last several years trying to pair me with a man here in town—as if hoping that somehow, if I married well enough, we could all escape to a distant city or kingdom and forget fae even existed—her efforts had been unsuccessful. As much as I wanted to help my family, I'd never believed Father would pass so soon, so suddenly. I'd foolishly believed I had time to find a match that wasn't simply smart and secure, but also one that gave me a chance at love. Most men didn't even give me a second thought—we were too poor, without a tempting dowry—or they found that my beauty paled in comparison to Grace's radiance. They wanted to court her until they realized she was betrothed; and then they turned to me as an alternative. I'd always been quick to spurn their advances.

What woman wanted to be a man's second choice?

I wasn't ugly by any stretch of the imagination. Sometimes, when the light fell across my face just right, I could fancy myself almost as beautiful as Grace. But where she possessed glowing skin, golden hair, and a perfectly full mouth, I had a pale complexion paired with dark hair. My blue-grey eyes were my one flash of color in an appearance that I sometimes worried appeared more ghostly than alive. Grace was like an angel descended from heaven; I was like the apparition that haunted her steps.

I resisted the urge to snort—my thoughts were turning as dramatic as Isabel and Bridget could be. But it was hard not to feel that way, not when I was constantly ignored for Grace. If I hadn't loved her so dearly, if she wasn't my best friend, with a heart that matched her stunning looks, I probably would have envied her. As it was, I'd grown comfortable living in her shadow, in being the one who was overlooked.

At least it meant I didn't carry the burden of being engaged to a fae.

"Tomorrow," Maggie mused, startling me. She tugged at a wild curl that had escaped her bun, frowning at the fire. "Do you think they will set a date for the wedding then? Do they know Father..." She let the sentence trail off, swallowing her unspoken words.

Mother dabbed at the sweat on her brow with a handkerchief. "I'm sure they know," she affirmed. "And I'm sure they'll set a date. After all, I received word just yesterday morning that your cousin, Mr. Cantrell, will be here within the week."

Isabel gasped while Bridget choked on a sob. "And then he'll take all our things! What will he even want with all our dresses and bonnets?"

Maggie rolled her eyes. "He won't cast us out without clothes or compassion," she protested. "I'm sure he'll wait until we our settled in Brytwilde—with our belongings—before he takes residence here." She turned to Mother for confirmation.

"I do hope you're right," Mother sniffed. Bridget and Isabel had inherited her penchant for dramatics.

I turned to Grace, noting her rigid posture, her tense jaw. Squeezing her hand, I rested my head on her shoulder and whispered into her ear. "It will be all right." It was an empty promise, and I knew it.

Nothing had been all right since Father had died.

CHAPTER TWO

The familiar squeak of the hinges as the door to Fletcher's Bookshop swung inward was a soothing welcome in my swiftly changing world. At least this shop, dimly lit and full of the lovely scents of leather and ink from the countless books filling the shelves, remained the same amidst all the other chaos in my life. I drew in a deep breath, despite the dusty air that also greeted me, tickling my nose.

"If it isn't the lovely Miss Elle Blackford," Mr. Fletcher called out, dipping his head with a smile. His warm brown eyes twinkled as he set down the book he'd been reading. "I've missed seeing you around."

Normally, I frequented Fletcher's Bookshop several times a week, but ever since Father's funeral, I hadn't had the heart to venture into town and face all the half-hearted condolences and whispers about fae deals and their far-reaching consequences. I didn't want to hear comments on how awful it was that he'd passed so soon, or what a burden losing the home was on us all. We were merely fuel for the town gossipers, and nothing more.

"Good day, Mr. Fletcher." I dropped into a shallow curtsey, my mourning skirts whispering across the floor, like an unwanted messenger forever sharing the news of my loss for all nearby.

Mr. Fletcher eyed my black dress for a moment, his brow pinched. I tugged at the ribbon on my bonnet, suddenly feeling as if there wasn't enough air in the shop. *More condolences,* I thought.

But Mr. Fletcher spoke gently. "I considered your father a good friend," he said at last, and it was the sincerest remark I'd heard from anyone since Father's passing. "I missed him when he stopped coming to our...meetings." He cleared his throat. "But I understood his choices."

My gaze was steady as I said, "I've decided it is my time to visit for the same reason he once did."

Mr. Fletcher's eyes widened, but he didn't question me. No one else occupied the shop, so he handed me a freshly lit candle and opened a drawer, withdrawing a single ornate key hanging from a cord. As soon as he gave it to me, I folded my fingers over it.

For a breathless moment, a question hovered on my lips. It was almost too much to hope for—a passing rumor I'd clung to stubbornly ever since losing Father. A fool's dream. I was terrified that if I voiced it aloud, only to have it dashed, I'd break all over again.

The weight of Father's locket, one I'd worn constantly since he'd died, seemed heavier around my neck as I considered. "Do you have any books on spirits?" I murmured, my words so low, I wasn't even sure if Mr. Fletcher could hear me.

I hadn't thought his eyes could widen any further until they did, telling me that he had heard me, and that he knew the question I was truly getting at. "Downstairs, with the others, if you want to study the subject." He frowned again. "But please note, Miss Blackford, that I don't have any information on the subject I believe you're referring to. It's not something we mortals know much about. It's such a closely guarded secret that few of the fae even know about what you're seeking. Not to mention the fact that the act itself is nearly imposs—"

"Thank you, Mr. Fletcher," I said, gently but firmly cutting him off. I couldn't bear to listen to him continue listing reasons to shatter my hopes. "I understand quite what you mean. I'd still like to take a look."

Mr. Fletcher didn't press the matter, merely nodding and allowing me to shuffle silently into the depths of the shop, toward the corner with the trick bookcase. Though I'd never used this secret entrance myself, Father had spoken about it—and even used it often enough in my presence while I'd innocently browsed the shelves of the shop—that I knew exactly what to do. I inserted the key into the lock and pushed the bookcase inward. Unlike the front door, this one swung on silent hinges. My candlelight danced on the stone walls and the staircase leading into shadow.

Murmured conversation reached my ears, and my heart picked up its rhythm, a mixture of dread and eagerness slithering through me.

Pulling the case shut with a muted click behind me, I descended, letting my candle spill warm, golden light over the stone steps. There wasn't any dust or cobwebs in sight. This hidden space underground was frequented even more often than the bookshop itself.

When I reached the bottom, I scanned the large room, with rows upon rows of bookshelves extending into shadow, so that I could not see where they ended, and another side open to small tables tucked into corners and alcoves. Hooded forms occupied some of these, exchanging hushed conversations, but many more figures kept to themselves and avoided eye contact.

Father had cautioned me about associating with anyone here—another reason he hadn't brought me on any of his own visits. While he'd admitted many frequenters were some of our own neighbors, he'd also warned that it wasn't unusual for strangers to venture here from other towns, seeking illegal information or trading forbidden charms.

Those were the sorts of people who would just as easily threaten a fellow mortal if it helped them gain the powerful magic they craved.

Goosebumps trailed along my flesh, and I pulled my coat a little closer, cursing how threadbare it was becoming.

"Elle!" Sophia Hart's voice echoed off the stone walls as she rushed forward. The warmth of her embrace contrasted with the cold, musty atmosphere. Her rich brown hair was pulled into a knot, and her dress was a little worn, but her grey eyes were full of joy. Ever practical, ever kind, Sophie was one of my favorite people.

"Soph, what are you doing here?" I demanded, my words muffled against her neck.

My friend drew back enough to meet my eyes with a solemn expression. "Because I knew this was the first place you would go."

"Have you been here before?" I whispered, my gaze darting toward the shadowy figures at the corners of the room.

"Father brought me here before."

I was surprised. My own father hadn't even let me come with him. Then again, he'd also stopped frequenting in recent months, claiming it was too dangerous and that he could continue to study magic on his own.

"Well, it's good to see you," I said, squeezing Sophie in another embrace. I didn't want to cry, but the burning sensation in the back of my throat told me I was losing that battle.

"*Finally*," Sophie emphasized. "I was worried about you."

For weeks after Father's death, I'd remained confined to my house, trying to accept the fact that I not only had lost my father, but that I also had to part with my childhood home. Even when Sophie had tried to call on me, I'd found excuses, asking Hannah to say I was indisposed.

Sniffling, I pulled back and gracelessly wiped my eyes with my sleeve. *God forbid Mother see me now,* I thought. "Please forgive me. I was..." My voice trailed off, and I realized I didn't have words to describe what I was, not then and certainly not now.

I was aching, full of too much and too little all at once. I was a violent rainstorm of emotion, and yet I was also emptiness itself. There was anger and panic, hopelessness and defiance, sorrow and regret. And there was an all-consuming numbness. A void in the place where Father had resided in my heart. A space where all hopes for a happy future and somehow avoiding our parents' ill-fated deal were dashed forever.

"You don't need to explain it," Sophie said, taking my cold hands and squeezing them in her warm ones. Though both her parents were living, and she couldn't know the terror that came with knowing one's entire life was about to be uprooted, I believed she understood my pain. Much like Grace, Sophie was always cool and collected in a way that made many assume she felt little, when I knew the truth: my dear friend's emotions ran deep; she simply knew how to hide them.

"You came to learn more about Brytwilde before you're forced to live there, didn't you?" Sophie asked gently.

I nodded, falling into step beside her as she started for a row of book-shelves on the far side of the room. Flickering candlelight cast shadows along the grimy stone walls.

"I wish you would have waited for me outside," I confessed.

"It *is* rather eerie here," Sophie agreed. "But as I said, it's not my first time being here." She arched a brow. "Though hopefully my last." Like myself, Sophie believed the fae laws were unfair, but unlike me, she found no logical reason to fight against them. She hadn't inherited her father's rebellious spirit. *You can't win against the fae,* she'd often told me.

I clasped Father's locket as I scanned a row of shelves. *But what if I can?* It was a dangerous thought, growing alongside a dangerous plan I had barely let myself fully consider, let alone admit to anyone.

Heart pounding, I leaned in close to whisper in my friend's ear. "Queen Griselda summoned us to a ball *tonight*. I believe she's determined it is time to make good on the deal she made with my parents."

Pulling back, Sophie inhaled sharply. She didn't make some trite remark about the fortuitous timing that would prevent my family and me from becoming homeless and destitute. Instead, her eyes filled with pain and worry. She'd known for a long time this day would come, that eventually we would be forced to say goodbye—and we might never see each other again. "It isn't right, to be forced to part with your father and your home—your whole life—all at once," she said fiercely, drawing me into another hug.

We stayed that way for a long time. I fought back tears as she held me close, as if her willpower and friendship could keep me here.

"You are my dearest friend, Elle," she said at last, her voice breaking in a rare display of emotion.

"And you mine." I sniffled, swiftly plucking a handkerchief from my coat pocket and dabbing at my eyes. "But I promise you, I will see you again. I'll find a way."

Sophie smirked. "If anyone can, it is you, of that I have no doubt."

I hesitated between the shelves, wondering if I dared let Sophie even see the book I was looking for. She'd never judged me for my reckless behavior, but she'd surely worry. No one in Riverton knew much about the ghosts that lurked within Ashwood Forest, but we'd all grown up hearing stories about how dangerous angry spirits could be. She'd assume I wanted to find Father's soul and say goodbye, at the risk of facing other dangerous ghosts.

The aching void in my heart didn't want to hear my friend's reason and logic. It wanted a solution. It wanted magic.

I reached for a somewhat-innocent looking book on the history of the fae. Surely *that* wouldn't invoke any suspicion. But if I wanted to research the ghosts, even if the topic I really wanted to know about wasn't here, I would need to convince her to leave me.

A masculine voice jolted me from my thoughts, and I dropped the book I was holding. It thudded dully against the stone floor, sending up a cloud of dust.

"Well," the voice said, its tone amiable, bordering on flirtatious, "I've never seen two such fine ladies in a place like this before."

Sophie and I stiffened at the same time, plastering smiles on our faces and dipping our heads in acknowledgement. The man himself was leaning against a bookcase at the far end of the aisle, his grin carefree and warm. Despite the unsavory atmosphere, I couldn't help but grin as soon as my eyes met his familiar form.

It was Mr. Reid, a young gentleman who also happened to be an old family friend, one who'd often spent afternoons in Father's study talking about the fae and magic. As a messenger to the fae royal family, he'd grown up in Brytwilde.

Mr. Reid's eyes were as grey as an overcast day, but full of openness and charm that were undeniable, making them sparkle in the dim light. A single dark lock of hair swept over his forehead as he lifted his hat and bowed graciously to us both, picking up my book and holding it out to me.

Suddenly, I felt as ridiculous as my younger sisters. What would Grace think of me right now, gaping at our friend? I'd always thought he was the handsomest man I knew, but I'd managed to conceal my feelings. Now, a traitorous blush crept up my neck and warmed my cheeks. *Don't be a fool.*

"Miss Blackford, I heard the news," Mr. Reid said sadly as I hurriedly plucked the book from his hand, studiously avoiding touching his fingers. "My sincerest condolences. I wish I could have made it to the funeral, but unfortunately, word didn't reach me until it was too late."

"Thank you," I whispered.

"I meant to call on your family after I finished my business with Mr. Fletcher," Mr. Reid went on. "I'm surprised to find you here."

"You know that Grace is engaged to one of the fae princes," I blurted out, my words tripping over one another in my haste to release them. He knew I'd studied endless books on the fae already, but surely he wouldn't be surprised that I'd want to pore over a few more when I'd be making my home in Brytwilde so soon.

Mr. Reid's eyes flashed with an emotion—there and gone so fast I couldn't place it. Pity? Sorrow? He extended his hand again. "As you know, I could share far more than these books ever could. Would you walk with me, Miss Blackford? Let's see if there's anything I haven't yet shared with you."

Sophie arched a brow at me, but she didn't protest when I accepted Mr. Reid's arm and he led me toward a corner table, out of the hearing range of others. Sophie trailed mutely behind us, a faithful shadow. Mr. Reid pulled out chairs for my friend and me before settling into one across from us.

For a moment, Mr. Reid's gaze turned distant while he glanced around the room, as if gathering his thoughts. Then he cleared his throat and forced a smile. "The fae..." He hesitated. "They aren't *all* bad."

"So you've said before." I squeezed my fingers together in my lap to silence the protests that came to mind. Magical immortals who thought nothing of stealing women away from their homes, of making cruel deals with humans, of forcing us into arranged marriages with their sons? Of course they were bad. I despised them all, and I always would.

"Some have been kind to my family," Mr. Reid went on, "and their world of magic can be cruel, but it is also enchanting. It's why so many humans are lured into Brytwilde. To enjoy the power. The decadence. The beauty."

I scowled. "It sounds to me as if you are defending them."

Mr. Reid shrugged, looking helpless. "In a way—I am. But that isn't to say there aren't terrible fae, too. There are plenty who hate humans, who want nothing more than to see us be destroyed. They think that we are lesser without magic, and they take great joy in abusing their power over us. Those are the ones who make the deadliest of deals, or corner you on a dark night, alone and frightened." He stiffened and cleared his throat. "Forgive me," he said, his eyes flicking between Sophie and me. "Not the sorts of topics that human ladies sit about discussing. I forget myself. The world of the fae is different."

I snorted before I could cover it, and then stifled a laugh. "You don't need to pretend with all of these formalities, Mr. Reid. Father shared many of the stories you told him with me." My lips twitched into a wistful smile, there and gone again in an instant. I reached up to clutch his locket, the familiar weight comforting me. "And considering my family and I are about to live among these fae, I'd rather be prepared for all dangers," I added pointedly. "Ignorance isn't a luxury we can afford anymore."

Mr. Reid leaned forward, his expression turning earnest. His eyes churned with emotion as he scanned my locket before I tucked it away. "I remember seeing that before. It's a charm....one that belonged to your father, did it not?" he asked softly. "Did he leave it to you, then?"

"Well, I was the only one who knew about it and its...magical properties. Even if we don't know how to use them," I confessed. "It's a comfort to keep it near." I hesitated before changing the subject. "Is there anything else you can share?"

Mr. Reid swallowed. "I can try to prepare you for the world of the fae, but it's not exactly something one can prepare for. No matter how fearful or disgusted you are now, once you are in those woods, surrounded by their magic...it's a bit intoxicating, to be frank. The most important thing is to cling to your fear. It will keep your mind sharp, rather than letting it grow muddled with fae tricks and their glamour. I'm sure your father already warned you about the food and drink. Don't consume anything unfamiliar. They have meals as we do, but there are also fruits and wines that can be dangerous to a mortal. They cause a variety of symptoms, from making one more prone to their glamour and commands, to stealing away your appetite until you starve yourself to death."

I scowled. "Mr. Reid, you're very kind, but most of these things I already know." I glanced pointedly around the room. "Father kept nothing from me, from his borrowed books to your accounts and even those of your own father, when he was alive."

He scanned my face, searching. "I understand. And those are probably the most important things to know, for now," he mused. "Always be on your guard. I know any mortal living in the shadow of Ashwood Forest knows better than to strike deals with the fae. But understand that your parents knew better too. They were quite desperate, and the fae are masters of discovering your weaknesses and preying upon them. They understand temptation, and they wield it as a weapon."

"And what of the ghosts?" I asked, picking at a loose thread on the sleeve of my dress. Despite my attempt at appearing casual, I could feel the weight of Sophie's gaze on me. She had an idea, now, of what I hoped to learn. But she couldn't even begin to guess what I wanted to do.

"I believe it's all more that you already know. The Ashwood family is bound to protect the spirits that linger. Their mission is to help the souls pass on to the hereafter. Until they pass on, they are meant to stay in the glade of souls..."

"Yes," I sighed. "That's nothing new."

Mr. Reid's face darkened. "Then I'll warn you of a new issue: do not venture into the forest or the castle grounds at night. Some of the spirits have taken to wandering outside of the glade, and I know you've already been warned about how dangerous they can be." He smirked. "Though I must say, if any are haunting the Ashwood family in their own castle, that's something I'm not upset over. The royals, I'm afraid, are among the fae I'd warn you about."

"Ah," I said wryly, "so now you tell me that the ones I'm to make my home with are the worst? Father didn't share that information with me."

Mr. Reid's expression turned solemn. He leaned forward further. "I'm afraid so," he whispered. "You'll need to be especially guarded among them. And..." He hesitated. "I assume Miss Grace is meant to marry the eldest, the heir to the throne?"

I shrugged. "It wasn't specified, but I imagine if he's unmarried, it will be him."

"Crown Prince Fitz," Mr. Reid breathed, tone full of disgust. "I do not envy your sister. He's dangerous, that one. I don't think he would harm you, not when your family has made a deal with the queen. They keep their word, and they don't glamour humans. But understand that all deals can have loopholes. Your safety won't be his prime concern. He would want to keep his wife alive, simply to produce heirs at the least, but the rest of you..." He frowned. "Be very cautious, Miss Blackford. And know that I won't be far away. Royal messengers live on the castle grounds. If you need anything, I'll be near."

I dipped my head in gratitude. "Thank you."

His smile was bittersweet. "We humans must band together."

CHAPTER THREE

"Well?" Grace asked, tipping her chin bravely as she met my eyes in the mirror. "How do I look?"

"Like a dream," I murmured, my heart pinching as I scanned her from head to toe. It was true. Even the proudest fae prince couldn't deny that my sister was a vision, human or not. Her golden hair was twisted into an elaborate braid that crowned her head like the true ornament that would soon adorn her brow. I'd woven asters and thistles from along the forest's edge into her hair, giving her beauty a wilder edge, one I imagined might be appealing to the Fair Folk. A few ringlets framed her face, and her eyes were bright and blue, full of hope that I wouldn't have possessed in her place.

You're better than me, I thought as I retrieved her slippers, delicate and white with gold beading that matched her dress, and kneeled to help her into them. *I would have let go of hope and settled for daydreaming of ways to cut out the prince's heart by now.*

They were violent words that a lady wasn't supposed to think, let alone say aloud. Yet it seemed time to start thinking that way, when our survival would depend upon being prepared for an unfamiliar world. Besides, we were about to leave the propriety of mortals behind, where it could molder and rot like all the other belongings we'd part with. I hoped the house would do the same, for our cousin's sake. Let it fall to ruins around him—I couldn't bring myself to feel sorry for my hateful wishes, not when he hadn't mustered an ounce of sympathy for our plight. Not when he was so swiftly shoving us out of our home and into the fae world.

I was especially irritable tonight, not only because of my nerves over the upcoming ball, but also because my search for more information about the ghosts in Ashwood or the glade of spirits had yielded no results. After speaking with Mr. Reid, I'd searched the bookshelves with Sophie until she'd had to gently remind me that I needed to return home to prepare for tonight. I'd known it was unlikely I'd find what I needed at Fletcher's, but I'd still felt glum coming home empty-handed.

"Your turn," Grace said gently as I stood. The tremble of her fingers as she laced up my corset, buttoned me into my gown, and styled my hair with a few of the leftover wildflowers was the only indication that she was terrified.

"Mother and Father should have known better," I muttered. "They should have let us work as maids or governesses rather than send us to the fae."

It wasn't the first time I'd complained about this, but Grace responded patiently anyway. "Who would have hired us, inexperienced as we are?"

It was true. I sighed, hating the way the world was. In Riverton, or even neighboring towns, gentleman's daughters who didn't marry to secure their futures were mocked and turned away from jobs. We were seen as castoffs, unfit to sully our hands with honest work. Rejects who hadn't managed to capture the interest of well-to-do gentlemen. Father and Mother had spoken of others like us who'd lost their homes and tried to work, only to find themselves struggling to survive. When we humans should have looked after one another, we failed each other, forcing our own into Brytwilde.

I knew all this, but I still thought trying to live a new life among humans seemed better than casting in our lot among the fae.

"Grace, are you truly all right?" I whispered, but she shook her head, refusing to speak, refusing to let me stop her as she worked. Determination filled her eyes as I studied her in the mirror. She set her mouth into a fixed smile that nothing could shatter.

My heart ached. My dear, sweet, brave older sister, who had always known she was the sacrifice to save our family. Who had spent a lifetime preparing for this moment, loving Father and Mother and her sisters without begrudging us anything despite the fact that the rest of us didn't have to bind ourselves to a fae for our family to survive. I wanted to cry and scream at the injustice of it all, but for my sister's sake, I held my tongue.

When she asked me to stand and placed my slippers on my feet, I turned to the mirror and smiled as if I was about to attend any other ball, any other night. "Beautiful," I whispered. "Thank you."

While Grace wore bridal white accented with gold that made her shimmer like precious treasure, I was clad in white and silver. At her side, I was overshadowed by her light. Just the way it was meant to be. Her beauty was her curse, and I couldn't fully envy her, not even when the other villagers raved about what an angel she was, as if my sisters and I didn't exist, didn't notice the way they ignored us. We'd all learned long ago not to take those comments personally. We were all beautiful in our own ways, but not ethereal and stunning like Grace. Our average, perfectly *normal* beauty was our protection, the armor that would guarantee when we attended tonight's ball, the fae queen wouldn't choose one of us instead of Grace.

I hated myself for being relieved.

Even though I'd gladly give myself in my sister's place to save her, the fact that the fae would never accept me was still soothing. I wasn't fearless, after all.

"Grace! Elle!" Bridget's voice turned shrill with pleasure as she burst into our room, Isabel on her heels. They were both clothed in pale shades of pink and lavender, blushing colors that fit their youth and innocence. I prayed that and their sunny naivety didn't make them tempting for the crueler, more cunning sorts of fae. "You look *stunning!*"

"Like a true princess," Isabel agreed, curtseying prettily and giggling as she took in Grace's appearance from head to toe.

Ever the dutiful older sister, Grace beamed and laughed along with them, like she was delighted and excited for the night and her upcoming nuptials. She pretended to adjust the flowers in her hair. "Soon I can trade this crown for a better one," she said with a wink.

Isabel clasped her hands. "What do you think the castle will be like? Will the music be irresistible? Will they use their magic? Do you think they'll dance with us, even if we're human?"

"I think you should be concerning yourself more with being on your guard," I cut in crossly. "Do you know to check that the food and drinks you accept are familiar? Will you avoid letting them lure you into making any tricky bargains? Will you remember not to let them sway you with their beauty and glamour you?"

Bridget sighed, settling her hands on her hips. "Don't be a worrywart, Elle. We know about the fae ways. If we must live among them, can't we at least have some fun?"

I chewed my lip, suddenly at a loss for words. Perhaps all my sisters' silliness was simply their own way of coping with the grief and change we were facing. "Of course," I muttered, turning away to peer in the mirror and fidget with my dress.

"It'll be all right," Grace promised softly, setting a hand on my arm.

I drew a deep breath and tugged on my gloves. Normally, we didn't wear fine gloves to the local balls our neighbors hosted, but to the castle, Mother had insisted we spend the extra money to look our finest. She claimed it was important to make a good impression.

Whatever that meant.

"Girls!" Mother called from downstairs. "The coach has arrived. It's time to go."

Maggie was already in the hallway, scowling as she stomped down the stairs.

"Do try to smile," Grace hissed as we followed Maggie. "Better to be agreeable and hope that our friendliness endears us to them."

It was the closest she'd ever come to admitting that the fae might be less than kind to us, even while upholding a marriage agreement. My heart thundered. If Prince Fitz was as awful as Mr. Reid made him sound, if he did anything to make me question how he would treat my sister...

My whirling thoughts drew to a halt as Hannah threw open our front door and a chill breeze washed over us. The coach outside was somehow magnificent and ominous, all at once. Adorned in contrasting shades of onyx and ivory and drawn by sleek horses in matching shades, it obviously did *not* belong in the simple town of Riverton. The driver was human, but not a fae messenger or servant I'd seen before. He swept the door open with an impassive look, his eyes scanning us without seeming to really notice us, but his gaze didn't hold the glazed look I'd heard glamoured humans wore. Maybe he didn't care about fellow humans and their fates within Brytwilde. Maybe he thought we were eager for this new life. Or maybe, having chosen a life of serving the fae, he was as cruel-hearted as they were, and wouldn't mind watching us suffer.

Mother, my sisters, and I climbed inside to find a black interior of cushioned velvet, more comfortable than anything I'd ever ridden in before.

As my youngest sisters oohed and ahhed, I sank back and stared out the window, watching our home and everything familiar disappear behind us. Though I knew this wasn't the last time we'd see home, that Grace's marriage date still needed to be arranged, this moment felt final.

After tonight, everything would change.

I'd heard that normally, all sorts of fae balls and feasts and parties were held outside, where the immortal beings could be closer to the natural world from which they harnessed their power. But tonight, perhaps in a show of hospitality and generosity to make us humans feel more comfortable, Mother had informed us that the ball was being held within Ashwood Castle.

I couldn't help but scoff as our coach rumbled along the dirt forest road and the castle came into view. There was nothing about this ball that would seem familiar to us, not when we were used to simple country dances held in our neighbor's homes—not extravagant affairs held by immortal royalty.

Beside me, Isabel shrieked in delight. "And this is to be our *home*?"

I couldn't deny that the sight of the castle was breathtaking, if in a somewhat melancholy sort of way. It was a massive structure of grey stone and spires, draped in moss and wreathed in mist. The only warmth emanated from sputtering torches lining the walls and battlements or shimmering through countless windows. Ashwood Forest towered around it, vivid greens and oranges and reds showing off the full glory of autumn and contrasting richly with the dark castle.

My pulse ratcheted in my ears as I imagined the ghosts that, according to Mr. Reid, now wandered the forest. Instead of fear, hope filled my chest. Not even the chill breeze, full of the eerie music of rattling leaves, could douse the warmth building inside me as I stepped from the coach and approached the castle with my family. *Father. Are you near?* I pressed my hand over the clasp of my coat, to where I knew my locket was tucked away. Near enough to comfort me, but hidden so none of the fae would notice an object that was supposedly a charm, though Father and I had never learned how to wield its powers. I didn't want to be forced to convince the fae that the locket was an old gift to my family. What if they didn't believe me, and accused me of possessing something illegal?

Several human servants stepped forth at our approach, curtseying and bowing to welcome us, but I found the sight chilling rather than reassuring. Were they treated well? Had they chosen this life, or were they paying the penalties of making bad deals with the fae? I scanned each one, seeking any signs that they had been glamoured and were at the mercy of the Fair Folks' commands, but their gazes were all clear.

Fae guards pushed open heavy double doors, carved with all manner of forest creatures and ancient looking trees, as if to bring the surrounding woods even closer. Distant music greeted us, the notes wild and achingly beautiful, unlike anything I'd ever heard played in the mortal world. Tears stung my eyes and gooseflesh rose on my arms, despite the warmth of the hall that lingered even when a servant took my coat. I gaped at our surroundings, taking in the lush carpet, the curving staircase ahead, and a chandelier that cast dancing shadows over walls adorned in tapestries. The art depicted everything from peaceful landscapes to violent hunts, where I couldn't tell if the fae were seeking animal or human prey.

My stomach churned, but I forced a smile on my face as a mortal man, his expression stiff and void of any feeling at all, led us down the hall, toward the music. At my side, Grace slipped her gloved hand into mine, and I sensed the way she trembled. I squeezed, trying to offer her courage I didn't feel. Even my younger sisters had gone quiet, too awed by the decadence of the castle to know what to say. I cast a sidelong glance toward Mother, who kept pace with me at my other side, and found a brief crack in her usually peaceful expression. There was pain and fear in her eyes, there and gone in an instant, but easily recognizable since they were the same emotions haunting me.

What had she and Father done?

We paused in the entrance to a grand ballroom, full of more flickering chandeliers and woodwork adorned in carvings of forest life. Laughter and music and conversation flooded the room, which was so vast we could have placed our own home a dozen times over within it and still had space left over.

"Announcing Her Majesty's honored guests, the Blackford family," the man ahead of us announced, causing a hush to descend.

Countless inhuman faces turned toward us, taking in our mortal appearances, clothes, and terror. Their own beauty was unspeakable, harsh and powerful and awe-inspiring, almost to the point that it hurt to look at them. The women were adorned in vibrant colors, their gowns ranging from elaborate to simple, and some showing off far more skin than I'd ever seen in polite human society. Some wore nature in their hair the way Grace and I had added flowers to ours, except they wore moss, leaves, and branches—adornments that would look ugly on us but were stunning on them. The majority of them looked like us except for their unnatural beauty, pointed ears, and the hungry gazes they pinned on us. But some had wings ranging from dark to gossamer, or eyes in colors that I'd never seen before, or animalistic characteristics such as horns or hooves or fur. Sprites flitted through the air and some goblins hovered at the edges of the crowd.

And all—all had an aura about them that made a primal part of me scream *danger* while feeling drawn to them at the same time. I was frozen in place, as entranced as I was afraid. It was like Mr. Reid had warned. Being around magic could make me let down my guard, I realized, if I wasn't cautious.

"Come in, come in." The voice was rich, full of a subtle sort of power that made the hairs on the back of my neck rise. As kind as the words and tone were, my mind instinctively knew that the speaker was not someone to underestimate.

Though I'd never met her, I knew immediately that the voice belonged to Queen Griselda Ashwood. I peered through the crowd, but there were too many bodies to catch a glimpse of her. Or perhaps she was standing among her courtiers, and I'd never know which of these fantastically dressed creatures was her until she stepped out and introduced herself.

As the honored guest and the reason we were all here, Grace made the first tentative step into the room. Then, gathering her courage, she straightened her spine and swept forward as elegantly as a future princess would. My heart burst with pride as I trailed in her footsteps, keeping my eyes straight ahead, on her. I didn't want to turn toward the fae, didn't want to meet the pairs of eyes boring into me like daggers. Even from the corner of my eye, I could tell their expressions were not curious in the way humans would be interested in newcomers, but more in the way predators would assess new prey. Or perhaps the way children would study a potential new toy.

Somehow, that last thought was more terrifying than the first.

Behind me, Isabel whispered something to Bridget, too soft for me to hear, but not too soft for fae ears.

A woman to my left sneered, and I froze. "They think they deserve to be here?" she spat to her neighbor. "That marrying into the Ashwood family makes them...*equal* to us?"

I glanced up, meeting eyes as pink as a dawn sky and full of malice—and focused on my younger sisters. My blood raged in my veins, overcoming all thoughts of caution.

"Oh no," I said, keeping my tone low and cold, "we would never deign to imagine ourselves equal to you."

She dragged her gaze from Isabel and Bridget to pin me with her stare, and I welcomed it. I stood taller, the heat of my anger burning away my earlier fears.

"In fact," I went on, fighting a smile, "we pride ourselves on being nothing like you."

Pointed teeth bared at me, the woman stepped forward. Her extravagant, gauzy green skirts swirled like leaves in a storm. "How dare you—"

"That is quite enough." Queen Griselda's voice cut like a blade, dropping every fae and human into bows and curtsies. The music crashed to an abrupt halt, even the musicians in the corner freezing either out of respect or fear.

Dipping her head reverently, Mother cast me a wide-eyed look. My skin tingled. Had I ruined our chance at a life here? Had my words destroyed that old fae bargain and left us homeless and destitute? Half of me wondered if that would be such a bad thing, except for the fact that I was sure, deep down, that if we offended the fae that deeply, we would never leave this forest alive.

"Which one of you is the eldest Miss Blackford? Miss...Grace Blackford, is it?"

At last daring to lift my head, I watched as Grace straightened and faced the queen. "I am Miss Grace Blackford, Your Majesty," she murmured.

"Well, for a human, you are quite beautiful." Her eyes scanned Grace and then turned to each one of my sisters and me in turn, assessing us with a detached air. "Easily the best-looking in your family, just as I expected you would turn out to be. Very good. You will do nicely for my son."

Queen Griselda turned back to me.

Fury licking at my stomach like flames, I returned the queen's scrutiny, taking in her surprisingly short stature but no less intimidating presence. Though it was said she was ancient and ageless, I noted she was not immune to wrinkles, as a few gathered around her piercing blue eyes. Her rich brown hair, however, gleamed with health and showed not a single grey strand, while her skin was porcelain white and without blemish. Her jaw and cheekbones were as sharp as the edges of her pointed ears, emphasizing the fact that she wasn't human.

"And you," she said, her tone dark. "What name do you use?"

"Miss Elizabeth Blackford, but I go by Elle," I said, keeping my own words carefully neutral. It wouldn't do to enrage the queen any more than I'd likely already had.

She arched a single haughty eyebrow. "For being absolutely no one, you possess a lot of pride."

I only wish to protect my family from your hateful kingdom. But I swallowed back the comment and dipped my head.

For a long moment, Queen Griselda continued to stare. No one in the ballroom moved. Everyone was studying the Blackford family and our pitiful human attempts at being beautiful.

Finally, the queen tore her gaze away and gestured, a silent signal for two young men to approach. I couldn't tell if they were both truly around Grace's and my ages, or if their fae blood made them appear more youthful than they were. As they stopped on either side of the queen, I realized they were her sons, though they couldn't have been more different from one another.

One stood tall, dwarfing his mother with his long limbs and square shoulders. His hair was as dark as a night sky and pulled back from his chiseled face, while his eyes were pale like his mother's, with a gaze just as sharp. He possessed the sort of good looks that left a human breathless—myself included, unfortunately. His expression was cold, and when his eyes met mine, sweeping over me in half a second before glancing away boredly, I couldn't help but feel a rush of anger. To him, I was no more interesting than an insect crossing his path.

On Queen Griselda's other side stood a man nearly a head shorter than his brother, but no less handsome. His hair was golden, while his eyes were a rich brown that radiated warmth and kindness. His mouth twitched in a smile, friendly and open, as he bowed his head in greeting.

"Mrs. Blackford, Miss Grace Blackford," Queen Griselda announced, "I would like you to meet Crown Prince Fitz." She gestured toward the dark-haired man. My mouth soured. Of course my sister was betrothed to the cold one that looked dangerous and cruel. "And this is Prince Holden." She waved a breezy hand toward her other son, who beamed at us. Grace grinned right back at him.

Prince Fitz gave a single dip of his head toward my sister. "Miss Blackford." And then, without another word, without an attempt to get to know her or invite her to dance, he spun on his heel and disappeared back into the crowd. My breath caught at his rudeness.

Prince Holden stepped forward quickly, his dimpled smile turning a little sheepish. "Please forgive my brother, Miss Blackford," he said, offering a hand to Grace. "He is not fond of dancing, but I would be honored if you would join me."

"Come, speak with me," Queen Griselda said, barely sparing a glance toward my mother as she gestured for her. Mother knew better than to refuse, so she curtsied and trailed after the queen, further into the crowd.

And just like that, the music started again, Prince Holden and Grace strode arm-in-arm toward the dance floor, and my younger sisters and I were left alone among the fae courtiers.

CHAPTER FOUR

"Have you ever considered selling these lovely locks?" A woman who looked far too old and wrinkled to be one of the high fae sidled up to me, plucking one of the flowers from my hair to tangle her knobby fingers through the strands. She was a hag, known for their ugliness where the high fae were known for their beauty. Perhaps she liked to collect mortal hair for spells—or curses.

"Not at all," I gritted out.

Her grip tightened, twisting my neck so that I faced her. "You have fine eyes," she crooned. "Surely you could spare one of those. Two is indulgent, don't you think?"

Catching my breath, I slapped her hand away, freeing myself. My fury melted into fear, and I stepped backward as a vision of her cutting off my hand for my brazenness flitted through my mind. But the hag merely cackled, baring yellowed teeth before sweeping away into the crowd.

"Messengers," Isabel breathed, and before I could snag her arm, she and Bridget were racing off toward a group who appeared blessedly human.

My heart jumped in my chest, a mingling sense of hope and dread colliding within it. Could we really trust these human men who had committed their lives to the fae? We knew and trusted Mr. Reid, but what of the others? I scanned their forms, searching for our friend, but I didn't find him.

"I suppose it's safer with other humans," Maggie groused. "This whole night is..." Her eyes settled on a pair of winged fae twirling and laughing wildly, spilling the wineglasses they held carelessly, leaving gold droplets in their wake. Her brows knotted. "Frivolous."

"And dangerous," I agreed. "Go with Isabel and Bridget. I'm going to find Mother. I don't like her being alone with the queen."

Maggie tossed me a sidelong glance, but she didn't protest. I watched as she slunk toward the corner, slumping against the wall as she watched Isabel and Bridget giggle at something one of the men was saying.

Satisfied that they were surrounded by company that would shield them from danger, I pressed through the ballroom, avoiding curious glances from all manner of creatures. The high fae were the most familiar to me, as they were the ones most often depicted in the books I'd read. They were the ones who possessed the strongest magic. But there were others, like the darting sprites or the wrinkled hag or sneering goblins.

A tall, willowy woman possessing long, dangling ears rather than pointed ones blocked my path. "Astonishingly ugly. I can't believe the queen is so desperate for heirs that she would bind the crown prince to the likes of you." She shuddered.

In a blink, another woman was beside her, this one with dark skin and perfect curls. She fluttered her lashes at me, but her laughter was mocking and cruel.

"Excuse me," I said, picking up my skirts and attempting to shuffle past them, but then another stepped up behind me.

My lungs hitched when I realized I was surrounded, slowly being hemmed in by leering fae women with glittering eyes. Hands plucked at the flowers in my hair, the fabric of my dress. They giggled, tossing the petals across the floor. "You're not worthy of wearing the finery of the forest," one snapped. I felt the rake of too-long fingernails slicing through fabric and drawing blood along my arm.

With a hiss, I reared back. "I am an honored guest of your queen," I forced out. "No matter how you feel about it, my sister is to marry your prince, and I am under royal protection. Let me pass."

The women pulled back as swiftly as they'd surrounded me, leaving me blinking my stinging eyes and trying anxiously to gather myself. When I smoothed back my hair, I found they'd ripped it down, leaving it to cascade in wild strands down my back. Every flower Grace had carefully arranged lay crushed and shredded on the floor. A glance down told me my dress was ruined, torn in multiple places and stained with my own blood. I wasn't terribly injured—their nails had only scratched me—but I would have been lying to myself if I'd claimed I wasn't frightened.

I slipped through more bodies, these ones thankfully too distracted with one another to take notice of me. They clung to each other in scandalous ways as they danced. I'd never seen a man and woman more than clasp hands together in public, so seeing a couple pinned to the wall, the man trailing kisses down the woman's jaw and neck, made my cheeks heat with embarrassment.

At last, I found a shadowed, unoccupied corner. I sank to the floor, ignoring the way a chill seeped into my bones. I breathed in and out, in and out, telling myself my family would survive this world. Desperately willing that declaration to be true.

Scanning the dance floor, I found that Grace was still in Prince Holden's arms, twirling until her eyes shone and her cheeks pinked. She was laughing with such unadulterated joy I almost couldn't believe it. Since Father died, I hadn't seen her smile like that, not so wholeheartedly. Prince Holden pulled her close, swaying to the music as he dipped his head to whisper something in her ear. My eyes widened. Grace hadn't ever permitted anyone to embrace her so closely—by our mortal standards, dancing with someone like that would be considered an embarrassing display of public affection, not to mention a clear indication that they were engaged.

My happiness for my sister melted into fear. Where was Prince Fitz? Surely he'd be furious to see his brother dancing and laughing with his betrothed like that. But I could find no sign of the man. Instead, my gaze snapped on Mother, who stood rigidly at Queen Griselda's side, nodding along to something the fae was saying.

Safe. Everyone in my family was safe, for now. I leaned against the wall, letting my shoulders sag with relief. Some of the laces of my corset were undone from the faes' earlier attack, and I found myself able to take my first deep breath all night.

I choked back a laugh at the scandal of it all. My skin was covered, but if anyone from back home could see me now, they'd be horrified.

"Absolutely not." The words were bit out so forcefully I heard them easily over the strains of music and chatter filling the room.

I peered around, discovering I was standing near a door that was cracked just a sliver, opening into a dim hallway. Outside, two men were conversing, one beaming as he gestured out toward the dancing, while the taller one scowled at him.

"It would gratify your mother to see you at least dance *once* with your bride-to-be," the cheerful man said. I dared to lean a little further toward the door, catching sight of a young fae man with chestnut hair and bright green eyes.

"I think my brother has already taken that upon himself...for the foreseeable future." I drew back at that statement, realizing this second man was Prince Fitz.

"Well, someone must be agreeable toward her!" the other man protested. I wondered who he was, that he was so comfortable speaking familiarly with the stony crown prince. "If your brother likes Miss Grace Blackford this well, perhaps you could leave her to him and marry one of her sisters."

"Mother gave her word," Prince Fitz said coldly. "No matter how Holden feels about Grace Blackford, he knows his place, and I know mine."

"Fine, but you need to dance with *one* of them to welcome the family. If you don't want to cut into your brother's dance, ask another Blackford. The one with the dark hair—did she say her name was Elle?— she is quite beautiful too."

The prince scoffed. "I'd sooner dance with one of the squirrels outside."

"I'm sure that could be arranged."

"Kinsey, I'm not even sure what makes you think she is beautiful—"

I'd had enough, storming away before I could hear more of the prince's insults. It wasn't as if I cared for his opinion, but a personal attack on my beauty was more than I felt like I could bear. I'd heard enough comments about my shortcomings compared to my sister all my life; I didn't need to listen to those same remarks repeated by a cruel fae.

To my relief, there was another door nearby, and when I swung it open, I found that the hallway beyond was quiet and unoccupied. Floorboards creaked beneath my slippers as I passed endless paintings of imposing fae staring back at me. One was in the likeness of Queen Griselda. The painting made her look so youthful and stunning that I decided it must have either been from years before, or from a generous painter's hand smoothing away any slight imperfections. Beside her were paintings of the princes, Fitz and Holden, and these I found to be exact, even down to the scowl on Fitz's face and the friendly smile on Holden's.

A chill breeze whispered down the hallway, and I glanced about, wondering if there was an open door or window somewhere nearby. Out of habit, I slipped a finger beneath the neckline of my dress to tug at my locket's chain, reassuring myself with the feel of the metal warmed by my skin.

You have an aura of grief about you, like you know death's touch.

The voice was feminine and musical, but distant, as if coming from another room. I startled, glancing around the hall again to reassure myself that no one else was around. Sweat beaded on my brow, and I shook my head to turn away fanciful illusions. I knew ghosts lingered in Ashwood Forest, away from the castle. Although—hadn't Mr. Reid hinted the castle might be haunted?

Refusing to entertain fear, I pressed further down the hallway, finding a single door framed by two windows that permitted a view of tangled tree limbs and fiery leaves burning against the velvety night sky. My heart leapt, and without letting myself second-guess the action and worry about vengeful ghosts, I turned the knob and slipped outside. Finding Father would be worth risking any danger.

A breeze welcomed me with a chilly caress, pebbling the skin along my bare arms and reminding me that I'd stepped into a cold autumn night without my coat. Leaves crunched underfoot as I strode through the castle gardens, full of decaying plants and a few autumn flowers.

Beyond lay the forest, and I couldn't help but wonder where the glade of spirits was. Could it be close? If the royal fae were bound to help the spirits into the afterlife, then surely it wouldn't be far. This time, I pulled out my locket and cradled it in my palm, studying the flowers engraved on its surface. Maybe no one at the ball would miss me if I ventured out into the forest to find the glade. Maybe I could find Father and speak to him, and he would know what I needed to do, what magic I'd have to acquire to bring him back.

Another breeze whispered through the leaves, making branches creak. I shivered.

Are you here to save us?

This way...

Come and play, won't you?

They were words carried on the wind, mingling voices of men and women and children.

I gasped, leaning against a nearby trunk. *Spirits.* They had to be close.

A heavy hand landed on my shoulder, and I choked back a scream as someone spun me around. Fitz's dark eyes blazed with cold fury. "What are you doing here?" he demanded, his gaze flicking down to my hand, fisted around my locket, and back to my face. "Is nothing sacred to you mortals?"

I clenched my jaw until it ached, terrified he would pry my fingers apart and see what I wore. Though Father claimed the fae had gifted it to one of our ancestors, I wasn't sure Prince Fitz would care. Back when this locket had been given, laws had been less strict, and the fae had shared magic more freely. Now, I had a feeling Fitz would insist the locket didn't belong to me and that I deserved to be punished for daring to touch it.

Even if I had no idea how to use its magic. I couldn't even open it.

"I was going for a walk," I said. "The ballroom was too warm, and I needed some fresh air."

Prince Fitz scanned me again, and to my mortification, I remembered my ripped dress and wild hair. "I didn't think humans considered it proper for a woman to be wandering alone in strange places." His eyes sharpened. "Why are you lying to me?"

I straightened my shoulders, determined to not let his immortality, magic, or status intimidate me. "Perhaps I grew tired of your court's hospitality," I quipped. "I was in need of an *agreeable* dance partner, so I was seeking a squirrel."

As I strode past him, I couldn't help the warm rush of pleasure in my chest when I realized I'd left him standing there, speechless.

CHAPTER FIVE

"**E**llie! Did you drink their wine?" Mother asked shrilly.

As I settled into our coach, I tugged my coat tighter around my dress, hoping neither she nor my sisters noticed the blood or rips in the fabric. I considered telling them about the brutal women, but I noted the flush of joy on Grace's cheeks, and decided it wasn't worth ruining the night with fear. My family already knew to be on guard around the fae; at least now, they'd also tasted some hospitality that gave hope of a secure future. After all, we had the Ashwood family's protection. Even the women who'd attacked me had stopped at the reminder.

"Only a sip," I lied, glancing out the window to avoid Mother's cutting gaze.

She began to fuss, her hands fidgeting with her coat buttons as she listed endless reasons and reminders and rules—everything I'd grown up hearing, everything I already knew.

"And you were the one warning *us*," Isabel huffed, crossing her arms. "You thought we would be foolish—"

Mother waved a weary hand, cutting my youngest sister off as the coach jolted over a bump in the road. Every now and then, I caught a glimpse of mist slithering through the trees, and I wondered if those signaled where ghosts wandered or where the glade of spirits lay.

"The most important thing is that you're all right, though your hair is in a disgraceful state." Mother sighed, taking in the locks cascading freely down my back. I could only imagine how tangled they were.

Grace was a silent, reassuring presence at my side as she laid a hand over mine. I knew she didn't believe my story and I'd have to confess the truth to her later, when we were in the privacy of our own bedroom.

"Queen Griselda explained that normally a ball of this magnitude would have lasted through the night," Mother went on. She leaned back, her black lace gown emphasizing her pale features. Grief and worry had added new lines to her face, and my heart pinched in empathy. Her pale eyes landed on Grace. "However, they cut tonight's short, as your wedding ceremony is set for tomorrow evening."

Bridget, who'd been leaning drowsily against Maggie, sat bolt upright. "Tomorrow? We leave tomorrow? How will we prepare? How will we pack?"

"We already knew we would have to pack in a hurry," Mother said. "Besides, we'll only take what few clothes and items we can't bear to part with. The queen promised to provide generously, and the furnishings belong with the house anyway."

Bridget sniffled, and even Mother's lashes fluttered, but I turned toward Grace. *Tomorrow.* My sister's fingers tightened over mine, but her expression gave away nothing.

"The fae will send your dress beforehand," Mother added, and Grace nodded.

Isabel's brow pinched. "How could they have it ready so soon? They don't even have her measurements."

"Apparently their seamstresses are quite skillful." Mother's eyes were distant. I wondered if she was as terrified of tomorrow as I was, if she felt guilty or doubtful. Or if she was thinking of Father, longing for him to be alive and for none of this to be necessary.

"We'll get some rest tonight," Mother announced with a weary sigh.

The coach rattled out of the forest, and at last, I could glimpse home. The house that would be ours for only one more night. "We'll wake early to pack our trunks and prepare Grace." She reached across the coach to clasp my sister's free hand. "You'll be a beautiful bride, my dear."

I wondered, in that moment, if even my sweet older sister felt the same resentment boiling inside her that I did.

Grace whirled on me as soon as she'd clicked our bedroom door shut. "Tell me what happened."

I shimmied uncomfortably out of my coat, which Hannah had unsuccessfully tried to take from me earlier when we'd stepped into the front hall. Mother had cast me a reproachful look when I'd refused our maid's offer, but she'd apparently been too tired to press the matter, and had instead retired to her room, claiming a headache. Maggie had quietly disappeared to her own room, no doubt seeking the solace of one of her books, while Isabel and Bridget had tearfully departed upstairs, saying they wanted to start packing. I wasn't sure what they thought they had such a desperate need to take with them into Brytwilde. I had a strong suspicion none of our human fashions would be considered fine enough once we lived in the castle, and all our dresses would be replaced.

Now, Grace gave me a firm expression I wasn't used to seeing on her face. Her eyes skimmed over my wild hair and every place my dress and skin had been torn.

I swallowed thickly, averting my eyes to watch a drop of wax run down the candle Hannah had set on my bedside table to prepare for our homecoming. "Some of the women were...angry that I will be a part of the royal family through your marriage. They surrounded me and..." I shrugged, meeting Grace's eyes, finding tears pooling in her blue gaze. "When I told them I was under the protection of their queen, they stopped."

"They never should have started," Grace said, rushing forward to brush a strand of hair away from my face. "Let's get you out of that dress and clean you up."

I was silent and numb as Grace rang for Hannah, requesting a bowl of water and a cloth. Then my sister set to work helping me out of my ruined dress.

When Hannah knocked and Grace went to fetch the bowl, my sister didn't close the door fast enough. Our maid's wide eyes landed on the cuts tracing my arms, and she gasped. "Miss, are you all right? Do you need anything else?"

I shook my head fiercely. "It's nothing." I forced a smile. "They don't even hurt anymore."

"I'll take care of her," Grace soothed, gently pushing Hannah back into the hall and shutting the door behind her. She returned to crouch beside my bed, wetting her cloth and dabbing at the dried blood flecking my skin.

I hissed.

"You said they didn't hurt anymore," Grace reminded me crossly.

"They only hurt a little," I amended.

She frowned but didn't pause in her work. "I'll speak with Prince Holden of this," she declared. "I know he will ensure this never happens again. Not to a single one of us."

I drew back, surprised. "You don't plan to request the protection of the man whom you are to marry tomorrow?"

Another furrow formed between Grace's brows as she swept a golden curl behind her ear. "Elle, I have always resigned myself to a loveless marriage, you know that. But Prince Fitz didn't even lower himself to dance with me. We barely exchanged two words all night! I hope he will be agreeable, if for no other reason than because he needs children." She swallowed, uncomfortable. "His brother, however... He gave his word that we would all be under his and his family's protection, and told me I can come to him with any concerns."

I ducked my head to peer into her eyes, trying to better study her expression, but she glanced at the cloth in her hand to avoid me. "You care about him."

"You and I both know that I cannot afford the luxury of feelings," Grace whispered.

I clasped her hand in mine. "That knowledge doesn't change your heart. Answer me honestly. You spent all night with him, dancing and laughing."

Grace's lips trembled. "I do care for him. I hardly know him, yet in one night I feel as if I understand him better than anyone else in the world—apart from you."

I gently plucked the cloth from Grace and took both her hands in mine, tugging her onto the bed beside me. "Could he...have used glamour?" I asked hesitantly. I knew my sister was no fool, yet I couldn't help but worry for her.

Grace shook her head adamantly. "He promised never to use glamour on any of us. He vowed it almost as soon as we began dancing, saying he wanted us to be comfortable with them, to know we are safe."

I smiled. "He sounds kind indeed."

"Am I mad, to have grown attached to a man I've only known a few hours, all when I'm promised to someone else?" Grace asked, her laughter tremulous.

"Absolutely not," I insisted, my eyes burning with tears I wouldn't shed. I didn't want to cry and remind us both that whatever joy Grace had found with Holden could never last. Life seemed impossibly cruel in this moment, when all I wanted was to see the sparkle of hope in my sister's eyes last forever. "Tell me all about him."

And so, like any other young woman in our town who could giggle and blush over a handsome and charming man, Grace described Holden's many virtues. "He introduced me to a number of the human servants, Elle!" she exclaimed. "He treated them with respect and kindness, and I could tell by their regard for him that his friendship with them is sincere. Their admiration for him was obvious, which is what convinced me that he meant what he said about ensuring our every happiness once we moved into the castle." She sighed, a dreamy look on her face. "He listened to my foolish hopes and dreams, or what is left of them." As if remembering herself, she straightened and frowned. "But he knows as well as I do that anything between us can never be."

I pulled her to me, wrapping my arms around her slender form and noting the way she trembled.

"He was only being friendly; but tonight, he felt a little like my savior, sweeping me away from all my nightmares of the fae and a loveless, miserable marriage," Grace admitted. "I think in him, I saw an escape. A perfect, impossible dream to be infatuated with. I'm so afraid. Nothing about Prince Fitz appears kind...and now, to know his brother is his opposite..."

"It's not fair," I said, my fury lashing like flames at my heart. I squeezed my sister more tightly, as if by sheer force of will, I could stop tomorrow from arriving. "You are the best person I know, and you, out of anyone, deserve happiness and love. It's not fair that *you* bear the burden of ensuring our family's security."

Grace's voice cracked. "Mother and Father had no other choice—"

"I refuse to believe that," I said bitterly. "I love them, I do," I added when Grace tossed me a look. "I miss Father so much it hurts to breathe. But we've always been taught that striking a deal with the fae ends poorly...yet that is exactly what they did. I know they believed our circumstances were desperate, but surely they could have turned to the generosity of a neighbor, a friend...someone!"

I slipped out of bed, tugging on a nightgown and sitting before our vanity to brush out my hair. One lone petal fell out as I worked through the tangles the fae had snared in my locks with their angry fingers.

Still on my bed, with her ballgown spread around her, Grace shrugged. "I suppose they had exhausted all other options at the time. You've seen how little our neighbors have stepped outside of their comfortable lives to help us. We became outcasts the instant Father died. They're already living as if we've moved into the forest."

"That sounds positively unforgiving of you," I teased.

Grace frowned, but if it was out of guilt or frustration, I couldn't tell. "One runs out of kind things to say when everyone calls you doomed and turns away from you."

Setting down my brush, I stared at Grace's solemn reflection in the mirror, at her straight back and carefully folded hands. "If Father were still here, he wouldn't stand for anyone disrespecting or ignoring us like this."

Tears glistened in her eyes. "He couldn't convince them to help before he and Mother betrothed me to Prince Fitz. And anyway, he's not here, and we have to go on without him." She peered around the room. "Without our home. Without..." She choked off her words, shaking her head and wiping away her tears.

Without his love, I finished in my head. *Without safety. Without the comforts of home and neighbors who don't want to kill you.*

My fingers itched to pluck out my locket and try opening it again. It refused to budge—it never had opened, not even for Father—yet in that moment, I could feel the magic within calling out to me. I didn't think it alone contained enough power to raise the dead, though whispered tales brought from Mr. Reid and relayed to me by Father had claimed some magic could do such things. Though my search for books on necromancy at Fletcher's had failed, those rumors I'd grown up hearing wouldn't leave me alone.

There had to be a shred of truth to them. And maybe a way to save Father.

"Try to get some sleep," I told my sister, helping her out of her corset and gown and then taking down her hair.

Red-eyed and silent, she let me settle her into bed and tuck the bed-clothes around her. She'd fought to be strong and obedient, gentle and kind, for so long, and to bear this weight for our entire family and never complain about it to our younger sisters. To ensure they weren't afraid the way she was, or the way I was. She'd smiled and pretended almost all her life.

Now, she was utterly exhausted, and even on the night before her life as she knew it would end, she couldn't fight that weariness. She blinked bleary eyes as she thanked me, and my heart eased. She'd be asleep soon, hopefully lost in a dreamless escape.

Muttering an excuse about needing tea, I slipped from our bedroom and closed the door behind me. I wouldn't be sleeping tonight.

Heart thundering in my ears, I crept barefoot downstairs, avoiding the places I knew would creak. I swung open the door to Father's study, inhaling the scents of tobacco, leather, and ink. Sinking into his armchair, I stared blankly at the bookshelves. Spines with labels about human history and finance and other dull topics that would be of no use stared back at me. I already knew where all of Father's forbidden books were hidden, and I'd memorized their contents years ago. There was nothing on necromancy but a few hints, enough to tell me that I needed an important object from Father's life to tie him to his mortality, and plenty of fae magic.

I already wore the locket that I trusted would tie Father to his mortal life. And in Brytwilde, I could find more information on necromancy, as well as the magic I needed.

Outside, the wind rustled, and the branches of our old oak groaned.

Many fae in Ashwood Forest possess such powerful magic that they imbue objects with it, called charms, I recited in my mind, closing my eyes and recalling everything I knew. *Though a few charms are sealed with powerful magic, meaning only their creators can wield them, most are not. Unsealed charms can be stolen and used by anyone, granting even a mortal a portion of fae magic. The Ashwood family possesses the most potent magic of all, and it is said that even their human wives are gifted a portion after their weddings, so that they might be accepted as true royalty.*

Drawing the locket from beneath my nightgown, I squeezed it in my palm, feeling the warmth emanating from it. It was unnatural, like a jolt of lightning. Powerful and beautiful. A reminder of the magic it possessed.

With the locket, I had magic that I didn't know how to use. A sealed charm that would do me no good, not on its own, anyway. Perhaps I could find a way to use it, or I could steal more charms in Brytwilde.

Or...

Or I could trick the tricksters and claim their magic for myself.

My hands trembled. I could take my sister's place. The books I'd read explained that the fae honored mortal weddings, much like they'd hosted a ball that was demure and human-like for us this past night. Likely, it was their way of lulling potential brides into a sense of peace before they were bound by their vows.

I closed my eyes again, not even needing to find Father's book to recall the picture on the page depicting a human dressed to marry a fae and the words around it. I'd read it so many times, I'd long since memorized it. *Fae garb their human brides in dresses in our own mortal style, but they add a long veil crafted with magic. The veil allows the bride to see, but it conceals her face from view. Some claim this is because the fae are disgusted by human appearance, and do not want to reveal the human bride until she is royalty, gifted with magic. Others believe it stems from a desire to avoid having to behold a bride shedding tears on her wedding day.*

If I wore that veil, I could take Grace's place, and no one would know the difference until the vows were spoken. Even fae wedding vows were simple, as Father's book had shared. The fae wouldn't even deign to say the bride's true name, which gave me the perfect loophole. When Prince Fitz spoke his vows, they would be to the human woman standing beside him, *whoever* she was.

As a princess, granted magic of my own—or close enough to steal a charm from my new husband, if need be—I would be in the perfect position to rescue Father from his premature death.

And if I rescued Father, none of this would matter. We could flee Brytwilde and find a distant human city where the fae would never find us. We could be *free*.

But could you really? If you were the crown prince's wife, their princess, a human woman capable of giving the Ashwood prince heirs...would the fae ever rest if you disappeared? What if you can't escape?

I swallowed thickly. "Then so be it," I whispered into the shadows. "I will help my family escape. Father could find honest work to support them. I can bear a life apart from them, among the fae, if I only know they're safe and happy." I blinked at my gathering tears. *But I won't give up hope that I can share that happy fate.*

Emboldened, I stood and paced the length of the study as I considered my plan. Prince Fitz would likely be furious, and I knew he wasn't one to underestimate. But fae were creatures of their word, bound to the truth and unable to lie. For them, vows were sacred things that could not be undone, no matter how much they wished. And in the end, all he needed was a human woman—any human woman. He would still be marrying into the Blackford family, fulfilling Queen Griselda's vow to my parents.

Perhaps Prince Fitz would turn out to be not only cold and arrogant, but also dark and vicious. My mind conjured up dark visions of a violent immortal bent on using his magic to hurt and kill. Weeping. Blood. Bodies strewn in his wake.

I repressed a shiver, dispelling the images. *He can't harm me, not according to the promises of protection his family has made. And not if he wants me to bear heirs.* I cringed at the thought. *But maybe he'll find other ways to torment me.*

I squeezed my hands into fists. *It doesn't matter.* If I had to, I'd steal all his magic. I'd survive in the cruel fae world, long enough for my family—and hopefully me—to escape. He might have power, but the very fact that the royal fae married humans to ensure their lines continued was proof that I would have a sort of power of my own, too.

He could destroy you, a voice whispered in my head, one that sounded very much like my father's. *Rumors say the Ashwood family is dark and dangerous. Their only duty to mortals is to usher the dead into the afterlife. They don't care about us when we are alive. Crossing Fitz by tricking him is a dangerous game to play...*

I brushed the worrisome thoughts away. If it gave me a chance to save my family, I was willing to risk my safety. Now that the idea had formed in my head, there was no banishing it. For my sister, for my father, I would bear anything.

My resolve was greater than my fear and hatred of Prince Fitz.

If he was the darkness, I was the flame that would destroy him.

CHAPTER SIX

"Wait, I have one more!" Isabel shrieked, rushing down the stairs and hugging a dress to her chest. A human servant that had arrived with the fae coach this afternoon hefted her trunk in his arms, prepared to load the coach and take us away.

Mother glanced anxiously between her youngest daughter and the servant, whose expressionless mask was swiftly dissolving into annoyance. "Izzy dear, I don't think any of your dresses are fine enough for life in the Ashwood court. I'm sure Queen Griselda will provide you with ones more befitting our new life when we're settled in the castle."

Isabel bit her lip to stop it from trembling as another servant joined the first, carrying our six trunks one by one from the house. It only took a few minutes for the remainder of our lives to be stuffed into the back of a single coach.

"It's not dresses I want to take with me," Maggie muttered from where she stood at my side. She glanced around the hall, her gaze distant. Her eyes were dark when they settled on mine. "Elle, do you think Father and all our memories will feel further away once we've left?"

I blinked against building tears and squeezed her hand. "I hope not."

One of the servants returned, carrying a box that he offered to Grace. "The queen requested we bring Miss Grace Blackford's wedding dress," he announced with a reverent dip of his head. "You are to try it on and ensure it fits properly, but do not wear it on the ride over and risk damaging it. She will provide a place within the castle for you to prepare for the ceremony."

"I'll help you, Grace," Mother said, pulling away from the doorway and trailing Grace up the stairs toward our bedroom. "Ellie," she called, "be sure that your sisters are settled into the coach. We'll only be a few minutes."

Stifling my sigh, I turned to Maggie, Bridget, and Isabel each in turn, bidding them to wipe their eyes with their handkerchiefs and straighten their dresses. We were all clothed in our finest, though I knew that just like last night, they would pale in comparison to fae extravagance. Perhaps Queen Griselda would also have wedding clothes awaiting us and demand we change to suit her whims.

"Come on," I said, clasping Bridget's hand and gently tugging her toward the door. Both servants were standing by the coach, prepared to hand us in.

"I want to say goodbye," Bridget whimpered.

"What, will the pianoforte cry over your leaving?" Isabel mocked around her own sniffles. "It's only a house, but if I could have taken my dresses..."

"Dresses mean nothing," Maggie cut in. "This house, though? It is full of *memories*! Let Bridget cry." She stormed out the door and swooped into the coach before a servant could offer her his hand.

As I stepped outside, half-dragging Bridget, Isabel frowned. "She's been cross with me all morning," she whined.

Sometimes, I had to remind myself that Isabel was only fifteen—although more self-absorbed and fixated on silly things than I'd ever been at her age. I wanted to tell her that Bridget and Maggie were right, and they were crying for the loss of something intangible, not the clothing they had been forced to leave behind. But I knew Isabel was mourning in her own way. Her dresses were how she expressed herself, and though Father hadn't been able to afford all the latest fashions, he'd doted on us as much as he could. He'd once gifted Isabel several lengths of beautiful ribbon to add to her bonnet, all because he said he thought the colors would set off her eyes.

Pausing to pull Bridget into a comforting embrace, I sighed. Maybe it wasn't about the clothes for Isabel, either.

"No fae deal can take our memories of Father away," I declared. Bridget sniffled, likely covering my dress in her tears, and Isabel sighed, turning away from the house. "This isn't the end of our happiness," I vowed.

The return journey into the forest was silent. Even Mother had run out of things to fret about, and all our tears had run dry. The somberness of the occasion gripped us firmly. Fear writhed in my chest, a winged creature beating against my ribcage.

When I glanced at Grace, I found her skin pale and her eyes glazed with a terrible look of resignation. I couldn't help but wonder what she and Mother had spoken of when they'd been alone, fitting Grace into a wedding dress she didn't want to wear.

Slipping my hand into the pocket sewn inside my dress, I ran my fingertips along the vial within and thought of the day Father had shown it to me.

"Nightsweet," he'd declared proudly *as we stood at his desk within his study. "I purchased it at Fletcher's, though you musn't tell a soul, Elle. This drug is made from special herbs found only in Brytwilde, and slipped in a mug of tea, for instance, its mild flavor is hardly noticeable. It only takes a splash to put a grown man into a deep sleep for a few hours."*

I frowned. "Why did you want that? We have the locket. If we can't learn how to use it, then perhaps we can sell it for money. Or bargain with the fae. Surely they'll want their charm back."

"They would kill us merely for possessing such a forbidden object," Father said solemnly. "Never let them see it. No—this nightsweet I'll keep hidden, in case of the worst."

Rolling my eyes, I bumped my hip into his. "You have many years left, Father."

"Still." Father's eyes were entreating when he turned to me. "I want you to know where it is. In case you and your mother and sisters have no choice and must venture into Brytwilde, I want you to have something. It could be used as a last resort, a way to put the fae prince to sleep so you can escape."

"They would never stop searching for us," I murmured despondently.

"You are clever." Father clasped my hand, squeezing it gently. "I know it's a fool's hope, like everything we've tried. But give me this small sense of peace. Remember where I'm hiding it, and take it with you."

"I promise."

Now, I thought about my plan, how I'd be using the nightsweet in an entirely unexpected way.

As the coach rattled over the dirt road, I stared out the window at afternoon sunlight burnishing the leaves still clinging to the trees. At last, we rounded the final bend and the castle itself loomed ahead. The wind picked up, whistling through the forest.

My stomach churned when we eased through the gates, horse hooves clattering against the courtyard's cobblestones. Fae servants scurried out to tend to us, bowing low when our coachman opened the door and handed us out one by one. I left last, trailing behind Grace.

A tall, thin woman with soft violet eyes and green curls that reminded me of moss stepped forward. Though her smooth, pale skin made her appear youthful—perhaps no older than I was—I knew that among immortals, there was no easy way to judge age. She could have just as easily been older than my entire family combined. "Welcome," she said, and I was both surprised and relieved that her tone was not unkind. "I am Lina, servant of Ashwood Castle, and honored to welcome you into Queen Griselda's court. Which of you is Miss Grace Blackford?"

"I am," Grace said bravely, tipping up her chin and smiling with a warmth I knew she didn't feel.

"Pleased to meet you," Lina said, curtseying gracefully. "The others will guide your family members to their rooms and help them prepare for the wedding, but as your personal maid, I will lead you to yours and ensure you're ready for the ceremony."

Grace cast a nervous glance my way. It was the briefest instant of hesitation, but Lina's sharp eyes caught it.

"If you would prefer," Lina started, "a member of your family could accompany you..."

"Yes," I blurted. "I would love to help Grace prepare."

I felt Mother's gaze on me, but I ignored her as I took Grace's hand and followed Lina, sweeping past the servants unloading our trunks and through the castle entrance. The plush carpets dulled our steps as we left the hall and the ballroom from last night behind to ascend several sets of curving stairs, rising toward a painted ceiling and glistening chandeliers. My legs were burning, and my hand was clammy in my sister's grasp by the time we stopped on an upper floor.

"How many floors are there?" I gasped, and Lina glanced over her shoulder with a smile. I decided I liked her, even if I desperately needed to find a reason for her to leave Grace and me alone. And soon.

"Six, and your rooms are all on the fourth," Lina explained. "Miss Grace's is next to the crown prince's suite, and the rest of you have rooms close by. Her Majesty thought you would prefer to be near one another."

Grace squeezed my hand, probably in relief. This castle was enormous, and I was already lost. At least we wouldn't have several floors between us; it should be easy to find one another.

It was difficult for me to relish this knowledge, though, when my heart was pounding in my ears, dulling all other sounds. I was conscious of Lina saying something else, but I could no longer make out her words. We paused before a white doorway inlaid with gilded carvings, and Lina made a grand gesture as she swept it open and stepped aside, letting my sister and I enter first.

There were multiple rooms, from a cozy sitting room with armchairs arranged before a fire, to a vast bedroom with a canopied bed of white and gold large enough for my entire family, to a dining room and washroom, all for Grace's personal use.

My personal use, I corrected myself. Once I took my sister's place, I would be living here, close to the prince.

Or I'd be dead.

I refused to linger on that possibility.

In an instant, a whole group of maids rushed through the doorway, filling the room with chaos as they laid out Grace's wedding dress, fussing over it more than needed, I thought. Another brought forward a tea tray, but Grace waved it away wearily, too overcome to nibble on a pastry or try the offered beverage.

As the maids urged her to sit before the vanity, my sister reluctantly released my hand and staggered over to the stool with the look of one lost in a dream.

My eyes latched onto the tea tray, which one of the maids had left on a side table. Relief filled me, knowing I wouldn't need to waste more time requesting refreshments.

"Wait," I managed, voice surprisingly firm.

Multiple pairs of fae eyes turned on me, their expressions ranging from inquisitive to annoyed.

"I...I need to speak to my sister first," I managed. "It's a custom," I went on, gaining courage as my lie took form, "for us mortals. Perhaps newer, one you likely don't know of yet. A member of the bride's family does her hair alone, so she has time to reflect quietly on her upcoming marriage."

For a long moment, Lina didn't speak, and I feared she didn't believe me. But then she smiled and dipped her head. "I'll knock when we return, to help Miss Grace into her dress."

The maids followed her out as swiftly as they'd arrived, leaving the rooms mercifully empty and still. I released a breath, sinking onto the bed as Grace whirled on the stool to face me.

"Thank you. You don't know how much I needed these last moments of peace," she said, tears glistening in her eyes.

My heart pounded in my ears as I strode across the room toward the tea tray. "Fetch your veil," I murmured. "I think we need some tea, something soothing before...well. Everything."

Smiling wanly, Grace nodded and rose, walking to the bed where the maids had left her dress and veil.

Stomach clenching, I cast a swift look over my shoulder to ensure my sister was occupied with studying the magical veil before I uncapped the vial of nightsweet and splashed some into one of the mugs. Shoving the vial back into my pocket, I poured two mugs of tea and approached my sister.

"Interesting how the fabric is magical," Grace mused. "How they don't want to see my face until it is all over."

"Because they think they're better than us," I said sharply. "I changed my mind. Set it down. Let's rest on the bed and sip some tea before I do your hair."

My sister looked too weary, too sad, to even make a remark about how we shouldn't have been wasting time. She collapsed onto the bed with a heavy sigh. I perched beside her, poking her gently in the side until she sat up and accepted her mug of tea.

"Mmm," I said, taking a long sip of the tea. It was delicious—mildly sweet and refreshing and unlike anything I'd ever tasted in the mortal world. Perhaps it had been the right choice. It certainly seemed to steel my nerves as I inhaled the steam curling up from within.

Grace smacked her lips. "Mine tastes a little bitter."

I shrugged. "It's different from our tea, but it does seem to soothe the spirits, don't you think?"

"Indeed." She took another long gulp, risking burning her mouth in the process. Leaning back, her eyelids fluttered. "Thank you for this, Elle. I needed a moment to breathe." She cradled her mug in her hands, looking so delicate in that moment that my heart pinched.

I hoped she would forgive me. "You're welcome," I whispered, but Grace was already drooping, and I wasn't sure she heard me.

Before she could drop the mug and spill the hot liquid across her front, I caught it. As Grace sank back onto the bed, head lolling, I scurried across the room to deposit both our cups on the tray. When I whirled around, my sister was lightly snoring, lost to the world.

I had to hurry.

To my relief, the maids didn't waste time questioning me when they re-turned to find I'd drawn the curtains closed around the bed. Magical veil firmly in place, they couldn't see my face or even my dark hair. When I explained that Elle had taken ill with a mortal sickness, they'd happily kept their distance from the bed and followed me out into the sitting room to help me don the wedding dress.

Lina alone appeared uneasy as her fellow maids finished lacing my dress. "You look lovely," she said. "Are you sure your sister will be all right?" A frown creased her brow. "The queen...she will not be pleased by her absence."

I cleared my throat, doing my best to imitate Grace's softer voice. Thank-fully, I knew none of the fae were as familiar with its timbre as I was, so my ruse would be easy to maintain. "She would be more displeased if Elle vomited during the ceremony," I said.

Lina's complexion turned a shade paler. "Indeed. Well then, I suppose you are ready. Everyone is gathered outside. Follow me."

Please understand, Grace, I thought as we swept from the rooms and left my sister to her deep slumber. I'd dumped both mugs of tea and found a basin of water to clean out any remnants of nightsweet. The vial itself I'd dropped into a vase of silk flowers on the mantel, praying that it wasn't something any servant would do more than dust.

I had to stifle a groan when Lina led me toward the staircase again. My gown wasn't overly ornate, but it did have a small train in the back that I feared would prove deadly while descending the endless steps. As if reading my thoughts, Lina quirked a smile and shifted until she stood behind me, bending to lift the fabric in her arms. "Hold the banister," she advised, "and walk slowly. Better to arrive late than fall to your death. It's not as if the wedding can begin without you, anyway."

Beneath my veil, my lips twitched into a slight smile.

At last, we swept outside, where I was thankful for the layers of my dress. The afternoon was growing chillier, a whispering breeze tugging at the end of my veil and promising a cold night. Leaves crackled beneath my slippers and filled the air with the crisp scent of autumn.

Lina didn't need to guide me far into the forest beyond the castle grounds before the sound of murmuring voices signaled the site of the wedding.

Time rushed forward all too swiftly as we stepped into a clearing, where the boughs of trees laden with crimson and golden leaves swayed gently like a delicate ceiling, crowding out the sky. Dappled sunlight danced over the forest floor, dusted in wildflowers and moss. Birdsong and rustling leaves filled the air, mingling with the soft whispers of fae as they leaned toward one another to gossip while I approached. Their inhuman eyes took me in, scanning the gown I wore. I was thankful for the veil that concealed the frustrated blush suffusing my cheeks.

The gathering was small, clothed in the same variety of extravagant or barely-there attire I'd witnessed the night of the ball, and mostly barefoot despite the chill air. Many were already holding goblets of fae wine aloft, sipping generously. A few sprites fluttered about, circling my veil and tugging at the material until a single sharp look from Queen Griselda sent them darting away. My gaze fastened on the queen, who stood beneath the largest tree I'd ever seen, its trunk easily wider than four men and so tall its blood-red leaves seemed to brush the sky. Several of its mossy roots broke through the earth, creating a sort of natural barrier that kept the queen and the crown prince separate from the rest of the court.

Nearby, Mother and my sisters stood in lovely dresses in deep shades of burgundy, plum, and gold, mimicking the autumn leaves. The clothes were human in their style, proving that the fae queen wasn't without a heart and wanted us to feel welcome. Or that she knew how to make us comfortable until she'd fully lured us into her world.

My stomach fluttered as Lina paused at my side, bowed, and stepped away. I was on my own.

"Where is the other one?" Queen Griselda demanded, her voice deep and annoyed.

I froze, uncertain if I should advance without an invitation. Behind me, Lina bowed and scraped some more. "She is afflicted with an illness, Your Majesty, and remains in Miss Grace's rooms. She did not want to cause a scene with her...mortal weakness."

Queen Griselda sniffed, but she let the matter go. Her eyes traced my form, critical even though I wore the dress her seamstresses had made for me. She herself was clothed in a deep red dress, its shade making me imagine she'd carved out the heart of some poor human and dyed her clothing in the blood. A fine crown of silver, with rubies glistening along its points, adorned her hair, which cascaded almost to her waist. "Come forward, girl," she ordered, and an angry part of me wanted to ignore the rude command.

Lifting my head, I proceeded until I was directly in front of her. Crown Prince Fitz was on my left, silent and unmoving, but I refused to turn and glance at him. Out of the corner of my eye, all I saw was a blur of darkness, his rich attire of a deep blue velvet that reminded me of something a human royal might wear. Another strange way the queen was either comforting or deceiving us.

The queen sighed, cracking open a book, and raised her voice to address the crowd. "You are here to witness the marriage union of my son, Crown Prince Fitz Ashwood, to the human, Miss Blackford. Your presence signifies your approval of this marriage, and your acceptance of Miss Blackford as your princess and future queen, if the magic of the forest accepts her as well."

My heart throbbed in my throat. *And what does that mean? What happens if the magic denies me?* My palms turned clammy. Would it see through my deception and reject me?

The rest of the ceremony was a haze.

"Do you take this woman as your bride?" Queen Griselda asked her son stiffly.

His voice was cold and deep. "I do."

"And do you accept Crown Prince Fitz Ashwood as your husband?" Queen Griselda asked, pinning me with eyes that seemed to pierce through my veil into my soul. For one terrifying instant, I thought maybe she could see through the magical fabric and my lies. But she didn't stop the wedding, didn't shout any accusations.

I spoke the words through numb lips. "I do."

As Queen Griselda bid us to turn together, her court bowed to us, my family included.

"And now, we will retire and leave you for the rest of the ceremony," the queen announced. Her people left in a flurry, taking my mother and sisters with them. Queen Griselda followed, her dark red dress standing out among the crowd as her guards formed a circle around her.

The birdsong sounded muted in my head, but the wind whispering through the trees was louder, seeming to carry voices speaking words I couldn't quite make out. My head spun, and I resisted the urge to shiver. It was done. I'd tricked the fae.

I turned hesitantly toward Fitz, realizing we were utterly alone.

CHAPTER SEVEN

"Are you ever going to lift that hideous veil, or must I?" Prince Fitz's tone was dry, and for a brief instant, I thought I saw the shadow of a smile on his lips. Up close, I realized his blue eyes weren't exactly like his mother's. They were deeper, richer—and though they still reflected a cold, withdrawn attitude, in that moment, they didn't seem unkind.

Surely I was imagining it.

I threw my hands over the fabric, as if bracing myself for him to rush me and rip it off. "And why do I need to remove it here, in the middle of the woods?" I gestured around, as if the prince had forgotten we stood within his forest.

"For the magic ceremony," he said, stepping closer. Close enough to touch me. My heart slammed into my ribs, and I sucked in a breath. "How did you think we royals transferred our magic to human wives?"

"You don't do that through the vows?" I asked weakly.

Fitz shook his head, rustling his dark, chin-length hair. "Our magic is in our blood." He pulled open his velvet coat to reach for a dagger hanging from his belt, sliding it with a hiss from its sheath. Its hilt was inlaid with rubies that matched his mother's crown, though—for the first time, now that I dared to study him closely—I realized he didn't wear a crown of his own. He pressed the blade to his fingertip until a drop of blood welled. "It's for this transference that you must remove the veil." He spoke patiently, not annoyed but not eager either. This was a business transaction for him, just part of his duty as a prince.

Hysterical laughter bubbled up. I'd known I couldn't put off this moment forever, though I would have been lying to myself if I hadn't hoped it would happen later, after I'd had even just one instant to myself to plan my next step. With trembling fingers, I seized the fabric and tugged it back, letting it cascade behind me.

Shock and then anger flashed in the prince's eyes. "You—" He shook his head, at a loss for words. Taking a step back, he gathered himself, letting his cold mask fall back into place. "Is this a joke to you?" His words trembled with suppressed fury, but I stood straight, hands fisted at my sides, refusing to let him see how terrified I was.

"No."

"Then why the trickery? You are not the one my mother bargained for."

"Surely it doesn't matter. All your mother wanted was a human so you could—" I swallowed. "Produce heirs."

"She requested your mother's eldest daughter." Fitz's eyes flashed. "And she does *not* like to be crossed." His jaw flexed. "And neither do I."

I spoke my next words with more confidence than I felt. "We've already exchanged vows in front of her witnesses. What will she do? Kill me despite those vows?"

Fitz stared at his bleeding finger. "No," he murmured, "but there are many other ways an immortal queen could make a mortal's life hellish, without laying a hand on you."

I stepped forward, hoping my boldness would be rewarded. "And what will *you* do? You cannot break your word."

When he lifted his face to meet my gaze, his smile was wry. "No, my word is worth considerably more than yours, it would seem. I cannot lie or deceive you. I spoke the words to accept you as my wife, even if I thought you were another. Those words cannot be changed or undone."

He stalked forward, and I stepped back, my pulse skipping a beat.

"Why did you do it? To mock me?"

I blinked. "What?"

Fitz crossed his arms. "You overheard me at the ball last night and threw my words back in my face. I take it that I hurt your vanity, and now you hold some sort of grudge and wanted to exact revenge."

This time, my laughter rang out harshly. Loudly. "If I wanted to punish you, I wouldn't *marry* you. How self-absorbed can you be? Do you really think my choice had *anything* to do with you?"

For a moment, Fitz's wrath seemed to cool, overtaken by his surprise. "Then why did you take Grace's place?"

I crossed my own arms, mimicking his arrogant smile. "She deserves better than you."

"Fine," Fitz snapped. "Don't tell me." He lifted his finger, still blooming with a drop of bright red blood. "A mortal life—that was the bargain. The risks you take are your own. It is your folly." With those words, he seemed to wash his hands of me, his anger returning to his customary indifference. "There is nothing else to do but finish this."

I remained still as he brushed his blood onto my skin, tracing a pattern that must have had some sort of significance along my cheeks and chin. His finger was calloused and warm, but his touch didn't linger longer than necessary. He kept his eyes rooted on his task, studying only my skin and the blood he painted upon it, rather than meeting my gaze.

"As our vows have sealed us in marriage, may the sharing of my blood tether Ashwood's magic—*my* magic—to you. May you be bound to this land as I am bound to it. May this land be bound to you, as it is bound to me."

As soon as he was done, he stepped back, like he couldn't stand another moment near me. My shoulders sagged with relief. Even if that was foolish. I was as bound to this man as he'd proclaimed his magic would be. Distance between us was an illusion, when I might be trapped with him, in this dismal land with his ghostly castle, for the rest of my mortal existence.

"Is that all?" I asked.

Fitz sheathed his dagger. "The rest remains to be seen. Either the magic will accept you, deceit and all, or it won't."

I wanted to ask what a magical rejection would entail, but he was already striding back toward the castle, his leather boots scattering leaves and snapping twigs in his path. Without turning or pausing, he called to me. "Come, and pull your veil back down. No sense in angering Mother any sooner than necessary."

My heart lurched as I tugged on my veil and hurried to reach his side, wondering what the queen's anger would mean for me.

"I take it Grace is the one hiding back in your rooms," Fitz went on, tugging on his collar as if it was bothering him. He was likely more used to loose shirts like the one he'd worn the night of the ball, not constricting human clothes. "She can help you dress for your coronation, but that will be where your charade ends. No more veils."

I nodded gravely, and a moment of silence passed between us as the castle came into view, its edges gilded by light from the slanting sun.

"Why did you take your sister's place?" the prince asked, pausing and pinning me with his gaze.

"You already asked that."

He sneered. "Perhaps I hoped to catch you in a lie."

Though he couldn't see my face beneath the veil, I refused to flinch. "Not at all. My answer is unchanged. I couldn't subject her to a lifetime of misery."

"So you are the hero of her story, taking her place by sacrificing yourself to the villain?" He smirked, and I wished he could see my scowl.

"She is the best, most selfless person I know," I said fiercely, "and she deserves the world."

He lifted his brows, yet turned away as if the matter only half-interested him. "And you do not?"

I ignored his question, trailing him silently until we reached the door to my rooms.

"Was your sister complicit in this?" Fitz demanded, turning on me one last time.

"She's innocent. I tricked her too and left her behind. I alone should bear the queen's wrath." I fisted my hands. "And yours."

Fitz shrugged, but he didn't protest. Without another word, he strode a short distance to another door—the entrance to his neighboring rooms.

I nearly tore the knob off my door as I wrenched it open. "Insufferable, unfeeling, nasty man," I muttered under my breath, but Grace interrupted by flying toward me, her expression livid. She scanned me head to foot, taking note of the veil still in place.

"Awake already?" I asked faintly, tearing off the veil and tossing it to the floor.

"Elle, what have you done?" Grace's hair was a wild, frizzy halo about her face, her cheeks still flushed from her sleep. "They'll hurt you. Tell me it isn't over—tell me it isn't too late."

I braced myself. "The wedding is over. Prince Fitz and I are married, and he saw who I am. He thinks I'm petty, or maybe that I was jealous of you. Better he thinks that."

Grace's eyes flashed with repressed fury. It wasn't often I saw my mild-mannered sister so roused, and extremely rare for me to see her anger directed toward me. "You drugged me."

"I'm sor—"

"You tricked me! You knew this was my duty, my way to protect all of you, and you took it from me!"

Shock thrummed through my veins as I gaped at my sister's face, taking in the tears glistening in her lovely eyes. "I saved you!" I protested. "I'm going to save us all. Father and I studied magic. I'm going to find a way to bring him back using necromancy. I'm going to find a way so we can all escape and leave this awful life behind."

Grace blinked. "Are you mad? They'll never let us leave."

"Perhaps not me," I admitted, "but they'd let the rest of you go. I had to do it. For Father. For you. For all of us." Tears burned my own eyes. "Please understand, Grace. I have to try. And I saw how miserable you were...and how happy you were with Holden... You deserve a *choice*."

A tear snaked down Grace's cheek and I dared to lean forward, pulling her into an embrace. Sighing, my sister wrapped her arms around me, pulling me close. "We *all* deserve a choice."

"I know. And I made mine."

"I don't know about this magic, or the risks you're taking, or necromancy to save Father," Grace said, "but I trust you. Though I wish next time you wouldn't trick or drug me. Tell me your plan!"

Sniffling, I pulled back and lifted my chin. "We didn't have time to argue, and you know you would have."

Grace shrugged, but then froze, her eyes darting to the dried blood adorning my face as if just noticing it for the first time. "Are you all right?"

"Oh," I said. "It's not mine. It was part of the ceremony so the prince could share his magic." I hurried through the quarters to the immaculate washroom. I found a bowl of water and a cloth, scrubbing my face until it was clean.

My sister trailed after me. "Will they hurt you?" Grace whispered. I turned, and she pulled me into another tight embrace. I hugged her back fiercely.

"They cannot hurt me, for I am their princess," I said with courage I did not possess. I didn't want Grace to know that the magic might reject me, or that Fitz had claimed his mother had plenty of other ways to torture me. I'd made my choice, and I refused to let anyone but myself suffer for it.

"Someone left a dress for your coronation while I was still asleep," Grace went on. "I found it hanging in the open wardrobe when I awoke. I can help you into it."

I squeezed her tighter. "Thank you. I promise, everything will be all right."

"The queen will be furious," she murmured, and I could feel the way she trembled.

"None of her fury can touch me," I lied.

Resting my hand over the place where my locket was concealed beneath my wedding dress, I left the washroom for my new bedroom. In the open wardrobe awaited a dress of silvery-blue with floral detailing along the bodice. It would be the perfect complement to Fitz's dark blue outfit. I'd be the moonlight beside his shadows while I claimed my crown.

And then, I'll find a way to save you, Father, I thought, tugging out the locket and relishing its weight in my palm. If Ashwood's magic accepted me, would I gain the power to finally open it? Would I have enough magic to perform necromancy and bring back Father, or would I need to steal a charm from my new husband too?

I caught a glimpse of more fabric behind the dress and frowned. "What is this other dress meant for?" I asked, stepping forward to brush the silver-blue gown aside to better reveal the gauzy white gown behind it.

"That is in the fae style, and is for their celebration later tonight," Grace explained.

"Another one?" My voice faltered. I'd hoped that perhaps after the coronation I'd have a chance to be alone, to breathe and plan and maybe even slip away and search for the glade of spirits.

"Mother told me that the wedding is more of a mortal custom they do for us, and that the coronation will be more like we're accustomed to, but that afterward there will be a true fae celebration."

I squeezed my eyes shut, inwardly cursing the fact that I'd be fortunate to have a single second to myself the entire night. But on the positive side, that meant I'd also be unlikely to be left alone with Fitz anytime soon either.

"Come," Grace said, striding to the wardrobe to pluck out the dress, "let's make you look like a future queen and force all those fae to bow before a mortal."

We shared a smile, and for a moment, all my fears eased.

The knock on my door made my heart stop. "He's here."

"That means it's time for me to dress in my rooms," Grace announced. "I'll call for Lina and explain everything."

I shot her a look. "Are you sure? I could help you dress and…"

Grace shook her head, guiding me gently toward the sitting room and the door that was slowly creaking open. "It's important that you're on time."

She vanished deeper into my rooms before I could protest, leaving me standing in my sitting room with my mouth dry and my new husband stepping inside to assess my appearance. His eyes inspected the careful way my sister had arranged my hair, hanging freely down my back to allow room for a crown. His brow scrunched when he noted the hem of my dress, just the tiniest bit too short since I was a couple inches taller than my sister.

I swallowed, a familiar inadequacy sweeping over me. I had the sense that Fitz didn't want any human wife, but that if he'd been allowed to choose, he would have preferred my sister. And could I blame him, when I'd spent my whole life hearing how she was superior in every way?

"Acceptable," he muttered, swinging the door open and stepping out while gesturing for me to follow.

Shame and annoyance burned through me. *Acceptable?* But I swallowed it down. I wasn't Grace. I'd spent a lifetime understanding that I would always be "acceptable" and "pretty enough." It wasn't as if I *wanted* the prince to find me beautiful, either. My pride was wounded, but that was all.

As Fitz clicked the door softly shut behind us, he offered his arm, and I slipped mine through his. I hoped he didn't notice the way my hand trembled. There was no room for fear, not now.

"I heard there is to be another celebration after this one?" I asked.

"A true fae feast."

"Where you dance barefoot under the stars?"

"And howl at the moon, yes," he quipped.

I glanced at him askance, but when I met his eyes, there wasn't mirth in them, only annoyance.

"You seem to think we are barbaric, wild creatures, so I thought that would meet your expectations."

"All my life I've been taught that your kind are deadly and untrustworthy, that I must always be on my guard, and that the humans who survive are the ones who never trust you."

Prince Fitz scoffed. "That's rich, coming from the woman who lied her way into my bed."

Stiffening, I dropped my eyes to my slippers, hoping he didn't notice the blush flooding my cheeks. "I haven't—I'm not—I certainly *do not* want—"

He stopped in the middle of the hallway, tugging me toward an alcove where a window faced a late afternoon sky, the sun already turning ruddy. Some of that crimson light reflected in Fitz's eyes as he spun me to face him. "Let's make one thing clear. I may be bound by my word, but I do not trust you or your motives. And your status as my wife and the princess of Ashwood is tenuous until you show signs of possessing magic. That means you can parade around here as haughtily as you'd like, but my ability to protect you is limited. The people will probably not accept you until—or perhaps more accurately, *if*—my mother accepts you. They will be forced to honor our marriage bond and our word to protect you and your family, but that doesn't change the dangerous position you've thrown yourself into. If something happens to you, it is on your head, and not mine."

I glared. "Don't resent me because you feel duty-bound to shield me from your own court. I never asked for your protection."

For a long moment, he didn't say anything. His eyes swirled with annoyance and anger. "Then you are a fool," he said, releasing my arm and stepping back. "But regardless of what you do or do not request, it *is* my responsibility to keep you alive. What sort of future king would I be if I couldn't protect my own wife?" His eyes flicked toward the window and the swaying leaves of the forest. "However, if you make a habit of tricking fae and running off into the woods, I can't promise you'll survive long."

Contrary to the emotions he was surely trying to instill in me, I felt a flood of relief loosen the tightness of my chest. Fitz stepped back into the hall, turning toward the stairs, and I followed him, fighting the urge to smile. "So you're saying you won't forbid me to explore or hold me hostage in your castle?"

Fitz cast an annoyed look over his shoulder. "Did you think we were powerful, immortal beings, or nannies?"

Despite myself, I laughed. He turned away, like the sound offended him.

I tempered my amusement as I descended the stairs behind him, running a hand along the carved banister and trying to take in the sights of the vast castle—the endless rooms, plush carpets, and paintings of past royals whose immortal lives must have been taken violently long ago, for sustaining a fatal injury was the only way I knew of that a fae could die.

"How do you suggest I survive your mother?"

Fitz paused on the first landing and shook his head. "I would have suggested not marrying me," he said drolly. "Since it's too late for that, perhaps you can attempt to be as little like yourself and as much like your sister as possible."

The urge to hurl an insult at him consumed me.

He noted my wrath and sighed, crossing his arms. "I meant, you should stop voicing your opinions so freely and keep them to yourself around the queen. The best way to survive her is to bow and scrape and obey her. You've already crossed her, though, and that's the deadliest thing anyone could do."

I glanced at my palms, as if I'd be able to see light swirling around them, tangibly indicating I possessed the magic Fitz had imparted upon me. But, though I knew little about magic in a practical sense, I didn't think it would manifest in such a blatant way. "Will she kill me if the magic...doesn't take?" I hesitated. "Would you let her?"

Fitz turned to me, raising his eyebrows. "Would *you* defy your own mother for someone you just met?"

I set a hand on my hip. "If it was a matter of life and death, and my mother was a cruel tyrant, certainly."

A muscle in his jaw twitched, and I had the strangest impression that Fitz was trying not to smile. He took a step nearer. "I've already told you that I don't trust you or your motives in taking your sister's place. Maybe you were being charitable, or maybe you're after something."

I ground my teeth, begging my face to give away nothing.

"My loyalty is to my people," Fitz continued. "If you do anything to harm them, it won't be my mother you should fear. No vows I've taken will prevent me from protecting my kingdom and stopping you."

Cool air tickled the back of my neck. *You're toying with things you don't understand, foolish mortal.*

I glanced around, but Fitz didn't react to the ghostly voice, and there was no one in the hall but us. Sucking in a breath, I turned back to the prince, who likely thought my reaction was to his threat.

He plastered a half-smile on his face. "Come, wife, let's pretend we're overjoyed at this union and celebrate."

He held out his hand, cold and calloused, and I took it.

CHAPTER EIGHT

Flickering chandeliers sent shadows dancing like wraiths in the corners of the ballroom as Fitz swept through the doorway, leading me on his arm. He didn't even pause for the servant at the entrance to announce us, though he and every courtier whose eyes landed on us appeared speechless anyway. Silence descended, heavier than the music that came to an abrupt halt, louder than the gossip and laughter we'd crushed like glass. My heart was a battering ram against my rib cage, begging to be set free.

I searched the crowd in vain for my family. Instead, I noticed Holden, his dark eyes widening when he noticed that I was *not* Grace.

Pausing, I extended a hand for him, and he rushed forward at my silent bidding. Fitz cast me a warning glare, but I ignored him as I leaned toward Holden and whispered. "If you care at all for my sister, find her and keep her out of this room for as long as possible."

Holden nodded and vanished into the press of bodies, and I allowed my disgruntled husband to tug me deeper into the room. I prayed that the younger prince truly did care for Grace, and that he could protect her from whatever wrath I was about to encounter.

Every courtier parted and bowed and stared, leaving an open path directly to the dais set up at the far end of the ballroom, and the extravagant throne upon which Queen Griselda sat. Daring to lift my chin, I met the queen's stormy eyes.

Fitz's fingers clasped my arm and squeezed, a silent reminder that my survival depended on appearing humble, not defiant. I lowered my gaze, focusing on the way the candlelight reflected in the hardwood floor as my slippers whispered across it.

When we stopped before the dais, Fitz led by example, bowing respectfully toward his mother. I swallowed, grasping my skirts to dip into a curtsey.

"You." The queen's voice came out in a low purr, like a contented cat entertained at the sight of a mouse presenting itself. "Tell me, did you seduce my son and force him into this?"

I was supposed to be quaking in fear, but the question made laughter bubble up. Clamping a hand over my mouth, I forced it back down and cleared my throat to cover the sound. When I met the queen's gaze again, I saw a furrow between her perfect brows, the only sign of her annoyance. The rest of her was a calm, cool mask that reminded me of her son's demeanor.

"I took my sister's place without his knowledge, Your Majesty."

"So you lied and tricked your way into a royal marriage," the queen observed, settling a hand over the arm of her throne. She leaned forward, and I couldn't tell if there was amusement flickering in her stare, or a gleam of bloodlust. "Do you crave power, Elle Blackford?"

"Doesn't everyone?" As soon as the words were out of my mouth, I cursed my impulsive nature. That wasn't the tone of a humble subject. At my side, Fitz was motionless as stone, a statue carved of marble. I wondered if he'd remain still if his mother descended from her throne and lobbed my head off.

To my surprise, Queen Griselda's full lips twisted into a wide smile. "You're surprisingly confident, for such a young, mortal thing. I suppose only time will tell if you truly belong in this position." Leaning back, she clapped her hands. "Come. Since there seems to be no avoiding it, it is time for you to receive your crown."

Fitz seized my hand to pull me onto the dais. As I turned to face the court with him, countless inhuman eyes stared back at me, some unblinking and full of barely disguised hostility. Near the front, a woman with wings so full they touched the floor tossed her hair over her shoulder and bared her teeth in an unfriendly smirk. Not far from her stood the hag who'd seized my hair the night of the ball—had it only been last night?—and asked for my eyes. She mouthed something with her withered lips, something that appeared uncannily like she could have been asking about my fine eyes again. I resisted the urge to shudder.

At last, I found my family in the crowd, dressed in unfamiliar gowns. Bridget and Isabel clung to one another, whatever shock they'd felt when they'd seen me in Grace's place already replaced with their rapture over the finely dressed crowd, the elaborate throne, and the tables filled to the brim with food and drink that I'd failed to notice earlier. A part of me longed for even a portion of their enthusiasm, wished that I could be celebrating a wedding to a human back home, one that loved and cherished me as opposed to the cold man who'd threatened me only minutes ago. Maggie stood with her hands clasped before her in an effort to make herself as small as possible, her eyes darting about uncertainly. When they latched onto mine, I found fear and shock and horror simmering in her gaze. *Why?* she mouthed, as if I could explain it to her from across the ballroom. Beside Maggie, Mother scowled, but there wasn't anger in her eyes—only fear.

A jaded corner of my heart wondered if she feared for my life or her own.

Grace was noticeably, blessedly absent.

Queen Griselda's voice rang out over the crowd. "It seems we have a surprise, which, for immortals who must endure endless days of sameness, is rather amusing, don't you think?"

A chill shuddered down my spine, though I didn't know why. I glanced over my shoulder, looking for the source of the draft, but there were only rows of bored-looking guards lining the back of the dais. Surely their bodies would block any breezes creeping through the castle.

I turned to the crowd, shaking off my curiosity.

"But as interesting as this is, someone must pay the price for allowing this mortal trickster to connive her way into our royal family." The queen's tone turned darker, and I tensed, imagining her drawing a knife and slipping up behind me.

But she'd told me I would receive my crown. Would she punish my family in my stead? Terror clawed up my throat.

"Bring Lina." Queen Griselda snapped her fingers, and several servants who'd been standing at attention near the wall darted from the room.

My blood pounded in my ears. The maid who'd been meant to tend to Grace. My terror melted into guilt. I'd never considered that anyone but myself or Grace would be punished.

In moments, the servants returned, leading Lina toward the dais. The young woman's pale skin appeared even whiter, the effect stark against her green hair. When she lifted her eyes, though, she betrayed no fear.

Dropping into a curtsey, she waited for the queen to declare her reason for summoning her.

"Lina, were you the one assigned to attend Prince Fitz's bride as she prepared for her wedding?"

Lina dipped her head. "I was, Your Majesty."

"And did you place the veil upon her head?"

Pressing her lips into a firm line, perhaps to hide the tremor running through her, Lina shook her head. "Miss Grace's sister, Miss Elle, wanted that honor."

Queen Griselda laughed and gestured to me. "And do you now see why?"

Lina's eyes darted up, meeting mine for the first time and widening in shock. Then terror. "I-I'm sorry, Your Majesty." She curtsied again.

"Well," the queen said, sashaying down the steps in her blood-red skirts to stand before Lina, "you should have remembered the fact that *humans are liars*. You should have remained true to your task, and never allowed another to take it from you. Extend your hand."

Lina held out her left hand, her whole arm shaking.

In a gentle movement, almost like a caress, Queen Griselda seized the maid's wrist in one hand while drawing a sword from a sheath at her side with the other. "Mistakes of this magnitude must be punished," she said, her voice as even as if she were discussing the weather.

By now, Lina was so pale she looked like she would faint, but she knew better than to pry herself from the queen's grasp. There was a flash of silver as the queen lifted her sword and sliced straight through Lina's forearm. Scarlet sprayed and Lina screamed—or maybe the sound came from me—as the young woman's hand dropped to the floor, landing in a growing pool of blood.

I swayed on the dais, afraid I'd be the one to faint or be ill. A cold hand grasped my arm, holding me upright. I couldn't look at Fitz and see his callous gaze as he watched his mother dole out a punishment I should have expected. He'd all but warned me of it. I knew the fae were cruel, and yet knowing something and seeing it play out before my eyes were vastly different things.

Through hazy vision, I watched the servants act so swiftly it made me think such violent punishments in the court were regular occurrences. A pair carried Lina away. I had no idea how much blood a person could lose and survive, had no understanding of how one would recover from such an injury. Until now, I'd lived a sheltered existence, where only stories of distant horrors reached my ears. More servants removed the severed hand and mopped up the blood, leaving the floor gleaming and perfect for the celebration.

My mouth tasted sour as the queen casually wiped her dripping sword on her stained gown. The dark splatters of Lina's blood were hardly noticeable on the red fabric the queen wore, but it was impossible not to stare at the drops on the queen's cheek and in her strands of black hair. She sheathed her sword, strode to my side, and spun to face her court.

"Please bow as Prince Fitz bestows a crown upon his bride." Queen Griselda laid a chilly hand on my shoulder. "Our new princess, *Elizabeth* Blackford, will kneel, showing her subservience to her husband and to you, the people she will serve."

I forced my breath to steady and my body to stop shaking. I'd witnessed why I should never cross the queen again, and though I hardly knew Lina, it was all I could do to resist the tears burning the back of my throat. My skin crawled while I did as the queen said, turning to Fitz and kneeling like a poor subject. Just as the fae preferred their humans. I swallowed when I met his fathomless dark eyes. He held no crown, and the queen wasn't producing one. Fitz wasn't even wearing one.

Before I could wonder further, Fitz raised his hands, and this time, a breeze rippled throughout the ballroom—but this one wasn't cold. It tasted warm and electric, similar to the air moments before a thunderstorm. Gooseflesh rose on my arms when darkness pooled and danced around Fitz like living shadows. Like clouds gathering for a storm. Within them, miniature tongues of lightning flashed. Then the energy changed, and the darkness turned gentler, a blanket of velvet. It was the sky at midnight. Pinpricks pierced the blackness, forming glowing, ethereal constellations that spun and danced until they enveloped me. Shades of emerald and violet washed over the darkness, performing a colorful dance.

For a moment, my terror and guilt faded. I was breathless with awe, lost in the power and beauty of Fitz's magic. It wasn't terrifying like I'd expected, though this blatant display of power warned me that he was capable of being fearsome. Light twisted through the darkness, a silver object draped in black gems. It alighted on his head—a crown he'd woven from storm and starlight and shadow. With another gesture of his hand, something settled on my head, and I swallowed, lifting my hand to feel the points of my own crown.

Something flashed in Fitz's eyes, almost like confusion, but it was gone before I could register it.

Queen Griselda muttered from behind me. "This doesn't mean the magic has accepted you, even if the crown that formed matches his," she snapped in a quiet voice only I could hear.

"A princess of dusk and shadow, to match Fitz's might," she announced loudly as Fitz's magic slowly dispersed and the flickering glow of candlelight steeped the room in gold once more. She clapped her hands together. "Play a song and let us dance and drink for the new couple!"

The court roared, wings fluttering and feet stomping and goblets of wine spilling as they welcomed a chance to celebrate.

The queen turned to me, a warning in her icy eyes. Her voice was only for me as music pulsed through the air. "You may desire power," she murmured, "yet let me make one thing clear. Even if our magic does accept you, the abilities you'll possess will never match ours. If you do *anything* to threaten my kingdom or my son, I promise no vow will keep me from severing your head from your neck and displaying it in my court, for all your family to see."

I met her stare unflinchingly, until she sniffed and strode away. Apparently, I was not worth another moment of her time.

Fitz approached, taking my elbow and leading me off the dais. Another chill wind brushed my neck, and I scowled over my shoulder. At nothing.

"You look like you need a drink before we intervene for the real celebration," he said coolly, pushing effortlessly through the crowd and toward the tables where countless goblets awaited, already filled with wine—thankfully, plenty of it with familiar varieties and not only with the golden wine of the fae.

I seized a goblet and lifted it to drink, but as I did so, my eyes fastened on a window in front of me and I froze. A woman with a ghastly grey face peered back at me, eyes hollow and shadowed in dark circles. I blinked, swallowing my gasp, and when I opened my eyes, the face was gone.

Surely I'd imagined it. Breathing a sigh of relief, I turned away from the window to face the dancers. The same grey-faced woman stood in front of me, her dress coated in dirt and grime and her mouth a black hole of emptiness. Her pupil-less eyes darted toward my crown, and a look of pure fury flashed across her face. Her hands reached for me...

I jerked backward, wine sloshing from my goblet and down the front of my dress. Fitz shot me a sharp look, lowering his own goblet of gold wine. "What was that?" he demanded.

"I—" Glancing around, I realized the woman was gone. I set my drink on the table behind me, feeling too unsteady to not spill more. Was I going mad? I rested my hand over my bodice, where my locket was hidden.

You don't deserve to wear that, a voice hissed in my ear, and I resisted the urge to shudder.

Dimly, I was conscious of two goblins growling and threatening one another in a nearby corner, bringing me back to reality. To the sounds of the crowd around me, not whatever phantom I was seeing and hearing in my own mind.

Before I could come up with a response to Fitz, a group of women approached with fluttering eyelashes, bowing and scraping before their crown prince. Their skin was in shades ranging from palest white to brown to mossy green and sky blue, and some possessed horns or wings or even leaves and branches that grew from their flesh. They cast sour looks in my direction, as if I'd willfully stolen their chances of having him.

Give me a few weeks or months, and he will be all yours, I thought.

"We offer you our sincerest congratulations, Your Highness," the woman with blue skin said. Her irises were so pale they were almost white, and she made no attempt to hide the way she ogled Fitz.

A shout broke out, and my eyes landed on a fight that had started on the dance floor. A man with horns butted into another fae who looked much more human. The human-looking one roared in fury and slammed a punch into the horned man's face. Blood burst from the injured man's nose as he ducked his head to plow into his opponent. Around them, the dancing stopped, and the music screeched to a halt. Cheers and applause erupted as courtiers gathered, screaming for blood.

The horned man drew a dagger. Sweat coated my forehead. I turned and reached for my half-forgotten drink, needing something to stabilize my nerves. But the wine tasted bitter this time, like ashes and rot.

In the blink of an eye, a slicing sound cut through the air. A copper tang filled my nose. Blood spurted in a gruesome arc, followed by a thud. More blood splattered across dresses and faces and shirts and wings. Wild eyes tracked the progression of the losing man's head as it rolled off the dance floor and stopped at my feet.

Do not *be sick. Do* not *scream. Don't show fear.*

I'd already shown weakness earlier when Queen Griselda had cut off Lina's hand. I couldn't afford to look afraid again.

I tasted blood and realized I was biting my tongue to hold back my rising nausea. The weight of countless fae gazes pressed on me. None of them looked surprised—giving me the impression that fights that ended in death were a regular occurrence at court. Perhaps they'd reined in their violence for our first ball, but now that my family and I lived among them, they had returned to their usual behavior. And they were watching me for my reaction. Would I be a ruler that could stomach their ways, or one they would prey upon?

My eyes found Mother in the crowd. She looked like she was holding back a scream, or the urge to be sick. Never in our lives had we seen such gore, such violence, such cruelty.

I wouldn't let the fae see my terror, wouldn't let them know bile singed the back of my throat.

Already, servants had rushed forward, their faces blank as they hastily mopped up the blood and removed the severed head from the ballroom. All finished in moments. All done with the efficiency of an action carried out countless times.

That fact, more than anything, terrified me.

Forcing a smile upon my lips, I deposited my drink on the table and lifted my chin. "Enough of this ruckus!" I shouted. "Play a song. It's time for my dear husband and me to dance."

Everything quieted. With a single stern glance from Fitz, the musicians settled in and started a new song, one reminiscent of a popular tune from home, yet more lilting and mysterious, as if even in this moment, the fae were determined to unnerve me.

Fitz drew me onto the dance floor, which had emptied to make room for us. My heart continued to pummel its way up my throat until the room spun. I knew I hadn't had nearly enough wine for that yet.

Maybe I was panicking.

Twisting, turning, I followed each step of the dance precisely, and Fitz matched my every move, as if he'd grown up among humans and danced this way all the time. We dipped and curved around one another, stepping in close only to brush hands and spin away again. In my world, it was a flirtatious dance meant to give couples the chance to smile and exchange short pleasantries, just enough to pique curiosity.

I forced everything else to fade away, letting my mind relish the familiarity of the moves and the music, praying it could sink into my blood until all my fears and doubts melted away. There were no ghoulish women breathing down my neck, no bloodthirsty fae decapitating one another. There was only the music and me, twirling in an endless cocoon of flickering, golden warmth.

But when I glanced up, Fitz's eyes were the darkest I'd ever seen them, like a sky clouding over. The dance brought us near again, and he dipped his head low, breath tickling my ear. "What are you doing?"

"Dancing," I said flippantly, spinning away. My skirts swished around my legs, and I breathed deeply.

Everything was fine.

A chill brush of air licked at my arms, but I turned again, circling Fitz.

Everything was *fine*. And I realized I wasn't merely thinking that to try to convince myself anymore. I was light, carefree, unafraid. My fear was gone, replaced with something warm expanding through my chest. No more grief, no more doubt, no more horror.

Only joy, the thrill of the music, the rapid beating of my heart to the point I thought it could burst. I smiled, letting laughter escape. Fitz's scowl deepened, which only made me laugh more.

Everything else faded. There wasn't another sound beyond the music and my laughter and the rush of blood in my ears.

I'd thought my dress was too short earlier, given the fact that I was taller than my sister, but it seemed too long now. My slipper caught on its hem, and I stumbled. I choked back my cry as I crashed to the floor, sliding along the freshly mopped surface.

Once more, the music crashed to a halt. Sneering voices and vicious laughter echoed, until a stern command stifled them. Lifting my head, I found a storm cloud swirling above, blocking the warm light of the chandeliers. Electricity flickered within the grey mass, its power crackling through the air.

"Tonight's celebration is canceled," Fitz announced.

Strong arms lifted me, and the room spun. Something tangled and caught in my hair before falling to the floor. My crown.

I swallowed back my shame, relishing the way the clouds blocked my view of the crowd as Fitz swept me from the ballroom and back up the stairs leading to his rooms.

CHAPTER NINE

With my ear pressed to his chest, Fitz's voice was a low rumble. "Are all mortals as impulsive and careless as you?"

I had the impression that deep down, I should have been angered by his words, but instead I felt surprisingly light, my earlier terror consumed by overwhelming peace. The world still spun, but my breathing had steadied.

"Careless indeed," I said with a laugh. I couldn't remember the last time I'd felt this carefree, this wonderful, without any uncertainty or pain weighing on my heart. It was delicious. Perfect. I wanted this sensation to last forever.

Fitz was already shoving open the door to his rooms.

"Do you have a death wish?" Fitz went on, kicking the door closed behind us. "Surely you know better than to show weakness and carelessness like that."

I nearly choked on my laughter, burying my face in his jacket. He smelled like crisp autumn leaves, which wasn't surprising given we'd spent the afternoon in the forest. It was lovely. I inhaled deeply, causing him to freeze, prying me away from his chest and frowning.

"Dancing seemed like a good way to prove I wasn't frightened," I said, fighting another urge to giggle. "How do you smell *so wonderful*?"

Fitz didn't respond as he walked through his rooms. The warmth in my chest expanded until my whole body seemed full of light, glowing and content. "Warm and careless and incandescent," I rambled, sighing and closing my eyes. In Fitz's arms, I had the sensation that I was flying, but I wanted to pry myself away and dance again. "Shall I change into my dress for the rest of the celebration? I want to *dance*."

"That's not happening tonight. Stop talking." Fitz's tone was sharp with annoyance. At his command, I clamped my lips shut without complaint. For reasons I couldn't understand, I wanted to obey him. Wanted to please him.

Fitz's grip tightened, and when I opened my eyes, I found that his churned with fury. "I thought you knew better than to drink fae wine."

I squinted, trying to focus but finding the edges of his face had gone blurry. Blinking, I reached up, brushing my fingers along his cheek as if that would help me see him more clearly. "I've not had a drop."

"You wouldn't be so obedient to my command, or so carefree after watching that man die, if you hadn't consumed some of our wine. Did you set down your drink?"

My brain turned sluggish, making it difficult to recall the events of the night. "You made me spill some. No, *she* did." A shudder rippled through me when I remembered the ghostly face that had startled me.

"And did you set down your goblet?" Fitz demanded.

"I...I think so."

Anger lit his eyes again, reminding me of the lightning he'd wielded. He strode into his bedroom, which consisted of dark, soothing hues in burgundy and black, and deposited me on his bed.

I stretched out, sighing with pleasure at the softness of his bed cover. I hadn't realized until that moment how exhausted I was, with the world turning hazy. Without an ounce of shame, I pulled back the bedclothes and buried myself in the silky sheets.

"I take back what I said earlier," I announced. "I would gladly trick you into marrying me again for this bed."

Fitz ignored me. "Someone drugged you."

I sat up, his words eliciting enough fear to sober my mind a fraction. "You mean someone put fae wine in my drink?"

"You sound surprised."

"I thought all those angry members of the court would do something a bit more violent than drugging me so I'd make a fool of myself." I laughed again.

"It's far more malicious than that. Under the influence of our wine, you're far more compliant to requests and orders. Even someone without glamour would be able to command you, and you'd find it difficult to resist. And if you'd drunk *more* than a sip or two of wine? Humans have been known to overdose to the point of poisoning and drinking themselves to death."

I frowned. "It tasted awful."

Fitz stepped closer, his eyes boring into mine as if he were determined to make his point clear. "It always does for mortals at first, but once you experience its effects, it's more difficult to resist." He spun on his heel, storming about his room, opening and closing dresser drawers and fidgeting with his fine coat. "You're staying in my rooms tonight. If nothing else, the fact that you were drugged makes me look weak. A prince who cannot protect his wife cannot protect himself either, and there are plenty of courtiers who would love to end our entire royal family and take the throne."

Leaning back against the pillows, I stifled a yawn. Fitz's words sounded distant. Everything was warm and soft, and he cut an imposing, fierce figure with his handsome face set in angry, determined lines. I knew he was talking of serious matters, but all I felt was a lightness, an urge to giggle. To curl up like a contented cat in this bed, or to stand up and dance some more. Either sounded like a perfect way to spend the night.

I couldn't remember the last time I'd experienced such joy. Grief and fear had crushed me so heavily. Now, I couldn't quite remember why I'd been so sad or afraid.

"Tomorrow, when the influence wears off, you'll carry yourself with dignity to show them we are unintimidated." He held up a dagger, frowning, as if lost in thought. He swept toward the bedroom door.

"What are you doing?" I asked.

The threat in his eyes was clear. If I weren't mindless with fae wine, I might have been afraid. "Finding who did this."

"You're quite handsome when you want to murder for me." I paused. "No, I don't mean that. I think I hate you, and I'm sick of death."

Fitz continued to ignore my ramblings. "I'll send my brother in to keep you company until I return."

"I suppose he might be more entertaining. You're so solemn."

Fitz shot me a sharp look. "He will guard you, not entertain you. I can't trust that you won't wander off and get yourself killed." He strode toward his sitting room, where I heard him ring a bell. Soon afterward, there was the quiet murmur of his and what I assumed was a servant's voice exchanging words. The servant retreated, and a few minutes later, the door opened again.

"This is quite the favor you're asking of me, dear brother." Holden's tone was light and teasing, and I perked up. Perhaps he'd be up for dancing, or playing cards, or drinking more wine.

My mind halted at that last thought, something like fear tugging at my heart. *No. Fitz explained why that would be a terrible, dangerous idea.*

But I could vaguely recall how I'd felt before, and I desperately didn't want to feel that ache in my chest again. Perhaps it would be better to drink fae wine forever, even if I drank it until I died.

What about your family? Father? I shook my head, clearing my thoughts. *Remember why you're here. Endure the pain until you can save him and end the grief.*

Holden and Fitz exchanged murmured words too low for me to hear, and then the door closed and Holden strode into the bedroom. He pulled out a chair from a desk set near the heavily curtained windows and sank into it with a cheerful smile.

I smiled at him blearily. "So you are to be my bodyguard while Fitz commits unspeakable acts of violence?"

Holden quirked an eyebrow. "You seem less horrified by the idea than you did by the violence at your coro..." He cleared his throat, catching himself and cringing.

The memories of that severed head rolling across the floor, of Lina's hand falling in her own blood, made bile sting the back of my throat. My eyes shot to Holden's warily. "Will Fitz be severing more heads?"

Holden glanced down, fidgeting with the sleeves of his coat. "He is not known to be forgiving."

A chill raked down my spine. My mind was clearing more and more, and with the absence of my delicious, wine-induced haze came a tangle of emotions. "Like your mother?" I whispered.

He met my gaze steadily. "Fae can be greedy, power-hungry creatures, always sniffing out weaknesses and searching for ways to take advantage of one another. My mother and brother both believe that the surest way to secure their power and their safety—and the safety of those they care about—is by being swift to exact punishment on anyone who oversteps or makes the smallest hint of a threat."

I pulled the bedclothes up higher, the chill growing, spreading throughout my body. "And what do you believe?"

Holden smiled sheepishly. "I like to hope that strength can also be found in mercy."

"No wonder my sister speaks so highly of you."

His grin broadened. "Grace?"

I rolled my eyes and laughed teasingly. "Who else? Since she thinks so well of you, I'm tempted to think the same way." I shrugged and picked at a thread on the duvet. "Even if you're acting like my guard tonight to keep me in your brother's bed." I scowled in distaste.

Holden laughed outright, leaning back in his chair as if he didn't have a care in the world. "Firstly," he said, lifting a finger, "I am not forcing you to stay in my brother's bed. Feel free to wander these rooms, or even to return to your own. Though I think us being alone in your quarters might look a little more suggestive?"

My cheeks turned pink.

Holden shook blond locks away from his face and lifted another finger. "Secondly, you're not a prisoner. I could be your escort as you wandered the halls, but honestly, even with company, you don't want to do that at night." Sorrow flashed in his eyes and tugged on his features, but he forced another smile before letting me study it too long.

I thought of whispered words and cold drafts and the ghostly woman's face. "Why wouldn't I want to walk around the castle at night?"

Holden stood, pacing the length of the floor. His boots sank into the thick carpet, making no sound. "That is my brother's secret to share."

"Your brother doesn't seem like the type to be forthcoming." I stood, feeling steadier and more sober than ever. Crossing the room, I laid a hand on his arm, forcing him to whirl around and face me. "Are there ghosts within the castle? Souls that escaped the glade?"

Holden's mouth pinched. "Yes."

"Souls that were never meant to be wandering freely in your castle?"

"Yes."

"Why? Wouldn't it be your mother's duty to send those restless souls on?"

Holden shook his head, looking agonized. "That is Fitz's responsibility now. As heir, he acquires more and more of the crown's duties until our mother chooses to pass them all to him. Now that he is married, I'm sure that day is coming sooner than later. Immortality eventually makes ruling wearisome, I'm told, and Mother will be happy to rest." His mouth twitched, but his smile didn't quite reach his eyes.

I scanned the room, thinking of Fitz's magical display in the ballroom. The flashes of lightning, the sparkle of stars, the crackle of power, and the twisting shadows. It had been beautiful, but I had a feeling it was only a portion of what he was capable of wielding and could be equally terrifying when he wanted it to be. "Then why isn't Fitz sending the souls on?" I demanded.

My voice wavered with growing agony as I thought of the mortal spirits, unable to find the peace they so desperately craved. Though I didn't want Father to leave, I couldn't help but think about him as well. What if he was wandering beyond the glade's limits, lost and alone? What if I couldn't find him? What if he was tormented with sorrow and the knowledge he'd never be able to find rest, either by returning to his life or by moving onward? I couldn't stand the thought.

Holden glanced toward the windows, as if the answers were hidden beyond the drawn curtains, out in the night, among the dying leaves and whispering wind.

"*Holden.*"

His eyes snapped back to mine. "I'm sorry. It's his secret to tell."

A tear trickled down my cheek, and I lifted a hand to dash it away. "I think the wine has worn off. Could I please return to my own rooms? I cannot bear to be in here a moment longer."

Holden's gaze softened, and I had a feeling he was about to agree, but the door to Fitz's quarters burst open and the man himself entered the bedroom.

"Thank you, Holden," he said gruffly. "You may go."

I curled my hand into a fist as I took in Fitz's disheveled hair, fallen loose from its tie, his clenched jaw, and his crimson-stained coat. The tang of blood was unmistakable, as were the flecks of red adorning the stubble lining his cheek. His eyes gleamed with something dark and powerful, something that leeched the blue from them and made them look black as the night sky.

The room spun, and I wondered if maybe I wasn't sober after all.

"Are you hurt?" Holden asked, ignoring his brother's order and extending a hand toward one of the stains on Fitz's coat.

"I'm all right." The words came out short and clipped, another clear dismissal.

Holden froze, frowned, and shook his head. "If that's what you want, I'll leave. Goodnight, Fitz."

Fitz turned away, peeling off his coat as the door closed behind Holden. This was an opportunity to learn about the crown prince's magic and perhaps even find his charm, something that might be powerful enough to bring back Father, but between the lingering effects of the fae wine and Holden's recent revelation, the last thing I wanted to do was remain in Fitz's bed. Even if there might be no avoiding it in the future, surely tonight of all nights I could escape and try to forget this nightmarish evening.

I turned to Fitz. "I assume all that blood means you found the one who drugged me?"

Fitz tossed his coat across Holden's recently vacated chair, followed by his stained cravat. When his hands went to the buttons of his once-pristine white shirt, I averted my eyes.

"As you know, fae cannot lie, and I can be quite convincing when I want to extract the truth from someone."

"Then I am out of danger. I feel much better now, and I promise not to wander outside of my rooms. I only want to rest in the comfort of my own be—"

"Come here." Fitz said it gently, not in the commanding tone he'd used with his brother. My heart skipped a beat, urging my feet forward despite the part of my mind that remembered I could barely even stand the sight of this man. He was allowing souls to suffer, forsaking his duty despite all his proud words about keeping his word and protecting his people. As part of his kingdom, the human souls waiting to move into the afterlife *were* his people. And he was failing them.

But I kept walking forward anyway, compelled by an irresistible need to be close to Fitz. When I was near enough to touch him, I dared to lift my eyes. He'd peeled off his shirt. Despite the heat that bloomed in my cheeks, a sense of daring seized me, and I let my eyes slowly trace each inch of smooth skin and the planes of his muscles. Even speckled in blood, he was beautiful. He was arrogant and cruel, but that didn't stop me from inching even closer and extending a hand.

Fitz laughed, pulling back and shaking his head. "I didn't use a hint of glamour on you, and you still couldn't resist."

I swallowed hard, glancing up to meet his eyes. His earlier fury had cooled, and his mirth didn't seem to be at my own expense, but I couldn't help the wash of humiliation that seized me. I'd made a fool of myself, nearly drooling in front of this man that I *did not even want.* Fitz was correct—if I'd been in my right mind, I never would have ogled his bare chest so brazenly.

I stumbled back, covering my face, wanting to use every foul word I'd been told to never speak as a lady.

Fitz's amusement melted away, his expression turning solemn. "You're staying here tonight for your own safety."

If I could keep my wits about me, if the wine's effects continued to dissipate, I could use this night to search his rooms and seek out an object that could be his charm.

I straightened, trying to summon every last ounce of dignity I possessed. "Very well, but you will sleep on the couch." My eyes flicked toward the sitting room, where a comfortable couch larger and finer than my bed back home rested.

Fitz snorted. "Absolutely not. I will sleep in my own bed."

I opened my mouth.

"And so will you. I won't have you alone out there by the door, trying to sneak off as soon as I fall asleep."

I swallowed my protest, knowing if I tried to convince him I didn't want to slip out of his room while he was asleep, I'd only draw more suspicion. I was sure he already believed that I would try to steal his charm. He'd made it clear he didn't trust me, that he believed I was after power.

He wasn't wrong.

I imagined even just a sliver of his magic would be enough for me to bring my father back. If it was Fitz's responsibility to send the spirits in Ashwood Forest on, then surely it would be easy for him to bring one back to our physical world.

Satisfied that I'd relented, Fitz turned, the silver light filtering through the drapes highlighting the muscles of his back. Swallowing, I glanced away, afraid that whatever wine remained in my blood would encourage me to make a fool of myself again. "Are you truly all right?" I asked stiffly as I pulled back the bedclothes and slipped into bed.

I exhaled with relief as Fitz vanished into the washroom. "Unlike you, I cannot lie."

I rolled my eyes at the wall.

A few minutes later, Fitz reentered the bedroom, clothed in loose pants and a tunic with a neckline that dipped dangerously low and fabric that was too thin to conceal much of anything. His skin gleamed and his hair hung free and damp. Not a single drop of blood remained.

When his gaze latched onto me, his mouth twitched. "Are you sleeping in that gown?"

I pinched my lips together. "It isn't as if…"

My voice trailed off as he reached into his wardrobe and tossed a nightgown at me. "The servants stocked my room."

My cheeks burned. Of course they had. They expected me to sleep here regularly. I ground my teeth.

"You can change in the washroom," Fitz suggested.

I stared at him, frozen.

He raised his brows, annoyance and amusement battling for dominance in his eyes. "Is this how you think I'd lure you into my bed?" He shook his head, as if shocked by my foolishness. "Trust me, if I were trying to seduce you, you would know."

I curled my fingers into the nightgown's fabric, a confusing mixture of fear and desire rushing through my veins. The room was too warm, and my head was fuzzy. *Curse this wine.*

Fitz turned away, as if I weren't worth another second of his time. "But I'm not. I promise I'll never glamour you. We Ashwoods don't believe in that. And I won't touch you tonight, either." His lips quirked, but there wasn't any mirth in his smile. "That's not why you're here."

"You have to."

Turning, he stared at me, shocked at my proclamation.

I fidgeted with the nightgown, twisting it between my hands. "I mean, unless you want to call for a servant to help, which I assume you want to avoid so they don't see me in this state" –I giggled, and this time I wasn't sure if it was a result of the wine or my nerves– "you will have to undo the buttons on this gown." I swallowed. "And unlace my corset."

Silence thickened the air, and for a few seconds, I didn't think either one of us breathed. No emotion showed on Fitz's face, and nothing flickered in his eyes, yet I could have sworn his discomfort was as palpable as mine.

"Well," he said at last, clearing his throat and gesturing, "I think that would be better accomplished if you stand over here, unless you *want* me to do that while you're in my bed."

Wiping my sweaty palms on my gown, I nodded and rose, striding forward as if this was exactly what I'd hoped for on my wedding night. If he could jest about something he didn't even want—something he was likely repulsed by, since he'd made it clear he thought I was no beauty next to my sister—then surely I could temper my own embarrassment. Fitz's eyes latched onto mine, and for a terrible instant, I was breathless again, my head swimming with lust.

I didn't want him to like me, but a petty, proud part of me wanted him to find me as beautiful as I found him. Probably that was also the part of me that resented the attention Grace received, the part that longed to be told that I was as worthy as she.

The shadow of a smile darted across his lips, and I realized I was staring. At him. At his mouth. He leaned forward and for a moment, I thought he would kiss me.

I sucked in a breath to clear my head and lifted my arm to slap him.

Laughing, Fitz seized my wrist. "Turn around."

He released my arm, and I sighed. Spinning on my heel, I nearly lost my balance, preventing a fall by grasping one of the bed posts. "I hate fae wine," I muttered as I righted myself.

"You might not say that by tomorrow evening," Fitz said, his hand lightly brushing my neck as he swept my hair over one shoulder. My skin tingled.

"Why not?" I wanted to keep the conversation going to distract myself from the sensation of Fitz's fingers deftly moving down the row of buttons along my back. I had whole layers beneath the gown to separate my bare skin from his, and yet somehow, his warmth soaked through them. He was scarcely even touching me, moving as swiftly as he could to prevent his hands from lingering, but it was still the most intimate moment I'd ever shared with a man.

I squeezed my eyes shut. *This is what you need,* I reminded myself. *If he keeps his charm on his person...getting close to him is the only way you'll ever find a chance to steal it.*

"Because once you've experienced fae wine," Fitz said, "even if you hate the taste, you'll start to crave it."

"I don't even like how it's making me feel." My voice was too high-pitched and unconvincing as Fitz finished with the buttons of my dress. I stepped out of it, air whispering around my bare ankles.

It struck me how vulnerable I was in that moment, left with trusting this fae's word and honor. He might not be able to lie outright, but that didn't mean he couldn't twist his promises or find loopholes. That didn't mean he couldn't do any number of things, claiming them as his right as my husband. Perhaps, even if he didn't find me desirable, he'd want to exert his power, or even try glamouring me.

I glanced down, reassuring myself that my locket was tucked beneath my chemise where he wouldn't see it.

Fitz's fingers started tugging on the laces of my corset. This time, I could have sworn they were less sure, a little clumsier. More than once, his fingers brushed the bare skin of my back, where my undergarments dipped lower than my dress. He wasn't working as quickly, and he'd gone quiet.

I dared a glance over my shoulder, and Fitz frowned, jerking his gaze away. "You might not like how it feels tonight," he said, his breath warming my neck. I swallowed back an embarrassing urge to gasp at the sensation. "But the danger of the wine to humans is how addicting it can be. You'll forget the bad moments and only remember the good—the joy and lightness and freedom it gives you. You'll have to be particularly cautious around it now."

I nodded, not trusting my voice as Fitz finished with the last of the laces and my corset fell, joining my dress pooled on the carpet. Even though my back was to him, I hugged my arms across my chest and resisted a shiver.

"Thank you." I darted back to the bed, seizing the nightgown and draping it across myself to cover my petticoat as I turned.

Fitz was staring, or at least I thought he'd been. He turned away, striding to the windows and brushing aside the curtain to peer into the night. Something like both fear and hope bloomed in my chest as I dashed into the washroom and changed. It felt shockingly revealing to exit in only a nightgown, when I'd spent my life covering my ankles and avoiding the possibility of seeming too flirtatious or forward around humans.

But Fitz was my husband, and tonight, being a shy, modest lady wouldn't suit me. I needed to be confident and assured, to at least gain his friendship and trust in a way that would help me find what I needed. And then, when I'd saved my father and had a way for my family and me to escape, perhaps I'd also confront Fitz about his cruelty toward the souls wandering throughout his own castle.

Maybe, with enough magic of my own, stolen or acquired through our marriage, I could force or threaten him into changing his ways.

I sank into the bed, soothing myself with daydreams of Father's cheerful laughter and warm embrace, of freedom for my sisters and me. Fitz climbed into the opposite side and blew out the candle on his nightstand.

Exhaustion made my eyelids heavy, but I stared resolutely into the shadows, determined to stay awake. Once Fitz drifted off, I would begin searching his room. That, finding a book or other information on necromancy, and discovering the glade of souls were my top priorities.

Overly conscious of the limited space between Fitz and me, I forced myself to relax my muscles and lay motionless, hoping to reassure him I wouldn't sneak out of bed. In the darkness, I listened to the rhythm of his breathing. His back was to me, another reminder that he wouldn't try to move closer. He wouldn't touch me. He didn't *want* to touch me, for I was not the beautiful sister he'd been engaged to.

But a flash of that look in his eyes when I'd turned to find him studying me came to mind, and my skin grew hot. *You were imagining it because you're drunk on their wine. And you don't need him to touch you to steal his magic. He might not even keep it on himself. Maybe it's not like this locket.*

Laying my hand over my heart where the reassuring weight of my locket rested, I closed my heavy eyelids and thought of Father. *I'm so close to saving you.*

CHAPTER TEN

My head was going to burst. Groaning, I opened my eyes to a too-bright room, vastly different from the cozy dark space I'd fallen asleep in. Dust motes danced in the sunlight gleaming through the windows. Why was it so bright? I turned, finding that the curtains were open, revealing that the windows were actually glass doors leading to a balcony. The scents of coffee, bread, and sugar swirled through the air, and my stomach growled.

Sunlight. The wine must have made me too exhausted, too comfortable, and I'd not only fallen asleep against my will, but also slept through the entire night. I sat up so quickly my head pounded, my eyes first darting to Fitz's side of the bed, which was blessedly empty, and then to the figure wheeling in a cart of food.

Blinking blearily, I rubbed at my eyes, sure they were playing tricks on me. "Lina?"

The young woman looked weary, her smile appearing pasted on. Her green curls hung limply about her face, and there were dark circles beneath her violet eyes. When she turned to me, I saw the way she held her left arm close to her body. Heavily bandaged, it ended in a shapeless lump.

Guilt and relief swirled in my chest. "Why are you—how are you—I thought you would need more time to heal," I stammered. Tears stung my eyes, and I ignored the way my head ached as I leapt from the bed. "Lina, I thought that only I would bear the punishments for my deception. I'm so sorry."

My heart pounded as I imagined all the vile things Lina could force me to do, even if I was her princess and under Fitz's protection. It wouldn't be difficult for a clever mind to glamour me into committing harm against myself that Fitz wouldn't discover. Ways Lina could torment me and never be found out. All I could do was hope my apology and humility would be enough to appease her.

Or perhaps I could bargain my way out.

Before my wild thoughts could race any further, Lina shook her head, curls bouncing. "Don't be." She lifted a teapot, adeptly pouring a cup one-handedly without upsetting the lid. "Queen Griselda is known for her harsh punishments, and it is true that I am to blame for not ensuring I delivered the *correct* bride. I am aware of the dangers this job entails."

I gaped. Was this part of some fae trickery? Perhaps Lina meant to lull me into a false sense of security.

Lina gestured to the newly poured cup of tea. "This tea has some herbs that will soothe your headache."

Stepping back, I gritted my teeth. *More fae wine,* I thought, terror seeping into me.

"Fitz told me about what happened and swore me to secrecy," Lina went on, perhaps mistaking my fear for surprise. "As your maidservant, I am in the perfect position to watch over you and ensure no one else tampers with your food or drink. Now, do you take sugar and cream in your tea?"

"I'm not thirsty," I lied.

Lina rolled her eyes. "If I was foolish enough to add anything nefarious to your tea, Prince Fitz would find me out immediately. I can live without a hand, but a head?" She laughed outright.

"How can you be so cavalier about losing your hand?" I burst out. "And surely...surely you're not well enough to go about your duties today."

Lina sighed, utter weariness descending on her features as she studied me. "You don't know the extent of healing magic and its powers. Trust me, I am well enough."

I frowned, and she went on. "Princess, I have lived in this kingdom all my life. I have seen many awful, violent things. I've always known the queen to be unforgiving, but I've also seen her generosity toward those who serve her faithfully. Could I leave and take my chances elsewhere? Perhaps, but this world is cruel. Fae with greater power will always be on top, and those like me, with little magic and weak glamour, must make the best of our circumstances. Yes, I am tired, and I am sad. But I have many advantages compared to you." Her eyes scanned my nightgown and her lips pursed. "I do not live in a mortal body. And lowly as my power is, I still have some. No one can glamour me."

Frowning, I finally accepted Lina's proffered teacup. As she'd pointed out, she couldn't drug or poison me without dire consequences for herself, which meant the food and drink she brought me personally was likely the safest out of anything else in the castle. I took a long sip, finding she'd added the perfect amount of cream and sugar.

As I drank, I contemplated the fact that Lina and many like her struggled in Brytwilde almost as much as humans did. In all my years, I'd never once considered that some fae might be less powerful, less happy. I'd imagined they all thrived on human suffering, enjoying the magic they horded for themselves and the people they stole, blackmailed, or otherwise tricked into living in their world.

Against my better judgment, this information made me trust Lina a little more.

"Don't you wish for something different?" I asked.

Ignoring my question, Lina turned away, busying herself with removing Fitz's bloody attire from the chair and my discarded clothes off the floor. My skin heated with embarrassment, but I reminded myself that Lina wasn't judging me. In fact, I had the sense that she pitied me, and I wondered what sorts of stories she'd heard of fae taking humans to bed. I swallowed.

And yet, Fitz hadn't laid a hand on me except when I'd asked him to help me undress. He'd kept his word. I hadn't thought I'd find any virtues in the man I'd married, but it seemed he was, at least, honest.

"Why did you take your sister's place?" Lina asked as she started making the bed. I marveled at how swiftly she'd adapted to working with one hand.

Cradling my teacup, I studied the steam curling from the beverage and debated my answer. I couldn't share the whole truth, but a partial one would be most believable. "She's spent her whole life bearing the burden of keeping our family safe once Father died and we were inevitably left with nothing," I said. "She is the kindest, bravest soul I've ever known, and seeing her afraid and sad..." I shook my head. "I thought she deserved better."

Lina paused, looking up and meeting my eyes. "You love your sister very much."

"She is my dearest friend."

A knock on the door halted our conversation. Lina glanced up from fluffing Fitz's pillow. "I'll answer that," she said before I could set down my teacup.

While I waited for Lina and whoever had knocked, I picked up a pastry from the tray and nibbled on it. I wondered where Fitz had gone, and if he'd be away long enough for me to search his rooms undisturbed.

An angry voice rang out from Fitz's sitting room. "She is my daughter, and you will not bar me from seeing her."

I stiffened and glanced at my nightgown. Lina might not have blinked twice at the sight of me in the prince's bed, but Mother would be furious about the way I'd undone her plans. She didn't know I was fighting to save us all.

Setting down the pastry, I shuffled out barefoot to meet my mother in the sitting room.

Mother took one look at my tangled hair and nightgown and crossed her arms with a huff. "Ellie, how could you?"

Lina slipped out on silent feet, retreating to the bedroom to give us a semblance of privacy.

This time, Mother's censure only ignited my anger. "Did you even bother to look in Grace's eyes the day of the wedding and see how afraid and hopeless she was?"

Taking a step back, Mother wiped a hand across her face, looking utterly exhausted and suddenly much older. The early morning light sifting in from the bedroom highlighted the bits of white threading through her hair and the wrinkles gathering around her eyes and mouth. I was startled to find tears glistening in her eyes and stark fear on her pale face. "The queen specifically requested our *eldest* daughter," she murmured. "You saw how violently she retaliated against that servant girl." She gestured wildly toward the bedroom. "What will she do to us for breaking our word? For spurning her generosity by deceiving her?" Her eyes raked over my nightgown. "Has...*he* done anything to you?"

I drew a deep breath, wishing I could tell Mother the extent of my plans. But I knew they were dangerous and could as easily fail as succeed. She would be horrified enough to know I was concealing a charm on my person, even if Father had reassured me it had been gifted to our ancestors. I wasn't sure what she'd think of my hopes to steal Fitz's magic and escape Brytwilde, or to at least help the family escape while I remained behind, bound by my wedding vows. "He hasn't touched me," I said. "He gave his word to protect me, and last night he fulfilled it when someone slipped fae wine into my drink."

Mother's eyes widened.

"They are not happy about the switch," I went on, "but they have honored it, and they have given us a place to live, haven't they?"

Mother's brow furrowed. "Why did you do it?"

My throat was thick with unshed tears as I repeated the words I'd told Lina only moments earlier. When one escaped and slipped down my cheek, Mother's expression softened, and she stepped forward, enveloping me in an embrace. Her shoulders shook. "This burden is more than any one person should bear."

It was, perhaps, the closest to an apology regarding the bargain that I'd ever heard from her lips. While Father had constantly bemoaned our situation, helping me pore through illegal magical texts in the vain hope we'd find a way to use our family locket and become so powerful the bargain would be obsolete, Mother had behaved as if it were an honor.

For the first time, I wondered if she'd been wearing a mask, playing a part to seem strong and unafraid as much as Grace had been. After all, she'd been the one to teach her daughters about the dangers of the fae world, instilling caution in us. She'd done everything in her power to prepare us for this world, in the ways she knew how.

As I pulled back, wiping my eyes, I realized I still wasn't sure if I could forgive Mother, but I was at least beginning to understand her. "I think we can trust Holden," I whispered. "He seems kind, and he has been good to Grace. We should keep Maggie and Bridget and Isabel busy, occupied with normal activities that will keep them far from the courtiers and the danger."

Mother nodded. "That's my plan. I've already reminded them that they must keep up their studies—music and knitting and painting and all the talents that I suppose the fae won't value as much. But I told them we must keep to our ways and make Father proud. Perhaps I can also ask the prince to escort us on walks around the grounds and to picnics. Maybe we can write to friends in Riverton and ask the royal messengers to deliver our letters."

I smiled. "That's perfect!" I thought of Sophie and my heart warmed at the idea of being able to exchange letters.

"I'll leave you to get dressed," she sniffled. "My rooms aren't far. If you need anything..." Her words trailed off, as if she were embarrassed by all the times in recent days when she'd been too vacant, too lost in her own grief, to offer help or comfort. But I knew she meant to try harder now, so I nodded and squeezed her hand.

When I reentered Fitz's bedroom, Lina was humming and laying out an outfit on the bed for me.

"You work quickly," I said.

"Come, finish eating and let's prepare you. You have a busy day ahead."

I froze, dread seeping into my veins. "Why? What must I do?" I hadn't been naïve enough to assume I wouldn't have duties as a princess, though perhaps I'd hoped that as a human, the fae would only trust me with simple things, like hosting parties.

Lina frowned regretfully at the clothes, lost in her thoughts. "I'll have to call on another maid to help you into your clothes." A pang of guilt shot through me, but before I could apologize again, she went on. "All humans married into the royal family need tutelage, of course. You'll have to learn about our customs and magic and kingdoms."

"Kingdoms?" I exclaimed around a mouthful of food, completely forgetting the years of etiquette Mother had drilled into me. "I thought this was the only one."

Lina laughed at my ignorance. "This one, the kingdom of Ashwood, is the only one your little mortal town has had to concern itself with, but there are four fae kingdoms in Brytwilde, and it's rumored there are others on continents around the world. Each one is mighty and magical. Though not all the kingdoms of Brytwilde are friendly with ours," she added, a pointed warning in her eyes.

I swallowed my bite of pastry, my appetite dwindling.

"It is a dangerous world for all, but especially humans," Lina said, noting my mounting fear. As if I hadn't already been terrified enough. "But learning about it will help shield you." She grinned at the outfit she'd chosen for me, and for the first time, I realized it wasn't a gown like I was accustomed to. Instead of layers of petticoats and a corset, there was a strange set of undergarments with barely any fabric at all, the upper one acting like a corset in the way it fastened and laced up. A set of fitted leather pants and a long, loose tunic and heavy coat lay beside them. "And wearing fae clothes—that will also be your armor," she added.

"You want me to wear men's clothes?"

Lina shook her head. "These are sized for a woman. They might not be an exact fit, as they were made for your sister, but our seamstresses will make a new wardrobe for you."

"I thought as royalty, I'd have to wear something more formal."

"Not on a training day. You'll do more than simply sit in a study and pore over books all day." Lina swept toward a dresser where a mirror rested and opened a drawer, retrieving a hairbrush. Clearly, she and the other maids had thought of everything when supplying Fitz's rooms with everything a woman would need. Part of me wanted to request if we could go next door and settle into my own rooms, where I'd feel less awkward and out of place, but I shook that emotion away. I belonged here, and the more I claimed this space, the more opportunities I'd have to scour it.

Leaving the tray behind to follow Lina, who'd strolled into the washroom and begun filling the tub with a spout right there in the room, I settled onto a bench and watched. Steaming liquid spilled out like a waterfall, directly into the tub. "Back home, we have to fetch our water," I said.

As she poured in soap until bubbles popped, Lina giggled. "This is one of the many benefits of magic. Connected to nature as we are, it's easy to manipulate nearby water sources to flow toward the castle and move through a system of pipes. And servants who can control fire warm the water regularly."

I sighed contentedly when I settled into the tub, insisting that I didn't need Lina's help to bathe. She left, presumably to call on another maid to aid in dressing me when I was finished. "If there's no corset, I don't need help dressing, either," I called. Not only did I feel ridiculous being waited on when my mother and sisters and I had always helped each other with our clothes, but also I couldn't risk stripping in front of the fae when I was wearing my locket. Surely they'd know it was a charm.

Lina's voice came from just outside the closed washroom door. "Let us at least do your hair, Princess!"

"Very well." I scrubbed at my hair and remembered Lina's earlier words about my studies and how I wouldn't only be sitting around. "What else will I be doing today, aside from being tutored?"

"You'll also be training with Fitz."

I nearly slipped in the tub. "What?"

"You'll need to learn about our magic—specifically, *his* magic. Did he explain how the ceremony after your wedding vows worked?"

Hope rose in my chest. I'd have the chance to learn from Fitz, one-on-one, about his magic? I couldn't have asked for a better opportunity. "A little."

"If the magic of Ashwood accepts you, then you'll wield power similar to his. It's best to start learning about it before it manifests, rather than afterward when your lack of knowledge could prove dangerous."

My tunic and leggings, as the maids had called them, proved to be remarkably freeing compared to the restrictive, heavy dresses I was accustomed to. Even better, the bath and Lina's tea had nearly eliminated my headache, as she'd promised. Now I only had a dull throbbing at my temples to endure.

Lina led me through the hallways and up sets of stairs, which in the daylight were warm and golden and full of the laughter of passing courtiers and servants. It was difficult to reconcile the horrors and violence of last night—from the queen's brutality to the ghostly figure to the deadly brawl—with today's serenity. Plenty of light shone through the windows, glistening with the colors of late autumn, adding to the sense of loveliness and comfort.

I knew it was a farce. The blood and fear from last night were seared into my memory, replaying easily in my head now that the effects of the wine had worn off.

Lina guided me up a narrow staircase that seemed half-forgotten, tucked away in a dim corner of the castle. When she opened the creaky door at the top of the steps, excitement thrummed in my veins. An entire library awaited me, a vast expanse of shelves filled with tomes. I could only imagine the depths of knowledge about magic and history this room contained.

"I'll return when it's time to take you to your training with Fitz," Lina said, closing the door behind her and slipping back down the steps.

Left alone within the library without a tutor in sight, I began scanning the shelves. Would one of these books contain information about necromancy? Or perhaps one would explain where I could find the glade of souls. Beneath my tunic, my locket pulsed. Maybe the secret to opening and using it would be here, and I wouldn't have to rely on stealing Fitz's charm or hoping for the land to grant me power.

"Ah," came a clear, feminine voice. "I see someone else appreciates books and knowledge almost as much as I do. How refreshing. Too many of the courtiers, and even the servants, take far too much enjoyment in partying and over-indulging rather than in sharpening their minds."

I spun away from a book with a title written in a language I didn't recognize to face the speaker. She was the exact opposite of what I had imagined when Lina had spoken of a tutor. Naturally, my imaginings of a wrinkled old man didn't make any sense in Brytwilde, but the cheerful blonde woman in front of me looked nothing like how I would expect a wise old fae to appear either. A braided crown topped her head, and a mischievous smile adorned her lips. Her eyes were deep green and twinkled with delight. She was clothed in a simple emerald-toned dress that set off her eyes and accentuated her curvy form. A pair of wings fluttered at her back, smaller than any I'd seen in the ballroom last night. If it weren't for the fact that she was only a head shorter than me, I would've thought she was a sprite.

"Oh, forgive me," she said with a laugh, extending her hand. "I'm your tutor. I should have introduced myself. My name is Dahlia."

"Elle Blackford," I said with a curtsey, accepting her hand to shake it. My eyes widened. "Or rather, Elle Ashwood now."

Dahlia waved a hand as she spun away, leading me toward a cozy alcove containing armchairs and a small table laden with books. I hadn't noticed it before, which explained how I hadn't seen my petite tutor. With a playful flutter of her wings, she plopped into a chair and gestured toward another. "In Brytwilde, we don't worry so much about women taking their husband's names. You can be Elle Blackford and still be the princess of Ashwood, if that is what you prefer."

I smiled shyly as I seated myself. "I think I would like to keep my name. It connects me to my father, and he was very dear to me."

Dahlia cocked her head to the side, studying me shrewdly but not unkindly. "I heard about your loss, and I'm sorry. Grief is a strange and foreign concept in this world, even if our immortality sometimes has its limits."

"What do you mean?"

Dahlia settled her hands into her lap, as if preparing herself for a long story. Perhaps this was my first lesson. "I mean that not all fae live forever. Sometimes, we sacrifice our immortality for various reasons. Some simply grow tired of living after thousands of years and choose death's peaceful embrace. And of course, violent acts and curses can take our lives. So Prince Fitz, for instance, is considered quite young as a fae, but in the end, his lifetime might not be any longer than a mortal man's from your hometown."

I crossed my ankles. "And what is considered young in Brytwilde?" I asked awkwardly. Was my new husband decades older than me? I knew the fae didn't age like humans, which meant his appearance could have been deceiving.

"I suppose that is a relative term," Dahlia said with a smile. "I mean he is not much older than you." She sighed. "As for his experience with death and grief... His father passed when both he and Holden were quite young, and they don't have memories of him. And... Well, suffice it to say, when death does enter our world, it is as awful as loss in yours, but we struggle to understand how to cope. We don't handle it nearly as gracefully as you mortals do."

Tears stung my eyes. "I don't think I've handled it gracefully at all."

Dahlia leaned forward, laying a gentle hand over mine. Hers was warm and soft, but when she squeezed my fingers, she possessed unexpected strength. "*I* am not considered young among the fae. From the little I observed of you at your wedding and coronation, I think you've shown more bravery and strength than most fae and humans I've known in my many years."

As she sat back, picking up one of the books stacked on her table, I wiped away my tears and breathed out a soft chuckle. "You're not going to ask me why I took Grace's place, like everyone else has been doing?"

"It's not my business. My duty is to teach you. If you want to open up to me, you'll do so when you're ready." She glanced up from her book, and I noted the depth of wisdom in her eyes. Her cheerful demeanor certainly didn't make her naïve; it was clear there was much more to her than merely a sweet disposition. I could only imagine how many human lifetimes she'd experienced.

"Thank you."

"And now," Dahlia said, casting her book aside with a laugh, "I suppose that means we don't need to delve into history quite yet. Simple facts about Ashwood and how we live will do for today. Prince Fitz can complain to me directly if he finds that insufficient, but I think practical matters are what you need first and foremost. And," she added, rising and crossing over to a cupboard set within the nook, "I don't know about you, but studying makes me hungry. Would you like some scones, and I'll ring for some tea?"

This time, my smile was relieved. "I'd like that very much."

CHAPTER ELEVEN

Fae healing magic truly must have been remarkable, for Lina kept a brutal pace as she led me out a side door of the castle and into the grounds. An unseasonably warm breeze greeted us, rich with the crisp scents of leaves and the mums blooming along the stone pathway.

"Do humans always dawdle?" Lina groused, tossing a frustrated look over her shoulder. Her cheeks were rosy from exertion, and her curls damp with sweat.

"I was taught that ladies aren't supposed to run—" I began, but my maid rolled her violet eyes.

"Firstly, you aren't in the mortal world anymore, Princess. And secondly, you don't want to upset your husband. We're already late. You and Dahlia went over your scheduled time."

There was no mistaking the accusatory glare on Lina's face, so I picked up my pace, jogging at her side. "I'm sor—"

"You'll also need to practice your mannerisms," Lina interjected, and despite her sweaty face, she didn't sound breathless at all. "Princesses do not go about constantly apologizing."

As we swept from the gardens, Lina tugged on my arm, taking me through a courtyard that led past the stables, and down a path that brought us to a large building. A gate encompassed it, blocking my view of its extensive yard until Lina and I drew nearer. The sounds of shouts, jeering, and the clash of steel filled my ears before I noticed the men and women sparring with all manner of weapons. The yard was sectioned off into different training areas: one where fae were practicing with magic, another where archers shot at targets, and a final one where opponents sparred with their hands as well as weapons.

Near the center of that last area was Fitz himself, his shirt discarded in the grass as he faced another bare-chested man in a swordfight. Memories of last night swam through my mind unbidden, reminding me of the painfully embarrassing way I'd ogled Fitz's muscles.

Unfortunately, fae wine was unnecessary to appreciate the prince's beauty. He fought with fluid grace, the muscles in his back rippling as he lifted his blade and effortlessly parried the other man's attacks. When he moved in for his own offensive strikes, he stepped with the ease of a dancer, each action precise. Sunlight gilded his dark hair, and—

"You're staring," Lina interrupted, stifling a giggle. "I suppose that means you don't entirely loathe him." She cast me a sidelong glance, turning serious. "He isn't as bad as his mother. And if he ever *does* lay a finger on you, I'll..." She sighed. "Well, I hope I have the strength to stop him."

Warmth spread through my chest at Lina's ferocity. She'd known me less than a day, but she'd already proven kinder and more loyal than some of the people in Riverton I'd known my entire life. Whether it was all trickery and manipulation was still to be seen, and yet her sincerity was starting to convince me that maybe she truly did want to be my friend.

"Thank you," I said, meeting her eyes and hoping she could see how deeply I meant the words. "But he hasn't hurt me, nor has he tried. In fact, it seems like he's a man of his word, and he vowed to protect me, if only to prove to his kingdom that he's strong enough to defend his wife." My grin turned mischievous. "I can appreciate his good looks from afar, but trust me when I say I'm quite confident I'll *always* loathe him."

"I can't decide if I should be flattered that my wife finds me handsome, or hurt that you find me so loathsome."

Lina's face turned pink. I whirled in time to see Fitz finish tugging on his shirt, though it was half-unbuttoned and did little to cover him. He was only a few feet away, when I'd sworn he'd still been sparring only seconds ago.

He smirked, clearly enjoying my discomfort. "Did you forget how strong fae hearing is, my princess?"

My princess. How I loathed those words. I hardened the shock on my face into a glare. "Maybe I *wanted* you to hear me insult you, the way you insulted me."

Fitz blinked at the reminder of his refusal to dance with me at the ball, and how I'd later thrown his words back at him. Instead of responding, he turned to Lina and dipped his head. "You may go, Lina."

She vanished without a word, so quickly I could have sworn she'd flown. I wished I could disappear as fast.

"Come," Fitz said, turning on his heel and strolling away from the castle grounds and toward the forest.

For a moment, I considered ignoring his summons and escaping back into the castle and Dahlia's cozy library. We could eat more scones and sip more tea, and maybe she wouldn't raise a questioning brow if I sought books on necromancy. But the weight of the locket around my neck reminded me that spending time with Fitz and learning about his magic was more useful than scouring the pages of old tomes. Stifling my sigh, I followed him as he took a well-worn trail, leading past mossy rocks, drooping branches, and old trunks draped in ivy.

After rounding several bends, Fitz approached a clearing with a pond in its center. I paused, studying the brilliant shades of orange and crimson reflected in the water's smooth surface, creating a riot of bright colors that threatened to bring my headache back with a vengeance. If I were home, it was exactly the sort of beautiful day Father and I would have spent walking or reading beneath the trees near our house. Or perhaps studying magic.

The reminders felt like too much. I had another urge to return to the castle, this time to climb into my huge bed and shut out this strange, lovely, dangerous world. I was about to uncover more fae secrets, to be *trained* in their magic, and Father wasn't here to see it.

Tears burned my throat, and I swallowed to force them back. *This is for Father,* I reminded myself, closing my eyes.

Fitz paused near the pond and turned, noting the way I'd stopped at the edge of the clearing like a terrified deer. He scowled impatiently and began to finish buttoning his shirt. Despite his earlier exertion, his hair was still pulled back, only a couple loose strands escaping and framing his annoyed face. It seemed as if the laws of nature conspired to ensure the fae always appeared pristine and attractive, even under circumstances that would normally be unflattering.

"Please inform me when you've finished admiring the view," Fitz called dryly, "as I haven't all day to waste."

Snapping my gaze away, I trudged forward, doing my best to appear nonchalant.

"I suppose we should start with what you do know," Fitz said as soon as I was a couple feet away, staring into the pond rather than looking at him. "Have you learned about the source of our magic?"

"Nature." Branches swayed overhead and gold leaves fell like the softest rain, one catching in my hair.

Before I could reach up and untangle it from my braid, Fitz stepped forward, seizing it. Startled, I glanced up and met his gaze. His eyes widened and he dropped the leaf.

What was that?

But he'd already broadened the space between us, gesturing toward the glimpses of sky visible through the forest canopy. "You're correct, though it's a little more complicated than that. Magic runs through our blood, bequeathed to us by our ancestors who were also connected to nature, but it's also granted to us by the land we're born upon. If my mother had traveled to another kingdom and given birth to me there, I might wield winter magic."

I quirked an eyebrow.

"The sky under which we're born also affects the sort of magic we possess. Those born under a night sky, in the middle of a storm, have the power of shadows and lightning." A dimple formed beside his mouth, the barest hint of a self-satisfied smirk.

"So that is where your magic comes from. I suppose that grants you quite a measure of power," I said, crossing my arms.

"The measure of one's power doesn't lie in the type of magic wielded. It's actually quite random."

"You mean, even the non-royal fae might be born with powerful magic?"

Fitz dipped his head in acknowledgement. "Anyone can have powerful magic. The land chooses whom it will. However, the greatest measure of magic is always granted to the royal family, as we are also the ones tasked with specific responsibilities."

Like sending the spirits on, I thought. I glanced at my leather boots and the muddy leaves I'd trampled on my way into the clearing. "Does the land ever reject a fae born here?"

"Rarely, but if so, the fae journeys to another kingdom where he or she is accepted."

"What about humans who are rejected?"

"Only those wedded to fae are granted magic, and in the past, that has never been a problem."

I pursed my lips. "But there might be one now?"

Fitz's eyes flashed. "Of course there might be. You were not the one promised to me. The land honors our customs, our traditions, our sincerity, and our desire to protect our kingdom. You are a usurper." His gaze flicked over me, scanning the leggings that revealed far more of my curves than I'd ever shown in public before, my loose tunic, and the column of my neck where my locket's chain was visible. Discomfort and fear squirmed in my stomach. Did he wonder about the necklace I wore? Did he sense its magic now that I was near?

Was that why he'd been staring last night? Had he suspected something then?

He stepped closer, so near I had to lift my chin to meet his stare. "If the land senses that you are insincere, it won't accept you."

I swallowed. "Would that give you the right to cast me and my family from your kingdom?"

The intensity in Fitz's eyes abated, and he turned away. "My mother and I made a vow to protect you. Though being refused by the land would dissolve our marriage, according to Ashwood law, you would remain here. As long as you didn't prove to be treacherous. But if you made a move against my kingdom..." He cast me a sidelong glance, his eyes burning with his unspoken threat. "In the meantime, I'll train you, as my ancestors trained their human wives, with the hope that the land finds you worthy."

"How quickly does magic manifest in a human?"

"If our land accepts you, yours would reveal itself by the end of autumn." He lifted a hand, brow furrowed in concentration, and a grey cloud swirled into the clearing. More followed, until the air was damp with mist, and strands of loose hair clung to my forehead. "As you already know, my power stems from the night as well as the land of Ashwood. I can summon clouds and storms, darkness and stars, but I could never control ice or snow. The land I was born upon does not offer those abilities. Neither can I influence the sunlight. Your magic, if it comes, will be like mine."

"Do all the kingdoms have different magic?"

"Since we're all granted magic through nature, we can possess similar abilities. Some fae in Ashwood can manipulate fire, for instance, and some in Ravenheart—the summer kingdom—can as well. But yes, each kingdom also has unique powers."

Fitz stepped forward, taking my hands in a surprisingly gentle movement and cupping them before me, positioning my arms like a child catching raindrops. "In the past," he went on, "members of the Ashwood family found that humans wielded magic more easily after spending time close to the land." Mist swirled in my palms, dancing to a tune only Fitz knew.

"Will my magic also involve sending the souls on?" I dared to ask. I glanced up to watch Fitz's reaction carefully, hoping to begin to understand why he wasn't performing his responsibility.

But his expression remained an unreadable mask. "That is a task borne and inherited by the Ashwoods only."

I decided not to press the issue, for now. "So my training involves standing outside and watching you use your magic?"

"For today."

I studied the mist, contemplating all Fitz had told me and all I still didn't know. "If you leave your kingdom, does your connection to your magic vanish?"

"Not entirely. The more powerful a fae's magic and their connection to the land is, the less they are affected. My—" He cut himself off and shook his head. "Even the strongest, though, feel a difference. This is why many store their magic in objects they can carry, helping them access their full power no matter where they venture. Those charms also help us draw on our magic when we're tired. If you use too much power at once, you'll grow too weary to keep wielding your magic. But with the help of a charm, you have additional power to pull from when you grow weak." His eyes met mine. "Those charms are highly coveted."

My stomach churned. I knew he was all but accusing me of exactly what I hoped to do: steal his charm.

Questions tingled on my tongue, but I was afraid to sound too eager. Fitz was already suspicious; I didn't want his theories to be confirmed. Instead, I feigned surprise, hoping he would believe my expression and think I'd never learned about this aspect of magic. "Could I do this as a human too? In case...my responsibilities as a princess take me away from Ashwood?"

Fitz cocked his head, this time smirking outright. "Isn't that something you would already know, given that you long for that type of power?"

I raised my eyebrows. "I would like some measure of *protection* if I'm ever forced to travel, considering even the fae here seem to want me dead."

"Don't lie," he said, pushing closer until I could feel his breath on my face. I wanted to shiver or retreat, but that would look weak. I tipped my chin up, meeting his gaze with equal ferocity, refusing to back down. "Even if it's a favorite pastime of yours. I don't care what excuses you gave about protecting your sister. We both know there are only two reasons why a human would willingly choose to marry a fae." He curled a hand behind my neck to tilt my face up, burying his fingers in my hair. "Either for power," he whispered, "or for desire."

His lips were mere inches from mine, and I had the dizzying thought that he was going to kiss me, simply to test my reaction. Maybe he took pleasure in goading me on, in seeing the mingling disgust and desire that warred in my expression. He was exactly what I'd expected every fae man to be: revolting, yet beautiful. I gritted my teeth, furious at him and at myself for feeling desire.

He's manipulating you. Stroking his ego by seeing you react to his looks, and perhaps hoping to weaken your defenses against him. He wants you to fall for him, to be a lovesick girl easily persuaded by his charm.

Sneering, I set my hands on his broad chest and shoved as hard as I could, forcing him to release my hair and stumble backward. "Desire?" I mocked, my voice a little too shrill. "You're the vainest man I've ever met. Why don't you believe the reasons I gave for marrying you?"

Fitz laughed bitterly. "Because you're a liar."

I fisted my hands. "I did it for my sister, so she'd have a chance at real love. She deserves something better than this—than *you.*"

His eyes flashed with annoyance. "Indeed. You've already made that point quite clear, more than once."

"Perhaps I wanted a portion of your power so I could learn to glamour you. To command you to apologize, or perhaps even to humble yourself before me."

Fitz laughed again, the sound still mirthless. "Firstly, glamour doesn't work on other fae who can also wield it. Anyone who can use glamour is immune to its powers."

I scowled.

"And secondly, I said that you will possess my *magic*. I did not say that you'll gain my ability to use glamour. That is a purely fae gift, one that never passes on to humans."

I waved away his explanations, my fury building to the point that now I couldn't hold back my grievances. "And I certainly didn't marry you out of desire. The first night we met, you insulted my appearance and my intelligence with your rude comment about refusing to dance with me. Then last night, your mother took Lina's hand, yet you did nothing. And you refuse to send the souls on, letting them suffer and linger here, lost and alone and hurting. I know they don't know peace outside of the glade—and even then it's nothing compared to the peace they deserve from being able to pass on into the afterlife." Tears swam in my eyes, and my voice broke. Though I wanted Father to stay long enough that I could save him, I was also haunted by the idea that he might be wandering the woods, hurting. At least, back in Riverton, when I'd imagined him in the glade of spirits, I'd known he'd have a bit of rest until I found him. Now I knew that was unlikely to be true. Every story I'd been told shared that wandering spirits were tormented. Lonely. Broken.

Drawing a deep breath, I lifted my chin. "You're abhorrent and I despise you, but at least this way, Grace doesn't have to spend her life suffering your presence."

Without a backward glance, I stormed out of the clearing, back down the path, and toward the castle. My erratic heartbeat muffled the sounds around me. When I reached the castle, I was relieved to find that Fitz hadn't bothered to follow. I was alone.

It was time to get to work.

CHAPTER TWELVE

As I stormed through the castle, giving my blood time to cool, I started to regret my impulsive declaration. I shouldn't have been so swift to spout angry words at Fitz. The thought that he might not hide his charm within his rooms, but that it might remain on his person, had already crossed my mind more than once, and if that were the case, stealing it would require getting close to him. It would have been smarter to pretend like I wanted him to kiss me rather than shoving him away. Perhaps I could have pretended to be overwhelmed by attraction, or petty and jealous of the attention my sister received. Anything to assure Fitz I wasn't dangerous and to stroke his ego. It might have reassured him I wasn't after his power and made him let down his guard, if only a little.

Instead, I'd let my temper get the best of me. Sighing, I began the arduous climb up the stairs. The castle was a dizzying maze, and the few times Lina or Fitz had escorted me through it had only made me feel more lost, but thankfully, the route to the stairs and our rooms was simple enough. Sweat dotted my temples by the time I reached the fourth floor. I turned from the staircase and followed the hall past a statue I recognized. It was a king, with haughty features chiseled into marble and a long cape flowing down his back.

This was it. Fitz's rooms were two doors down.

An open doorway beyond the statue made me pause. I'd never seen any of the doors on this floor left open before, and the hall was vacant and silent. I crept toward the doorway, taking in the dusty sunshine pouring through a dirty window, illuminating the quarters in watery light. The sitting room was small but luxurious, with a plush blue carpet and matching blue and silver armchairs. Paintings of the autumn forest and floral arrangements hung from the silver walls. It reminded me of the royal luxury of Fitz's quarters, but these had a distinctly feminine feel.

I frowned, noting the dust coating the tables that sat beside the armchairs. A side table across from the fireplace held a tea set that was just as grimy, like it had been neglected for months or years. Even the air smelled stale.

My locket pulsed, low and steady like a second heartbeat, and a thrill of curiosity and fear make the hairs on the back of my neck rise. Was it recognizing the presence of magic? Something about these sad, abandoned rooms drew me in irresistibly. I crept into the sitting room, taking note of the trinkets set atop the fireplace mantel: a miniature figurine of a couple in a passionate embrace and a worn envelope without any markings. When I inspected the envelope, I found the wax seal was broken and the letter was missing.

Glancing behind me to reassure myself that no one was in the hall, I gently clicked the door shut. If these rooms had been left uninhabited and untouched long enough to be dirty and musty, I had the distinct impression neither Fitz nor his family would take kindly to my poking through them. But if the door was closed, no one would think to look for me here. No one need ever know.

I slipped past the sitting room and into the bedroom, studying the large four-poster bed draped in faded white curtains. The bedclothes were also blue and silver with tiny floral patterns, and every piece of furniture was carved with depictions of flowers and trees, leaves and tangled vines. On the vanity, a comb and brush and stunning pearl necklace were laid out, as if the owner had only stepped out for a few minutes and would return soon. A beautiful jewelry box painted in blue and silver flowers rested before the mirror, but when I lifted it, none of the pieces felt magical. Nothing made the locket pulse further. There were gold and silver rings, pearl and ruby earrings, and a necklace of sapphires and pearls. All stunning and expensive, but all normal.

Next to the vanity stood a wardrobe. It opened easily, revealed rows upon rows of fine dresses in every imaginable color, from gowns that I might have seen in the mortal world to lavish, ethereal-looking fae attire. There were also tunics and nightgowns and some carefully folded leggings in drawers, along with beaded slippers and sturdy boots. Every outfit spoke of youth and beauty. Even the more practical outfits had little embellishments:

embroidered flowers along the collars of tunics, beading on the hems of the leggings, and tiny gems sewn along the tops of the boots.

Turning away, I approached a bookshelf on the opposite wall, scanning its leatherbound spines. Maybe there was a book on magic, or something else containing a trace of power that called to the magic within my locket. But disappointment settled in my chest when I realized the books were all novels, works that sounded romantic and whimsical and utterly unhelpful to me.

Who had this woman been? In my inexperienced eyes, the quarters seemed too opulent for any average courtier. And why were her rooms like this, neglected and layered in dust, left as she'd kept them? Had she passed away, or had she left Ashwood? But if she'd left, why did her belongings remain?

A floorboard creaked and I spun, surveying the room. What if a maid had left the door open because she'd been ordered to finally clean the quarters? A shadow flashed in my peripheral vision. Someone was in the washroom.

Get out of here.

I turned toward the sitting room when more movement flickered. I whirled, finding the room empty, and faced the vanity with its mirror.

A woman stared back at me, her face blurred and indistinct in the reflection. The only clear image I had was of her eyes, the whites bloody with burst vessels. My heart lurched and I spun once more, but there was no one behind me. When I glanced again at the mirror, only my pale face peered back.

Am I going mad? I couldn't tell anymore if it was my own heart or the locket pounding against my chest.

I had to leave these rooms. An overwhelming sense of wrongness seized me, like a silent scream warning me that I didn't belong, that I was unwelcome and in danger. I lurched through the quarters and toward the sitting room door, clammy palm seizing the doorknob. It refused to turn. Chill air licked the back of my neck, and I imagined the ghost of that woman behind me, whispering enraged words only she could hear.

"No," I breathed, pleading with the restless spirit in the room. "Let me out."

I rattled the door, desperate tears stinging my eyes. Holden had warned me not to wander the halls at night, but what if they weren't limited by the hour? What if this ghost was capable of attacking me now?

I twisted to face the room. "I'm not here to hurt you. Please let me leave."

A rustling sound filled my ears, and shadows danced in the corners of the room. I glanced toward the clock over the mantel, realizing it must have stopped working a long time ago, its hands frozen at one. One in the morning? Or one in the afternoon? Did the time have any significance?

I placed a hand over my chest, right where my locket was concealed. "I'm sorry if someone hurt you, but I don't mean any harm. I'm sorry I entered this place. I only want to leave."

Breathing deeply, I waited, hearing no other sounds, and seeing nothing else out of the ordinary. No whispered words. No darting shadows. The air warmed, becoming less oppressive. I dared to turn despite the prickling sensation along my back and the way I felt unseen eyes watching me, trying the knob again.

A rush of relief swelled when it turned, and the door swung open. I burst into the hall and clicked the door shut, then promptly ran to my rooms.

CHAPTER THIRTEEN

shamed by the flight of my courage at the first sign of a hostile ghost, I collapsed onto my bed and stared at the ceiling. I vowed that next time I wandered, I would not fall into the role of helpless victim so easily. I'd find a weapon, even if I had to steal a dagger from Fitz's rooms.

Despite the mystery of the woman and the fear that encounter had instilled in me, it also offered me hope. If souls were active in the castle at all hours of the day, I had more opportunities closer at hand to search for Father. Maybe he wasn't even in the glade of souls, but right here in the castle, and I wouldn't have to find a way to sneak into the forest undetected. Though the castle was a vast maze, full of courtiers and servants and guards who would become suspicious if they caught me poking about, searching it still felt more manageable than scouring an entire forest in the dead of night.

Rising from the bed, I steeled my nerves. There had been guards out in the hall who thankfully hadn't been close enough to the strange rooms to see me emerge from them. Stationed closer to my own door, they hadn't even blinked at the way I'd ran to my rooms like a coward. But I couldn't expect them to be so casual about an attempt on my part to enter their crown prince's quarters alone. Could I pretend as if I'd been sent there to retrieve an item for him? Or that I'd forgotten something of mine?

I glanced out the windows, where the afternoon sun was already sinking. My stomach growled. Dahlia and I had feasted on scones and sandwiches for luncheon, but I was already growing hungry. Dinner would be soon, and the queen would likely make it a formal occasion with my family in attendance. The fae were known for their frequent celebrations and feasts. Perhaps I could pretend that I needed an article of clothing for dinner.

Before I'd even made it out of my bedroom, there was a light knock on my door. "Come in," I called, and Lina entered, another dress in her arms. A second maid trailed her.

"You and your family have been summoned to a feast to celebrate your recent marriage and to further acquaint yourself with the court, Princess," Lina announced.

"Oh," I said, rather stupidly, as two more maids scurried inside. Once again, my opportunity was gone. My stomach clenched, and I wondered if I could feign illness at dinner and leave early. Perhaps, while the courtiers were occupied, it would be easier to sneak around the palace as the light faded and the spirits began to roam in earnest.

"We haven't much time to prepare you," Lina added, "as this dress was just finished, but you'll be thankful to hear it's in *your* size. Now hurry. The queen won't tolerate your being late."

Knowing a threat when I heard one, I stood and let the maids get to work.

Fitz was already waiting in my sitting room when my maids finished, leaving me to stare dazedly into the mirror at the unrecognizable woman they'd transformed me into. I was clothed in frothy layers of green and teal, my sleeves thin and swooping off my shoulders. Silver beads and embroidery flashed across my skirts each time I moved. The maids had left my hair to fall in a straight curtain down my back, only curling the strands that framed my face. Even more unusual for me was the rouge dusting my cheeks, the silver brightening my eyelids, and the deep red staining my lips. I looked like a stranger.

Like a princess.

"Have a good evening," Lina murmured, dipping into a curtsey. She and the other maids slipped from my rooms, leaving me to face Fitz alone.

I wondered how furious he was at the way I'd left him during training. Sighing, I turned and strode toward my sitting room, knowing that stalling would only provide further grief in the form of Queen Griselda's wrath.

Fitz lounged in one of my armchairs, one booted foot propped on his knee, staring at a crinkled paper. From the doorway, I could make out nothing of the inked words on it, but the flowing, elegant script looked like a woman's handwriting, and the letter was worn, as if it'd been read many times.

I frowned, my mind darting back to the blue and silver rooms and the ghostly woman. Could the letter have belonged to her? Had she been Fitz's lover? Or was I trying to draw connections where there weren't any?

Stepping forward, I entered the room and Fitz folded the letter, tucking it into his pocket and standing. He was dressed simply, in a loose shirt and trousers, but his black coat was of fine material, its silver embroidery mimicking the leaf and star patterns on my dress. Without a word, he extended an arm.

Pursing my lips, I accepted it, and we strode silently from my rooms and down the hall. Annoyance tugged at me, though I couldn't pinpoint why. "So we've returned to cold hostility and unpleasantness?" I asked at last.

My skirts whispered along the polished steps as we began our long descent toward the first floor.

Fitz cast me a sidelong glance. "Do you always feel the need to fill the silence?"

"I simply think it's pleasanter and more agreeable if, when two people encounter each other, they at least exchange polite greetings instead of being reticent."

A muscle worked in his jaw. "I forget how formal you humans can be."

"You're a crown prince—surely you see the necessity of formality?"

He sighed. "Hardly. It becomes tiresome. And after your parting words earlier, I assumed you'd prefer silence." He shot me a pointed look, blue eyes piercing. "Wouldn't you prefer that the man you hate keeps his distance?"

I imagined what it would be like if Fitz avoided me altogether. My mind flashed back to how often I'd already been forced to be closer to him than I wanted. The memory of Fitz's fingers tugging the laces of my corset darted through my thoughts. Those same deft fingers in my hair, digging gently into my scalp, making my skin prickle.

I blushed and looked away, nearly slipping off a step. Fitz's fingers squeezed my arm to steady me. "Flustered?" His mouth twisted in a grin. "Were you lying earlier? *Again*?"

"Why would I lie about hating you?" I rolled my eyes and pulled on his arm none too gently to keep us moving.

The stories hadn't exaggerated fae beauty, but I was relieved to know it wasn't true that they were irresistible. I might be foolish around Fitz at times, but I wasn't utterly senseless.

Unless he glamours you, I warned myself. But he'd vowed he wouldn't, and I could only pray he didn't have some secret loophole that would allow him to break his word.

But it would be better to play the part of a beguiled woman, I reminded myself. I couldn't afford for Fitz to be aloof; I needed him near. Since I'd already been too rash to fool him into thinking I was interested, perhaps I could pretend to gently relent and become friendly. I didn't even have to earn his trust, only to gain enough time with him to take what I needed.

"I...may have spoken a bit harshly earlier," I said, tempering my voice. "I have no reason to like the fae, but given that I hardly know you, hate might be too strong of a word."

It's not strong enough of a word, I thought. *Anyone as heartless as you—leaving the spirits to suffer and thinking nothing of the way his mother disfigures her own servants—is a monster.*

As we rounded a bend and swept down a hallway, passing the ballroom to approach a different set of double doors, the sounds of conversation and laughter drifted toward us.

I stiffened. "Are we late?"

"A little," Fitz admitted, pausing. A pair of impassive guards stood outside the doors to what I presumed was the dining room, scarcely seeming to notice us. "It's not your fault. The maids barely had time to prepare you."

"The queen will not see it that way," I said feebly, studying the doors with dread. Suddenly, being locked in the blue and silver room with the red-eyed ghost seemed preferable to this meal. I didn't think I'd have to pretend to be ill, either.

Fitz tightened his grasp on my arm, whirling me to face him and shoving me unceremoniously against the wall. I choked on air, lifting my hands to strike him, but he was already moving, burying his hands in my hair and mussing the perfectly brushed strands into chaos. Our noses grazed as he brought his lips so close I was afraid if I even breathed more deeply, his mouth would be on mine.

"What are you doing?" I whispered, horrified at the way his hands, trailing down my bare shoulders and arms, sent bolts of heat through me. His eyes were bright, filled with an emotion I couldn't place, but one that was not at all like the distant expression he'd been wearing.

Glamour, my mind screamed. *He's toying with you, making you want him despite how you really feel.*

"Giving you an excuse," he said, pulling back as swiftly as he'd pressed himself against me. I heaved a sigh of relief, reaching up to fix my hair. Fitz frowned. "Don't. My mother won't mind our tardiness nearly as much if she imagines that I couldn't keep my hands off you when I saw you in that dress."

I blushed furiously. "Your mother hates me."

Fitz raised a brow. "My mother wants heirs, so I imagine she'll overcome her feelings if she believes her desire will come true." He extended his arm. "Come, let's play the role of infatuated couple."

"Will your mother really fall for that?" I groused. "I'm sure she knows how mad you are about what I did."

Fitz leaned in close to murmur in my ear. "Since it's in your best interest that she does," he said, mouth brushing my earlobe, "I suppose that means you'll have to be convincing."

Gooseflesh rose on my arms at the feel of his warm lips against my ear, and I jolted away, embarrassed. *Because he surprised you,* I reasoned, ignoring the way my cheeks heated.

When I dared a glance toward Fitz, his expression was blank, his eyes straight ahead. More proof that whatever had just happened between us meant nothing to him. *And nothing to me, because I am not so foolish as to become enchanted by a handsome face,* I promised myself.

As the guards pulled open the doors, I reached again for my hair, this time pretending to hastily brush it back into place as we entered the dining room. My stomach dropped at the sight before us, taking note of the vast gathering. To the queen, this was probably an intimate occasion, with only her most favored members of court and my family present, but to me, it was like attending my coronation all over again. And this time, my appearance was—less than ideal.

Although, as I scanned the pairs of eyes raking over me, noting the way one of my sleeves had fallen lower off my shoulder and how my hair was tousled, I realized that, strangely enough, Fitz had granted me more power.

Eyes widened and heads dipped as they realized their crown prince had accepted me. It went without saying that if their prince was enamored with me, I was under his protection, and they had no choice but to offer me deference. My eyes snagged on Dahlia's knowing smile in the crowd, and I couldn't help my answering grin, happy to have a kind fae present.

Near the far end of the table, Mother and my sisters sat together quietly, their hands in their laps. Grace scanned me from head to toe, a quizzical expression on her face. *Are you all right?* she mouthed, and I knew she feared for me. I longed to rush to her, to find a private place to bare my soul to her. I'd stop keeping my doubts a secret. I'd tell her about the ghosts and magic and my fear. I'd confess the way Fitz had made desire curl low in my stomach when he'd pressed me against that wall, when I had no evidence he'd been using glamour. And then I'd tell her how much I loathed him, even more so because of my attraction.

Then my gaze snagged on Holden sitting near Grace, and I blinked at their intertwined fingers. In our world, it would have been a scandalous display of affection even if they'd announced an engagement. But here? It seemed unremarkable. I wasn't sure if I was overjoyed for my sister and this chance she had to explore possible love and happiness, or fearful for her. Though I liked Holden, I couldn't help but worry that some of his mother's cruelty lurked within his own heart.

I wanted to ask Grace about Holden and the short time they'd spent together. I wanted to know if *she* was all right and happy.

But it was not to be. Queen Griselda, raising a wineglass of sparkling gold liquid that made my stomach twist, turned the full weight of her stare upon me. "Welcome, Prince Fitz and Princess Elle. How good of you to deign to join us...at your leisure." Her eyes combed over my gown and fastened on my tangled hair. "Do sit down."

Fitz took the empty chair on his mother's right, while I sat next to him and across from Grace. When her eyes met mine, I glanced meaningfully at her and Holden's clasped hands. She smiled gently, reassuring me. I wondered what the queen thought of it.

As Queen Griselda called to her servants to bring the first course, I scanned the table and noticed that my family and I were not the only humans. A group of young messengers sat talking quietly amongst themselves. My heart leapt when I found Mr. Reid among them. Maybe, if I was careful in how I worded my questions, I could glean information about the glade of spirits—or maybe he'd have an idea of what Fitz's charm could be. Feeling the weight of my gaze, he turned from the man he spoke with and offered me a dimpled smile.

A fanciful, girlish part of me—the one that wished life could have been different—melted a little. But those feelings didn't matter anymore. Even if I could escape the bonds of marriage, even if there was a corner of the mortal world I could hide in and never be found by the fae, I knew Mr. Reid had chosen Brytwilde. An attachment between us simply wasn't meant to be.

My husband took note of my wandering gaze. "Not convincing, Blackford," Fitz murmured in my ear, purposefully letting his mouth linger before dipping his head and brushing his lips against my neck.

I froze, certain I was turning scarlet. He wasn't kissing me, only letting his mouth explore in the suggestion of a kiss. Enough to make a statement. I'd never witnessed such a blatant display of public affection in my life, much less been the recipient of it. Recovering myself, I pulled away, forcing a smile that I hoped looked coy and turning to Fitz. "I think we made a persuasive enough entrance," I whispered.

Fitz's eyes bored into mine. I wished that I could elicit even the slightest bit of embarrassment or surprise from him, after the reactions he'd managed to pull from me. "That will all go to waste if you're eyeing other men."

Dropping my napkin into my lap, I seized my spoon and dipped it into the soup set before me. "Noted," I said, hoping Fitz was done with his "convincing displays" for the evening. I wondered if I'd be able to complain of a headache and escape dinner early not only without the queen's wrath but also without Fitz following me to play the role of doting husband. My chest tightened with worry and frustration. It might have only been my second evening in the castle, but I couldn't bear the wait. The idea that Father's spirit could be roaming the halls—so close yet so far—was agonizing.

Would he recognize me? Would his spirit remember his mortal life, or would he be confused? If he did, perhaps he'd also have ideas about how to save him. Father had always been the most intelligent person I'd ever known.

"Tell me, how do you find Ashwood, Elle?" Queen Griselda asked, jolting me from my thoughts as I swallowed my first spoonful of soup.

I wasn't sure what the soup was supposed to taste like, because with my tangle of grief and worry dancing in my stomach, the only flavor I detected was bitterness. "It's very comfortable, Your Majesty, and everyone has been most accommodating."

Fitz shot me a look out of the corner of his eye, and I could have sworn he was fighting the urge to laugh. Was he thinking of how *unaccommodating* some courtiers had been by drugging me? I was seized with a desire to stomp on his foot.

"And your family?" the queen glanced across the table at Grace and Mother, who both sat perfectly poised. Beside them, Maggie looked fretful, and Bridget and Isabel were whispering furiously. Isabel nudged Bridget, who stifled a giggle and darted a not-so-covert glance toward the messengers.

I gritted my teeth, unsure if I was more furious at their lack of etiquette before a queen who casually severed hands, or at their unabashed interest in men who'd *chosen* to live in this world. Aside from Reid, whose character we were familiar with, we had no reason to believe those other men were any less greedy or cruel than the fae they lived among. Talking with them was one thing. Courting them? Another.

"We are most obliged, Your Majesty," Mother said with a dip of her head. "You have been nothing but generous to us."

Queen Griselda sat back in her chair, clearly pleased.

More servants entered the room, bearing glasses filled with wine sparkling in every shade imaginable. Most, though, gleamed a rich golden in the flickering candlelight. To my horror, longing gripped me as I remembered the light-hearted, carefree feeling the fae wine had elicited. There hadn't been room in my heart for sorrow or fear.

My mouth went dry. "Would it be so terrible to try one si—"

Fitz turned to me, his gaze sharpening. He seized my hand and squeezed it. I hadn't even realized I'd been reaching for one of the passing trays until he did. "Don't make a scene," Fitz muttered under his breath.

I wanted to be angry and pull away, but he'd rested our hands on the table, in full sight of everyone. Not to mention, I wasn't sure I could trust myself as long as there was fae wine within reach. Thankfully, Fitz declined some for himself and requested two glasses of red wine. On my right, a female courtier with smooth, dark skin and wide mossy green eyes studied me intently as she lifted her own golden drink to her lips.

"Interested in the taste of fae wine?" she asked, her tone rich and musical.

My skin prickled. Was she hoping to tempt me further? Did she know what Fitz had done to the one who'd drugged me last night? I shook my head too quickly, and the woman's lips curled into a smile at my unconvincing display.

"I've heard that it tastes like rot and ash to mortals anyway," she said, setting her glass aside, thankfully far out of my reach. "At least the ones who haven't been accepted by the land yet, the ones who have no magic in their blood." She glanced at me pointedly.

Fitz made a sound, tugging on my hand until he'd nearly pulled me out of my chair and into his.

The woman laughed lightly. "Easily jealous, Prince Fitz? I wouldn't think one such as you would feel the need to fight for your wife's attentions." Her eyes scanned his face appreciatively.

Fitz ignored her, whispering to me instead. "Don't trust her."

I almost burst into laughter. "I trust no one here, including you."

Running his thumb over my knuckles as if we were murmuring sweet words of adoration to one another, Fitz smirked. "Good."

"Have you ever tried fae wine, Elle?" Queen Griselda called.

My entire body went cold. Fitz's thumb stilled and his fingers tightened over mine. For the first time, I wondered if his protection of me would end if his mother forced his hand. Would he give in as a dutiful son and prince? Or would he, as heir to the throne, feel the need to exert his own authority?

Nausea danced along my tongue as the queen lifted her glass to her lips, drinking deeply. Awaiting my answer.

I wanted some. Only a sip. Just a short escape. My blood thundered in my ears so loudly it was difficult to hear the murmurs of other conversations happening around us. I sensed my sisters' and Mother's eyes on me, could practically feel their concern.

If the queen made me drink her wine, what would she compel me to do next? It was said that even powerful glamour could be resisted with a strong enough will, and I supposed in some ways I'd already proven how headstrong I was to the queen and her court, but their wine was a different story. If I lost myself once more in that beautiful daze, if I drank more than the small dose I'd had last night, I could only imagine the things I could be forced to do. Perhaps Queen Griselda would use the wine as a loophole in her vow to protect me. Maybe she would convince me to drink a little, and then I'd continue of my own accord and drink myself to death.

A fitting end to the girl who'd stolen her son.

"I..." Words failed me as I stared at her wineglass, sweat beading on my forehead.

Fitz stood suddenly, pulling me with him. "Forgive us, Mother. This isn't the time. I believe Elle is ill."

He didn't even wait for a dismissal before sweeping me from the dining room and out into the blissfully cool hallway. Pulling away from Fitz, I slumped against the nearest wall, catching my breath.

"Your mother will be more furious at me if you miss dinner too," I said, turning to Fitz with an accusatory glare.

He watched me, unmoved.

"I can return to my rooms, and you can return to dinner and give my excuses."

Still, Fitz didn't make a move to leave. Something flickered in his eyes. "You do realize the sun has almost set and the halls won't be safe for you to walk alone."

"I'll go straight to my rooms," I insisted. "*Please* leave. I don't need you." My voice cracked, and I despised myself for the pleading tone, but I needed to be alone. I dearly hoped now wasn't the moment Fitz chose to have a heart and concern himself about me for my own sake, and not merely his reputation.

Fitz arched a brow. "Such words of gratitude, Blackford," he said, dipping his head and turning away.

The doors creaked as the servants opened them again, and, without a backward glance, I straightened and strolled toward the stairs. Outside, the sun was slowly descending, bright and bloody. It streaked red light across the floor, strange and otherworldly, but the sight eased my mood. I only needed to wait a short while for it to grow dark. If everyone believed I'd retired to my rooms, no one would come looking for me.

I'd be free to search for ghosts.

CHAPTER FOURTEEN

I brushed a shaking hand across my forehead, relieved to find the rest of the castle silent and still compared to the noise and bustle of the dining room. Striding past the ballroom, I turned down a quieter, narrower corridor. Sconces lined the walls, but the candles had burnt to stubs, threatening to flicker out at any moment. Studying the portraits lining the walls, I remembered discovering this space before, the night of the ball. The whispered words I'd heard. The side door that led onto the castle grounds.

As before, I could have sworn I heard murmuring voices. Queen Griselda and her sons watched me sternly from their portraits, along with other fae I did not recognize. This time, I studied each depiction more closely, singling out the humans among them, previous wives and husbands persuaded to join this world or stolen into it. Some had convincingly cheerful smiles that made me wonder if they'd found happiness here. Others appeared grim, a haunted look in their gazes that made me shiver. Most stared with glazed eyes and foolish grins, indicating they'd been glamoured into oblivion.

A mingling sense of relief and curiosity gripped me. If it were truly that easy for the fae to force humans into submission, why hadn't the queen or her sons done so to us? Had the Ashwood glamour weakened over the years, or was Mr. Reid's claim that the Ashwoods no longer used it really true? Was it because there was something wrong with their magic? I rested a hand over where my locket was hidden beneath my dress.

Fitz's magic didn't seem weak.

Did his mother agree with his earlier vow to not use his glamour on me? Was that a family choice? It seemed more honorable than I'd expect Queen Griselda to be, but perhaps she preferred for her human and fae subjects to submit to her willingly.

A cold whisper of air shifted my hair, like fingers plucking it away from my ear.

I will stop you.

The words were clear, whispered in a furious feminine voice.

I whirled to face my unseen company.

"I didn't expect to find you here." I gasped and glanced toward the end of the hallway, where Mr. Reid leaned against the wall, his mouth twisted in amusement. "I thought you'd retired to your rooms."

"Mr. Reid," I said, dipped into a hasty curtsey. "You startled me."

"You needn't stand on formality like in the mortal world here," he said, pushing off the wall and striding toward me, his smile melting into concern. "I'm nobody, so you could just call me Reid. Or by my given name, James."

"That seems too intimate, given I'm a married woman now."

"It doesn't work that way here."

"Very well," I relented. "Reid then."

Reid's smile faded as he scanned me. "How have you been? Did he...has he hurt you?"

I shook my head. "Surprisingly, he's been a gentleman."

Reid's eyes narrowed. "Truly?"

The memory of Fitz's fingers in my hair, of his body pressed close to mine when he pushed me against the wall flashed through my mind. I'd never asked him to stop, though given the way he'd kept his word the night I'd spent in his bed, I knew if I had, he would have listened. But in the quiet of my own thoughts, I could admit that I hadn't wanted him to.

No, I wasn't afraid of Fitz touching me when I didn't want him to. I was afraid of *wanting* him to touch me despite my aversion. Of wanting him to push me against a wall and kiss me rather than pulling away at the last moment. My mingling desire and disgust was confusing and terrifying.

"It's not what I fear," I told Reid, shrugging helplessly. "He and his mother have shown themselves to be cruel and cold in other ways, but thankfully, not that."

Reid's mouth pinched together. "Why did you do it, Elle? Why did you take Grace's place?"

My first name on his lips was jolting and unfamiliar. I'd once longed to hear him warmly say my given name in such a way. Now, I took comfort in the fact that we could be friends in Brytwilde.

Still chilled, I hugged myself. Reid noticed and shrugged out of his coat, offering it to me. I draped it over my shoulders gratefully. "Grace and Prince Holden danced together at the ball, and it was the first time in as long as I can remember that I saw my sister truly carefree and happy." I hesitated, looking up to search Reid's eyes. "Is Holden a good man?"

Reid stuffed his hands into his pockets and studied the wall of portraits behind me. I turned, finding his eyes lingering on the one of Holden. "I believe so," he said at last, voice lowered, "though I don't fully trust anyone in the Ashwood family."

"Understood." I frowned and gestured to the portraits of glamoured humans. "Why haven't the queen or princes glamoured us?"

"Supposedly, Queen Griselda prefers to blackmail and bargain. She feels powerful that way, and I think she likes a challenge."

I tilted my head to the side. "Is it that, or is their magic somehow not as strong as it was in generations past?"

Reid smiled at my musings. "If that's the case, they have done an excellent job of keeping that a secret and showing off their other magical abilities." He held out an arm. "Come, you shouldn't be out in the castle when the sun sets."

Instead of taking his arm, I whirled on him, excited. "Can you tell me more about the escaped spirits?"

Reid nodded solemnly. "Crown Prince Fitz is a truly heartless wretch, to not let the ghosts have their peace. What else do you want to know?"

"Do the spirits *only* wander at night?"

Reid's eyes narrowed. "What do you mean? Have you seen one?"

I swallowed. "Perhaps." Reid took my arm and gently led me back down the hall as I shared my earlier encounter with the ghostly woman in the blue and silver rooms. As I spoke, Reid's face grew darker.

"Do you know who she could have been?" I asked.

Reid shook his head, running his free hand through his dark locks. "I could guess, but I can't be sure. Probably she was a royal who lived here long before us and met an untimely end. That would explain her anger."

"But the ghosts haven't always roamed beyond the glade—so wouldn't the ones trapped in the castle now only be from recent deaths?"

Again, Reid shook his head. "No, any spirits who had refused to move on could have wandered beyond the glade."

I mulled over this information. "Would that explain her ability to show herself before the sun set? Would an older fae or a previous royal have more power as a ghost?"

Reid's jaw tightened. "I'm not sure. I think that's unusual, although it's not unheard of for souls to reveal themselves at any hour—they're just insubstantial before nighttime. Nothing but shadow and spirit, unable to physically touch or harm a living person. But her showing herself at all to you in the daylight is more proof you need to be in your rooms tonight. The ghosts do not intrude upon locked quarters in this castle. Ancient magical wards placed on those locks when the castle was built will keep them out. As a stranger, you are in the most danger if you leave your rooms."

I arched a brow. "And you are not?"

"The spirits are more familiar with those who have lived in the castle or on its grounds for years. They're less likely to trouble us. It's new blood that upsets them. They grow confused and feel threatened, especially if they met violent ends."

I swallowed, remembering some of the whispered words I'd heard, the sense that I wasn't welcome.

Reid and I neared the staircase, and I turned to him, desperation burning the back of my throat. I didn't want to cry, but I feared my stinging eyes would rebel. "But don't you understand? It might be dangerous to search the castle at night, but I need to find Father." My voice broke. "If Fitz isn't sending the spirits on, that means he's still here, that there's a chance..."

Reid froze, every muscle in his body stilling. A strange mixture of pity and fear flickered across his face. "I understand your desperation, Elle, but please don't go looking. Besides, none of the spirits in the castle would belong to your father. The only ones who linger here are those who died on the grounds. And it's possible he isn't wandering at all. If any spirit would keep his wits about him in death and remain in the glade of souls, even without Fitz's magic helping him, it would be your father."

My stomach clenched, disappointment momentarily draining the fight out of me. "Do you know where the glade is?" I whispered.

"Elle..."

I wrenched away from him, furiously brushing away the tear that had escaped and trickled down my cheek. "Don't scold and warn me like a child, Reid. You knew my family for years. You know what this means to me, and you must feel something akin to grief too, after all the time you spent with Father. All those meetings in his study. So much of what he knew about the fae and magic came from you, and much of your news of the mortal world came from him. Don't fail me now. Don't fail *him*. I need to see him again."

Reid studied me. "Is that all you want, or are you hoping to bring him back?"

I hesitated, but Reid understood immediately. His eyes darted to the hall behind us. Though we were too far from the dining room even for fae ears to overhear, Reid lowered his voice even more. "We don't even know how necromancy works. I've only heard rumors. It's a great secret, even among the fae. Enough so that I fear you'd be in danger if anyone realized you were trying to learn more about it, let alone perform it." A beat passed as another realization dawned and new horror widened Reid's eyes. "Please don't tell me you're planning to steal magic from *Prince Fitz*. That's why you married him, isn't it?"

I lifted my chin stubbornly. "If you're afraid for me, then help me."

Blowing out a breath, Reid leaned back, once again scrubbing a hand through his hair, tugging some of the strands loose from its tie.

"You were always a good friend to our family. Please be a friend now, when we need you most."

Seeming to decide on something, Reid grasped my wrist and tugged me up the stairs. When we'd reached the next floor and he'd assured himself the hall was clear, he unclasped a sheathed dagger from his belt and placed it in my palm. "I don't expect you to listen to me, but I ask that you don't go wandering the forest alone. Knowing you'll probably disobey me, take this. Spirits can only become corporeal in the night hours, meaning that's the only time they can touch or harm you. And like I said, even then they will not pass your locked doors. Some ghosts are peaceful, but others are vengeful and deadly. Don't hesitate to fight back if one attacks you. They're already dead, after all, but I've been told they still experience pain, or the memory of pain, if you strike true."

"Why not come with me now? Help me find Father?" I asked.

Reid's eyes filled with regret. "I'm afraid I have to leave tonight. I have another message to deliver to the human world, one that will take days of travel and perhaps days more to...convince the recipient." He scowled. "The queen's spies have uncovered a scandal, and she's hoping to blackmail another mortal into joining us in Ashwood. And I'm the fortunate man chosen to deliver her threats."

"Hasn't she enough servants, fae and human?" I asked. "And now her heir has a human to...help produce more heirs. What more could she want?"

Reid's frown deepened. "It isn't only the royals that need humans. If enough humans didn't come to reside in Brytwilde, the fae population would languish. The elders would grow old and tired, or they'd murder one another in wars until they all died out. The more fertile humans there are to produce fae, half-fae, and humans, the more Ashwood can continue to grow and thrive."

I shook my head, disgusted. "Maybe when all of this is done and I've saved Father," I whispered, "you can leave this world too. Run away with my family."

Reid's brow pinched. "For all the evil here, there are also good, wise fae. And Ashwood...it's the only reminder I have left of my life with my father before he passed. It's all I know." He shrugged helplessly as he stepped back. "Please stay safe, Elle. When I return, we'll find the glade and speak with your father."

Reid had been right to doubt my ability to heed his warnings about staying in. With the knowledge that, if my magic didn't manifest, my position could become even more precarious, I was deeply aware of how little time I had. I wasn't going to hide in my rooms for days while I waited for Reid to return and be my escort, not when I could spend that time trying to make progress on my own.

As I closed the door to my rooms after bidding Reid goodnight, I leaned back against it and pulled my locket from beneath my bodice. The metal was warm and alive in my palm as I traced the flowers etched into its surface. I'd heard whispers the night of the ball, giving me the feeling that the locket's magic connected me with the spirits. Maybe I wouldn't need to scour books or ply Dahlia with questions or wait for Reid's help. Maybe my locket could guide me to the glade.

I placed my ear against the door, reassuring myself that Reid was gone. Since everyone was supposed to be at dinner, I hadn't noticed any guards in the hall either. They were probably busy prowling downstairs, assigned to watch over the dinner guests and ensure my family returned safely to their quarters once darkness fell.

Unlike human clothes, my fae-made dress was easy to slip off on my own. I hurried to my wardrobe, tugging on a pair of leggings, boots, and a tunic. I even found a belt tucked away in one of my drawers, which allowed me to attach Reid's gifted dagger to my hip.

Without wasting another moment, I crept from my rooms and approached the door to Fitz's quarters. Heart pounding, I waited, listening to ensure that he hadn't left dinner early. Nothing.

The door swung inward silently, and I set to work inspecting every table, drawer, and shelf. There was a desk filled with paperwork and maps, but none that felt magically significant. Nothing warmed or pulsed or drew me to it the way my locket did. I sifted through pots of ink and quills, papers, and dull books full of history, politics, and battles—all feeling ordinary beneath my touch.

In his bedroom, I found an extra dagger, clothes, candlesticks and matches, and more books. I scanned the titles, hoping some of the tomes were about magic, but these, too, were about history and politics.

Everything was sterile and dull. Either Fitz was a terribly boring, dutiful prince who had no hobbies, or—more likely—he had cleared his room of anything important or personal before our wedding. He must not have wanted his human wife to snoop into his life and interests, and certainly not his magic.

I slumped in defeat. This meant either he had another hiding place for his charm, or he kept it on his person. *But where?* It couldn't be a necklace, because I hadn't noticed a chain around his neck. He only wore one ring bearing his family crest, but that seemed far too obviously important for him to imbue with his magic. Did he conceal the object in his pocket? Under his clothes?

My skin flushed hot, and I stifled a frustrated, half-hysterical giggle. The idea of attempting to seduce my husband sounded awful. Maybe it would be easier to curse the consequences and drug Fitz with the remainder of my hidden nightsweet, search him, and then flee with my family.

Pretending to seduce him will be your last resort, I promised myself, turning to exit his bedroom and wondering if I still had time to sneak out of the castle.

The sitting room door burst open, two frustrated voices talking at once.

"That's a foolish idea, and Mother will hate it. *I* hate it." Fitz's voice.

"Please, if you'd only listen—"

I whirled, searching for a hiding place. But that would still leave me trapped in the rooms with Fitz and his guest, potentially for hours. My gaze snagged on the doors leading to the balcony. Could I climb down from there?

"Fitz," Holden went on, "she's not your fiancé anymore, and I've already made my feelings known. What's the difference between spending time with her now and announcing an official courtship?"

I froze, hand on the doorknob. The men hadn't left the sitting room, where they'd presumably settled to have this conversation. About my sister.

"The difference is that Mother doesn't care about your passing fancy for a human. She doesn't care who you flirt with, but she cares whom we *both* marry. And after what we saw with Elle Blackford—"

"Oh," Holden cut in, "so you mean to tell me you're hoping for a loophole? You're waiting for our law to declare that Elle is not your legitimate bride, proven by her lack of magic, so you can cast her aside and marry Grace? Is that it?"

Fitz's voice was low, so low I couldn't make out his words.

I couldn't help it. I didn't want Fitz to care about me, but hearing him meddle with Holden and Grace's growing feelings made me livid. I knew I needed to move, but I continued to strain my ears, hoping to hear more of their conversation.

Holden released an exasperated sigh. "I care about Grace."

"You've known her for all of two days."

"I only needed to know her for two hours to see that she was the kindest, gentlest, wisest soul I've ever met," Holden snapped.

My chest expanded at his defense of my sister and his feelings. It seemed he truly did care about her.

There was a pause, the silence growing heavy. I gently turned the knob, waiting to open the door until the men started talking again. One gust of wind or hoot of an owl could give me away.

"What about Elle?" Holden's tone turned gentler. "You haven't known her long, but you've spent more time with her than her sister. Are you sure you aren't intrigued by her at all?" A beat. "Are you so eager to push her away?"

"She's a distraction."

I ground my teeth, wishing I could stay to hear the end of this conversation, but knowing that lingering would mean being discovered.

If Fitz was counting down the days until he could marry my sister, I really didn't have time to waste. He'd said magic in human spouses typically revealed itself within a few months. That meant I needed to find and save Father before then.

I inched the door open and slipped outside, only breathing easily when the latch clicked softly behind me.

Thankful for my flexible leggings, I shimmied over the side of the balcony and reached for a crack in the stone wall of the castle. My muscles screamed, unused to this level of exertion, but I was determined. And desperate. The need to escape Fitz's rooms undetected gave my quaking muscles strength to scramble down the wall, shoving my booted feet into crevices and cracks where the mortar had crumbled with time and weather. More than once, I blessed all the long walks and hours of dancing I'd indulged in, likely the only reasons my body found the endurance to continue clinging to the castle wall.

By the time I dropped the last few feet to the grass, my skin was clammy with sweat, and I was breathless. Every muscle in my body burned and my fingers ached. I already dreaded the return climb.

A welcome breeze stirred leaves across my path and whispered against my face as I turned toward the forest. Tucking my hand into my tunic, I withdrew my locket and cradled it in one palm, relishing the way it warmed and pulsed at my touch. Like it recognized other magic nearby—or ghosts.

Take me to Father, I thought, praying that it could be that easy, that my charm could obey a simple command.

For a while, there was no other sound but the crunch of leaves and twigs beneath my boots and the rattle of leaves each time the wind stirred. There were no signs of wildlife, which stoked my uneasiness. Perhaps that meant spirits were near. Maybe no living creature wanted to be close to the souls still clinging onto this existence.

Can you see me? Can you help me?

The voice was so soft it could have been a mere thought in my mind. I paused and scanned the trees, shimmering in an unearthly red aura thanks to the fading sunlight trickling through the forest canopy. I'd rather encounter spirits early, while I still had some light to see by and they weren't fully corporeal. When they couldn't harm me.

I curled my fingers around my dagger's hilt and plunged deeper into the forest, determined not to waste the waning light. Soon it'd be gone, and I'd have to turn back to the castle and wait for another chance when I was more prepared to wander in the dark, with a lantern and a better idea of where the glade might be located. I was already risking enough, but getting lost in the forest at night would be deadly.

The sound of footsteps raked cold fingers down my spine. I squinted against the slanting light, finding a short figure approaching through the trees. I knew instantly from his deathly pale skin and shadowed eyes that this was no living human child. He was a soul who'd wandered beyond the glade. This poor child might have perished mere days ago, or long before my time. His clothing was nondescript, ragged and faded to the point of being colorless. Judging by his scant frame, either hunger or illness could have claimed him.

My heart dropped. He wasn't any older than ten summers.

When the boy's eyes met mine, a smile crept across his face. "Hello," he said, his voice soft and almost shy. "Are you stuck in the forest too?"

I shook my head, throat tight with sadness, even while my blood burned with fury. How could Fitz leave children to suffer, alone and lost and sad? Did he plan to let the spirits continue to venture through the forest forever?

"But how can you see me?" the boy went on, frowning.

"Probably because the daylight is nearly gone." I stepped forward, eager. "Do you know where the glade of spirits is? You should return, where you can rest with the other souls, and you can lead me as you go. I have someone I wish to speak to."

The boy cocked his head. "But you're already speaking with me. Can't you stay?"

"Are you lonely? The other spirits can keep you company."

He frowned. "Other spirits?"

The wind picked up, tugging at my loose tunic, and making me shiver. As the light started to vanish, the chill crept in quickly. I glanced desperately toward the sun, low on the horizon and threatening to slip away at any moment. I wasn't sure I had enough time to travel to the glade, even if it was nearby. And this boy seemed confused. Maybe he had perished recently, and he didn't even know he was dead.

"Have you seen a glade? Or anyone else wandering the forest?"

"It's lonely here," the boy said, shaking his head. "Can you stay and play?"

"I can't; I'm looking for someone," I murmured, fighting back the sting of tears over my inability to send this little boy on and out of this lost, sorry state.

The boy stepped closer, dark eyes wide and desperate. "Please. Don't leave me alone." He reached for my wrist, his cold fingers whisper-soft against my skin. My heart lurched, though I struggled to keep my expression composed so he wouldn't notice my reaction to his *very* corporeal touch.

Maybe night was close enough that his spirit had formed early. Or maybe the locket I wore, already throbbing against my throat like a second heartbeat, had some influence over the spirits.

"I'm sorry, but I have to go," I said, tugging away. The light was almost gone, and so was my chance. I'd return to the castle and try to ply information about the glade from Dahlia, along with some answers regarding why Fitz wasn't sending these poor souls on.

"No!" The boy stomped his foot, eyes flashing with fury, and for the first time, fear instead of pity seized me. "You can't." His eyes latched onto something over my shoulder. "Father, make her stay."

I spun to find a burly man behind me, his grey eyes bloodshot. A gruesome slice through his throat and a bloody trail down his shirt indicated that his death had not been peaceful. He was lurching for me, a knife glinting in his hand and appearing solid enough to cut me. Biting back my cry of panic, I drew my dagger, ducked low to avoid his wild swing, and charged through the woods, back in the direction of the castle.

Breath steaming the air, I made it only a few steps before a blur of motion from the side collided with me. The boy slammed into my stomach, dropping me onto my rear. I caught a glimpse of a bloody knife protruding from his back—apparently, he'd been murdered along with his father. "Let me go!" I shouted, kicking and punching until I'd knocked the boy away. I didn't want to lift my blade against a child. Which, I realized, was ridiculous when he was already dead.

Pounding footsteps charged toward us, reminding me that the larger, more murderous father was not far behind.

Leaping to my feet, I sprinted, dodging trunks and stumbling over roots. A branch snagged in my hair, wrenching me backward. I lost a precious few seconds struggling to rip my hair free, enough time for the man to draw near again, his ghostly face twisted in fury as he drove the dagger downward, straight toward my chest.

I lunged, slamming a fist into his arm to knock his strike awry while kicking his shin. My attack caught him by surprise. He grunted in pain, or the memory of it, giving me a chance to flee.

Cold air stung my eyes and throat as I pushed my aching muscles to go faster than I'd ever driven them before. Over the sound of my frantic breathing and the blood rushing in my ears, I listened for the sound of pursuing footsteps, but all had fallen quiet again.

Several more minutes passed before I dared to slow, gasping for breath and glancing around to find no one else in sight. I feared my mad dash through the forest had been loud enough to draw anything living or dead for miles.

The sun had fully set, leaving nothing but swiftly fading twilight to guide me through the trees. The castle wasn't yet in sight, but I knew it couldn't be far.

The sound of whistling off to my left jolted me from my frantic thoughts. My breath caught as I froze to listen to the familiar melody. It belonged to "Crown of Forget-Me-Nots," a song I would recognize any-where. *Father.* It had been his favorite tune, one he hummed or whistled during many an afternoon walk.

"Father?" I called, turning to push toward the sound. My dagger was still in my clammy palm, and I used it to knock vines and branches out of my way with abandon, determined to catch up with my father before he ventured too far. "*Father?*"

The whistling stopped, and the sound of cracking leaves filled the air in its place. "Elle?" came a hesitant voice, one I'd longed to hear. One I'd feared I'd never hear again.

I choked back a sob as I circled a large tree and finally caught sight of my father, standing in a small clearing a few yards away. He was in the same shirt and coat I'd last seen him in, his skin sadly battered and darkened with ugly bruises. They were an awful reminder of the accident that had claimed his life. One arm hung at an odd angle, and when he strode toward me, he limped, his face twisted in pain.

"Elle." His voice broke as he repeated my name. "How are you here?"

"I came to find you," I said, rushing forward, tears blurring my vision. It was awful to see Father so broken, but it was him. That was his hopeful smile, his warm voice, and his kind, loving gaze.

Father reached for me, like he couldn't bear to wait for his half-kilter gait to cover the distance before he touched me again. I extended a hand, trying to fight back my tears, trying to be brave for him. I had so much to say, and little time to linger.

"I came to find you too," Father said, but this time, his voice was wrong. Foreign. His hand latched onto my arm, and in a blink, something entirely different leered at me. Hollow eye sockets and a hungry, slobbering maw with long, bloody fangs lunged forward, its spittle dripping onto my face and its rotten breath filling my nose.

Screaming, I tugged to free myself, but what had looked like Father's hand was now a long, bony one ending in wickedly curved claws. They pierced my skin, drawing blood and a flash of pain. Lifting the dagger in my free hand was more instinct that a conscious thought. I arced it toward the creature as it snapped, greedy as a starving dog. Blood spurted from its chest, warm and sticky as it gushed over my hand. My first strike had landed true.

It released me as I pulled away and teetered, nearly losing my balance. The creature snarled and slashed with a gangly arm, claws slicing through my tunic. Something soaked my front, and chilly wind bit through the ruined fabric. I glanced down. The monster's claws had shredded through my tunic, leaving multiple claw marks, and there was blood—a lot of blood—but my fear and drive to fight back were too strong for me to register my pain.

Staggering back, I blinked through my blurring sight. Darkness shifted overhead, a shadow blocking the starlight. I glanced up in time to find the creature looming over me, reaching out to slash again with its claws. Too exhausted to dodge, I dropped, landing hard on my knees. The monster continued to tower over me, distorted by the darkness creeping in at the edges of my vision. As it snapped its maw, I lifted my dagger to ward it off.

Hot blood trickled down my hands. I blinked, realizing the creature had bitten the blade in its frenzy to reach me. Shaking, I took advantage of its pain and surprise to slam the dagger upward with every ounce of strength left in my body. Once. Twice. Thrice. Over and over, until blood was raining on my face, and the monster stopped screeching and collapsed in the dirt.

Tears streaked my cheeks, mingling with the blood as I dragged myself to my feet, lurching in the direction I hoped the castle lay in. Night had fallen, and I'd lost all sense of where I was in the forest. My lungs were heavy, struggling to take in air, but my head was light. Teeth chattering, I wondered dully why I was so cold when I was drenched in sweat, pulse pounding from my encounter.

What was that thing? Had it really been my father, transformed into something horrible in death? I refused to contemplate that idea, terrified I'd collapse sobbing in the dirt, too weak to go on. I had to believe he was still out there, still able to be saved.

Panting, I shuddered as I collided with a trunk, the impact jarring my bones. Everything was so dark that I felt blind, surrounded by impenetrable shadows.

And I couldn't breathe. Couldn't think. Leaning against the tree, I willed my trembling legs to hold me a little longer. Surely the castle couldn't be far. I hadn't walked for long. Pushing off the trunk, I stumbled onward, tripping over roots. Branches sliced at my face.

Please... I pled to gods who hadn't heard me when Father died and the fae had come to collect on my parents' promise. I pled to the magic of this land, the power that was supposed to accept me and claim me as its rightful princess—if it didn't reject me for being the wrong woman.

My knees gave out and I slammed to the earth, ears ringing. I closed my eyes and thought of Grace. Maybe she would be happy here with Holden. But then I pictured Isabel and Bridget and Maggie, terrified and lost in this cruel world. I imagined Mother, bereaved not only of her husband but also of a daughter.

Please don't let this be the end, I begged of anyone or anything that would listen. *Let me save them.*

The dull thud of footsteps and crunch of leaves drew my focus, and I resisted the urge to scream in frustration. Not another ghost. Not another ravenous creature. My fingers were numb around the hilt of my dagger, and I knew with a terrifying, hopeless certainty that I didn't have the strength left to fight off another attacker.

Hands seized me, but they were warm and gentle, without the bite of claws. "What were you bloody thinking?" a voice muttered. I blinked bleary eyes to fight off the haze and shadows as strong arms lifted me, and I met Fitz's steely gaze. "Who—or *what*—did this to you?"

There was blood flecked on his face, matching the scarlet I knew streaked my own cheeks. What monsters or ghosts had he encountered in the woods? I shuddered to think of what else lurked out there.

"I..." But the words wouldn't come. Even if I had the energy, I didn't have a name for what I'd fought off tonight.

Instead, my head lolled against his chest, and I found I was too tired to care. He radiated warmth when I was so cold, and I could feel the taut muscles of his arms even through his coat as he carried me. Maybe he was a scoundrel, and maybe he saw me as nothing but a burden, but he *had* vowed to protect me. I let myself take comfort in that. As much as he resented me, I was safe with him.

As I drifted out of consciousness, I felt Fitz's voice rumble through his chest. "How many times will I have to kill for you, Blackford?"

CHAPTER FIFTEEN

My eyes snapped open to a young stranger leaning over me, his hand pressed to my wounded stomach and his forehead scrunched in concentration. I registered pointed ears, chestnut hair tied neatly back, and intent green eyes before pain punched through me, radiating from my torso throughout my body. Startled, I couldn't stifle my cry of pain. I flailed, reaching for a dagger I no longer held, and resorted to throwing clumsy punches instead.

Calloused fingers seized my wrists. "It's all right. Kinsey is healing you." I turned to find Fitz standing over me as the other fae worked. Warmth steadily replaced my agony, clearing my head a little.

I blinked at my bloodied tunic, or what was left of it. Sometime in the minutes I'd been unconscious, the men had cut the torn fabric to reveal my wound. With the man called Kinsey's magic working through me, miraculously knitting my skin together, I'd never know how grievous the injury had been, but I could imagine. There were three gashes closing, and the amount of blood soaking my tunic, slicking my skin, and staining the sheets was alarming.

I leaned against the pillow, grateful for the comfortable bed I was in—Fitz's bed.

"I'm ruining your sheets," I said weakly. Stupidly. That was not the first thing I wanted to say, but my brain was muddled.

"Drink," Kinsey said, lifting hands stained with my blood to press a cup of water to my lips.

I gulped greedily, until Kinsey plucked the cup back. "Not too much at once," he chided. He set a hand on my forearm, where my sleeve was torn and revealed another scratch. The pain was mild this time as his magic sealed my skin. "You'll need rest. Healing magic drains mortals more than us. My power simply sped up your body's healing time, which means it undertook a considerable amount of work in mere moments."

I already felt exhaustion coursing through me, an inexorable wave bidding me to drown in its warmth.

When I opened my eyes again, seconds or minutes or hours later, I was being lifted. Fitz set me in an armchair by the fire, urging me to sit up.

An unintelligible groan left my lips, something I'd meant to sound formidable and confident, such as *Don't touch me, you scoundrel.*

I glanced up to find that Fitz's eyes were as dark as storm clouds. The set of his jaw and the furrow between his brows warned me that he wasn't going to give in to my pitiful protests. A quick scan of his bedroom told me that Kinsey was gone and we were alone. Fitz's bed linens had already been replaced with fresh, clean ones. It was a relief no longer having to see all that blood spreading across the sheets, knowing it was mine.

"I'm trying to clean off the blood," Fitz said crossly, "and then I need you to tell me exactly what happened." His fingers bunched in the fabric of my ruined tunic, pulling it away from my body as if to lift it over my head, and I made a strangled sound.

Suddenly, I was very much awake.

He froze, and for the first time, something like fear flitted across his face. "I'd forgotten about human modesty." He cleared his throat and went on more formally, "If you permit me, I'll only remove this to wipe away the blood, and then I'll find you a fresh shirt."

Mouth dry, I slipped a hand down my tunic and tucked my locket into my underclothing.

Fitz blinked. "What are you...?"

I glared at him.

He shook his head. "Never mind."

Slowly, he lifted his eyes to meet mine in a silent question. Knowing I was too weak to do much more than sit there and not wanting my blood to dry and crust on my skin, I nodded.

Fitz drew my tunic up carefully, never letting his gaze linger as he urged me to lift my arms so he could pull it over my head. I held my breath, hating how vulnerable I was in nothing but the strange, half-corset undergarment Lina had given me. For a horrible moment, our eyes met, and then Fitz dropped his gaze to the blood staining my stomach. Flinching, he turned away to dip a cloth in a bowl of water near my feet.

I knew he wouldn't cringe at the sight of blood or the pale scars where my wounds had been. Instead, I thought of the way he'd insulted me when he'd refused to dance with me, and I wondered if he was disgusted by my bare skin. Trying to dispel the burning sensation in the back of my throat, I asked lightly, "Repulsed?"

"I wish." His muttered response was so quiet I was sure I'd imagined it.

The silence grew so heavy it pressed against my ears. Without meeting my gaze, Fitz ran the cloth over my stomach gently. Gooseflesh rose on my skin despite the warmth of the crackling fire. It bathed Fitz in its light, gilding his dark hair. I couldn't reconcile this side of him with the one that was distant and cold.

He's tricking you, pretending to be gentle and kind. Don't let a handsome face fool you.

"Who attacked you?" he asked, his tone low and rough.

It wasn't the first question I'd expected. No demands to explain how and why I'd escaped. No threats because I hadn't remained in the castle.

"I don't know," I admitted, swallowing as the memory of the attack assaulted me, filling me with fresh pain. "I saw...I saw my father in the woods. He was whistling his favorite song, and when I called for him, he answered and—" My throat was too tight, and I blinked back tears. Fear that my father was lost consumed me.

Fitz's eyes flashed. "That wasn't your father. It was a phouka." He said the word like a curse.

"A what?"

"They can read their victims' minds, enough to take the form of someone dear they've lost or haven't seen in a while. Someone they'd be desperate enough to venture deeper into a dangerous forest to see."

I pressed my lips together, refusing to look guilty or ashamed for being tricked. I'd been warned all my life that the fae weren't the only dangerous, deceptive creatures in these woods, and yet I'd been so easily duped.

Fitz pulled back, his fist clenching around the cloth until his knuckles turned white. "I'll kill the monster."

I laughed wearily. "I already did."

Fitz turned to me, lifting the cloth to wipe at the blood staining my cheeks. His eyes flicked to mine, unable to conceal his surprise. Then he looked away again, refocusing on his task. He absentmindedly brushed strands of hair from my face with his free hand as he scrubbed at the blood.

"Why did you leave the castle?" he finally asked. One hand grasped my chin, fingers firm yet careful as he turned my face upward to wipe my neck. The cloth tickled, and I gasped.

Embarrassed, I kept my eyes trained on the ceiling. Fitz chuckled and leaned in closer than he needed to be, until it was his breath tickling my neck instead. "What were you doing in the forest, Blackford?" he prodded, lips brushing my ear.

Scowling, I shifted to glare at him, immediately regretting the movement when it brought my face centimeters from his. "Fae allure won't wheedle answers from me," I said crossly, and to prove my point, I offered him another lie. "I was trying to connect with the land's magic."

One side of his mouth pulled into a crooked grin. "You admit you're allured?"

I narrowed my eyes, refusing to let him fluster me. "Why aren't you sending the spirits on, Fitz?"

Fitz's eyes widened, and he reared back like I'd slapped him. "Don't pretend you know anything about our magic, mortal," he snapped, standing and turning to rifle through his wardrobe. He tossed a shirt at me. It smelled of him, and I almost wanted to refuse it, but going without a shirt was unthinkable. Especially since I assumed that after finding me half dead, Fitz would insist I slept in his rooms tonight.

If I was entirely honest with myself, even if he'd suggested I leave, I would have tried to find an excuse to stay. I didn't want to be alone. Even staying with a husband I didn't trust was preferable to that. At least Fitz had a reason to keep me alive.

I stood on shaking legs, glancing down to find my leggings were blood-stained as well.

Fitz noticed my gaze. "The shirt will be plenty long enough."

"Maybe according to immodest fae standards," I grumbled. "What happened to the extra nightgowns?"

"The servants only left one. I'll have them bring more in the morning."

I frowned, and Fitz sighed. "Or you can sleep in your bloody clothing, but you'll be staying on the floor, so you don't stain more of my sheets."

"Fine. Turn around."

He obliged, and I hurried to tug off my boots, stockings, and ruined leggings. The shirt was comfortable and light and hung nearly to my knees, but that left my legs startlingly bare. I'd never allowed a man to see so much as an ankle before, and now I felt half-naked.

Sensing I was finished, Fitz turned, his eyes flicking over me before he tore them away and frowned at my bloody leggings. Lifting them and my discarded tunic gingerly, he fed both to the fire. I teetered on my feet as I watched the flames crackle and lick at my clothes. The memory of the monster's slicing claws sent a shudder through my frame.

Fitz approached, offering his arm and guiding me toward his bed.

"Wouldn't it have been easier to let me die?" I asked bitterly as I sank beneath the covers.

For a long moment, the fae prince's face was blank as he studied me. "I gave my word."

"But my wandering off and getting myself killed wouldn't qualify as a failure on your part. You didn't need to search for me. If you'd left me, I'd be dead by now, and you could marry Grace instead, like you wanted."

"I don't want to marry your sister."

I frowned. "Then why the anger when I took her place?"

"I didn't want to marry *any* human," Fitz clarified, narrowing his eyes. "But you proved to be even more troublesome than I expected a bride to be."

As Fitz settled into bed and blew out the candle on his nightstand, he sighed. "Did you marry me over some petty jealousy regarding your sister?"

Heat flooded my body, and I was grateful for the darkness so he couldn't see my angry blush. "I suppose that would be preferable to me being a power-hungry threat," I snapped, rolling over.

Fitz chuckled. "A threat?" he repeated.

I refused to allow him to rile me more, instead closing my eyes and letting my exhaustion take over.

When I awoke, only a few hours had passed. The fire burned low in the hearth, and despite the vast space between Fitz and me when I'd fallen asleep, I was immediately aware of a lack of warmth. Glancing over, I found his side of the bed was empty, the room silent and dark with only the dying embers casting an eerie, dancing glow.

Where had Fitz gone in the middle of the night?

I sat up, blinking to dispel the lingering bleariness of my vision, and strained to hear beyond the occasional muted pop of the fire. Outside, the wind whistled, and a branch scratched against a windowpane. Otherwise, the world was still. There were no whispers of restless ghosts, no footsteps from wandering fae in the halls.

Fitz's coat lay discarded on a nearby chair. *His charm.* Though I doubted he would leave it for me to find, I still had to search everything. I had to know. Standing, I strode across the plush carpet and hastily rifled through his pockets. Nothing. I checked the inner pockets, but those were also empty. Almost as if he'd carefully emptied it before leaving. As if he'd expected me to wake and search his belongings.

That meant Fitz kept his charm on him at all times. My stomach churned. I would have to grow closer to him. My mind flitted toward the nightsweet concealed in my rooms, but I immediately discarded the thought. Even if I managed to slip something into one of Fitz's drinks without being caught, once he awoke from his drugged sleep, he would know what had happened. I couldn't risk making myself even more suspicious.

No, the nightsweet would be the perfect drug to use *after* I'd already found a way to save Father. When it was time to escape, and my family needed time. Especially if I thought there was a chance I could leave with them.

Stepping away from Fitz's coat, I spotted my sheathed dagger on his dresser and seized it before turning to the sitting room.

My heart thundered and gooseflesh rose on my bare legs. Was I a fool for leaving the safety of Fitz's rooms so soon after being grievously wounded? And yet, I'd escaped the ghosts and slain the creature that had attacked me. If I succumbed to fear, cowering in my husband's quarters, how would I ever find my father? He might not be in the castle, but perhaps uncovering some of Fitz's secrets would provide answers I desperately needed. Grasping the sheath so tightly my knuckles went white, I gathered my courage and strode forward.

The door swung open, and as Fitz stepped inside, I froze. Closing the door behind him, he leaned against it, scanning my bare legs before his gaze flicked to the dagger in my hand and then back to my face. "You must truly have a death wish." He stalked closer, effortlessly plucking the dagger from my hands. "Haven't you already learned not to stray beyond a locked door at night?"

I gritted my teeth. "Where were you?"

Fitz's face was inscrutable. "I don't believe I owe you any information. My business as crown prince is my own."

I opened my mouth, but he reached forward with his free hand, pressing a finger to my lips.

"And before you protest, remember that I promised to keep you alive. That means when you prepare to throw yourself headlong into danger, it *is* my business to know what you plan to do." Fitz pulled back, brushing his finger along my bottom lip. My heart skipped in surprise.

As if just as startled by his own action, Fitz's brow furrowed and he drew back, flexing his hand. *Disgusted with the way I feel. Trying to forget he ever touched me,* I thought wryly.

"Return to bed, Blackford," he said, interrupting my thoughts. "I don't want you sustaining any more deadly injuries and ruining more of my sheets tonight. I'd like to get some sleep." He smirked. "Maybe tomorrow you can bleed out on them again."

Stifling my sigh, I stormed after him, climbing back into bed. He slipped under the covers silently, and for a long time, I did nothing but stare into the dying embers of the fire, wishing Fitz didn't infuriate me so much. Or wishing I hadn't been foolish enough to fall prey to the phouka's tricks. I could have had more time to search the forest, or a chance to sneak up to Dahlia's tower library to search for books on necromancy. I could have wandered the castle halls in search of answers. Anything other than wasting away another night, weary and shaken from a near-death experience.

All I'd succeeded in doing was reaffirming Fitz's beliefs that he'd have to keep a close eye on me, not only to keep me alive but also to prevent me from threatening his kingdom and power. I'd been impatient and impulsive, and now any hope of gaining his trust was likely out of the question.

Fitz's voice was low and soft in the darkness, drawing me out of my reverie. "You thought the phouka was your father. Is he why you went into the forest? Do you hope to see him again?"

"Yes," I said, thankful he didn't guess the whole truth, that I dared to hope I could bring Father back to life. But I wasn't surprised. That was information Mr. Reid had insisted few knew. It was perhaps the most closely kept fae secret of all.

"It's too dangerous," Fitz murmured, sounding like he was speaking to himself, musing through possibilities. I rolled to face him, despite how dim the room was. The faint glow from the fire's embers and the moonlight sharpened the planes of his face. "The ghosts don't take kindly to strangers, and as I'm sure you already know, some can be aggressive."

I thought of the boy and his father in Ashwood Forest and shivered.

Fitz leaned against his pillows. "It's a great risk, all for the chance that your father hasn't already moved on."

"You haven't been sending the souls on," I snapped, "so I didn't think there *was* a chance."

"It's not that simple."

Before I could try to push for more information, Fitz continued. "But if the land accepts you and your magic manifests, you'll seem familiar to the ghosts, not to mention you'll have the power to calm restless souls."

"I will?" I breathed, awe and hope swelling in my heart.

"It will be a small portion of my magic," the prince reminded me. "You won't send souls on—nothing of that nature. But it will grant you safety."

"What if my magic never manifests? You'll have me waiting in vain—and if, as you claim, there's a chance Father could move on in the meantime—" I let my voice break, not bothering to conceal my distress. If Fitz had enough of a heart somewhere beneath his cold, cruel exterior to offer to take me to my father, maybe my pain would be enough to sway him.

Fitz surprised me by reaching out, setting a hand on my arm. "We'll wait a month. You'll continue to train with me. Whether your magic shows or not, I'll still take you to look for your father at the end of that month. No matter if he's in the glade or roams the forest, we'll find him. But you will obey my every word, and we won't linger for long. Do you understand?"

I nodded, knowing that in the dark, Fitz's fae eyesight could see me far better than I could see him. Satisfied, Fitz pulled away and rolled over. "Get some sleep."

Despite my exhaustion, it took me a long while to drift off. I hoped that Reid would return and take me to the glade long before the month passed, but if not, I had Fitz's promise. If he could lead me to Father once, I could locate him again. Now the question remained if I could acquire the magic and knowledge to save him.

CHAPTER SIXTEEN

"Your husband visited this morning," Dahlia said casually, sipping daintily from her teacup. "He told me about your adventures last night." She shot me a pointed look, arching a brow. "I know mortal education is lacking when it comes to the details of Brytwilde, but surely you knew enough not to wander at night. The queen's jealous courtiers aren't the only ones who'd love to kill you."

My smile felt more like a grimace. "I...I know."

"And then there is the unrest at the borders," Dahlia added, "which makes any territory beyond the castle grounds and the Ashwoods' protection especially dangerous." She stood, setting her teacup on the table beside her armchair. "Perhaps today our focus should be on the four kingdoms, and the tension between them."

I straightened. "Are we on the verge of war?"

Dahlia smiled indulgently, like a mother comforting a distraught child. "We're always on the verge of war, Princess." She strode to her desk, digging through piles of papers until she withdrew a scroll, spread it out, and waved me over.

I peered over her shoulder at a beautiful map, scanning the Ashwood Kingdom near its southern border and then glancing toward the north, west, and east, where the kingdoms of Willowbark, Ravenheart, and Silverfrost lay. "The fae don't all live in Ashwood Forest?" I asked.

Dahlia laughed. "No, this forest belongs to Ashwood. Brytwilde refers to *all* our land." She tapped her finger on the countryside to the west, where the map depicted rolling farmlands and a twisting river. "This is Willowbark." She ran her finger toward the northeast, where trees clustered near a lake. "This is Ravenheart." Finally, she pointed to a mountainous region to the east. "And this is Silverfrost. All four kingdoms form a tenuous peace for trade among our lands, but there is frequent tension. Many of the other royal families—and I believe Queen Griselda herself—would love to rule *all* of Brytwilde."

"Where's the glade of souls?" I asked.

"Not on this map," my tutor said sharply. She rolled up the scroll and straightened to face me, immediately changing the topic. "Each kingdom draws its magic and power from its land, but they also take power from particular seasons: Willowbark the spring, Ravenheart the summer, and Silverfrost the winter. The Ashwood family is most powerful now, at the height of autumn."

I glanced out the windows to the swaying branches of Ashwood Forest. "Does that mean this land experiences perpetual autumn? And the others are forever in summer, spring, or winter?"

Dahlia shook her head. "No, but autumn weather lasts the longest here. If a single kingdom were to seize control of *every* throne, ruling every land, they would possess the power that comes with every crown. They would always be at the height of their power."

I frowned in confusion. "I thought the magic came from the land."

Dahlia nodded. "The *type* of magic. But the crowns also play a role—it's why those who rule each kingdom are the most powerful. When winter falls, Queen Griselda and the princes—and you too, if you come into your own magic—will still possess the strongest magic in the Ashwood kingdom, but Silverfrost will be the most powerful kingdom in Brytwilde."

I chewed on the inside of my cheek, ruminating on what this information could mean for me. If my magic came or I stole Fitz's charm, in autumn at the height of the Ashwoods' power, then surely that would be the most helpful. But if time passed and winter arrived, perhaps even Fitz's charm wouldn't be strong enough to practice necromancy. And if what Fitz had said last night was true—that some of the spirits passed on regardless of what he did or didn't do—my time might already be running out.

Head whirling, I stepped back, pressing a hand to my temple.

Dahlia's green eyes scanned me worriedly. "Are you still feeling weak? Do you need to sit down?"

I shook my head. "No, it'll pass."

Dahlia grasped my wrist and led me to my armchair anyway. "We haven't often needed to use healing magic on humans in recent years. You see, Queen Griselda was a rare woman among our kind. She married a *fae* man for love and managed to conceive children, without needing a..." She cleared her throat. "A human husband."

My eyes widened. "Truly?"

Dahlia laughed. "Queen Griselda's parents were furious. It has always been tradition for the royal fae to take human spouses to increase the likelihood of heirs being born. Our folk often struggle with conceiving, as you already know. I suppose enough human blood has blended with the royal line over the years to work in the queen's favor." She shrugged.

"Ironic that Queen Griselda is so hard on her sons. Fitz didn't even want a wife, and he was forced into this marriage." I crossed my arms, recalling his frustrated confession.

"But maybe that's also why Her Majesty hasn't been entirely upset to see Fitz's growing attachment to you?" Dahlia asked, shooting me a knowing smile as she deposited herself into the chair across from mine.

I opened my mouth to protest before remembering Fitz's and my show at dinner. I wasn't sure if Queen Griselda really wanted Fitz to settle for me or was still secretly hoping, like him, that the magic would reject me and provide an excuse to end our marriage. Instead, I asked a question I'd already been taught, but wanted fae insight on. "Most children born from a fae and human union are born fully fae?"

Dahlia gave a single graceful nod. "Every once in a while a child is born half-fae, possessing some magical abilities or a longer life than a human would. Very rarely, a fully human child is born." She scrunched her nose in distaste. "Unfortunately, Brytwilde hasn't been very kind to those children. Usually they leave. But don't fret," she added quickly, perhaps imagining I was worrying about my future children, "the Ashwoods have always been sympathetic toward humans."

I took a sip of my tea, even though it was growing cold. "Is that why none of the human servants or messengers are glamoured?"

Dahlia's smile was soft, but it didn't quite reach her eyes. "Yes, that is exactly why. Queen Griselda might be harsh in her punishments, but she is generous toward her loyal subjects, and she doesn't believe in using glamour."

"No lingering pain?" Kinsey, the green-eyed man who'd healed me last night, asked as I studied the dull practice sword he'd handed to me. Lina had brought me out to train with Fitz, only for his friend to approach instead and explain that he was taking the prince's place, as Fitz had to leave on business.

I'd glanced to Lina, who'd shrugged and brushed a lock of her green hair behind her pointed ear. Apparently it wasn't unusual for Fitz to disappear.

"None," I said, looking again to Lina and her bandaged arm, but Kinsey was already stepping forward to inspect it.

"And for you?"

Lina's grin widened. "None at all. You did a perfect job."

Kinsey's expression turned grim. "It was a job I never should have had to perform," he said darkly, gaze flicking toward the castle.

Lina shook her head fiercely, eyes roving about the training grounds, but no one else was near enough to hear—at least, not with human ears. "Enough of that." She dipped her head and scurried back toward the building before Kinsey could say anything further.

Clutching my practice blade closely, I followed Kinsey as he stormed toward the open area of the training grounds reserved for sparring matches. He swung his dull blade at the weeds we passed.

"You don't approve of the queen's punishments either," I observed.

Kinsey faced me, expression distant and annoyed. "I don't believe anyone does."

"Holden told me that Fitz agrees with their mother. He said Fitz and the queen believe harsh punishments are how rulers keep their subjects in line."

Running a hand through his shoulder-length hair, Kinsey sighed. "Well yes, on a certain level, Fitz has always believed that rulers must be strict. But he and Holden and I—we grew up among the staff, mortals and immortals. Punishing them so extremely isn't something any of us ever agreed with the queen on. At least, not before. Now...it's complicated." He stabbed his sword into the ground.

"How so?" I demanded.

Kinsey's smile was tight. "Holden and Fitz's father? He was murdered by assassins within our own kingdom, some greedy courtiers who wanted the Ashwood throne. And their sister? She was murdered more recently, on these very grounds, and they haven't found her killer."

I gaped. "Sister?"

Kinsey cursed under his breath, yanking his blade out of the dirt. "It's not my business to speak about these things. Fitz and Holden are my closest friends, and I won't share their story of grief before they're ready. I'm here to train you, so we can hopefully prevent future wounds like the one you sustained last night." He aimed his blade at me. "The first thing you need to do is relax your stance—and your grasp on your sword. It's not going to jump from your hand."

I laughed awkwardly. "Very well."

As Kinsey walked me through the basics of holding a sword and positioning my feet, I considered his earlier words. A murdered sister. The blue and silver rooms must have belonged to her, and she was the ghost who haunted them.

As I swung my sword the way Kinsey had directed, he easily sidestepped. "Fitz truly wants me to learn all this?"

Kinsey grinned and swiped his blade, forcing me to parry. "What, do you think he hopes the next time you wander off you'll be killed? He said he found you only armed with a dagger, and he feared you didn't even know how to use it. Human women aren't taught to fight, are they?"

I shook my head.

"Trust me, you've been driving Fitz mad. He knows no matter how many times he warns you that you'll sneak off again, so he wants you to learn how to defend yourself."

"I've driven him mad from the moment we met. He hates me."

Kinsey stepped back, giving me a moment to catch my breath and wipe the sweat off my brow. "I wish everyone who hated *me* was so quick to my defense."

I rolled my eyes. "You can't tell me *anything* about his sister?" I pressed.

Kinsey pursed his lips. "Perhaps you should ask your husband about her."

By the time Fitz arrived, leaning casually against the fence to watch as Kinsey and I finished a woeful sparring match in which my footing was all wrong and he barely even let me practice swinging my sword, I was covered in a thin layer of sweat and my muscles ached.

"You'll improve with time," Kinsey encouraged, patting my shoulder as he took my practice sword and gently gestured toward his friend.

I approached Fitz on unsteady legs, embarrassed by how awkward and exhausted I was already. Dancing and long walks back home had given me some stamina, but I could tell the work that Kinsey had put me through was going to wear on me. Fitz offered me his hand silently, nodding his thanks to Kinsey and then leading me along the path into the forest.

Birds flitted from branch to branch, dislodging leaves that floated down like colorful rain. Through the forest canopy, the sky was slightly cloudy with the suggestion of rain, but for now, the weather was perfect. Another kind of day Father and I would have loved to take a walk on and discuss our latest book, whether it was a fictional one we'd chosen for pure enjoyment or one about magic.

I glanced sidelong at Fitz, studying his chiseled features, always kept in a careful mask, and I wondered if he missed his sister with the same intensity that I missed my father. But before I could find the words to broach the subject, we entered the clearing and Fitz dropped my arm, slipping behind me and gently pressing his hands to my lower back to guide me toward the pond.

"Are you planning to push me in?" I asked wryly.

"That does sound tempting," Fitz said. His voice rumbled too close to my ear, and I had the urge to pull away. I didn't want to be one of those women beguiled by fae allure. I didn't want to be a silly girl caught up in the way his voice made me feel. Those reactions meant nothing, and they were a distraction from my true purpose.

But I made myself stand still, because pulling away wouldn't help me either.

"I don't know how to swim," I admitted.

Fitz went quiet, and I was tempted to turn, but instead, I glanced at the water. Today, it rippled softly, just enough to disturb the reflections playing along its surface and make it difficult to read Fitz's expression as he stood behind me.

"That may be a useful skill to learn eventually, though most of the ponds here aren't safe to venture into," Fitz said.

I shuddered as I imagined the sorts of creatures that must lurk within them.

"Hold out your arms." Fitz stepped closer, until his chest pressed against my back.

Frowning, I did, confusion and alarm filling me when he wrapped his own around my body, holding his hands palm upward below my outstretched ones.

"What are you doing?" I asked, my voice sounding strangled as my body went rigid. I was used to our performances for an audience, but I hadn't expected to be in Fitz's arms when we were alone.

He froze in response, as if he'd only now realized how close we were. He swallowed, and I could have sworn his laughter was strained. "Flustered?" he teased, and for a moment, I had the wild notion that he was trying to divert attention from his own nerves. But that would be madness. He was nothing if not confident and arrogant, in love with himself and convinced everyone else was entranced with him.

"No," I lied through clenched teeth, hoping he didn't see the humiliating flush spreading across my cheeks.

Instead of pressing the issue, Fitz answered my earlier question. "You might not have magic yet, but you can practice how it feels to wield it. I will still be the one controlling it, but I'll match your motions, let you have a sense of what it's like."

Gooseflesh rose on my arms as electricity filled the air and Fitz summoned a soft, miniature cloud to hover over our hands. My mouth went dry as I watched lightning flash within, a dancing, wondrous display mere inches from my shaking fingers.

"It won't hurt you," Fitz murmured, his breath warming the back of my neck.

I inhaled deeply, slowly relaxing my muscles until my body leaned into him, his arms enveloping me in a manner that was surprisingly gentle and comforting. His heartbeat drummed against my back, his chest rising and falling. I tried to ignore the contact and instead focus on the magic tingling in the air, and the taste of a building storm on my tongue.

Slowly, cautiously, I extended a hand, reaching for the miniature lightning as it forked from the misty cloud. It stabbed toward my finger, undulating like a candle flame, and I gasped when it jolted against my skin. But not unpleasantly. It was warm and powerful, and when I moved my hand, it moved with me, splaying until it encompassed all my fingers. I closed my hand into a fist, and the light vanished within. I opened my hand, and a crackling ball of gold and violet burst forth before transforming again into a display I could control with my movements, spiderwebbing toward each of my fingers.

I knew it was an illusion. Fitz was the one wielding the magic, mimicking my movements, showing me how I would one day be able to control my own power in a similar way.

"It's beautiful," I said, entranced.

"And deadly," Fitz reminded me. "But only when you want it to be. Your thoughts and emotions are connected to this power. As long as you keep those in control, wielding the magic will feel like a natural extension of your own will. After all our practice, when your magic manifests, it should come to you as easily as breathing."

Fitz released the electricity and let it return to flicker within the growing cloud. I lowered my hands, but Fitz didn't move away. He lifted his palms to manipulate the cloud, letting it expand until the entire pond was covered by a flashing storm. Lightning struck the water, turning it to liquid silver, restless ripples, and churning steam. My hidden locket warmed against my skin, as if coming to life in the presence of such intense magic. My heart thrummed against my sternum, but I was more in awe of this beautiful, powerful display than I was frightened. For as little as I trusted Fitz, I knew he had no desire to kill me, not now. He'd had plenty of chances to let me die.

As suddenly as the storm had grown, threatening lashing rain and violent wind, the cloud dispersed, and the lightning ceased. The pond went still, calm enough that I could make out my own reflection. Overhead, nothing impeded my view of the mild autumn sky.

I frowned, thinking of the training Fitz had insisted Kinsey give me earlier today. "When you possess magic like *this*, why bother using swords?"

"The very same reason we have the charms you were so interested in learning about," Fitz said, untwining his arms from me and stepping away. I hated that I noticed the lack of warmth. I didn't want him to make me feel safe, but the memory of his tender touch last night, of the fact that he'd rushed to save my life, clung to me stubbornly. "Using magic can tire you more than physical exertion. And depending on where you travel or what time of year it is, you won't always be at your greatest strength. Besides, you can practice controlling *my* magic all you want, but that's no guarantee you'll manifest your own." He stepped beside me to stand at the edge of the pond, shooting me a knowing smirk. "So you'll continue training with Kinsey."

"Not with you?"

"Missed me, did you?"

"Never." I turned away, not wanting to meet his piercing blue gaze. "Does the business that took you away today and last night have to do with your sister?"

Fitz stiffened so suddenly that I could sense it from a foot away. "What did Kinsey tell you?"

"Nothing," I said quickly. "Only that she was killed, and you didn't find her killer. He said it was your story to share."

"Good." Fitz spun on his heel and strolled from the pond, coat rippling behind him in the breeze. "I'm not sharing."

I chased him as he wound down the path, toward the castle. "I shared about my father. It seems only fair that—"

Fitz held up a hand to cut me off, and when he halted and turned, there was no dry amusement in his expression like before. Only a cold, hard look. He was like a statue carved from stone, immovable and untouchable. I couldn't tell if he was full of icy fury or grief, his blank expression was so complete. A chill ran through me. "Just because you like to fill the silence doesn't mean I do. However you mortals handle death, it must not be like us. It's *not* a conversation to gossip about over tea, or a matter in which one can curtsey and offer false sympathy."

I stomped closer, standing on my tiptoes so I could glare into his eyes. "*False* sympathy?"

"You obviously don't feel or care as deeply as we do."

"*What*?" I lifted my hand to slap him, but Fitz caught my wrist, leaning closer.

"One doesn't need to be immortal to feel the sting of death," I went on, furious tears burning my eyes. "Believe me, a single day in a mortal life—a single *hour*—without a loved one is infinitely long enough to feel the full agony of grief." To my horror, a tear slipped free. "I do not need to face the possibility of an eternity without my father to feel lost and alone. One moment is enough. And an entire lifetime already feels like an age, like a living death I'll carry with me until I finally reach my own grave."

For a long moment, we stared at one another. Fitz reached out slowly with his other hand, brushing my tear away with his thumb in an achingly tender touch. His hand lingered, and I couldn't breathe. I didn't know if I wanted to try to slap him again or accept this soft gesture. Outside of comfort from my own sisters, this was the sincerest consolation I'd been offered since Father had died. There was understanding in his expression, a matching grief and loneliness that, for the briefest moment, made me feel a little less alone.

None of my sisters had been as close to Father as I was, and Mother had withdrawn too much to offer any solace. Too often, I'd felt alone.

But if he is so troubled by his sister's death, why does he let the spirits stay and suffer? I flinched away from Fitz's touch.

He released me and drew back, shaking his head. "I will not speak of it."

Without another word, he strode off, and this time I was the one left standing by myself, staring after him. Furious at his curt manner, just when he'd begun to show a shred of kindness. Confused by the times Fitz had shown compassion and the conflicting knowledge I had of his callous, darker side. *More proof he is manipulating you,* I chided myself.

CHAPTER
SEVENTEEN

"About yesterday," Fitz began the next time we met for training. He kept his eyes locked on the pond, his words stiff and awkward. "We need to form a truce."

I crossed my arms, temper flaring. "I don't follow your orders."

Before I could finish taking a breath and continue, Fitz turned, his own eyes flashing with annoyance. "I meant—"

"My mortal mind is not so forgetful," I continued, refusing to let him cut me off. "Your comments were rude and presumptuous."

"Ah, and you are so perceptive and humble," Fitz snapped. "Very well. I accept your refusal to forgive me. There is no truce."

I stomped toward him. "Good!"

This time, a slow smirk crossed Fitz's face, but it was all bite, without any of his usual teasing. This was the true side of the man I'd married—his real fae nature. There was no deception here, only anger and cruelty and pride. *Perfect.* "Without a truce," he drawled, "there is no magical training." He lifted his hands as if to demonstrate, letting miniature storm clouds billow around him. "Your power will be severely limited."

Freezing, I stared at him, sucking in a deep breath to calm my whirling thoughts and emotions. "You wouldn't," I bit out. "You saw the danger I was in only last night."

Fitz shrugged languidly. "How awful for you that you'll be forced to rely upon my protection."

I gritted my teeth.

"When you tricked your way into marrying me, you chose to suffer my presence and my protection." Fitz dropped his hands, letting his magic vanish in the blink of an eye. "I, however, did not have a choice in the matter of suffering *your* presence."

I scoffed.

"So," he continued, "you can either accept a truce, and learn to protect yourself with magic, or you can leave now and accept that you'll forever rely on my power."

"I cannot forgive you without an apology."

"I'm not asking for forgiveness. Only tolerance." He paused before adding: "And maybe fewer insults."

Throwing my arms wide in exasperation, I relented. "Fine. A truce. But perhaps you can *try* to be a little more agreeable?"

That vain gleam sparked in Fitz's eyes—the one that I knew meant he was searching for a compliment and relishing my unfortunate reactions to his handsome features. "You prefer my...what did you call it?...fae allure? Well, that comes naturally."

I refused to acknowledge *that* comment.

With our tenuous truce declared, we fell into a rhythm. He continued to tease and provoke me each training session, enjoying the way he frustrated me, but I started to prefer that to his earlier cold manner. Even if he was only trying to fool me into a false sense of security, it gave me an opportunity to do the same to him. I stopped trying to conceal the attraction I felt for him, instead hoping I could convince him to no longer view me as a threat.

Two full weeks passed, full days of tutoring and training blending together. I understood the wisdom in Fitz's request to wait before we sought for Father. I told myself I could be patient at least until Reid returned and he could guide me to the glade. As a messenger, he was used to traveling through the forest, which meant he'd be prepared to fend off any dangers. He also wouldn't be as easily fooled as I'd been. He knew these woods intimately, as well as the tricks posed by its creatures.

I couldn't save my family if I was killed first.

Instead, I resorted to doing whatever I could to learn about necromancy and the spirits in the meantime. Unfortunately, my days were quite full, as if Queen Griselda had purposefully packed my schedule to prevent me from my own schemes.

Whenever Dahlia let me and I could linger after lessons, I scanned the books in her library and asked her as many questions as I could about life here. I even dared to inquire after Fitz's sister, but I received only a troubled look and an answer much like Kinsey's. Eventually, Dahlia agreed to let my family join us during our sessions, though Mother declined my invitation. Having Grace, Maggie, Bridget, and Isabel to giggle and study beside made my days less dreary.

Lina continued to be a kind presence, though after that first day, she grew more reserved. When I pressed her for more information about the castle ghosts, the deceased princess, or the glade of spirits, she merely shook her head and said some things were better left forgotten.

Frustrated, I scanned the castle for signs of this lost sister. Other than the blue and silver quarters that, since the day I'd found the door ajar, remained shut up and neglected, I found no trace that the princess had ever existed. No painting of her hung with the portraits of the queen and princes. I saw no depictions of Queen Griselda's husband, either. It was as if, in the wake of those losses, the entire family had determined to pretend as if they hadn't existed.

But I couldn't forget the grief etched on Fitz's face when I'd asked him about his sister. It was clear that he, at least, would not, or could not, forget her.

Each day after studying and taking luncheon with my mother and sisters, I trained with Kinsey in swordplay and Fitz in magic. Despite the ease I felt when Fitz let me experience the magic he conjured, I found no signs of an ability to wield my own magic forming.

To my dismay, I didn't have freedom at night, either. Every evening, Queen Griselda hosted fabulous feasts and dancing. Fitz explained that none of the spirits troubled my family or me on those evenings because we were among the familiar members of the queen's court. Only if one of us wandered off alone would the ghosts recognize a stranger and grow angry—and of course, he and Holden ensured that never happened, always providing us with guards or escorting us to our rooms themselves.

For every dinner and ball, Fitz and I continued our charade whenever we were around one another. He never did more than hold my hand, run his fingers through my hair, or lean in close enough for his lips to touch my ear while he made a show of whispering sweet nothings. Sometimes I thought

I noticed his hand trembling when he reached for me, and I was thankful for it. It was my reminder that he was disgusted by our farce. By me.

One night, I found myself leaning against the wall, watching the fae dance—or fight—on the ballroom floor as I tried to remain unobtrusive and far from the table of glistening gold wine. My mouth dried at the very thought of it, and my heart ached with longing to experience that bubbly joy, that exquisite lack of pain. *And then you'll be so much easier for them to control and kill,* I thought darkly.

Though I'd gained a slightly greater measure of respect among the courtiers since Fitz had made a public display of interest in me, I wasn't foolish enough to think the fae didn't still hate me. If they thought they could hurt or humiliate me when Fitz wasn't around, they would take advantage of that opportunity.

"A penny for your thoughts," Grace murmured, sidling up next to me and elbowing me. Her cheeks were flushed from dancing, and a quick glance over her shoulder showed me Holden wasn't far behind her. These days, he didn't even pretend to try to dance with anyone but her, though I could tell plenty of nobles were growing annoyed at his negligence. I supposed a prince was expected to dance with more of his subjects out of sheer etiquette, or to give his people a chance to converse with him, but it was clear each time I saw him and Grace together that he was smitten.

I shrugged. "I was thinking of how agreeable my bed sounds." It wasn't a complete lie. I was tired, but I was anxious for a chance to slip away. Too many days had passed with no progress. "All the training and tutoring I've undergone lately is exhausting."

Holden leaned against the wall beside Grace, extending a glass of red wine that she gratefully accepted. "Some for you, and some for your mother." He lifted another glass. "I seem to have lost her in the crowd?"

Grace laughed and took the second wineglass. "I'll take it to her," she said, striding away.

"I understand your exhaustion," Holden told me, shoving his hands into his pockets. "Kinsey and Fitz are both merciless. Perfectionists in their arts. Kinsey is a great healer, but also one of our best swordsmen; and of course, Fitz has the most powerful magic. Although there was one time that Cora nearly—" His eyes widened, and he feigned a cough, cutting himself off and pressing a fist to his lips.

"Cora?" I pressed, my interest piqued. "Was she your sister?"

"Cordelia." Holden cringed and dipped his head, lowering his voice. "But please don't speak of her, not here."

My brow furrowed. "Why not? Why wouldn't you want to honor her memory, to keep her close and remember her?"

Regret shimmered in Holden's eyes. The music reached a crescendo and couples twirled across the floor in a sweeping dance. A sprite fluttered past, and the golden-haired prince watched warily until the creature vanished from sight. "I assume you heard she was murdered. But...we never found her killer," he whispered. "That's the height of weakness for a royal family—to lose one of our own and never discover the murderer. We found her in the woods outside the castle, Elle. On our grounds! To speak of her and her death draws attention to our failure. And her killer is still out there. For all we know, it's an assassin, hoping to strike again and off the rest of the royal family."

My heart lurched.

Holden raised his eyebrows meaningfully. "It's one of countless reasons Fitz hates when you wander off."

"You have no idea who it could have been?" I asked.

Shifting on his feet, Holden glanced around, ensuring no one was listening. Couples continued to dance and other fae argued in the corners, some of those disagreements exploding into physical fights. No one heeded us. "Some. Before she died, Cora acted a little oddly. She disappeared at strange times and refused to explain where she was going or who she was seeing. She had some friends living in the city of Oakfell, so at first Fitz and I thought she might be visiting them." He swallowed. "But we think she had a lover. It must have been someone that Mother wouldn't have approved of—a servant or someone else with little magic." He cringed. "Fitz and I found letters she exchanged with this mysterious man, but none give anything away. They never used names. I worry he was the one to kill her."

For a long moment, we were silent. I processed the information, thinking of the blue and silver rooms I'd found. Of the letter covered in feminine handwriting I'd seen Fitz reading. As the pieces fell into place, I wondered again if Cordelia was the ghost I kept seeing.

A woman giggled drunkenly and lurched into Holden, grasping his arm to steady herself and spilling golden wine down his white shirt. "Oh, my apologies, Your Highness." She fluttered her lashes furiously, dipping a head topped with small horns that reminded me of those of a young goat. Her face was pretty, but the illusion of innocence was dampened by the cunning gleam in her black eyes.

I stepped back uneasily, wondering if the woman was truly intoxicated or trying to eavesdrop. Or simply wanting to gain Holden's attention.

After his revelation, though, my suspicions ran deep. I hadn't grown comfortable in this world, surrounded by ghosts and fae and monsters, but after days of kindness from Dahlia, Lina, and Kinsey—and even of Fitz's protection—I had become complacent. Not now.

As Holden played the role of gracious prince, withdrawing a handkerchief to dab at the wine dripping down his front and smiling in response to the woman's apologies, he shot me a covert look of warning. *Don't trust her,* he mouthed. I stepped away, starting to make excuses, when a hand landed on my arm. My heart jumped into my throat until I turned and found Fitz looking down at me.

Other than the night I'd nearly died, I wasn't used to experiencing relief at the sight of my husband. But once again, I did.

"May I have this dance?" he inquired, extending his hand. His tone was cool and unconcerned, but there was a flash of warning in his eyes that reminded me of his brother's expression. Neither of them liked me near that woman, giving me reason to believe she'd proven troublesome in the past. Did they suspect she'd played a role in their sister's death? Or did they think she'd try to harm me?

"You may," I said, accepting his hand and letting Fitz sweep me onto the dance floor.

"Holden and I don't trust her," Fitz muttered after a moment, his gaze on the woman still speaking with his brother. "She's always craved power. Always tried to gain favor and attention from us. She's the sort of cunning woman I would expect to pose a threat to you. I'd advise avoiding her."

I laughed mirthlessly. "I try to avoid as many fae as I can."

Fitz's hands tightened on me. "Unfortunately, you have to tolerate me."

I nodded sharply. "Unfortunately."

As we matched our steps to the music, silence fell between us. We swayed and avoided couples who were decidedly not moving to the rhythm of the song and following their own wild beat.

All the while, my mind churned. If Fitz's sister had been murdered on the grounds, why hadn't he used his magic to bring her back? *Was* the

Ashwoods' magic weakening, leaving them unable to save Cordelia? And if that were the case, could that be why the spirits lingered? Or was Fitz's choice to keep them here rooted in desperation for a chance to rescue Cordelia before she moved on forever?

It seemed incredibly selfish, and yet if I'd been in the same position, could I have resisted the urge to hold the spirits back to save my father?

"You're unusually quiet," Fitz murmured, pulling me closer as the music slowed. In the human world, men and women never danced like we did, with his hand clasped over my waist and my head almost resting on his shoulder. But here, physical affection was displayed publicly and generously, maybe too generously.

My pulse thrummed while I tried to sift through my feelings. If I was right in my new understanding of Fitz and his motives, he wasn't so different from me. He was still arrogant and cold and perhaps as cruel as his mother, but at least he wasn't vindictively leaving ghosts to suffer.

But what if my first impression *hadn't* been wrong?

He'd told Holden he'd prefer my sister—even if he'd later claimed to me that he wanted neither of us. He'd stood by when Queen Griselda took Lina's hand. And he'd told me that my father's spirit might move on, even without his help, which meant that Fitz wouldn't have any control over keeping his sister here, even if he didn't aid her soul in passing onward.

That led me back to the conclusion that his magic was weakening, or he was choosing to be cruel for another reason.

Fitz's fingers dug into my waist, firm yet gentle, and I hated the warmth that seeped through the fabric of my dress. Lifting my head off his shoulder, I drew back.

"What's wrong?" he asked.

I shook my head to clear it of my whirling thoughts. I'd been ignoring him for too long. If I wanted to continue the progress I'd made of *not* behaving as if I utterly despised him, I needed to force my churning emotions aside. I needed his friendship and trust. "I'm capable of being silent sometimes," I responded, letting my tone sound cross in a way I hoped he'd take as playful and warm.

Fitz spun us, his eyes darting over my shoulder toward where Holden and the horned woman stood, talking politely. "No need to fret," he said, leaning in so his breath tickled my ear. "She's nothing we can't manage. You're in no danger."

"That's what you thought the night I was drugged," I said lightly.

"I won't make that mistake again," he promised, his voice low and rough.

Confused, I tried to lean back to look into his face. I was used to his touches in public, our grand performance to placate his mother and to reinforce my position in the kingdom, ensuring anyone would think twice before trying to harm me. But this was different. Unless someone watched us closely, they wouldn't see Fitz's fingers tighten as he held me. He had no reason to grasp me that firmly, like he wanted to draw me as close to him as he could.

I searched for words, but I was at a loss. The song came to an end, and Fitz released his hold on me, stepping back and dipping his head.

"Thank you for the dance," he said in a clear dismissal, turning and vanishing into the crowd. I frowned after him, a little flustered but mostly relieved. I didn't think I could handle being that close to him a moment longer, and his quick flight had me hoping everything about that dance had simply been for show.

I'd only been imagining things.

Leaving the dance floor, I scanned the room for my sisters. I caught sight of Bridget and Isabel giggling with Lina, who, with the help of Kinsley's healing magic, wasn't even wearing a bandage anymore. Her arm instead ended in a healed stump. She was radiant in a violet gown that matched the vivid shade of her eyes.

She and my youngest sisters had become fast friends, much to my happiness. Usually servants didn't attend these events, but I had a feeling my youngest sisters had persuaded Holden to ask for the invitation from his mother. Perhaps the queen, in her twisted way, had considered the act to be a gesture of peace toward the servant she'd maimed.

In a corner, Maggie sat at a table with Dahlia, sipping water and poring over books. Mother looked on, stifling a yawn. My mouth twitched in amusement.

It was strange to see my family at home here. There was still much to fear, but with Holden, Lina, and Dahlia as trusted friends, my sisters and Mother had grown bolder. We had allies to defend us and help us navigate this new world.

A servant with ram's horns twisting through his curly hair approached, carrying a tray laden with wineglasses that glistened with golden liquid. I averted my eyes even as a rush of temptation coursed through my veins. If

I wasn't close to it, if I didn't look at it, I could avoid thinking about fae wine. But as soon as it caught my notice, it was difficult for my thoughts to fixate on anything else. He arched an eyebrow at me, his smile turning seductive. "Would you like a taste?"

No one in Queen Griselda's court had attempted to glamour me, at least not to my knowledge. But I had the distinct impression that this man was using it now. He'd been handsome before, but as soon as his grin showed his dimples, he became strangely irresistible. There was a radiant quality to his skin, making him stand out among everyone else. I opened my mouth to answer when a hand seized my arm and yanked me back.

"Elle!" Grace's voice was frantic as she clapped her hands on my shoulders and spun me to face her. "Don't listen to him. Don't even look at him."

As soon as my gaze tore from the man, his glamour's hold snapped. I couldn't even remember the color of his eyes or the shade of his hair, but I knew he'd had me transfixed.

Grace didn't wrench her stare from me, knowing better than to meet the man's eyes and fall prey to his power. "You are breaking the laws of this court, sir," she said, her tone strong and firm, full of an authority that surprised me. "Stop now or you'll be subject to its punishments."

Holden approached, laying a hand on Grace's arm and glaring at the man. "This is the last night you'll spend in my mother's service. Be grateful that is the *only* punishment you'll receive, unless you persist."

I didn't even pay attention to the fae's prattling excuses and apologies behind me, instead sinking into my sister's warm embrace, sighing in relief. "Thank you."

"I can't believe his nerve," Holden grumbled, eyes flashing with fury as he watched the servant retreat. He glanced between Grace and me. "He didn't force either of you to do anything, did he?"

Grace and I shook our heads. "I think I'm ready to retire for the evening though," I announced. "I've had quite enough. I'll find Lina to walk me to my rooms." Squeezing Grace's hand one last time, I bid them both goodnight and pressed through the crowd.

Glaring eyes watched me as I passed, some women huffing or snorting derisively. A goblin leered, eyes raking down my form—not in a lascivious way, but in the way a predator would eye its next meal. I swallowed and turned away.

Fingers latched onto my arm, long nails digging in. I spun, slapping the hand away as I met the face of the same hag who'd harassed me during our first Ashwood ball. "Your eyes are fine as always, Princess," she purred, dipping into a curtsey.

"What do you want?" I demanded.

"I could tell you things you need to know," she said, grinning wickedly. "Things about the past. Things about your future."

"If your information is as vague and unhelpful as your last two remarks, I think I'll be on my way." I turned.

The hag snatched at my hair, tugging strands out by their roots. I bit back my cry of pain, realizing a circle of onlookers had formed. The taunting, bloodthirsty faces warned me I'd find no help among them. "I am older than this earth, young mortal," the hag spat. "I've seen more lifetimes than you've seen years. I will *not* be dismissed in such a manner." She yanked me backward, the force burning my scalp and making my eyes water. A pitiful yelp escaped my lips. "Maybe I'll take your eyes as payment for your insolence."

I struggled in vain as she lifted a bony hand, her long, broken nails scraping along my cheek and drawing blood. Up, up, toward my eye. Bile filled my throat.

And then her hand stopped, spasming. Warm blood drenched the back of my gown, and I knew without having to turn, even before I heard the thud of her body, that the hag was dead. I straightened, panic overtaking my thoughts. I had to leave this ballroom, with or without Lina.

"No one thought to trouble themselves with helping their princess?" Fitz's voice rang out behind me, dark and ominous. Storm clouds formed, blotting out the flickering light of the chandeliers and slowly overtaking the room. Lightning flashed, filling the air with the tang of electricity and the threat of death. I stumbled backward, slipping in blood. Fitz caught me by the waist, tugging me upright and holding me against him. I glanced back to find his usual mask gone, replaced with deadly fury that made my blood run cold.

None of the courtiers who'd watched as the hag attacked moved or made a sound. Their wide eyes watched the growing storm and the prince who wielded it.

"*No one?*" Fitz repeated. "You were going to stand by and watch that hag murder my wife?"

Lightning forked from the clouds, the first strike dropping a sandy-haired man to the floor. The stench of burnt fabric and hair permeated everything. Electricity sparked as his body spasmed in a macabre sort of imitation of our earlier dancing.

Another flash of electricity. Another body fell. Thunder boomed so loudly I thought my ear drums would burst. My mouth was dry, my tongue heavy, but I forced out a scream. "Fitz! Enough! Stop!"

Rain exploded from the clouds, lashing at my face and mingling with the sweat on my skin. My blood-soaked gown turned cold from the icy droplets.

I tore free of Fitz's grasp, tripping and sliding across the slick floor, not caring what vengeful ghosts awaited me in the castle halls.

CHAPTER EIGHTEEN

The hallway was colder than before, its chill air nipping at my damp skin as I charged toward the stairs. Where earlier there had been guards posted, now there was no one, and I wasn't sure if it was because they'd rushed into the ball to aid their furious prince, or if they'd been within the whole time, standing watch over us. Teeth chattering, I lifted my sodden skirts and sprinted up the steps, my wet slippers nearly sliding on the polished wood more than once.

I reached the first landing, panting and dizzy, and paused to catch my breath. *Don't lose yourself now, Elle*, I chided. *Panic in the safety of your rooms, not here.*

A quick glance around reassured me that I remained alone, even though moonlight bathed the spiraling staircase in a silver glow, a constant reminder that the spirits would be active. And corporeal.

Picking up my skirts again, I charged forward, leaving a damp trail in my wake. By the time I arrived at the next level, my breath streamed from my mouth in a swirling mist and the air tasted of frost and blood. I wondered if I was smelling the stink of the gore coating my dress, or something else. I surveyed the empty hall and the wavering shadows cast by candles ensconced on the walls. Nothing. Besides the distant sounds emanating from the chaotic ballroom, nothing disturbed the quiet blanket draped over the castle.

"What are you thinking?" Fitz's voice echoed below as he burst through the ballroom doors. I scurried down the hall, searching for an alcove or an open door, anywhere I could hide. I didn't want to face him. I was too horrified, too furious. I'd already taken my chances with the spirits before, and in that moment, they seemed preferable.

The first door on the right was ajar, leading to a study lined with bookshelves. Though the fire was unlit, the thick carpet and cozy armchairs by the hearth made the room seem warmer. I stumbled over the threshold as Fitz's footsteps pounded up the stairs. "Blackford, stop and listen! It's not safe." His words were frantic, laced with panic.

I ground my teeth and fisted my hands. *Let him fret over what his subjects will think seeing his own wife fleeing from him. Let them know that I am not under his control, not trapped under his thumb. Let them see his weakness.* Every time I closed my eyes, I saw that man's body spasming.

The hag had attacked me, had maybe even wanted to kill me. I couldn't find it in me to be sad over her death. But the fae Fitz had killed? The way he'd unleashed his fury upon the whole ballroom? He'd gone too far. He'd reminded me of his cruelty, of how he followed in his mother's dark shadow. It made me think of Lina and her severed hand, of the blood and screams.

My locket hung heavily from my neck, suddenly cumbersome and warm, almost to the point of burning. I jumped, but before I had a chance to shove my hand into my bodice and draw the locket away from my skin, I detected a moving shadow out of the corner of my eye. A hand extended from the darkness, reaching.

"Little girl," came a man's rumbling words. "You don't belong here."

I scrambled backward, into the hallway, but the figure pursued. In the flickering candlelight, I found myself staring face to face at a tall, lithe fae man, his burning black eyes gleaming with bloodlust. Silver hair hung past his shoulders, and his body was strong and muscular. Except for the gaping hole in his stomach, spilling gore. My mouth soured with bile. He was eternally bleeding out, stumbling like a drunken man as crimson burbled on his lips. He drew a wickedly curved dagger from the sheath at his side.

Whirling toward the stairs, I ran, but my wet skirts impeded my progress and I tripped, slamming to the floor. Blood dripped behind me, and the spirit laughed roughly. "Pathetic. I thought maybe you'd give me some sport after all these long, lonely years."

Pulling myself up, my eyes landed on the decorative vase resting on a nearby side table. I lurched to my feet and seized it as the spirit reached me. His dagger flashed as it arced downward. The blade slammed into the vase, shattering it and raining shards around us. The ghost blinked, but I was already running for the stairs.

I collided with Fitz, whose eyes fastened on the spirit and turned dark and cold. Grabbing me by the waist, he swung me behind him as he shouted. The command shuddered the air almost as violently as the thunder had shaken the ballroom. "Begone! Leave the mortal lands and accept your eternal rest. I release you into the afterlife."

Peering over his shoulder, I choked on a gasp as the spirit froze, eyes widening. Almost before the prince had finished speaking, the ghost began to disintegrate, his form turning hazy and then drifting on a breeze that whispered through the castle, there and gone in an instant.

Fitz rounded on me, chest heaving. "You nearly became another spirit haunting these halls."

I couldn't breathe, couldn't meet his eyes. I stared at the place where the ghost had stood. Now, not a trace of him remained. No blood on the floor. No dropped dagger. Only the shattered remnants of the vase I'd used to defend myself. "You—you sent him on."

"Blackford, we need to get you to your rooms immediately."

I gaped. "You've let these other ghosts remain and suffer, and so I thought that you *couldn't* send them on...but—you just..." My words trailed off, and I realized I was whispering, probably incoherently.

Fitz grasped my shoulders, shaking me. "Did you hear me? There are many restless souls here, and others will be just as eager to kill you."

I wrenched away, repulsed. Before he could reach for me again, I tore up the stairs, praying I could reach my rooms before he overtook me. All I wanted was to be alone.

But of course, he pursued me the entire way, charging into my quarters before I could turn and slam the door. Instead, he closed and bolted it himself. Fuming, I stormed into my bedroom. I was still soaked, but I wasn't cold anymore. I was burning.

"Where are you going?" Fitz demanded, trailing after me. "Are you hurt?"

I spun, nearly colliding with his chest. He wrapped his arms around me, pulling me close before I could shove him away.

"Are you hurt?" he repeated, his voice ragged. Like he worried. Like he *cared*.

I was so sick of the manipulation, the games, the shows. So tired of trying to pretend with this awful, deceitful man.

I laughed, the sound coming out high-pitched and hysterical. There was blood all over my dress, blood that didn't belong to me staining the gauzy white fabric. My cheek stung where the hag had clawed at it. My hair hung in wild, wet strands that clung to my face. Perhaps I looked like an apparition myself.

"Elle." Fitz murmured my name almost reverently, and the laughter died on my lips. I stilled, not even breathing. "Please. You were attacked *twice* tonight." He drew back, pressing a calloused thumb to the blood drying on my cheek and tracing it so tenderly that this time, fear clawed at my insides for an entirely different reason. "Tell me only this blood is yours."

I nodded, startled into silence.

"I shouldn't have left you after that dance." Fitz pulled back, pacing agitatedly. "I should have stayed by your side the whole night, and none of this would have happened." He paused, turning to me. "I know you're frightened, but you're safe now. Please, come to my rooms tonight. No one will dare touch you there."

He stepped forward, taking my hands. "I'm sorry. For a moment I'd thought—I'd thought..."

I stared numbly, unable to comprehend his rambling words. His strange attitude. What sort of game was he playing at this time?

Fitz sighed and lowered his head, pressing his forehead to mine. Again, I couldn't react, couldn't move. "I fought in vain," he breathed, the words a whisper against my skin as he buried his face against my neck. One hand threaded through my sopping hair while the other dropped to my waist, tugging me against him.

"Fought what?" I choked out. A part of me wanted to pull away, but another desperately wanted to know, to understand. If Fitz was opening up, perhaps I'd learn some of his secrets. Maybe I'd finally earned his trust. Maybe I could clamp down my fury long enough to find out about his charm, or to steal it and run. Perhaps this was my chance at last.

Fitz straightened, ducking his head to meet my eyes. His own were swimming with emotions that frightened me. "Feelings." He laughed mirthlessly. "Distracting, all-consuming feelings, yet here they are, all the same. Every moment, every waking and sleeping hour, I have tried to push the thought of you away, but you haunt me. You were the wrong bride—reckless and infuriating and deceitful—and I told myself that was for the best. And yet I found myself struggling against this emotion building against my will."

I stepped back, and Fitz released me, his hands dropping to his sides. "What emotion?"

Fitz searched my face, vulnerability consuming his expression. Those bright blue eyes that were usually cold or masked or filled with dry humor now blazed with an inner light. He looked desperate, hopeless, lost—and he gazed at me as if I held the answers he needed. "Elle." The way he said my name almost made me shiver, but I wouldn't fall victim to fae allure. I wouldn't yield. "I love you."

Scowling, I shook my head, water droplets sprinkling onto the carpet. "No."

"I didn't want to, but I can't help it. You invade my every thought and dream."

I lifted my hand, as if I were warding off an attack. "This is some fae trickery. You're mocking me. You wanted my sister."

Fitz sighed, rubbing his hands through his hair, loosening it from the tie holding it back. It fell around his face, as unkempt and distraught as he was. I felt the urge to laugh again, or to cry or scream. "I told you, I didn't want anyone," he said slowly. "Why would I rejoice in the thought of marrying a mortal bride and giving up pieces of my magic—my own—" He cut himself off. "I married out of duty to my kingdom. Whether it was you or your sister, it didn't matter in the end. All I saw was a human distraction, someone to care for and keep out of danger when I have enough to concern myself with to keep my kingdom from falling apart."

"So you resented me," I spat, "as I resented you, for you too are only a means to an end, a way to secure my family's future, to keep us from poverty and homelessness back home. It is the same for us both. I'm glad you've admitted it, and now that's the end of it."

Fitz glanced up, eyes flashing. "No. That was how I felt at first, but not now. Instead of barely tolerating each other, Elle, we could try—"

"Is that how you show that you care?" I shouted, gesturing to my soaked ball gown. "You tell me how much you fought against loving me? You tell me what a burden I am? You murder your own courtiers because they weren't quick to my rescue?"

"You could have died!"

I stepped closer, hands clenched into fists. "My family was there!"

"I wouldn't have struck them," Fitz argued, quieter.

I lifted my chin defiantly. "You tried to keep Holden and Grace apart. I overheard you warning him not to love her. Even if I can believe it wasn't due to a selfish motive to have her for yourself, it was cruel to try to part two souls who so obviously care for one another!"

Fitz gaped. "How could I, in good conscience, ever encourage my brother to fall for your sister, when you proved yourself to be a liar? Why wouldn't I fear that Grace was trying to manipulate my brother's feelings and deceive him too?"

"And you have many more crimes than that," I went on, too livid to stop hurling my accusations at him. "You sent that spirit on just now, while you leave the others to suffer."

Fitz's eyes widened, his face paling. "It's not like that."

Tears burned my eyes. "My father's soul wanders somewhere in those woods!" I gestured wildly to the window and the forest bathed in starlight. "Knowing no peace, lost and alone!" I stormed closer. "I told you before how I felt about you. My feelings have *not* changed."

Fitz stiffened, pain flashing across his features before his mask fell back into place. "It seems you are determined to make up your mind about me without hearing anything else."

I threw my arms wide. "What else is there to hear? I've heard *and* seen plenty. And even before I came here, my friend who has lived here all his life, Mr. Reid, told me about you. He's struggled here, bound to the memory of his father but trapped in this cruel world."

Fitz sneered. "I'm sure your friend had many stories to share about his struggles."

I jabbed my finger toward the door. "Get out of my rooms."

For a half second, Fitz stared, as if he couldn't believe what I was saying. Perhaps in all his arrogance he couldn't comprehend the thought of a mere mortal rejecting him. But all he said was: "Lock the door."

Then he whirled and was gone, the door clicking shut with finality behind him.

I followed and bolted the door before turning back to my rooms, grateful for the fire burning in the hearth. A maid had already laid out a nightgown, as well as a tray of biscuits, sachets of tea, and a kettle of water that could be warmed over the fire. Sighing, I entered the washroom and turned on the faucet, letting blessedly hot water steam the air. I dumped in some soaps and stripped out of my ruined dress, climbing into the tub to scrub the blood from my body. My shivering ceased as the heat hit my skin, and I closed my eyes, trying to pretend the water wasn't turning pink.

For a moment, I let the horrors of the evening slip away, let my worry and grief for my father melt, and let Fitz's infuriating declarations disappear. I breathed deeply, pretending I was only Miss Elizabeth Blackford, daughter of a quiet, reserved man who loved to pass hours in his study or take long walks with me through the countryside. Deals with fae were far-off concerns, especially when Father and I clung to the hope of finding a way to open our family locket and wield the magic inside. We imagined all the ways in which we could forge a new deal with the fae, or become powerful enough to create our own home in the forest, where the residents would listen to us. Where we would never have to worry about mortal laws granting wealth to male relatives over female ones.

But when I opened my eyes, I was still in my rooms in Ashwood Castle. The bathwater was stained with someone else's blood, and my cheek burned from where the hag had scratched me. Mouth souring, I stood, toweled off, and changed into my nightgown. I went and sat before the fire to brush and dry out my hair, soaking in its warmth.

I love you. You invade my every thought and dream. I repressed a shiver. Fitz couldn't lie, yet I couldn't fathom how he believed those words. He wasn't supposed to fall in love with me, only grow to trust me. I squeezed my eyes shut and cursed in a most unladylike manner that would have made Mother cringe.

I should have rejoiced and accepted Fitz's profession of love. If only I could have overcome my anger and revulsion in that moment, I could have played my role in drawing him closer. I could have let those confessions lead to others, until he was sharing secrets he never told anyone else, like the location of his charm or some hint about how to resurrect a lost loved one. *Anything.*

I was weary of the close-kept secrets of this place, of the way I never seemed to make progress. My first night here, I'd been so sure that I could at least find a chance to speak with Father soon. But I hadn't even managed to find him.

Standing, I peered out the window at the autumn leaves and the swaying branches, wondering what lurked in the shadows beyond the places the silver moonlight touched. Tears filled my eyes. Even with the dagger I'd taken to keeping on my person at all times, belted at my waist or tucked into my bodice when I was forced to wear a gown like tonight, I was woefully vulnerable against fae and monsters and spirits.

For the first time, I dared to truly consider the possibility of the land accepting me. I glanced at my hand, turning it over to study the lines of my palm, and wondered what it would feel like. *If Fitz accepted me, despite his reservations and distrust, could that influence the magic in his blood and in this land?*

It was strange studying the forest outside and imagining it as a sentient thing, but according to the fae, it was. It responded to its people and creatures, fed them magic and helped them thrive. Would it see me as an imposter like the ghost that had attacked me tonight? Or would it see something in me worthy of being a ruler of its people?

At long last, I climbed into bed, ignoring the tea and biscuits. Weariness weighed down my limbs. All I wanted was to escape into blissful sleep for a few hours and to stop the spinning thoughts in my head.

I'd started to drift off when a sound startled me fully awake. I blinked my eyes open, wondering if a log had popped in the fire. Shadows danced on my wall, cast by the trees waving outside, their leafy branches reminiscent of hands. All was still. I sat up slowly to scan the room, and my eyes landed on the other side of the bed.

A golden-haired woman was stretched beside me on the covers, her bloodshot eyes staring, her chest motionless. Her neck was a ruin of mottled bruises, red and purple and swollen.

My scream died in my throat as the spirit sprang, slamming one hand against my windpipe while the other ripped at the locket chain around my neck. Her knees drove into my stomach with surprising force. She was heavy and strong, and she hadn't been kept out by my locked door.

"This doesn't belong to you," she hissed, her tone raw and hoarse. "*You* don't belong here."

I thrashed, trying to throw her off. Spots danced across my vision and my lungs burned. The spirit tightened her grasp, her fingers like a vise as her nails dug into my skin, fighting to tear the locket from my neck. Her hand was impossible to pry from my throat, so I aimed for her face, punching with closed fists like Kinsey had taught me only yesterday.

My knuckles smacked against her chin, but she continued to squeeze, so I struck again, summoning what was left of my wavering strength. This time, I punched her nose hard enough to send her reeling back. Her grasp loosened enough for me to roll out of her reach and seize my dagger from beneath my pillow. I gasped, sweet air filling my lungs and burning my aching throat.

Slipping off the bed, I rounded on the ghost, aiming the dagger's point at her. "Stay back," I rasped. "What do you want from me? How are you *in my room*?"

"You have my locket, and now you have my brother. I will *not* allow you to harm him."

Her brother? My mouth fell open, attempting to voice my thought: *Cordelia.* This ghost *was* Cordelia.

But before I could speak again, Cordelia snarled, her bloody eyes alight with fury, and darted forward with unnatural swiftness. My scream caught in my throat as I stabbed at her hand. The point lodged into flesh, but the wound didn't stop her, and there was no blood.

She could harm me, but I couldn't wound someone who was already dead.

Cordelia lunged again, her hair a wild tangle about her pale face, and I leapt backward, slamming into my nightstand and knocking it over. It crashed into the wall, dislodging the tray and scattering biscuits and water across the floor.

"Blackford?" Fitz called from his rooms, voice muffled through our shared wall.

Cordelia vanished as suddenly as she had appeared, my dagger falling from her hand and dropping to the carpet.

The shelves opposite me shuddered and swung forward, revealing an entryway leading into Fitz's rooms. The prince himself stood in the doorway, clothed in a loose shirt and pants, his hair mussed from sleep. But his body was tense, his eyes alert as they scanned my bedroom before fastening on me. "What happened?" he demanded, striding to my side and softly grasping my chin. He lifted my head to inspect my neck, his eyes bright and wild in the moonlight filtering into my room.

"It was...a ghost," I managed, my voice coming out strained through my painful throat.

Fitz scowled. "They don't pass through locked doors. They've always left our guests alone as long as they bolt themselves in each night." He ran a finger slowly, tentatively along my neck, his frown deepening as he took in my bruises.

I stepped back, forcing space between us. Crossing my arms, I glanced at my dagger. *Useless.* If a ghost attacked again, what defense did I have? I thought of Reid's promise to take me to the glade of spirits, and my heart sank. Was that plan suicide?

"I locked my door and fell asleep," I explained, "but a noise woke me. A spirit was in my bed." I gestured to the sheets as if they offered proof. For a moment, I considered telling him that I believed it was Cordelia, but it seemed cruel to tell him his sister had been the violent, angry apparition who'd nearly murdered me in my own rooms.

Fitz's sharp intake of breath jolted my attention back to him. I glanced up to find him staring, his expression full of disbelief and growing fury. My stomach clenched when I realized he was looking at my locket, plucked free of my nightgown thanks to Cordelia's attack. As if I could undo the moment he recognized the charm, I slapped my hand over the metal, which pulsed warmly against my palm.

"Where did you find that?" he asked slowly.

I swallowed, my throat feeling like it was full of gravel. "It's been in my family for years," I explained. "It was gifted to my ancestors, and my father always kept it near. It was his prized possession. When he died, I took it as a way to keep him close."

"*Liar.*"

I jolted back at the wrath in Fitz's tone, nearly tripping over the fallen tray. "I swear it. You've seen this chain around my neck since the day we were married. Do you remember? I have worn it daily. I brought it to Brytwilde with me. I swear on my father's soul!"

"Then you're saying your father was a murderer? Did you conspire with him?"

I stepped back still more, struck silent by Fitz's accusation.

For a long moment, we stared at one another. "What are you saying?" I demanded at last.

"That locket belonged to my sister Cordelia," Fitz said slowly. "The day we discovered her body was the day we realized it was missing and must have been her charm. So how did your father acquire that locket, if not through murder?"

I slapped my hand over the locket. "He'd never harm a soul. And *think* about it. Why would he want to harm your sister? It would do nothing to break the bargain he made with your mother and everything to endanger it. He needed your family to live and thrive so you could protect us when he died."

Fitz scowled. "Then how did he have it, and why did he lie about how he came by it?"

I shook my head. "I don't know, but...please believe me."

Fitz blinked, the anger in his eyes fading to something softer, sadder. Sighing, he turned away, his shoulders sinking. "I believe you. Our guards would have spotted a strange human wandering our grounds, and you're right. Your father had no motive to hurt my sister. It's possible the true murderer sold the charm."

"At Fletcher's," I murmured, thinking of the underhanded dealings that occurred in the dark rooms beneath the Riverton bookshop. "He must have been too ashamed to speak of how he'd bought it. I wish he'd told me. Maybe he could have described whoever he'd purchased it from."

"Another dead end."

I hesitated. "And will you take the locket from me, if it belonged to her?" My heart ached at the thought, even if now I knew the charm didn't have the sentimental value to Father I'd once believed it did.

There was sadness in Fitz's eyes—and understanding. "You wear it in memory of him, don't you?"

Throat burning with unshed tears, I nodded.

"It's dangerous," Fitz warned, his eyes flicking over me again. "But I suppose as long as you say in my rooms, you'll be safe. I'll call for Kinsey to heal you, and I'll let you have the bed to yourself. If any spirits dare to disturb you, I'll stop them."

I shook my head furiously, tucking my locket into my nightgown. "I don't want to stay with you. I want to stay with my sister."

"Blackford..."

"Please."

Fitz gestured to my discarded dagger. "The ghosts could *kill* you. And if you're drawing them beyond locked doors...they'd threaten your sister too. Nothing but my magic can protect you, not when the spirits are this powerful."

"I don't understand," I croaked.

"My sister's locket is drawing them to you. Her magic was powerfully tied to the dead. It's rare for more than one Ashwood in a generation to be able to command and send on the spirits, but both she and I could. Since that locket was her charm, her magic lives on in it. It calls to nearby souls, especially to her, and strengthens them. I'm assuming it was she who attacked you, perhaps assuming you were her killer and thief. Let's not have a repeat of that tonight." Fitz turned toward the hidden door and his quarters. "Come, you can hate me just as well in there as in here."

CHAPTER NINETEEN

"And you truly are all right?" Mother insisted, leaning across the breakfast table from her seat opposite mine and laying her hand over my fingers.

I nodded, not wanting to worry her or my younger sisters. Bridget and Isabel were giggling and whispering, discussing some of the messengers who'd captured their interest. Several handsome human men had been at the ball, dancing more than a few times with each of my sisters. Maggie read a book as she idly stirred sugar into her oats. At my side, Grace shot me a searching look that I refused to return. Her discerning glance the moment she'd entered the dining room had told me that I wouldn't fool her as easily as the rest of my family.

Thanks to Kinsey's ministrations the night before, my throat and cheek were both healed, without any lingering pain or marks. It was as if the attacks hadn't happened at all.

Fitz had given me the space I'd longed for, retiring to the couch in his sitting room and leaving the bedroom to me. Though I could sense he wanted to say more, to defend himself after the accusations I'd hurled at him or perhaps to ask for his sister's locket, he'd given me solitude. When I'd awoken this morning, I'd found Lina bringing a simple dress for me and announcing that Fitz and Kinsey had left to quell unrest at the border between Ashwood and Silverfrost. As a result, I wouldn't have any training with them for the foreseeable future.

"Prince Fitz is concerned about your safety," Lina had said, "so he requested that you and Miss Grace could stay in his rooms while he is away. Prince Holden will sleep in the sitting room to protect you."

I shrugged, unsure how I felt about this. On one hand, I would have more time alone with my sister than I'd had since we'd arrived in Brytwilde, along with time away from Fitz to plan and avoid his maddening talk of love. I also knew now that I possessed Cordelia's locket, one tied to magic that controlled the spirits, and I had time to do more research. On the other hand, I wouldn't be able to train in Fitz's magic or attempt to glean any further information from him.

Most shockingly, Fitz hadn't taken my locket last night after Kinsey's healing. Instead, he'd advised me to take it off and hide it in my quarters, so the ghosts couldn't trouble me while I remained in his rooms. But, considering the fact that he was making Holden watch over me while he was away, I had a feeling he'd known that I would continue to wear it anyway.

As much danger as I knew the locket posed, I also knew that, with its ability to attract spirits, it could help me find Father more easily. Besides, I didn't trust that I could hide it anywhere that it wouldn't be discovered and taken. I couldn't risk losing its magic to a nosy servant or courtier by letting the locket out of my sight.

Dressing, I asked Lina to invite my family to breakfast in Fitz's private dining room.

Now, I wondered if that had been a mistake. Isabel and Bridget's laughter grated on my nerves. I should have been grateful they'd found joy here, but I couldn't stop worrying that they'd foolishly drop their guard in their romantic pursuits. Maggie's disinterest was no better. Even Mother displayed a cool, collected air that set me on edge.

Had none of them seen the horrors I had? The wandering spirits, the bloodthirsty fae, or the deadly magic Fitz wielded? Had they forgotten that Father's ghost lingered in this land? Was I the only one who felt confused and angry and achingly lost?

When my sisters and I entered Dahlia's library later for lessons, we found her usual lighthearted manner gone. Quietly, Dahlia bid us take our seats and set about serving tea, her expression distant and troubled.

"Are you all right?" I asked, watching the way Dahlia's green eyes clouded over.

Starting, my tutor smiled and shook her head. "A little concerned about the unrest building, but it's nothing new. Come winter, your husband may be quite busy fighting." She spun to face us. "And so, that is why today we'll focus on past conflicts between the kingdoms."

Isabel whined. "In the human world, ladies do not fret over such dull subjects. We only concern ourselves with whether or not we can marry a handsome soldier."

Blushing, Bridget clapped a hand over her mouth to stifle her laugh.

Dahlia's usually cheerful face darkened into a scowl. "When the battles sometimes reach your doorstep, you make it your duty to worry. Besides, sometimes even those handsome mortal messengers you care so much for go to war, even if it is only to carry correspondences between regiments or across enemy lines."

Bridget blanched.

Dahlia sat primly and cracked open an old tome. "Listen closely."

When my three younger sisters filed out of the tower, I lingered, half-heartedly searching for books I was sure by now, after two weeks of failed hunts, either didn't exist or remained hidden. Grace waited, sipping the last of her tea, and I knew she was hoping to get a word with me alone in the halls when I left Dahlia's tower.

But I was determined to pull answers from my tutor. Plucking a random book off the shelf about the history of Silverfrost, I returned to the alcove, where Dahlia hummed as she picked up empty mugs and placed them on her tray, then set to tidying the stacks of books on her desk.

"As I said earlier, you needn't worry about Fitz," Dahlia said without turning. "His magic is at the height of its power this time of year. Silverfrost is only toying with us, preparing for whatever true attacks they have in mind come wintertime."

I hesitated. Until now, I hadn't given much thought to the possible danger Fitz was in, or how something happening to him could affect me.

"Actually," I began, clearing my throat and praying that this time Dahlia was more open to the subject, "I wanted to know...where the glade of spirits is."

Behind me, Grace set her teacup down with a thud. Dahlia turned, eyebrows raised. "You've been warned about the dangers the spirits pose toward strangers."

"Yes, but I..."

"Want to see your father one last time," Dahlia finished for me, eyes shining with understanding.

For a moment, I considered explaining my hope of using necromancy, but I held my tongue. Confessing that desire would also involve admitting that I'd married Fitz to steal his magic. And as kind and caring as Dahlia was, she was loyal to Ashwood. I couldn't be sure she wouldn't tell everything to the queen.

A human stealing magic was a death sentence, and from the swift and severe way Queen Griselda dealt her punishments, I knew even my status as Fitz's wife wouldn't save me. I had four sisters who could fill my role.

"Well," Dahlia said, waving me toward her table in the middle of the library. Grace stood and trailed us, shooting me a sharp glance I avoided for the second time that day. As our tutor spread out her map of Brytwilde, she pointed to various locations in the forest. None were marked in any significant way. "It's been here, here, and also here. Sometimes here as well."

I frowned. "What do you mean?"

"It moves," Dahlia explained. "Someone like your husband, a royal who possesses magic that allows him to interact with souls, could easily track it each night, no matter where it shifted."

I swallowed. "And while he's gone? Is there a way I could find it?"

Dahlia shook her head. "Short of wandering the forest, no. And I don't recommend that. The glade of souls is only visible to living eyes after dusk. And I know how your last excursion ended."

Disappointment swelled in my chest. Even if Reid was able to provide safety with his knowledge of Brytwilde and his years of training, he wouldn't be a reliable guide. It could take us days of hunting to even find the glade. *But you have the locket,* I reminded myself. Surely it could lead me to ghosts, both within and without the glade.

Unfortunately, wearing the locket into the forest posed a great risk. I deflated. Maybe it was wisest to wait and let Fitz lead me at the end of his promised month, if he'd returned by then. And yet, no matter his claims of love and even if he overlooked the fact that I'd married him in the hopes to use his power and leave, I couldn't imagine him ever agreeing to help bring Father back. After all, restoring Father would remove my family's reliance on the fae. Even if Queen Griselda mainly only needed me, I didn't think she'd be pleased if Mother and my sisters left. She wanted more humans in Ashwood, probably hoping my sisters would marry fae and have children too, keeping her kingdom growing and strong.

"Why isn't Fitz sending the spirits into the afterlife?" I blurted.

Dahlia's eyes widened, and even Grace started.

"I'm afraid that's his secret to share," Dahlia said, busying herself with folding up her map.

I crossed my arms. "That's what everyone says."

Dahlia gave me a warning look. "Because it's true. That's his responsibility, and none of the rest of the kingdom is privy to those dealings."

"You want to see Father?" Grace demanded as soon as Dahlia's door clicked shut behind us. "Why don't you ask Fitz? You might not like him, but he is your husband *and* the one with the power to interact with the spirits in a way no one else can. He's been protective of you, and his whole family has been generous. I don't see any reason why he'd refuse you."

I swallowed, focusing on each step as we descended the narrow, winding staircase.

"When he returns," Grace went on, "talk to him. And..." Her voice sounded small with grief. "I want to come too."

We reached the foot of the stairs, and I seized her arm. "Grace, he told me he loves me."

Grasping my hand, my sister tugged me down the hall, back toward her rooms, only a few doors down from mine. "What happened? Tell me everything. You seemed shaken this morning, and I saw the dark circles under your eyes."

Starting from the beginning, with the hag in the ballroom and then the ghost who'd stalked me in the castle, I explained everything. "And then he followed me into my rooms, acting worried about me."

Grace opened her door and ushered me inside, where we settled in her sitting room by the low-burning fire. "Well, you *were* covered in blood."

"I told him I was fine and then he started talking about feelings he was fighting and..." I groaned, dragging a hand across my face. "I know you always try to see the best in people, but you *cannot* defend him. He's not like your Holden. I'm sure if Holden had been near when his mother took Lina's arm, he would have tried to stop her. Instead, I asked him to keep you away, to ensure you were safe. But Fitz? He stood there like a statue, unmoved and uncaring. His heart is made of stone." I sighed and went on with my story, explaining what Fitz had said and how I'd thrown my feelings back at him and sent him from my rooms.

Something dark flitted across my mild-mannered sister's face. Anger I wasn't used to seeing. "He didn't bother you again, did he?"

"I was attacked again," I whispered, and told her of Cordelia and how she'd tried to murder me in my own bed.

By the time I was finished, my sister was nearly as white as the dress she wore. "I don't like this. Exchanging places was a mist—"

"No, it was my choice. I don't regret it."

Grace lifted her chin, turning her anger on me. "Well maybe I regret it. You could *die*, Elle. What would I do without you?"

I reached out, squeezing her hands. "You need to trust me. Besides, the marriage can't be undone."

Grace scowled. "You're not sleeping alone, not another night. I'm staying with you."

My lips twitched at my sister's proclamation, but I didn't point out that she didn't know how to defend against a ghost any better than I did. "You can stay with me tonight," I agreed. "And Fitz already asked that while he is away, Holden remains near to watch over us."

Grace tugged on a lock of her blonde hair. "Maybe you shouldn't wear Father's locket anymore, if it was Cordelia's and is drawing her to you."

"I can't risk it being stolen!" I lowered my voice. "It's a charm, Grace. And it was Father's. I *know* he wouldn't have stolen it."

Grace's brow furrowed. "Maybe he purchased it while dealing with someone in that underground group at Fletcher's bookshop. We should discuss this with Holden."

I clapped a protective hand over my bodice, where my locket was concealed. "He'll want it back. I'm surprised Fitz hasn't asked for it already."

My sister cast me a pitying look. "Elle, their sister was murdered, and they don't know who killed her. Don't you think that locket and the story behind how Father acquired it could help them find the culprit? I know it makes Father feel close, but if it wasn't even a family heirloom..." She shrugged helplessly.

I sighed. "All right. Tonight, we talk to Holden."

CHAPTER TWENTY

"Silverfrost is always striving to claim our kingdom," Lina said as she and another maid helped Grace and me dress for dinner. My sister had already moved some of her things into Fitz's quarters so she and I could spend the foreseeable future together. "Trust me, Prince Fitz will have no trouble sending them back into their land, not during the height of autumn."

"Then why does Silverfrost bother?" Grace asked. Earlier, Dahlia had explained that both princes never went together into a battle, to ensure that if the worst happened, there would always be at least one surviving heir. Those remarks hadn't exactly settled my sister's nerves. All she could think about was the next time, when Holden would have to enter the fray.

"They like to keep us always watchful, always wary," Lina muttered bitterly. She glanced up, noticing the way Grace and I studied her, and sighed. "They killed my parents when I was young. It's why I came to serve in the castle, where I'd have a home."

"I'm so sorry," Grace exclaimed, rushing forward to pull Lina into an embrace.

"That's awful," I added, staying back when I noticed the discomfort in Lina's expression.

"It was a long time ago," she said hastily, pulling away from Grace. "Silverfrost has yet to advance that far into Ashwood again in my lifetime. And they haven't breached the castle in many generations."

I hugged my arms to my chest. "But they did before?"

Lina's smile looked more like a grimace. "*Long* before my time, Ashwood nearly fell to Silverfrost. But we've never come so close to losing our kingdom since. You're safe here."

"Will it be more dangerous in wintertime?" I ventured.

Lina shook her head. "Queen Griselda and Prince Fitz are powerful." She glanced at Grace. "And Prince Holden too. They won't let the Silverfrost troops draw near."

As Grace and I finished preparing for dinner, I mulled over Lina's words. They had to be true. The Ashwoods' magic remained powerful, or else they would struggle to hold back their enemies, especially as autumn ended and their strength waned. I hadn't needed further proof after watching Fitz send on a ghost that he could, but this served as another reminder. He was *choosing* not to release them.

As soon as Holden, Grace, and I returned to Fitz's rooms after dinner, Holden turned to me, face solemn. "Fitz told me about what happened last night," he said gravely, eyes dipping toward my neck.

I touched my throat self-consciously, running my fingertips over the chain of my locket. "I assume he also told you who it was. And what I wear."

Holden seated himself in an armchair while Grace and I settled on the couch across from him. "He did," the young prince admitted, sorrow filling his eyes. In the flickering candlelight, I caught the glistening of tears. "Cora...she wasn't like that, in life. She was a gentle soul, one of the kindest people I've ever known. She brought light and joy everywhere she went. And when her magic started to show an affinity toward the dead, she helped Fitz send on the spirits with such compassion and care." He shook his head. "I still can hardly believe she's gone."

"She looked a lot like you," I observed. "Same golden hair. Brown eyes."

"I'm told we inherited our appearance from our father," Holden said wistfully.

I hesitated, picking at the folds of my dress. "It sounds like she was well-loved."

Holden leaned forward in his chair. "She was."

"Then who could do such a thing to her?" Grace interjected, shaking her head in astonishment. "Why kill her?"

Holden's expression turned dark. "For her power. Her magic was nearly as strong as Fitz's. When we..." He trailed off, swallowed, and continued. "When we found her body, her locket was gone. We were certain her killer had taken it. Maybe he or she did, and then when they found they couldn't use the charm, they sold it in a black market."

I sighed, undoing the clasp and removing the locket from around my neck. My heart ached, but if I couldn't use it, if it wasn't even a family heirloom, it wasn't the dear possession I'd thought it was. It held more meaning to Holden than it did for me.

Holden took it, running his fingertips carefully over the engraved floral pattern on its surface.

"Can *you* open it or use it?" I asked carefully.

"No. Cora's magic was so powerful that she was able to enchant her charm so only she could ever wield it." His fingers folded over the locket. "Few fae are able to cast such a spell, so her killer would have been shocked to find their efforts were in vain." Holden smiled bitterly. "Cora prevented her magic from falling into the wrong hands, but she couldn't save herself."

"Can her charm...help her in some way?" I asked.

Holden frowned into the fire thoughtfully. "The locket will draw her spirit out, make it more powerful. Maybe Fitz and I could finally see her. Ever since she passed on...we haven't found her."

I sat up stiffly. "You haven't?"

"It would mean a lot to us if we could use the locket to see her again. But I know you like to wear it in memory of your father." He offered me the locket back. "Would you consider letting us borrow it when Fitz returns?"

I raised my eyebrows. "You're not going to keep it? I was sure after Fitz said wearing it put me in danger that he would have left you with some command to take it off me."

Holden's gaze was piercing. "He wouldn't do that to you, Elle. It's your choice whether you continue to wear it or not. I may not be able to command the spirits to move on, but they recognize Ashwood blood and magic. They'll listen to me, and I can protect you, whatever you decide to do."

I sat back, stunned, clinging to the locket. Even though I knew it put me in danger, I couldn't help but feel attached to it. Was it because of my memories of studying it with Father, or because of its magic that warmed my palm, even now? "Thank you," I murmured. "And of course I'd let you use it to see your sister."

Holden smiled, the expression burning away the pain in his eyes. "If you're not ready to retire for the night, we could play a game of cards? We needn't focus on such dreary topics any longer."

At Grace's and my acquiescence, Holden fetched a deck from a drawer in Fitz's desk. We gathered around a little table in the corner and Holden dealt the cards as I ruminated on all he'd shared, wondering if he would be as forthcoming with information about other charms. Like his. Like Fitz's.

Time ticked by, full of laughter and conversation and enough flirting between my sister and Holden that I had to warn them I might be ill.

At last, during a lull in the conversation, I dared to venture toward the topic of magic again. "Do you fear the killer will try to attack one of you and steal your charms?"

Holden shifted in his seat. "Yes...and no. We're hoping the killer learned that stealing magic from the Ashwoods isn't so easily done." He studied us warily before adding in a whisper, "I trust you both enough to say that the truth is, protecting a charm as Cora did is not something anyone else in our family can do. But we're hopeful the killer will be more hesitant to steal from us again, afraid that our charms will be enchanted too. And of course, we've been vigilant, closely watching members of the court." He hesitated. "I think it goes without saying that this all stays among us. We don't need anyone else to know that they could steal Fitz's or my charms and be able to wield them."

"You're saying the killer could be anyone in the castle?" Grace asked nervously.

"Yes, but that's why we have guards stationed in the hall...and why tonight, you have me." He smiled until his dimples showed, though grief dimmed his eyes. "I'll dispel the ghosts and fight off assassins, if any dare come near. I promise you're safe."

A weeks' worth of nights passed similarly, without me having any luck in determining what Holden's or Fitz's charms were. It wasn't as if I could ask him directly, and I'd exhausted every way I could think of to broach the topic in hopes something he'd say would give me a hint. I failed to discover any books on necromancy, and I showed no signs of magic. To cheer myself up, I wrote a letter to Sophie, though I didn't dare give any incriminating details about my search or Cordelia's murder in case the messenger I entrusted its delivery to became curious. But even sharing the barest of details about my new life with my dear friend reminded me that Riverton still existed, that my past life wasn't entirely gone.

In addition to trying to find a way to save Father, I found myself drawn to the mystery of Cordelia's murder. Perhaps it was the fact that I wore her locket, making me feel connected to her and her magic. Or perhaps it was my hope that if we found who the true murderer was, she would no longer threaten me.

Whatever the reason, I found myself once again standing outside her rooms one afternoon. I'd excused myself from a walk about the grounds with Holden and my sisters by claiming I had a headache. When I checked the hall and listened at the door, I found everything to be vacant and quiet.

Cordelia's rooms were simple and elegant, as I remembered them. This time, I let the pulsing of her locket guide me. I scanned everything more closely, lifting books off her shelves and peering beneath the bed. Though I was sure I wasn't the first to scour her quarters, hoping for some clue, I had a feeling that Cordelia's locket might guide me to something of use.

I paused beside the hearth in her bedroom when the locket started to burn to the point of almost causing me pain. Gasping, I stepped nearer to the fireplace, running my fingers along the mantle to no avail. *I'm close,* I thought. I pushed on brick after brick until I found a small depression in the mortar. The brick in question popped out easily. Within the hole rested a small journal.

Heart pounding, I grabbed the book, sliding it easily into my bodice and replacing the brick. Without waiting to see if Cordelia would make an appearance in daylight, I retreated to my own rooms.

Nothing. Hours later, I found myself groaning. Cordelia's journal was as unhelpful as everything else I'd learned about her. The most recent journal entries spoke of a lover—kind and charming and handsome and forbidden—but she never gave specifics, as if she feared even her hidden journal would be discovered. No description. No name. Not even a hint as to whether the lover in question might have been a lowly human or fae.

The most information I could gather was from one of her later journal entries, which hinted at a secret meeting place:

If Mother learned of our desire to be together, I fear she would have him executed for daring to even think of loving me. She would say he is beneath me and would not approve. And because of this, I can't tell Fitz or Holden or Kinsey about him either. They might tell Mother. Fitz might even agree with Mother and kill the man himself.

All I have are our stolen moments and hopeless dreams. Trying to find clever ways to avoid the truth when I can't lie is becoming torture. Everyone is always wondering why I venture into the woods, and I'm constantly afraid someone will follow me and find our meeting place.

Mulling over that information, I tucked the journal away beneath my bed right before Lina knocked, coming to prepare me for dinner. It spelled the end of another nearly fruitless day.

The only good news came on the morning of the eighth day, when Isabel skipped into breakfast to meet Grace and me, Bridget eagerly following on her heels. Mother had sent a note claiming she and Maggie were indisposed, so it was only the four of us that morning.

"Guess who our second favorite messenger, Daniel, says has returned?" Isabel announced in a sing-song voice.

I blinked. "Izzy," I chastened, pouring myself a much-needed second mug of tea, "unless you're engaged to a man, you shouldn't use his name so familiarly."

Isabel rolled her eyes. "Rules here aren't like back home." She fluttered her lashes. "And you're not Mother." She sat back, withdrawing a note from her dress pocket with a flourish. "Anyway, Daniel says Reid has returned! He will be at dinner tonight." Isabel glanced up proudly, a wicked smile curving her lips. "Aren't you *pleased*, Elle?"

"It will be agreeable to see an old friend," I said primly.

Bridget scoffed, nearly choking on her toast. "Agreeable? You were half in love with him back home!"

I gritted my teeth. "And *now* I am a married woman. He is a friend."

Isabel curled her lip. "You don't love Prince Fitz, do you?"

"This isn't about love; it's about propriety."

"And," Bridget cut in, leaning across the table to look pointedly at Isabel, "it's about protection. If Prince Fitz caught her pining for another man, who knows what he would do!"

Isabel giggled. "Another storm, but this time, it would last for days!" she proclaimed dramatically.

I stiffened.

"What happened at the ball is no laughing matter," Grace said, laying a hand over mine and squeezing my fingers. I relaxed at her touch. "You were further in the crowd and didn't see the deaths. Don't make light of it."

Our sisters sighed but quieted, returning to their meals.

"I'm happy Mr. Reid has returned," Grace went on, steering the conversation to a safer subject. "He was always a good friend to our family, and it's comforting to have a familiar face. With the unrest at the border, it's reassuring to hear he's returned safely."

I squeezed Grace's hand back, silently thanking her.

As soon as I reached the dining room that evening, I scanned the expansive table, my eyes passing over fae whose gazes met mine with more challenge in them now that Fitz was absent. I lifted my chin and clung close to Grace and Holden, praying the courtiers would remember their places when seeing me so close to their other prince. When I caught sight of the messengers, with Reid among them, I couldn't contain my smile. He grinned back.

Tonight, he mouthed, and my pulse spiked.

Tonight, I would face the dangers of the forest again. Tonight, I might see my father.

But if Father had managed to remain in the glade, and the glade moved...there was a chance that we wouldn't be able to find it, regardless of Reid's knowledge of the woods and the magic in Cordelia's locket.

Dinner passed slowly, a succession of endless courses distributed with leisurely formality. I smiled through gritted teeth, praying I looked cheerful and grateful as Queen Griselda assaulted my sisters and me with insults covertly disguised as questions. Holden and Grace flirted as if the rest of the world had faded away. Across the table, my youngest sisters did their best to capture the attention of several handsome messengers, though only a couple seemed interested in conversation.

At last, Queen Griselda dismissed everyone, and I allowed Holden to start escorting Grace and me out of the room. I glanced over my shoulder, trying to seek out Reid in the exiting crowd, hoping he had a plan to sneak out of the castle.

"Your Highness," came Reid's voice as soon as we entered the hallway.

Grace and I turned with Holden, finding Reid dipping into a quick bow.

"If you don't mind, could I have a word with Elle?" Reid asked. "We're old friends."

Holden glanced at me, and I nodded.

"I'll escort her to her rooms safely," Reid added, his eyes darting toward the windows at the far end of the hall. Outside, the forest was growing dark, warning us that the spirits would soon grow restless within and without the castle.

The tension in Holden's shoulders eased, and he smiled. "Of course. Don't be long, and return her to Fitz's rooms." He stressed his words, adding the hint of a threat. It made me wonder what an angry Holden would look like.

Reid offered his arm and steered me toward a nearby bench casually as the other courtiers swept out, some toward the stairs and their rooms upstairs, and others out the doors to estates beyond the castle grounds.

As soon as the hallway cleared, Reid turned to me, voice lowered. "Fitz's rooms? I thought he was at the border with his soldiers."

"He is, but he has Holden watching over me while he's gone." I swallowed. "There was...an incident." Dropping my tone to a whisper, I relayed the events of that eventful night, from the ghost in the hall to Cordelia's attack, only leaving out Fitz's confession. That wasn't something I wanted to relive.

"Princess Cordelia," Reid breathed, his complexion pale.

"I'm sure you've heard much about her life and death," I said.

Reid shook his head, leaning against the wall. "The events of her death were kept rather secretive. I knew her when she was alive, of course. She was the youngest child, always a kind and gentle soul, nothing like her mother or our crown prince. She was also extremely powerful in her magic, so much so that there were..." He glanced about to ensure the guards were a good distance away before leaning toward me and lowering his voice even more. "There were whispers in the court that Prince Fitz envied her. As the heir, he didn't appreciate the fact that his sister's magical abilities rivaled his own, or that she could also commune with the spirits. Some say she was better at sending the souls on than he was."

The locket seemed heavy around my neck. "Really?" I mused. "I also heard that she might have had a forbidden lover. Someone the queen wouldn't have considered proper. Holden spoke of a servant or a fae with weak magic. But could it have been a *human* servant? Would the queen have rejoiced over possible heirs, or would romance with a servant have been scandalous?"

A muscle worked in Reid's jaw. "Perhaps. I think the Ashwoods suspected it was a servant, human or not. They did ask a lot of questions of us messengers after the princess died," he confessed. "Especially about one of my friends. I wouldn't ever believe it of him, but they thought it strange that Finley disappeared around the same time Princess Cordelia died." He shook his head. "The thing is, messengers vanish with regularity. Our travels take us through the treacherous woods and into the other fae kingdoms. As you already know, there are plentiful creatures in Brytwilde that can kill a human. Our profession comes with constant risks."

"But Finley...he hasn't returned?"

Reid's eyes filled with sorrow. "I'm afraid he's probably dead, lost to some monster in the woods. But I am sure he wouldn't have murdered the princess. He spoke often about how much he admired her. And they never found anything to prove he might have—nor did they find any evidence to convict any of us messengers."

I frowned in thought, mulling it all over. Though I wanted to believe Reid was a good judge of character, I also couldn't dismiss this information. What if Finley hadn't died? What if he'd run away after murdering his lover?

"But if Prince Holden expects you back soon, we must hurry." Reid glanced toward the windows and the swiftly darkening forest. "He'll grow suspicious, and who knows how far we must travel tonight."

"Because the glade changes locations?"

Reid nodded. "We'll find it, Elle," he promised, and I wanted to believe him. He seemed confident, but I was nervous.

Standing, he offered me his hand. "Pretend to be ill, and we'll insist you need fresh air."

I frowned. "They're going to grow suspicious with the number of times I've feigned being ill."

Reid shrugged. "Or they'll think you're a sickly human."

I stifled a laugh, knowing that wasn't something Queen Griselda would appreciate in the woman who was supposed to bear her son's heirs.

As Reid helped me up, I teetered on my feet and leaned heavily on him. When he tugged me toward the double doors leading into the courtyard, he glanced apologetically toward the guards. "I'm afraid the lady is feeling ill and needs some air," he explained.

One of the men straightened, his eyes flicking over me and then the human messenger I leaned on. If he was suspicious, nothing in his blank stare gave it away. "It's dangerous for a new human to be out after sunset."

"I understand," Reid said, patient despite the fact that the fae had explained something he already knew. "But I'll accompany her to ensure her safety, and we won't be gone long. Just a stroll through the grounds, and then I'll escort her back through the castle myself."

The guard hesitated, studying the sword and dagger strapped to Reid's belt. "Very well." His gaze turned sharp. "But if anything happens to the princess, Mr. Reid, you know who you have to answer to."

"Of course."

The doors opened with a groan, and Reid guided me down the cobbled path, avoiding the main gate in favor of the stables and a smaller, unmonitored side gate. It led out into the grounds, where we swept past mums and roses blooming by the castle walls, growing piles of leaves, and the outbuildings and training yard. Without the need to put on a show, I pulled away from Reid and hugged my arms to my chest. The air was chilly and damp, the heavy clouds promising rain.

My fingers drifted toward the chain around my throat. I could only hope the locket would be useful enough that any danger it attracted would be worth it.

"Forgive me, I should have thought of finding you a coat," Reid said, removing his and offering it to me.

It smelled of woodsmoke and the earthy aroma of the autumn forest, reminding me that Reid had been on the road recently. "Did your business...go well?" I asked, stifling a shiver and tugging his coat tightly about my frame.

Reid scowled. "I don't wish to speak of it. Most of the time, I can't complain about how Queen Griselda treats humans, and it's why my father and me remained in her employ. But she enjoys manipulation and blackmail. Humans are always in demand, as servants as well as for...breeding." His stride lengthened, twigs and leaves cracking under his boots as his expression darkened.

Finding myself falling behind, I tried to pick up my pace. My gown was heavy and extravagant today, layered in silks and elaborate embroidery and beading. Thankfully, slits were cut in the sides, reaching nearly to my knees. They allowed for some ease of movement as well as access to the blade I'd attached to my thigh, thanks to a new sheath Kinsey had gifted to me a couple weeks before. "But she has so many fae servants."

Reid slipped into the forest, surveying the area carefully. Mist swirled like a living thing through the trees, groping at bare branches and leaving droplets on the leaves littering the forest floor. But I didn't see any spirits, and my hidden locket didn't pulse or warm. "If you were immortal, don't you think you'd grow bored of serving the same family for hundreds or thousands of years?" He sighed. "Fae are always moving on to new things. They're vain and fickle, even those that aren't of royal blood, and it's far easier for Queen Griselda to blackmail, trick, or form deals with humans who will serve her faithfully out of fear or obligation. Most fae think they're above service, above the tedious duties they prefer to assign to us mortals."

My mouth soured.

"But Ashwood is known for its kindness toward humans," Reid added. "If you ever travel to Silverfrost..." His eyes darkened. "Well, don't."

"Is it that awful?"

"So awful, I won't tell you about the things I've witnessed."

For several minutes, we walked on in silence. The distant hoots of owls and the creaking of tree branches were the only sounds aside from our own footsteps. My breath swirled in the air, and wind whispered against my face. I paused, focusing on Reid's form as he marched ahead, unaware I wasn't right behind him.

Something about the breeze felt like it was more than just the wind. My skin prickled, and I scanned the trees to either side, expecting a figure to emerge.

Thief. Murderer.

Someone was breathing against the back of my neck.

I whirled, heart hammering in my ears. Cordelia stared, bloodshot eyes glaring into mine. Her ruined neck stood out starkly against her pale skin.

I reached for my dagger, not drawing it from its thigh sheath, but preparing to do so if Cordelia advanced. I didn't dare take my eyes off her to search for Reid, but his distant footsteps warned me he still hadn't noticed my absence. "Cordelia," I murmured.

Cordelia stepped forward, but at the sound of her name, she froze. Surprise flashed across her fine features, and her expression gentled. It was easier to see that in life, she had been a beauty, with flowing golden hair, rich brown eyes, and high cheekbones. She looked the part of a young, kind princess, not the angry specter she'd become. Then her expression hardened. "I don't know who you are, mortal, but just because you succeeded in killing and stealing from me doesn't mean I can't stop you from doing the same to my brother."

I stepped back. "I didn't kill you. I'm Elle Blackford, sister to Grace Blackford. We're the family your mother made a deal with. The ones meant to give your brother a human bride."

Cordelia hesitated, eyes studying me with renewed interest as the pieces clicked into place in her mind.

"I wasn't in Brytwilde when you died."

She pointed an accusatory finger toward my neck. "You wear my locket."

"Yes, but I didn't know it was yours. I was told it was a family heirloom—my father sometimes did business with the black market back home. He must have purchased it from someone and was too afraid to admit where he'd obtained it." I clasped my hand over the chain, praying Cordelia wouldn't launch herself at me. "Please," I added, as frown lines appeared on the dead princess's face. If I couldn't convince her I wasn't an enemy, I would have no reassurance that she wouldn't attack me again. "I'm not a threat. I...I could even help you. I found your journal. And when Fitz returns, I'm to lend your locket to him and Holden so they can speak to you—"

"Elle?" Reid called.

Cordelia vanished, and Reid's footsteps picked up their pace until he was at my side, breathless.

"Are you all right?" he demanded. "Why did you stop?"

I shook my head. "I'm fine," I said absently, wondering why Cordelia was so shy. Why even her own brothers hadn't seen her.

"I'm sorry for charging ahead, but I heard sounds," Reid went on. "We need to return to the castle. Immediately."

"Why?"

A horn interrupted me, and it was only then that I became aware of the pounding of hooves approaching the castle. I'd been too caught up in my conversation with Cordelia to register the noises earlier.

Reid's brow creased with worry. "Because your husband has returned."

CHAPTER TWENTY-ONE

Another setback. Another failure. My eyes stung, but I didn't want to embarrass myself by letting my tears fall, and I certainly didn't want to know what Fitz would do to Reid if he found us sneaking about in the dark amidst the ghosts.

"We'll have to be quiet near the stables," Reid whispered as we passed the training grounds and outbuildings. The castle gates were already opening, hooves pounding along the courtyard's cobblestones. "Prince Fitz likes to tend to his horse himself, so we can still make it back before him if he doesn't see us pass."

I glanced to one of the nearest buildings and frowned. "Isn't that where the messenger quarters are? Go now, and I'll sneak back into the castle alone. If Fitz sees me, it'll be all right. If he sees *you* sneaking me out at night..." I let my words trail off, not needing to voice what we both knew would happen.

Reid's eyes flashed. "Firstly, I'm not sure I believe you'll be fine either. And secondly, I'm not leaving you alone at night."

Grinding my teeth at his stubbornness, I hurried toward the side gate. Murmuring voices emerged from within the stables, one matching Fitz's timbre. "The gate *squeaks*," I hissed. "We have to climb."

Reid nodded, folding his hands together and offering them to me as a step so I could hoist myself over the wall. I seized the ledge, cold stone biting into my skin as I pulled myself to the top. Reid was at my side in an instant, leaping down first. Clinging to the shadows, he turned, his arms outstretched to catch me.

The courtyard itself was full of men and women dismounting and stable hands rushing forward to take the reins. Others on foot rushed to and fro, some carrying the wounded on stretchers. It was pure chaos, granting Reid and me the perfect chance to slip through the crowd unnoticed.

I released my grasp on the wall and jumped. Reid caught me by the waist and lowered me gently, his smile relieved.

But movement out of the corner of my eye made me freeze. I glanced over Reid's shoulder to find Fitz standing in the stable doorway, staring straight at me. At *us*, with Reid's arms still enveloping my body. Silhouetted against the buttery light of the lanterns in the stable, his expression was shrouded in shadow, but I knew it wasn't pleased.

"Reid," I whispered, pulling away and stumbling out of my friend's grasp.

Fitz was already striding forward, his fury so great I could feel electricity crackling in the air. I wasn't sure if I was imagining it, or if his magic was building, preparing for another strike. When he stopped mere feet away, his expression was terrifyingly blank, and his eyes were dark. "Mr. Reid, why are you out after sunset with my wife?"

I glanced around, as if to find someone who could intervene and distract Fitz from his building fury. But no one else in the courtyard paid us any heed, too distracted with their work of helping the injured and welcoming the warriors home.

"It's my fault—" I began, but Fitz shook his head and turned to Reid, silently demanding a response.

To his credit, Reid didn't balk or flinch. Instead, he nodded respectfully. "I beg your forgiveness, Your Highness. The princess wasn't feeling well and asked for some fresh air."

"Outside the castle grounds?" Fitz asked impassively. Before either of us could respond, he stepped closer, his height dwarfing Reid until my friend seemed to shrink in his shadow. "I have no tolerance for lies. You know that you endanger your princess's life by bringing her here, no matter how experienced you are in traveling through these woods."

This time, there was no mistaking the shadows building around Fitz, or the occasional flash of lightning forking through them.

"Don't!" I cried, throwing myself between the men and seizing Fitz's arms. "Please don't hurt him."

Fitz drew back, his magic vanishing in his surprise. His eyes searched mine before they dropped to the coat I wore. A muscle jumped in his jaw. "Mr. Reid, return to your quarters. You're dismissed."

Reid didn't give me a chance to return his coat as he turned to the gate and scrambled toward the outbuildings. Taking my hand, Fitz led me away from the stables and through the courtyard, his strides long but unhurried. I glanced his way, trying to read his expression, but there was nothing but focus shining in his eyes.

"Your Highness," the guards greeted at the doors, already open and waiting for his arrival. He nodded in acknowledgement before pulling me to the stairs, winding past endless floors until we'd reached our hallway. He stopped at my door and gestured for me to open it.

As soon as the door swung inward, Fitz drew me inside and shut the door behind us. "How well do you know him?" he asked, turning so I was backed against the wall in the entryway. Though he released my arm, I still felt trapped. He'd promised to protect me, even claimed he cared for me, but what did that look like to an envious immortal?

Instead of letting him see my nerves, I raised my chin. "He often visited my hometown. He's an old family friend."

Silence descended as Fitz drew back a little, his eyes raking over me as if he hadn't seen me in years. They snagged again on Reid's coat, overlarge on my figure and still smelling of him.

"Are you jealous?" Immediately, I regretted my question and cursed my quick tongue. Goading a fae didn't seem like a wise idea.

But there was no anger in Fitz's expression, only weariness. "Yes."

For the first time, I studied him more closely. Stubble shadowed his face, and his hair hung loosely to his chin. He'd just returned from battle, hadn't had a moment to rest or change, and he was exhausted.

I waited, but Fitz didn't elaborate on his answer or pull away, instead lifting his hand and tracing my cheek with his fingertips. His touch burned my skin. His hand was too warm; his presence was too overpowering. For a reason I couldn't explain, I held still, a pitiful victim entranced by a fatal spell. When I didn't move, he ran his fingers through my hair, over the shell of my ear, along my pulse pounding wildly in my neck. He set his hands on my shoulders and shoved off Reid's coat, letting it fall to the floor.

I choked on a gasp, dizzy and confused by my response.

When Fitz's eyes swept over me again, his gaze wasn't dark with lust. He looked worried. Feeling foolish, I sighed, realizing he was searching for blood. "I'm not hurt," I insisted.

"Your friend may be a messenger, but the spirits can harm him too. Especially when you're wearing Cora's locket."

Fitz inhaled sharply. He stepped back, swaying on his feet.

"Are *you* hurt?" I asked.

"Poisoned," he muttered, stumbling to the sofa.

I followed Fitz as he collapsed onto the couch, frowning at the sweat beading on his forehead. My rooms were cold with no fires burning, because Lina had prepared Fitz's quarters for me instead. Yet Fitz was clearly too hot. "What does that mean?" I demanded.

"It means an angry Silverfrost soldier stabbed me with a poisoned blade while I killed him, but Kinsey is knowledgeable, even in the poisons used by the winter kingdom. He healed the wound and gave me an antidote, but the antidote itself doesn't prevent all the unpleasant side effects as your body fights the toxin." Fitz sat up, unbuttoning his coat and blinking at the fireplace. "It seems I'm starting to feel them." He cast aside his coat and began to work the buttons of his shirt.

"You *cannot* stay," I said, rushing forward, "and you certainly can't undress here."

"Afraid you'll find me irresistible?"

I seized Fitz's hands, stilling his fingers. He froze, his too-warm hands clasping mine.

"How are you already so warm?" I muttered. No wonder his skin had felt so hot against mine; he was burning with fever. "I'll call for Kinsey."

I started to turn, but Fitz clung to my wrist, holding me back. "No, everything I need is here." He slumped against the couch. "Although, some water would be nice."

I hurried toward the washroom to fill a cup. "Shouldn't you inform Holden you're back?" I asked as I returned to the sitting room.

Fitz lay back with his shirt half undone and his gaze glazed as he stared at the ash in my grate. My stomach swooped at the sight of so much bare skin. I couldn't stop my eyes from running over the column of his throat and down the muscled planes of his chest before I forced the hazy desire away. This time, I couldn't lie to myself about Fitz using glamour. He hadn't even noticed me enter the room.

I stepped forward and he turned, eyes running down the length of my dress, taking in the way it hugged my form. "Blackford, come to torment me again," he teased, but I noticed the way he trembled.

I frowned. "Now you're shivering. Please, if not Kinsey, Holden can come. I know nothing of fae poisons or illness—"

Fitz grasped my arm and pulled me to him, sloshing the water from the glass and spilling it down his front. He tugged me onto the couch until I was sprawled next to him. "I sent a message to Holden. I'm sure by now he and your sister are settled in their own rooms."

"Then you can go to yours." I sat up, lifting the glass to his lips. "Drink, and then we'll take you to your own bed."

Fitz drank obediently, but his brow furrowed. He swallowed the last of the water. "There was something...something I needed to speak with you about."

Alarm filled my chest. "Oh no, you already did that before you left." I set the empty glass on a side table and stood.

"Yes, I don't want to repeat that either," Fitz said, smiling despite the pain in his eyes. "It was embarrassing for both of us, though I'm not sure why it caused *you* discomfort."

I looked away. "I don't take joy in making others hurt."

"Even if you hate them?"

Turning back, I met Fitz's gaze. His smile was surprisingly warm, his expression open. It reminded me a little of the ways in which he'd tenderly cared for me when I'd been drugged and hurt, except this time there was no mask concealing his emotions. It hard to accept that this man was the same one who'd killed his own courtiers. The one who'd been threatening my friend only minutes ago, even if he'd stopped at my bidding.

"Yes, even if I hate them." Sighing, I settled into an armchair to face him. "What did you have to tell me?"

Fitz ran a hand over his brow, mussing his hair. "Mostly, that you are unfortunately correct regarding many things about me. My mother is proud of our bloodline, and she trained me to take pride in it as well. Perhaps I'm as insufferable as you say." His words slurred and he smirked, belying his apology—if his statement was even meant to be one.

I raised my eyebrows, wondering if Fitz thought he was defending himself or proving my points. But he wasn't looking at me anymore, his eyes fixed on a painting featuring a lush autumn landscape.

"As for Lina, I regret it. I'm sorry I failed her."

"So you're agreeing with me?"

Fitz shrugged helplessly. "I grew up in a cruel world, Blackford. My Father was murdered by a jealous subject." He leaned back. "Some fae think humans are weak...like playthings. Because we're fascinated with your fragile nature. Always fighting to survive."

"You're rambling."

Fitz smiled lazily. "My thoughts are foggy. Am I not making sense?"

"And our lives aren't *that* bad," I went on, but Fitz pierced me with a look. "Well," I amended, "we *did* have to come here or risk being homeless. I confess, I haven't had the luxury of being bored for at least a month now."

My tone edged toward teasing, and I smiled, despite how truly heavy my grief was.

Fitz's eyes snagged on my mouth. "Your smile."

I fidgeted with the beading on my skirt. "What?"

"It was one of the first things that forced me to notice you, even when I didn't want to. And your eyes. There's...light and intelligence and laughter in them."

Now I *knew* Fitz wasn't in his right mind. The poison had addled his brain.

Blushing, I refused to look up. I didn't want this attention, but how could I *not* be flattered? I'd spent a lifetime hearing men drone on about every detail of Grace's angelic beauty. I hadn't believed there'd come a day when someone might see me the way they'd looked at her.

"But what first caught my attention," Fitz went on, "was how you faced my mother, even if it seemed foolish to me. You were courageous, even more so for having no magic to defend against her." He blinked, his words running together. "You defy her at every turn. You, Blackford, are a queen."

I stood quickly. "This conversation is wandering dangerously close to a subject we both agreed not to address again."

Fitz's expression hardened a fraction, his eyes clearing a little. "And all I've done is list the reasons you have to hate me. But...there was something else. You blamed me for the spirits that linger."

Crossing my arms, I stared at him. But it was difficult to be angry when he lay draped across the couch, his face shining with sweat and his eyes glistening with fever. "How could I not? It's your responsibility to send them on."

"I don't speak of it, because it is weakness," Fitz murmured, "but I haven't sent on a soul since my sister died. I've tried. But I wasn't *able* to. At least, not until the night you were in danger."

I plopped back into my seat. "What do you mean, you're not able to?"

Fitz's face turned troubled, full of a turbulent grief I understood all too well. "The spirits don't respond to me as they used to. Oftentimes, they don't even appear for me at all. It's as if all my spirit magic vanished with Cora. After all, magic without focus is futile, and grief has made it difficult to focus." He met my eyes briefly. "I failed her. If I'd been more vigilant, maybe I would have prevented her death. Seeing her body..." Fitz covered his face with his hands. "I blame myself. I haven't even seen her spirit since she passed."

Throat tight, I reached for my locket, pulling it from where I'd tucked it into my bodice. "Holden said that perhaps this would help you see her again."

"It might even help bring her back from the dead."

My heart leapt into my throat. *Necromancy.* Perhaps, in his fevered state, the crown prince would divulge some of its secrets. "That's possible?" I choked out, scarcely trusting my voice to not reveal my knowledge.

Fitz laid his head back, squinting his eyes sleepily. I feared he'd drift off. "Rarely, with powerful magic." His eyes shut, and I ground my teeth in frustration.

"Is yours powerful enough?"

"I hope," he murmured, eyes still closed.

Leaping up, I strode to the couch and rested my hand on his forehead. "I'm calling for Kinsey, so he can settle you in your rooms."

The prince blinked his eyes open. "Blackford, we brought home an entire regiment full of injured soldiers. Kinsey has more important things to worry about."

"What about your fever?" I demanded.

"It will pass by morning." He gave a crooked attempt at a smile. "We fae heal fast, even without immortality."

"*Without*?" I repeated.

Fitz inhaled sharply. "Never mind. Go to bed; pretend I'm not here."

I knelt beside the couch. "What do you mean?"

His gaze focused on me, clearer than it'd been earlier. He wasn't feverish to the point of being delusional, and he was a fae. He couldn't lie.

"I thought all fae were immortal," I pressed.

"We are, but wedding a mortal and sharing our magic requires...sacrifice." Fitz swallowed. "It's something I've always known would happen."

I gaped. "You're mortal now?"

"My life will not be as long as it would have been had we never married. It's the only way we can share magic with a mortal."

I sat back on my heels. "You were furious I took Grace's place, because you feared my deception would make the magic transfer fail, and your sacrifice would be for nothing." For the first time, guilt over the way I'd uprooted Fitz's life, and the way I planned to further uproot it, seized me in a cold grasp.

"It would have happened anyway, no matter who I married. A future queen must be granted magic and accepted by our land. Every royal who marries a human must do it."

"Will Holden...? If he marries Grace?" I asked, stunned.

"Since the burden of having heirs doesn't rest on him, that isn't a requirement. It would be his and Grace's choice, whether or not he would share his magic with her and give up his immortality."

I swallowed back my guilt. "I...don't know what to say."

Fitz shook his head. "Don't say anything." His smile was bittersweet.

Hesitating, I stepped closer. "I'll help you to bed."

"I'm not that weak," Fitz protested, but he was weary and unsteady on his feet. He didn't resist when I suggested he lean on my arm to shuffle into my bedroom.

When I guided him toward my bed, not the hidden door connecting to his quarters, Fitz cast me a questioning glance.

"I can't leave you alone when you're running a fever like this," I said, not meeting his eyes.

"Thank you," Fitz rasped. He sat on the bed, pulling off his boots and studying me thoughtfully.

I started worrying he was going to make another confession, so I turned away.

"You're not wearing a corset under all that, are you?" he asked instead.

My skin went hot at the memory of his fingers working the laces of my wedding corset. "No," I said, grabbing a nightgown from my wardrobe and scurrying into the washroom to change. Fitz's low chuckle followed me, echoing in my ears.

When I returned to the bedroom, Fitz hadn't fallen asleep. He met my eyes, his expression serious, his eyes bright. "Please don't sneak off into the forest again, alone or otherwise. I'll help you find your father, even if my spirit magic has weakened. I promise, Elle. You can trust my word."

And somehow, as I climbed into bed and slowly drifted off to the steady rhythm of my husband's breathing, it didn't sound so awful to consider trusting him.

CHAPTER TWENTY-TWO

I awoke enveloped in warmth and the scent of the autumn forest. As I squinted against the morning sunlight spilling through my windows, it took me a moment to realize that I wasn't only encased in the bedclothes. Fitz's arm was draped over my waist, hugging me close to his chest, which rose and fell gently as he slept. Last night's feverish warmth had left his skin, but his touch still burned through my nightgown.

A knock on the door made me flinch. Holden must have told Lina that I'd moved back into my own rooms. Sure enough, Lina entered whistling and pushing a cart bearing my breakfast tray.

I sat up, strands of hair hanging wildly in my face.

Lina halted, eyes darting from my shocked expression to Fitz's sleeping form beside me. "Oh," she said, lifting her brows. "Someone missed you, I take it?" She glanced hesitantly toward the prince, her eyes full of questions she dared not ask in his presence.

I shrugged, wishing I could explain, wishing I could untangle my own confused emotions. "Could you bring another serving of breakfast?" I asked instead.

Nodding, Lina left, giving me a moment to lay back against the pillows and sigh. At my side, Fitz stirred, drawing his arm away.

"I didn't mean to trouble you," he said, sitting up. "Did I disturb your sleep?"

"No," I said hastily, not meeting his eyes as a flush spread across my face. It wasn't as if we hadn't shared a bed before. But I hadn't woken in his arms any of the previous times.

"Good." Fitz hesitated before ducking his head, forcing me to meet his gaze. "Thank you for last night."

I hugged my arms across my chest. "I didn't do anything."

Fitz grinned—a true smile that took me by surprise. "You listened to me."

Fitz didn't linger after breakfast, leaving to change in his own rooms and check on his soldiers now that he was well. Lina tossed more than one curious glance my way as she helped me dress, but when I didn't offer her any details about the night before, she didn't ask.

My emotions were muddled, and I longed for a moment alone with Grace to try to sort through what Fitz had shared with me. My hope in rescuing Father had somehow both increased and diminished, leaving me uncertain and afraid. If Fitz couldn't commune with the spirits as he once had, I wasn't sure his magic would be great enough to save him. And if the locket I'd hoped would tie Father to the mortal realm—Reid had always claimed spirits needed something they'd kept close to them on earth to return—had belonged to Cordelia, maybe it wouldn't work for him.

I should have found one of his favorite books, I thought frantically as Lina finished combing through my hair.

"Are you all right?" Lina asked, wrenching me from my thoughts.

I started. "Yes."

Lina met my gaze in the mirror, her violet eyes solemn, searching. "You would tell me if you were not?"

"You have no reason to be so kind to me," I murmured.

"Because I'm fae?" Lina arched a brow. "Because I serve them?"

I shrugged. "You hardly know me."

"It doesn't mean I want to see you hurt. I know Queen Griselda, though harsh in other ways, doesn't glamour mortals, but that doesn't mean you're all right, caught up in all this. You've been sad and distant. Although, this morning..." She trailed off. "You seemed happy, for a moment. Do you care for Prince Fitz?"

"He was sick," I explained. "Nothing happened."

"He's different around you," Lina persisted. "More like he was before his sister died." She cleared her throat. "But I know you didn't want his attention, at least not before. I suppose I wanted to talk as friends, if you trusted me enough to share your feelings." She hesitated. "I know you haven't had much of a reason to trust us fae, and now you're a princess and I'm only a servant, but...I would *like* to be your friend."

I smiled. Lina had given me nothing but reasons to trust her and her intentions, and I realized in this moment that I no longer suspected her kindness was manipulative. She seemed sincere. "I would like to be your friend too." My mouth turned downward as I glanced at Lina's stump. "Fitz shared some things with me last night that helped me understand him better, but he still stood by while his mother took your hand. Don't you hate him?"

Lina shrugged. "He and Prince Holden grew up in their overbearing mother's shadow, living as her subjects too. It's only recently that Prince Fitz has had more power, as heir. I think, with the way you stand up to her, you might remind him that he can too." She frowned. "As a boy, he was gentle and shy. He's still quiet and reserved—just angrier and less trusting since his sister died. He doted on her, and this past year...well, it's been dark. I think he suspects everyone in the castle, servants and courtiers alike, and he lets fear and vengeance consume him. But for many long years, I considered both princes and the princess my friends. So no, I don't hate him. He wasn't the one who cut off my hand, and I can't blame him anymore than I'd blame you. The queen would have thrown her own son in the dungeons if he'd tried to stop her, and then taken my hand anyway. Or worse." She swallowed, glancing at her feet, and I wondered if she'd seen such actions play out before.

My eyes widened. "Intervening would have made it worse?"

"You've seen Prince Fitz's magic, but Queen Griselda's is powerful too. Perhaps he could defy her, but perhaps not. She's lived many more years than him, and those who bear the crown bear the most of our land's magic. Until she passes that crown onto him, she will remain the strongest fae in Ashwood."

"Lina, that's awful. Has she done other things..."

Gesturing, Lina cut me off and urged me to my feet. "Never mind that now. You'll be late for lessons if you don't leave. Hurry!"

Realizing she didn't want to talk, I bid Lina goodbye and left my quarters, shutting my door with a sigh and scanning the hall. Guards lined the walls, protecting my family and me from hidden threats, but otherwise the hallway was empty. Likely my sisters were already waiting in Dahlia's library.

The day passed swiftly, with Dahlia spending extra time on our lessons. I ate luncheon with my family in my quarters. Since Kinsey and Fitz were busy after their return, Lina informed me that I wouldn't have training today, so I spent the afternoon while Dahlia was away scouring her library, hoping for information on Cordelia, charms, or necromancy. Once again, I came up short, and I was running out of unexamined shelves.

At last, Lina dressed me for dinner in a sweeping violet gown and bid me not to be late, refusing to waste time on further conversation. I suspected she didn't want to discuss more painful subjects after this morning.

It was early enough that the sun hovered above the horizon and I didn't need an escort to the dining hall, so I set off on my own. As I approached the staircase, a chill crept down my spine. A draft of cold air whispered along my cheeks, and the locket warmed against my chest, pulsing with life. I halted mid-stride, searching.

By a window, clinging to the shadows, stood Cordelia. The daylight didn't appear to trouble her. Fully corporeal, she peered out at the forest. She could have been a member of court enjoying the view, but for her necklace of bruises. She turned, her bloodshot eyes meeting mine.

"Cordelia, what are you—"

"The longer my locket is near, the stronger I grow," Cordelia murmured. The rasp in her words had eased, enough to tell she'd once had a melodic voice. She didn't appear angry as she approached, her simple white gown rustling around her slippers. I remained still. "Did you mean what you said last night?" Her eyes dropped toward the chain around my neck.

"I did," I said. "Your brothers miss you and want to see you again."

"Holden and Fitz." Tears shimmered in her eyes. "I've been hiding, afraid to trust anyone. I don't know who killed me."

I stepped closer. "You don't? What about your secret lover? Do you remember who he was? Or if he hurt you?"

Cordelia shook her head, tears slipping down her pale cheeks. "I'm sorry. It's as if all those months leading up to my death are a blur. I never realized the pain the spirits face, losing so many pieces of themselves as their memories disappear."

I thought of Reid's messenger friend who'd disappeared so suspiciously close to Cordelia's death. "Does the name Finley mean anything to you?" I pressed.

Scrunching her face in thought, the ghost shook her head. "No. I don't remember. There is a vague memory of love, of happiness, of secrecy...but that is all. No name. No face."

I repressed a frustrated sigh. "Do you suspect anyone—anyone at all?"

"I didn't think anyone wanted to hurt me. And now—now I fear what could happen to my family, my kingdom, while my murderer is free. I haven't known who to trust, so I've spoken to no one."

"Not even your brothers?"

Cordelia looked away, grief twisting her face. "I want to trust them, but Mother taught us cruelty. She was bitter about losing Father, and she was always harsh toward subjects who stepped out of line. She was always paranoid there could be another assassination attempt or a dangerous rebellion." She shrugged. "Being a spirit, lost and unable to find my way to the glade, has been confusing. I don't know why Fitz hasn't sent me on, and that scares me. I thought I'd be able to appear to anyone I wanted in death, as other spirits do, but I think all my emotions—the betrayal and confusion and fear—have made it difficult. I can only appear around you, because you bear my locket."

"Fitz said he feels awful, like he failed you for not recognizing there was a threat to your life," I explained. "He hasn't been able to send souls on since he lost you. Seeing you again might help him heal and replenish his magic."

"You would share the locket with him? You aren't lying?" Cordelia studied me warily. "How do I know you aren't the one who killed me, come back to marry and murder my brothers for their power next?"

"I promise."

Her nostrils flared. "Humans can lie."

"Please, Cordelia, you've haunted the castle, alone and lost, long enough. Let me help you."

Cordelia hesitated. "I want to find my murderer and bring that person to justice. Then my family will be safe, and I should feel secure enough for my spirit to strengthen and appear to anyone I wished, without needing my locket."

"How can I help?" I asked.

Cordelia inched nearer, until she was close enough to lay a frigid hand on my arm. "I can show you my death."

Before I could respond, an icy sensation slammed into me, and my breath caught in my lungs. I blinked and opened my eyes to find the castle garden in full bloom, gentle sunlight dancing on the flowers and shrubs. Someone—Cordelia—was humming, plucking blossoms and lifting them to her nose. I saw and felt everything as if I were her.

I sensed the rich fragrances of her growing bouquet, the twittering of nearby birds, and the soft whisper of her dress flowing around her legs as she strolled.

Cordelia turned, exiting the castle grounds to follow the same path Fitz and I took to the pond, where we trained in his magic, but soon she veered off, plunging into the forest.

A footstep behind her made her pause and start to turn. She opened her mouth as if to speak, but whatever name she'd meant to say died on her lips. Wide, calloused fingers seized her neck, stopping her progress. She opened her mouth to scream, but those fingers tightened, sparking agony. Spots danced across her vision as she thrashed, trying to kick and punch her attacker. Her mind scrambled for magic, and vines rose from the ground, twisting, seeking. But it wasn't enough. She was too weak, with her lungs burning, her throat screaming, and the blood vessels in her eyes bursting.

Darkness enveloped her, and she collapsed.

Nothing. No sound. No scent. No feelings at all. Only blackness.

Gradually, the world came into focus again, distant and hazy around the edges, like viewing it through a foggy window. Glancing down, Cordelia found her body sprawled across the ground, her crumpled bouquet scattered about her form, and her locket gone. There was no sign of her attacker, nothing but a gold button.

When I peered closer, I found the button wasn't perfect, but tarnished. Upon its face was a small design: a flight of birds soaring over tree branches that were nearly barren of leaves.

I blinked, and I was back in the hallway again, Cordelia watching me eagerly. "What did you see?"

I frowned. "Only what you already experienced. I couldn't see who killed you, though there was a gold button on the ground."

Cordelia ran an anxious hand through her hair. "I knew spirits could share their deaths with the living, but I'd hoped you would see it differently, not through my eyes. It was a man's hands, right? I'm sure of it."

"Perhaps," I said. "Do you know anything about that button? I assume it fell off your attacker's coat when you struggled. It had a design—birds over mostly bare trees. Does that mean anything to you?"

"It feels familiar," Cordelia whispered, her eyes sad. "But I don't know why. I cannot remember. I wish I could remember. Everything is so hazy..."

"What about where you were going, in the woods? Did you die near the place where you used to meet your lover?"

Cordelia blinked, as if in a daze. "There—there was a tree. And flowers. White ones. I don't remember more..."

Footsteps interrupted us, and Cordelia vanished in an instant. "Miss Blackford?"

I turned to find a horned guard approaching. "The queen grows impatient, I'm afraid," he said.

My heart lurched as I followed the man down the hallway and toward the ballroom, wondering what sort of punishment the queen would exact for my tardiness. The door swung inward, and I entered to the sounds of chatter cutting short. I scanned the table, finding Grace's worried expression, Holden's frown, and Fitz's dark look. Holding my head high, I strode forward in a way that I hoped projected confidence.

As I approached the empty chair beside Fitz, he stood and pulled it out for me, his tension visible in his stiff movements. I sat primly, meeting Queen Griselda's piercing stare without flinching. "You're late," she said. "Do you care to explain what was more important than joining your court in a timely manner?"

The room was stiflingly quiet. I could feel the weight of countless stares as I tried to keep from panicking. I opened my mouth, but Fitz spoke first.

"In preparing her to rule, I believe we've given her a full schedule. It's not her fault if her lessons or the time it takes to dress in the extravagant clothes you send cause her to be late for dinner."

The queen's gaze snapped to her son. "Excuse me? I think Elle can speak for herself."

Fitz leaned closer to me, resting an arm on the back of my chair and running his fingers through the strands of hair Lina had left to flow loosely over my shoulders. "As my wife, she doesn't need to defend her actions to you. And as your future queen, she deserves your respect."

Queen Griselda sniffed, leaning back in her seat and glancing between us. "Are you a mortal or are you a witch?" she asked me, her lips twitching.

"I don't know what you mean."

The queen smiled, and some of the fear leeched from my body. Conversations at the table resumed, and the tension in the room dissipated. "Well, you certainly have bewitched my son, whatever you are," she said lightly. She lifted her wineglass and took a long sip.

As the meal commenced, I let myself relax and scan the table for Reid. He met my gaze with a taut smile, one that reminded me Fitz was sitting next to me.

Noticing my look, Fitz pulled me closer to whisper in my ear. "Tomorrow I must go into town, but afterward we can find your father together."

I searched his face hopefully. "Even without my magic manifesting?"

"Yes," he said. "It's nearly been a month anyway. I won't make you wait any longer." He hesitated, a smile slowly forming. "Would you like to accompany me into town first?"

I smirked. "Of course. I would love to meet some of my future subjects."

"You say that as if you don't believe you'll be queen."

I turned back to my meal, pushing a bite of veal around my plate. "What if the land doesn't accept me, and I have no magic? Won't you be forced to find a new wife?"

Fitz ducked his head to meet my eyes. "I'm the crown prince and future king. I can change the law. I'll make sure the kingdom accepts you. You'll remain my wife and become my queen."

I raised my eyebrows. "That's not what you said at first."

"I've changed my mind about a lot of things." His eyes dipped toward my lips, and for a moment I thought he'd kiss me right there, in front of everyone. "Forgive me. I won't speak like that anymore. I know you can barely tolerate me."

I bit my lip to hold back a laugh. "Maybe I can tolerate you a little more now."

Queen Griselda pulled my attention away from Fitz as she stood, lifting her glass of fae wine. "It is time for an important tradition as we accept Princess Elle into our midst."

Beside me, Fitz tensed. "Mother," he murmured, his voice low yet full of warning, "it's not yet time."

She glanced at him sharply. "I am your queen, and I say it is far past time," she snapped.

Fitz seized my hand, and alarm burst through me. What was wrong?

"To prove that the land has accepted our new princess and will grant her its magic, it is time for Elle to drink of our wine." She turned to me, eyes gleaming, as a servant bustled forward with a tray. He set the wineglass before me, filled to the brim with golden liquid.

My head spun, and my eyes darted to Fitz. *I'm sorry,* he mouthed. His expression seemed etched from stone, but his eyes were full of worry.

"If our princess can drink the wine without effect, it proves that she is worthy," Queen Griselda went on.

The silence around us had transformed into clapping and stomping. A few eager courtiers had begun a chant. *Drink drink drink.*

"Go on, Princess," the queen urged, drinking deeply of her own wine.

My fingers clasped the stem. An awful, mingling sense of foreboding and desire warred within my chest. I wanted the wine. I didn't want it. I loved it. I hated it.

If the wine affected me, would I be cast out? Executed? Or would the queen merely laugh and allow her people to command me? Was I about to become their plaything, ridiculed and tormented?

Fitz's fingers squeezed around my free hand. *No, Fitz will protect me.*

Drawing on my courage, I lifted the glass to my lips and took a long gulp. The wine...tasted like honey. Sweet. Light.

Not like ashes and rot.

Hand shaking, I set down the glass, blinking at it in wonder.

Did this mean the land had accepted me?

Lifting my head, I smiled, making a show of how delicious the wine was.

"And that's enough," Fitz said sternly, standing and pulling me up with him. "My wife enjoyed the taste, proving she's been accepted by the land. She will not be your entertainment any longer. Goodnight."

"Forgive me," Fitz said, his jaw tense and his eyes narrow with barely restrained anger as he escorted me back toward our rooms. "I would have warned you had I known my mother would subject you to such a ridiculous, outdated custom. You need not prove yourself to anyone. The magic will come soon enough."

"I'm fine," I interrupted, making the prince pause and turn to me, confusion furrowing his brow. "I don't feel the effects at all...and the wine tasted...like honey. I wasn't pretending to like it. Does that...mean the land has accepted me? But where is my magic?"

Fitz shook his head, not in answer, but in wonder. "I'm not exactly sure, but I think this means your magic will manifest soon. Not that I've doubted the land would grant you power. Like I said, you're a queen."

I glanced away to conceal my blush.

"But you're quite sure you don't feel strange at all?" Reaching out, he brushed his fingers along my cheek.

I blinked, startled to find myself leaning into his touch. "I'm all right," I said hastily, stepping back.

To take the attention off the subject of fae wine, I began walking again and shared about my encounter with Cordelia, though I didn't include the vision she'd shown me. I considered adding the fact that I'd found her journal days before, but something made me hesitate. Cordelia was so frightened, as if she suspected there were listening ears everywhere in the castle. Somehow, I had the feeling both her journal and her vision were secrets she wanted to share only with me. At least for now.

When I stopped outside my door, I undid the locket's clasp and handed it to him. "Maybe she'll visit you."

Fitz's brow pinched. "Or maybe not. She thinks I failed her."

I set my hand on my doorknob. "We'll find who did it so she need never fear again, and then we'll bring her back, like you said last night."

"Right." Fitz's fingers closed over the locket. "I hope so."

As I watched him cradle the locket, my heart squeezed a little. I hoped I wasn't making a mistake letting him have it, but I knew it was no longer mine to keep. It was a miracle Queen Griselda hadn't yet seen it and ordered me executed for the suspected murder of her daughter.

But I still couldn't help feeling as if my chances to save my father were slipping away.

"Necromancy," I whispered.

Fitz glanced around the hallway, as if afraid the guards would overhear. Suddenly, I wondered if the practice was so secretive and rare that it was knowledge the fae royalty kept close, concealed from their subjects. "Don't speak of that here." He nodded toward his quarters. "Shall we go to bed?"

I smiled demurely. "Since you have the locket, I'll be safe alone tonight. I promise not to sneak out. Don't miss me too much."

Fitz's eyes flickered with warmth. "Goodnight, Blackford. If you grow cold tonight, my bed is only a hidden door away."

CHAPTER TWENTY-THREE

The morning sunlight was soft, gilding the crimson and orange leaves overhead as a team of sleek black horses led our coach along the winding dirt path leading toward Oakfell, Ashwood's capital city. Lina had clothed me in a comfortable but luxurious gown of scarlet adorned with seed pearls. She'd assigned another maid to braid my hair in a crown atop my head, winding a matching scarlet ribbon through my dark locks.

"You'll be comfortable for traveling and walking through the city, but you'll be dressed to remind the people who you are: their princess," Lina had declared with a wink.

I'd expected her to press me about last night's test, when Queen Griselda had forced me to drink the fae wine. Surely word had spread throughout the castle and the servants had gossiped. I had tossed and turned last night just thinking about it, caught in numerous dreams in which my magic finally flared to life. But each time I'd woke and tried to reach for—something, I'd felt the same. A magicless human.

All I could do was hope that Fitz was right and my magic would manifest soon. If I could wield my own magic, perhaps I could also perform necromancy without Fitz's help. Maybe I could save Father without having to steal from or trust my fae husband.

Maybe.

There were infinite maybes, all threatening to drive me mad with anticipation and hope.

And yet, until my magic made itself known, none of those maybes mattered.

Now, I slumped back against my seat in the coach, trying to banish the exhaustion and tension from my mind.

Beside me, Grace wore a simple yet lovely silver gown that contrasted with her gold braid. Holden held her hand unabashedly, pointing out the window and sharing eagerly about the different sights as we neared the city. Tucked into the forest, some of its buildings were set atop tree branches or within their trunks. I couldn't deny that Oakfell was breathtaking.

On my other side, Fitz remained quiet, his scarlet coat matching so perfectly with my outfit that I knew it was no coincidence. He didn't try to flirt or reach for my hand, but I supposed in the coach with only our siblings and his friend Kinsey, he didn't need to do anything for show. And I'd already made it clear how I felt about him.

Then why did my chest ache—only a little—when I noticed the distance between us, differing so sharply with the comfortable closeness my sister enjoyed with Holden?

Across from us, Kinsey leaned back, smiling contentedly. "Even after the injuries we sustained, we didn't lose a single soldier. Those who aren't fully mended yet will be soon. This is truly a day to celebrate." His eyes met mine. "Your other sisters didn't want to come?"

"Maggie hates social events," I said with a shrug. "She'd much prefer to stay indoors with a book."

"And Bridget and Isabel convinced some of the messengers to join them for a picnic on the castle grounds," Grace added.

Kinsey raised an eyebrow. "They prefer the company of human men to fae? That's unusual, I hear."

"Don't be so vain," Holden teased, gently kicking his friend in the shin.

Glancing at Fitz, I smiled demurely. "You're not all as irresistible as you believe."

Kinsey's gaze darted between Fitz and me. He started to laugh before catching himself and pretending to clear his throat.

"That's enough," said Holden as our coach swept into the city, leaving the dirt path for a cobblestone one. "Let's let Grace and Elle enjoy their first view of Oakfell."

I leaned forward to peer out the window with Grace, studying the buildings lining the road and the way the city merged seamlessly with nature. Mighty trees twisted toward the sky, their massive trunks housing shops full of every ware imaginable, from baked goods with tantalizing scents that made my stomach growl to trinkets crafted from wood and spun glass.

A second city rose overhead, comprised of buildings and homes erected around tree trunks or settled within their boughs. Bridges, ladders, and winding staircases connected them to one another and to the ground below. Vines and twisting branches grew within and around every structure. Curious birds and squirrels twitched their noses at every tempting scent of food, hopping on branches or even landing on citizens' shoulders, where they rested comfortably as if they hadn't a fear in the world. Leaves drifted lazily through the air and littered the cobblestone street.

Banners of ribbons and canvas featuring the Ashwood emblem—a bare-branched tree covering a full moon—extended from structure to structure, waving merrily. Everywhere, men, women, and children of every size and color shopped and talked and laughed. Performers and musicians stood on street corners, calling to onlookers. Couples swayed and danced to countless songs all mingling together. Sprites darted from shop to shop, playing innocent tricks on their owners, who merely laughed at their antics and offered small gifts of appreciation.

Everywhere, the mood was joyful, far from the dark greed and bloodlust I'd experienced within the castle walls. I didn't even see a drop of fae wine being consumed—this was a sincere celebration, the result of their recent victory. It was a moment of unity and goodwill, rather than division and malice.

When we passed a row of goblins muttering together, my stomach clenched, remembering the violent ones I'd seen within the Ashwood court. But they merely waved at our passing coach, taking off their hats and bowing low.

"They know better than to cause mischief on a day ordained for celebration by the queen herself," Holden explained, noticing the way I'd sat up stiffly and clenched my hands in my lap.

As the coach rumbled to a stop in the middle of a busy market square, the men exited first. Holden offered his hand to Grace, leading her in the direction of a cluster of musicians.

"I'll see you later," Kinsey said, dipping his head to Fitz and me.

"Where is he going?" I asked as I took Fitz's proffered hand and descended from the coach.

"He has family in the city," Fitz said, the first words he'd spoken almost all morning.

I studied him thoughtfully, noticing the way his blue eyes darted from person to person and shop to shop. "Are you all right?"

He smiled absently. "Yes. Where shall we go first?"

I inhaled deeply, relishing the scent of something sweet and buttery. "Could we follow that heavenly smell? Lina hardly let me eat breakfast this morning, she was so adamant on dressing me to look the part of a princess."

Fitz's eyes warmed as they scanned me from head to toe, and he drew me nearer, until I was pressed so close to him I could feel his heart beating rapidly against my chest. "You do look the part," he murmured, then paused, pulling away. Once again, I noticed the renewed distance keenly. "Is that all right to say, or is that too close to the subject we won't name?"

I couldn't help but laugh, and Fitz's grin grew in response, revealing his dimple. "You can say that." I hesitated before laying a hand on his chest, feeling his heart pound against my palm. Everything started to fall into place in my mind: his silence this morning, his racing heart, and what Lina had told me before, how the crown prince had been a quiet, reserved child. "Fitz...are you nervous?"

He frowned. "Talking to strangers has never come to me quite as naturally as it does for you." Tucking his hands into his pocket, he cleared his throat. "But I've attended this celebration countless times. Just never with you." He searched my face, the openness I'd seen in his expression when he'd been feverish once again present. Nerves and uncertainty and hope danced in his bright blue gaze. Whatever he saw in my own expression seemed to reassure him, for he turned, again taking my hand in his. "Come, I know a place you'll like for breakfast."

"Did you see Cordelia last night?" I whispered as we followed a line of fae toward a shop set within a large trunk, a hole in its back pluming a steady stream of chimney smoke.

"Briefly, and then she vanished." Fitz's face pinched. "I wasn't able to speak with her. She's shy, and seeing her that way..." He shook his head. "It's awful."

I squeezed his hand, threading my fingers through his. "Then we won't speak of it anymore, not while we're celebrating. Protecting your subjects and not losing a single soldier in the process? That's impressive."

My stomach growled as we stepped inside the shop, the aromas of earth and moss blending with that of sugar and freshly baked bread. Patrons' eyes widened when they noticed Fitz, and they swept into bows and curtsies, stepping aside to let him move to the front.

"Your Highness, thank you," a man said, clutching a small child's hand. Horns protruded above both his and his son's curly hair, and hooves poked out from beneath the hems of their trousers. Fauns. "I'm forever grateful my son can grow up in safety, thanks to your protection."

Fitz's smile was genuine, his eyes brightening. "The pleasure is mine."

Releasing my hand, he stepped forward to speak with the father and son. More fae crowded around, eager to offer their gratitude. Behind the counter, a man with skin the texture of bark and hair like moss urged me forward. He gestured to pastries arranged in enticing displays behind the glass. "Take your pick, please, my princess. A gift for you."

I glanced back at the other patrons waiting in line. "Don't trouble yourself for me. You can serve us in order."

"I insist," the man said, lowering his head.

Knowing better than to refuse fae generosity, I smiled and pointed to a cream-filled pastry artfully dusted with crystalline sugar. Grinning, the baker wrapped it in tissue paper and handed it to me.

The first bite was still warm and exploding with flavor. I closed my eyes in delight. "It's perfect. Thank you."

"I knew you'd love it," Fitz said, at my side again. He turned to the baker, his words full of ease and pleasantries despite his claim that he wasn't talented at socializing. He inquired about business and the man's family before taking my arm, bidding all goodbye, and guiding me back into the busy street.

"You had no trouble speaking with them," I pointed out as we strolled past more shops. A wizened woman called to us, promising to prophesize about our future and coming heirs. I blushed, and Fitz pulled me away.

"I had no trouble because I frequent Oakfell, and that particular shop."

It became clear the more time we spent walking the streets and browsing the shops: Fitz's people loved and revered him. While the courtiers tended to be cutthroat, leaving Fitz on edge, his subjects here in the city let him relax. He seemed happy to enjoy these simple moments of celebration with his people.

On a corner, musicians burst into song, one of the women shooting me a suggestive grin as she waved at us to dance. I accepted Fitz's hand, and he pulled me in. The players switched from a quick tune to something slower, more seductive. We swayed to the rhythm, the prince drawing me even nearer. An audience started to form, citizens who watched with knowing smiles, apparently happy for us. Unlike the jealous courtiers, these people seemed eager to accept me.

"I guess they should have a show," I murmured, and laid my head on Fitz's shoulder, breathing in his scent.

He laughed, low and rich, and the sound rumbled in my chest. I wondered if he knew I was lying—that I hadn't moved nearer for appearance's sake, but because I'd wanted to. My pulse galloped in my ears, nearly drowning out the music and chatter of the crowd. Fitz wrapped his arms around me, resting his hands low on my back, and I relished the nearness.

Maybe I could lie aloud to Fitz, but I couldn't lie to myself anymore. I was enjoying this time with him, and when the song ended and we stepped away from one another, my chest ached with longing.

We made our way further into Oakfell, exploring and talking with the locals. Fitz was constantly pulled in different directions, men and women and children wanting to thank him, ask him questions, or make small requests, but I didn't mind. Seeing him interact with his subjects with such kindness and attentiveness made my heart swell. Gone was the vicious, angry man who'd been so quick to kill in retaliation in his mother's court. In its place was the quieter, gentler man I was starting to learn was the *true* Fitz, the unguarded version who wasn't attempting to avenge his sister or expecting betrayal and death at every turn.

For lunch, we visited a tea shop where a winged woman practically tripped over herself to offer her finest meals and most prized beverages. Whenever she tried to gift us anything, Fitz insisted that he had enough already, and paid her generously.

Afterward, Fitz purchased caramel apples from a confectionary. We exited the shop laughing around gooey bites of our treats.

As we finished the apples and edged toward the streetside to discard the cores, Fitz turned to me, still chuckling at our mess. "Holden, Kinsey, and I used to eat those all the time."

I tossed my core, watching it land and roll alongside Fitz's.

Grinning, I turned toward my husband to find his gaze on my mouth. My heart picked up speed.

"You have some caramel right..." Fitz began, reaching with his thumb to wipe caramel from the corner of my mouth. His eyes widened as he brushed my lip, realizing what he'd done. "Here."

Our eyes locked. A tense moment passed in which I dared not move, scarcely even breathed.

"Forgive me," Fitz whispered, his thumb hovering over my lip. He traced it slowly, reverently, and I swallowed. His calloused fingers grazed my chin, sending trails of fire along my skin, and he lifted my face to meet his, dipping his closer until our mouths were mere inches away. Encouraged by my stillness, he leaned forward until our foreheads touched and we were breathing the same air. "But this is not for show."

He brushed his lips against mine almost tentatively, and I wondered how such gentle caresses could make my blood burn. Gasping, I moved my lips against his, all the invitation Fitz needed. He slid his hand to the back of my neck and buried his fingers in my hair, while his other grasped my waist, tugging me against him. When he ran his tongue along my bottom lip, I shivered and threw my arms around him, pulling him closer, deepening the kiss. The world fell away, until I was completely lost in the smell and feel and taste of him. He ran his hands down my back, trailing kisses down my neck and along my collarbone, whispering against my skin. Fitz pushed me against the shop wall, caging me in with his arms, shutting out the rest of the town so that he was all I could see, all I could think about.

"*Elle*," he murmured. "You drive me mad. Please tell me you aren't pretending."

Drawing back, I gazed into his bright eyes, now dark with want. I was breathless, but so was he. His skin was flushed, and I imagined mine was too. "I'm not pretending."

He swallowed, eyes scanning my face with such hope it nearly broke my heart. Fitz tucked a lock of hair behind my ear and arched an eyebrow, his mouth curving into a playful smile. "So you don't hate me in this moment?"

I shook my head, meeting his grin with a tremulous one of my own.

"Good," he said, snaking his arms around my waist and lowering his mouth to my ear. "Because you taste like caramel, and I'd like to kiss you again."

I laughed, lifting my face to meet his in another kiss, this one more tender than before, like Fitz was taking his time memorizing this moment. Memorizing me.

"Well, you aren't feeling shy now," came a teasing voice.

Fitz and I broke apart, and I hurriedly lifted my hand to my hair, trying in vain to fix my braid, already coming undone in loose strands around my face. Cheeks flushed, I met Holden's cheeky grin. Over his shoulder, Grace studied me with wide eyes, no doubt remembering our conversation about how much I'd hated Fitz's declaration of love. Or maybe she was shocked about our open display of affection, even if we were away from the crowd. It would have been considered scandalous even for a husband and wife back home in Riverton.

"I take it you've been enjoying the celebration?" Holden went on, looking for all the world like he'd won a bet.

Fitz shot him a dirty look, but Holden chuckled. "Did you need something?" Fitz demanded. "Or did you come to ogle us?"

Grace glanced at her feet, embarrassed.

"I wanted Grace to try a caramel apple," Holden said, lifting the core in his hand as if it were evidence. "We decided to toss them, and found you... Which, actually, is fortuitous, as I wanted your help with choosing a birthday gift for Kinsey. It's only a fortnight from now, and he did such a fine job of keeping our soldiers alive." With a grin, he tossed his apple core into the trees beyond us, and Grace followed his example.

"Of course," Fitz said, slipping his hand in mine and following Holden and Grace back into the street's flow of traffic.

The sun was dipping low in the sky, its light already fading. A pang of anxiety struck me as I thought of Fitz's promise to help me search for my father. What did our kiss mean for tonight? Could I ask Fitz about necromancy and trust he'd want to help me, or would he feel too betrayed when I confessed I'd married him with the intention of running away? Could I still steal from him, now that these new, vastly different feelings for him were burning through my veins?

A woman with doe-like eyes, fur-tipped ears, and white freckles on her tawny skin paused me in the street. "Oh, Princess," she exclaimed, sweeping out her brown skirt as she dipped into a curtsey. "Please, would you give me the honor of accepting my finest necklace? It would be my greatest pleasure to have one of my pieces grace your throat."

I hesitated, glancing between her and Fitz. Though the woman seemed to have kind intentions, I also knew that as a human, I couldn't be too careful. Refusing a gift, however, could also prove dangerous. I'd been taught all my life how fae could be vengeful and petty.

"It's all right," Fitz said, squeezing my hand. He cast me a significant look. "You can go with Fayette. She made some pieces for Cora. I'll return to fetch you when Holden and I are finished." Lifting my hand to his mouth, he pressed a kiss to my palm without withdrawing his gaze from mine. The intensity in his eyes made my blood heat all over again.

When Fitz bid me goodbye and followed Holden and Grace, Fayette ushered me up a winding set of stairs and into her shop, built within the branches of a purple-leafed maple. I had to duck to enter through her doorway, even though I was only a head taller than her. Within, open windows allowed leaves to drift inside and birds to flutter in and out, pecking at seeds left on the sills and side-eyeing patrons curiously.

"Please give me a moment," Fayette said. "It's in the back."

I browsed rows of glass cases, studying gold and silver earrings, necklaces, bracelets, and rings laden with every color gem imaginable. All were crafted with carefully wrought metal, some pieces twisted into beautiful likenesses of branches, others shaped like leaves or butterfly wings and etched with tiny veins. They were delicate and lovely.

"Oh, Elle!" Isabel's voice startled me, and I glanced up to see my youngest sister blushing and giggling. "You're here too." She extended a hand to show off a twinkling silver bracelet. "Isn't it lovely?"

I frowned, glancing around the shop. "Are you here alone? I thought you were at the castle with Bridget."

"Alone?" Isabel scoffed. "Of course not." She pointed to the far corner, where messengers dressed in navy coats edged in gold were browsing other cases, one holding Bridget's arm.

"You shouldn't let these men spoil you," I scolded, striding over to confront the men. "Unless you're engaged, such gifts are too much. What sort of message are you sending?"

Isabel groaned as she trailed me. "You sound like Mother."

I whirled on her, dropping my voice to a whisper. "I'm not talking about etiquette, Izzy. I'm speaking of *caution*. They may not be fae, but they grew up among them. You shouldn't throw yourself at them."

My sister crossed her arms and glared. "You have an awful lot of gall, criticizing me after you *threw yourself* at the crown prince."

"One of us had to marry him, and it wasn't going to be Grace," I snapped. "She's sacrificed all her life for us."

"We're only having some fun," Isabel protested as I turned, stomping toward the messengers.

"Bridget and Isabel are most thankful, but I'm afraid they cannot accept your gifts and must return to the castle," I said.

A man with short ginger hair, still cradling Bridget's arm, turned first, blinking in surprise when he saw me standing before him. He dipped hastily into a bow, making Bridget giggle. She probably thought it strange to see everyone fawn over her sister.

Then the other messenger turned, and it was my turn to be shocked. "Reid?"

"I hope it's all right if an old family friend spoils your sisters," Reid said quickly, his smile warm. He glanced over my shoulder, finding Isabel and no one else. "Did you come into the city unaccompanied? We could escort you back to the castle."

I shook my head. "No, the shop owner has a gift for me. Fitz will be back to fetch me soon."

"Could I speak to you?" Reid asked, leaning forward and pitching his tone low. "Alone?"

His friend and my sisters exchanged confused glances, but they didn't protest as Reid grasped my arm and drew me into a second, isolated room of the shop. Isabel shot me a dark glance, eyes burning with envy. When had she set her eyes on Reid?

"I'm sorry about the other night."

"Oh, it's fine; of course I didn't want you to linger once Fitz saw us," I whispered, shaking off his apology.

His eyes darted to my neck, and his brows drew together. "Did he take your locket? Has he been cruel to you, since he saw us wandering outside the grounds?"

"No, not at all," I explained. "I gave the locket to him, so he can see his sister again. Cordelia's locket strengthens her spirit, and she kept appearing to me when I wore it."

Reid's expression darkened. "You mean she was haunting you?"

"No, I was able to speak with her. She wanted me to help find her killer. She even showed me the day she died, but all her spirit saw after her death was a gold button that must have torn from her murderer's coat when she tried to fight him off. But as I'm sure you can already tell, that was unhelpful. Everyone wears gold in the castle. You and the other messengers. The courtiers. Even Fitz himself."

Reid shook his head. "But why wouldn't Princess Cordelia's spirit appear for her own brother?"

I shrugged helplessly. "She's been so afraid..." I began, but Reid froze, face blanching of all color.

He caught my arm, leaning close. His whisper was scarcely audible even with his mouth inches from my ear. "Remember what I said before? I didn't give you all the details. Last year, before the princess was found dead, Prince Fitz and Princess Cordelia had a fight. The prince was envious of his sister's magic. She was powerful, and he was struggling to fill his role as heir. They argued. I'd delivered a message to Prince Holden that night, you see, so I was in their hallway, passing her rooms, when I overheard them."

"What are you saying?" I hissed, but my blood was already going cold.

Reid was quiet for a moment. "You've seen how harsh and violent the crown prince can be."

The storm he'd unleashed in the ballroom flashed through my mind. I felt warm blood drenching my dress, saw the man's thrashing body, and smelled scorched flesh all over again.

"What if there's a *reason* Princess Cordelia's ghost won't linger near Prince Fitz, even if she can't remember who hurt her?" Reid went on, worry lacing his tone.

Cordelia's words echoed in my head. The way she'd seen her brother grow crueler under their mother's encouragement. Her fear... Her reluctance to trust her own siblings.

"Just...be careful, Elle." Reid drew back, straightening when we heard the squeak of a door and Fayette bustle out of a back room. "And let me know if you want to look for your father again tonight," he added softly, before rejoining his friend and my sisters in the other room.

"Here you are," Fayette said proudly, holding out a delicate white gold chain dripping with diamonds. The necklace wound in a twisting, stunning pattern that mimicked a tree branch. Interspersed among the diamonds were small pieces of gold crafted to look like leaves.

"Thank you," I breathed as Fayette fastened it around my neck.

My stomach clenched and my mind whirled, preoccupied with the information Reid had given me. But it didn't prove anything. I'd seen Fitz interact with his subjects today, happy and at peace. He'd confessed to cruelty and pride, though he also seemed to show a genuine desire to change.

It was Cordelia's lover, I thought. *The messenger Finley, or someone else the queen wouldn't have approved.*

As the shop door opened and Fitz himself strolled in, eyes alighting when he caught sight of me, I smiled back. *Reid is wrong.*

"I'll give you two some privacy," Fayette said with a wink, and vanished into the back room once more, the door clicking shut behind her. Only Reid, his friend, and my sisters remained in the other half of the shop, murmuring and laughing together as the girls swooned over various pieces of jewelry.

"You look lovely," Fitz said, his eyes sweeping over me. "But you always do." Affection shone in his blue eyes, piercing my soul. Slowly, he withdrew Cordelia's locket from his coat pocket. "And as beautiful as that necklace is on you, I want you to have my sister's locket too. I know how much it means to you—and how it connected you to your father. Perhaps it will help us find him tonight."

"Oh," I murmured, shocked that Fitz would return it so freely. I'd feared that I would never see it again. "Thank you."

I turned to let him clasp it around my neck, his fingertips lingering on my skin.

My doubt made me queasy, refusing to disperse from my whirling mind. Could the same man who had been so tender toward me, who seemed to genuinely grieve his sister, also be the one who'd viciously strangled Cordelia?

When I turned, whispering my thanks, a furrow appeared between Fitz's brows. "Are you all right?"

"Where are Holden and Grace?" I asked, hoping to distract him from my distress.

"There was another shop they wanted to explore before they meet us at the coach." He glanced through a nearby window, where the way the sunshine slanted into the shop warned us evening was fast approaching.

"We will need to leave soon, but..." He stepped nearer, lowering his voice as he searched my face earnestly. "I wanted to talk about earlier."

I drew in a shuddering breath. I was too full of anxiety and uncertainty. Even if I didn't want to believe Reid's words, I still worried about tonight. Still wondered how Fitz would react if he knew I'd married him in hopes of using his magic and fleeing. "I don't think now is a good time."

The light dimmed in Fitz's eyes, and he swallowed, throat bobbing. "I know you weren't lying when you said you weren't pretending. Have you changed your mind?"

Fayette returned, sweeping toward where Reid, his friend, and my sisters browsed. She paused before she passed Fitz and me, dipping into a quick curtsey before asking the prince, "Doesn't she look lovely?" When she noticed Cordelia's locket, her eyes widened. "And she wears another piece of mine, I see. I remember that one..."

"She does," Fitz said, his eyes never leaving mine. "And the locket she wears belonged to Princess Cordelia."

"Of course," Fayette said, clasping her hands. "My sincerest condolences, Prince Fitz."

"We didn't come to demand gifts from our subjects," Fitz went on, turning to the shop owner. "I know you'll refuse payment for that necklace, so let me purchase another piece for the princess."

"Oh—you're too generous..." Fayette began.

"I insist." Fitz turned to me expectantly. I stepped toward a glass case, my eyes scanning rows of glittering jewelry. It was difficult to focus on anything, but a simple bracelet of intertwining yellow and white gold caught my eye, so I pointed to it.

As Fayette gushed about the beauty of my choice, Fitz withdrew his bag of coins from his coat pocket for at least the dozenth time that day. But this time, something fell from his pocket, clinking to the hardwood floor. He muttered a curse under his breath. At first, I thought the flash of rolling gold was a loose coin, but as it spun and stopped at my feet, I was able to study it better.

I knelt to pick it up, my breath trapped in my lungs. It was a tarnished gold button, with tree branches almost completely bare of leaves and a cluster of birds taking flight.

The same pulsing thrill that sometimes emanated from Cordelia's locket met my fingers as I lifted the button, numbly offering it to Fitz.

Fitz's charm was a *gold button*. The gold button that had been at the site of Cordelia's murder.

The knowledge collided with Reid's earlier revelation, and I thought I'd collapse from shock right there. I forced my face into rigid solemnity, pretending I didn't sense the magic, didn't suspect anything. Still, there was a sharpness in Fitz's eyes as he took the button from me, as if he could read my mind.

My mouth was dry as Fitz finished paying for the bracelet and turned to clasp it around my wrist. I hoped he didn't see the way my hand trembled.

How could Fitz have killed his own sister? He'd been devastated when he spoke of her loss. But what if what I'd seen hadn't been grief? What if it was guilt? Perhaps that's why he refused to talk much about her—he couldn't lie, and he couldn't risk being found out. Maybe he could claim, truthfully, that he'd failed her, because he'd failed her in the worst way of all: attacking and killing her.

The memory of our kiss seared through me. I didn't want to consider these new implications, didn't want doubt to take root in my heart, but I couldn't disregard what Reid had said.

Perhaps my first inclination to distrust and hate Fitz had been right.

But I couldn't accept this as fact, not yet. My heart ached, crying out that I had to be mistaken.

My mind flitted back to Cordelia's journal entry about her secret meeting place with her lover, and then again to where she'd died, so close to that location. *A tree. White flowers.*

Somehow, I believed that if I could just find the meeting place, I would find my answers.

It was time to leave. Time to find out if I could trust Fitz—or if I'd been duped.

CHAPTER TWENTY-FOUR

"I want to ensure my sisters return safely," I announced, staring at the sparkling colors of gold and silver enveloping my wrist.

Fitz turned to where my sisters stood with the messengers. "I see," he said softly. "You don't trust your old family friend to get them home safely?"

I stared at Isabel, who was leaning on Reid's arm, laughing loudly at something he'd said. As if sensing my gaze, Reid turned. I dropped my eyes hastily, afraid he'd notice the fear and shock on my face and give everything away. Fitz couldn't know, not now. "Well, he didn't inform Grace or me that he'd be bringing them here, and I'm sure you've already noticed that my youngest sisters aren't always easy to keep an eye on. I worry about them."

"Elle—" Fitz started, reaching for my chin. Those calloused fingers scraped my skin, and I had to repress a shudder as I remembered the feel of the callouses against Cordelia's neck, strangling the life from her. He lifted my face gently, peering into my eyes. "Are you all right? Are you nervous about finding your father?"

"Yes," I blurted out. "Please, while it's still light out, I want to walk back with my sisters. Walking always clears my head. I'll meet you there."

Fitz pulled back. "All right," he said. I'd feared he'd argue about his need to protect me. "I'll see you soon. But I promise, there is no need to fear." He pressed his lips to my forehead, and I closed my eyes, wishing I could feel the magic I'd experienced when we'd kissed only minutes ago. Now, there was only terror and the ache of betrayal.

I strode across the shop toward my sisters. "It's time to go. It's growing late," I said, interrupting Bridget as she gushed to Fayette about a necklace. The shopkeeper glanced up in surprise, before her eyes darted to the window in understanding.

"You're not Mother," Isabel whined, crossing her arms and scowling at me. She turned to their red-headed friend. "Please, Daniel, tell her you and Reid can keep Bridget and me safe. You know how to defend yourselves in these woods, no matter the time of day," she added proudly.

The man my sister so brazenly called by his given name turned scarlet, dipping his head deferentially toward me. "I think we should listen to the princess."

Isabel shot me a glare and tugged on Reid's arm. "You're just jealous we might have jewelry as fine as yours if we stay long enough to purchase some," she bit out.

"I can hold any pieces you're interested in," Fayette offered helpfully.

"Elle is right," Reid interjected, his gaze meeting mine, seeing the terror lurking in my expression. "It's growing late. Only a fool enters the forest at night when he needn't do so." His eyes tracked Fitz as he slipped out of the shop before turning back to me. "Are you walking with us?"

"Yes," I said, plastering a smile on my face. "I wanted more time with my sisters today."

Isabel rolled her eyes and huffed something under her breath.

As the five of us exited the shop, bidding Fayette a thankful goodbye, I was relieved to find that Fitz was nowhere to be seen. I hoped that meant he'd already returned to the coach to wait for Holden, Grace, and Kinsey.

While we joined the crowd flowing toward the city gate, Reid fell into step beside me, leaving my sisters to stroll on either side of Daniel, chattering away, oblivious to my distress. "Are you all right?" he murmured. His eyes snagged on Cordelia's locket, hanging freely outside my dress, and I wondered if it would have been wiser to tuck it away. Would a stranger on the street recognize it for the magical item it was?

I lowered my voice as I shoved the locket down my bodice. "Fitz's charm is a *gold button*, Reid. The same one that was by Cordelia's body."

Reid's eyes widened in horror. "I'd hoped what I overheard was nothing," he breathed.

"But I need to be sure," I went on, taking his arm, giving me an excuse to dip my head close to his. I was terrified that fae ears might overhear my whispers, but even more afraid of failing to share this critical information with my friend. There was no time to lose. "I'm going to look for Cordelia's meeting place with her lover."

Reid frowned.

"I need to *know*, Reid."

Something desperate must have shone in my eyes or rang out in my voice, for Reid's expression turned solemn, and he nodded.

We'd reached the gates, and when Daniel started to lead my younger sisters on the wide path the rest of the crowd followed, I gestured toward a narrower, more abandoned dirt road winding through the forest. Daniel frowned. "The sun will set soon. Shouldn't we be taking the faster route?"

Reid shook his head. "Elle is right. We'll be quick, but we need to follow this path. Trust me."

Bridget and Isabel cast confused glances between Daniel and Reid, but when Daniel relented, following Reid and me onto the narrow path, my sisters remained quiet. Like me, they knew Reid would keep us safe.

As we neared the part of the path that forked toward the pond, I plunged into the forest, drawing anxious cries from my sisters.

"It's nearly sunset," Bridget fretted. "What are you doing?"

"I'll be quick," I said, studying the trees, searching for anything familiar from the vision Cordelia had shared.

Behind me, cracking sticks and ruffling leaves signaled that my companions had followed. My heart pounded, and the locket started to burn.

I inhaled sharply, remembering how it had guided me to Cordelia's journal. *I'm close.*

Winding around a particularly large stump, I paused when a flash of white caught my eye. I staggered to a stop, drinking in the sight of row upon row of lovely white daisies growing thickly beneath a large, old oak.

"This is it," I breathed, rushing forward despite continued protests from my sisters. Even Daniel was muttering something, perhaps thinking I'd lost my mind.

I circled the tree, studying its rough bark, seeking any sign. Some hiding place for letters that might reveal something more, perhaps. Or any other clue that would point me toward Cordelia's murderer. *Because it can't be Fitz. It was Cordelia's lover—probably Finley.*

I staggered backward, moving deeper into the woods to try to see the tree from a different vantage point. My boot struck something hard and solid, and with a muffled cry, I fell.

"Are you all right?" Reid called, running toward me.

But as I stood, brushing leaves off my dress, my attention locked on the object I'd tripped over. My stomach lurched with revulsion. Bones. Bones, clothed in the ratty shreds of a royal messenger's uniform. My body went hot and then cold.

Isabel and Bridget shrieked, clinging to one another in fear. I couldn't hear them clearly, not with the ringing growing in my ears. My mind buzzed as Reid and Daniel studied the skeleton and cried out when they confirmed—from the belongings they plucked from the threadbare coat's pockets—what I'd already feared. The bones belonged to Finley.

Finley, whom I'd hoped was Cordelia's lover. And maybe he had been, until he was killed.

Had Fitz been the one to discover the lovers together? Had he murdered Finley and then, after heated arguments with Cordelia, killed her too?

I was sick. Sick with disgust. Sick with horror. All my hopes of finding another answer were dashed.

Tears burned my eyes. I could no longer ignore that all the signs were pointing toward Fitz.

I blame myself, he'd said. And Cordelia's journal had warned me: *Fitz might even agree with Mother and kill the man himself.* It seemed that he'd gone on to kill his sister too.

Murderer. Murderer. Murderer. My mind was screaming at me.

And if Fitz was capable of killing his sister, what did that mean about our relationship? The kiss, the looks, the tender caresses—I wondered what it all had meant to him. Fitz couldn't lie, but the fae were notorious tricksters. If he'd murdered his own sister in a jealous rage over her magic, had he spent all this time getting close to me to gain my trust and then take his revenge for deceiving him? Was this all about fury and vengeance?

Was anything we'd shared real?

Maybe I'd been wrong to start to trust him, to believe that seeing him interact so graciously with his subjects meant he was turning his back on his cruel ways. Maybe I'd been a fool to assume his gentle actions meant anything. All along, he was as violent and cruel and untrustworthy as his mother. Worse, because he'd turned those traits on his own flesh and blood.

And my family and me? We weren't safe, not even in the castle with the family that had vowed to protect us.

I turned to Reid, speaking through lips that felt startlingly cold and numb. "Can we trust Daniel?"

My friend gave me a single, sharp nod. "Absolutely."

"Good. When we return to the castle, you must help my mother and sisters pack. Can you secure a coach and leave with them?"

Reid hesitated, exchanging a glance with Daniel. "The guards might stop me."

"Pretend it's official business. Lie. Be convincing. They'll trust you as a royal messenger. Just get them out," I pled frantically. "Grace is with Holden, whom I pray I'm not wrong in trusting. But I'll look after her."

Reid glanced at me sharply. "And what of you and Grace? If you aren't coming with us, what do you plan to do?"

I clenched my hand, feeling the bracelet Fitz had fastened about my wrist slide against my skin. "We'll leave too, but first, I'm going to confront him."

"Is that—" Reid began, but I shot a dark look at him.

"I came here to find Father," I choked out. "If I can't stay any longer, let me at least have justice against the man allowing his spirit to suffer. If I can accuse him before Holden and Kinsey, or even the queen herself, I'm sure they'll want retribution for Cordelia. They'll punish him. I can't go until..." I swallowed. "Until I settle this."

I jogged toward my sisters. "You, Maggie, and Mother are leaving with Reid tonight."

Bridget froze. "What? What's happening? Where are we going? Why did you bring us out here to see this—this—" She choked on a frightened sob.

Isabel seemed too frightened for words, clinging to her sister.

"It's not safe in the castle," Reid said, coming up behind me. I was grateful he didn't expound on that, didn't send more fear into my sisters' hearts with a bloody tale of the murderous man whose roof we'd been living under. "I'm going to take you somewhere safe, and Elle will find Grace and join us later." He glanced at me, his gaze piercing. "Right, Elle?"

I gave a single, sharp nod, praying it was a promise I could fulfill. "Yes." I swallowed. "I need you to hurry. I'll explain more later, but you must trust me and not waste time on questions."

Faces pale, my sisters complied, hurriedly following Reid and Daniel's lead back to the path, until we were all half-running. Twigs snapped beneath my boots, and branches snagged in my hair and scraped my face. By the time the castle loomed ahead, the fading crimson sunlight making it shine like a beacon of warning, sweat sheened Bridget's and Isabel's faces.

"You'll be safe with Reid," I panted.

"I'll come too," Daniel offered.

"No," Reid cut in. "The fewer, the better. They never send two messengers together, so both of us would draw more suspicion from the guards. You'll better help if you stay behind and make excuses for me. Tell our friends I was sent away on business." He looked up. "And perhaps right now, you can chat with the guards. Distract them so we can slip into the castle without prying questions. Especially with Elle returning on foot and not with the princes."

Daniel nodded. "Of course."

As Daniel sauntered toward the guards clustered in the courtyard, loudly sharing about the day's celebration, Reid guided my sisters and me to the back entrance near the stables, unguarded at this time of day, likely because so much of the castle had emptied. No one stopped or questioned us as we entered the halls and traced our way up the winding staircase, nodding amiably at fae and human servants and pretending all was fine as we swept past posted guards. When we entered the hallway that housed our quarters, Isabel reached for my hand.

"Elle—"

"Hush," I said, squeezing her fingers. I was too conscious of the nearby guards. My pulse thundered in my head. "I'll meet everyone in your rooms in a few minutes."

She nodded, blinking rapidly as if fighting back tears. Bridget was silent and pale at her side. As much as it hurt my heart to see my little sisters afraid, I was also glad for it. Their fear would keep them alert and cautious, for once taking all the warnings they'd grown up with to heart.

Following Reid, they scurried toward their quarters, and I approached mine, breathing my first full gasp of air in many long minutes as my door clicked shut.

I'd left my dagger behind today—overly, foolishly confident that my outing with my husband would be safe and enjoyable. It waited for me in my nightstand drawer. The feel of it in my hand instantly brought me some relief. Against Fitz and his magic, it would do little good. But it was better than nothing.

"Elle Blackford?" Cordelia's voice pierced the silence, and I turned to find her standing behind me, her form solid in the waning daylight. The power of her locket had strengthened her even more, dulling the appearance of the bruises on her neck and the burst blood vessels in her eyes. Her ghost was looking more as she would have in life, vibrant and lovely, her gaze shining with color and spirit, her neck a smooth column of skin. Her voice was no longer raspy and strangled, but strong and musical. "Did you learn anything for me?"

"I hoped I'd find you here," I said gently, trying and failing to smile. "I did...but it's going to hurt to hear."

Cordelia laughed mirthlessly. "It hurt to die. I think I can handle this."

I stepped closer, searching her face. "Do you remember arguing with Fitz before your death?"

The ghost's expression darkened, her eyes clouding over. "I remember him being envious of my magic's strength, especially when it came to communing with spirits. He was insecure about his growing responsibilities, and fearful he wouldn't be the leader he needed to be. I told him it would be simple, that the power would come naturally. It's in his blood." She smiled wistfully. "He was angry though, and we argued. I said things I regret." She hesitated, trying to understand the look on my face. "Are you saying...*he* did it?"

"Cordelia," I whispered, "he carries the gold button we saw beside your body. It's his charm, is it not?"

Cordelia's hand flew to her neck. "I never knew what his charm was. It's habitual for us to keep those items such a great secret that even our closest loved ones never know." She frowned. "I remember something. There were gold buttons on an old coat of Father's that Mother kept. Maybe Fitz took a button to remember him by, something that would be easy to carry and imbue with magic, and something that would also hold sentimental value. Those are the sorts of objects that are simplest to fill with our power." Tears glazed her beautiful brown eyes, as if the implication of my words were just now sinking in. "Are you sure?"

"I saw it myself. It fell from his pocket, and when I picked it up, I could feel its magic. And the man I thought might have been your lover—Finley...well, I found his body near your meeting place. It can't all be a coincidence. Do you remember anything?"

Cordelia stepped back, swaying on her feet. "No, I don't remember, but... If you saw that button... I-I never would have imagined..." she murmured, as if to herself. Panic and pain warred with the doubt in her eyes.

"Listen," I said, hating myself for cutting into this moment, when I knew Cordelia needed to process and grieve. But I had to protect my family. "I'm going to give my locket to my sister Isabel. It's not safe for us to stay here. Your brother promised us protection in exchange for marriage, but now I know he can't be trusted. I'm sending my mother and sisters away—tonight. Can you defend them against the ghosts wandering the forest?"

Cordelia hesitated. "You're staying?"

I fisted my hands. "I'm going to accuse him. Holden and Kinsey and your mother must know what he did. And then Grace and I will run."

"Be careful," the ghost said.

"Can you protect my family?" I demanded.

Cordelia lifted tear-stained cheeks, setting her jaw. "I can, and I will."

"Thank you," I breathed as her form vanished, melting into nothingness.

"Ellie, are you sure?" Mother whispered when we all gathered in Isabel and Bridget's shared rooms. As I'd requested, everyone had packed light, only filling bags they could carry so they wouldn't draw further notice by requesting the servants' help.

Maggie hugged her arms to her chest, watching our youngest sisters' attempts to conceal their growing fear. "Queen Griselda and Prince Fitz gave their word that they'd protect us, and the forest isn't safe after dark."

"I know how to defend against the spirits," Reid promised, his expression solemn. His dark eyes flitted from me to my mother. "And though they gave their word, the fae are masters at finding loopholes in their promises. It's safest if you leave."

"What exactly did you discover?" Maggie asked, brow scrunched. "Why all this hurry and secrecy? We always knew it would be dangerous here. Isabel told us about the body you found in the forest, but I don't understand how that's any worse than the death we've already witnessed."

"Things are different now—far more dangerous than we expected. You must trust me. Reid will get you to safety. Grace and I will join you as soon as we can, and I'll explain everything."

Mother clutched my wrist, her eyes swimming with worry. "I know I've asked much of you and Grace, wanting you to watch over your younger sisters, but don't do anything rash. Please."

I crushed her into an embrace. "I promise. Listen to Reid, Mother. You'll be safe, and we'll all be together soon."

I turned to my sisters, hugging each in turn. When I reached Isabel, who was now sobbing openly, I unclasped my locket and slipped it around her neck. Her eyes widened as she blinked away her tears. "Wh-what is this?" she hiccuped.

"It belonged to Father," I explained. I considered sharing that it had also been Princess Cordelia's and would attract ghosts, but decided against it. Isabel was already terrified, and I didn't want her to refuse the locket, not when it would allow Cordelia to protect them. Instead, I added, "Let it give you courage until we're together again."

Isabel pulled away, nodding and wiping at her cheeks.

"We'll tell the guards I'm your escort to Riverton," Reid told my family, "but let me do the talking when we reach the gates. I'll say you have a friend back home who is deathly ill—one who couldn't take you in, but who is dear enough you'd want to say goodbye."

Mother and my sisters exchanged uncertain glances.

"Trust me, I'll convince them," Reid insisted. "And hurry."

I watched them leave, shuffling through the doorway. Reid paused, glancing back one final time. "I don't like leaving you here."

"I'll be all right," I vowed. "Besides, I can't leave without Grace."

As the door clicked shut, I waited in Isabel and Bridget's rooms, striding to the windows to watch my family slip through the courtyard and enter the stables. Moments later, a coach rolled forth, creaking to a stop at the back gates. Seconds passed like years as I listened to my throbbing pulse, hoping they'd be able to exit before Fitz's coach returned through the opposite gate.

At last, the gates squealed open, and the coach rumbled over the cobblestones and onto the forest road. I'd barely sighed my relief when the sounds of more hooves and wheels drew my attention. I couldn't see the opposite gate from this vantage point, but I knew those noises heralded the return of Holden, Grace, Kinsey, and Fitz.

Spinning on my heel, I left to confront my husband.

CHAPTER TWENTY-FIVE

I charged out the doors just as Fitz's coach rolled into the courtyard, its gates open wide to the darkening forest beyond. My boots crunched on the cobblestones as a cool breeze stirred through the strands of hair that had fallen free of my braids. The driver pulled up on the reins, forcing the horses to a sudden halt.

"Princess! Is everything all right?" he called, but I ignored him. My skirts swished around my ankles as I strode for the already opening door.

Fitz leapt out, Kinsey on his heels. On the opposite side, Holden and Grace scrambled from the coach, my sister calling frantically when she saw the expression on my face.

"Elle." The look in Fitz's bright eyes was pure concern. He reached for me, and I gritted my teeth. For someone who couldn't lie, the fae prince was a master at deception.

"What happened?" Grace called, her footsteps rushing around the coach.

Trusting that Holden and Kinsey would take my side, I didn't hesitate to slip my blade from the sheath on my thigh, shoving the point beneath Fitz's throat.

His eyes widened before darkening, churning storm clouds raging within their depths. "And here I thought you married me for my power, so at least my life wouldn't be at risk." He smiled grimly.

"You murdered her," I bit out, tears swimming in my vision. My hand trembled.

Frozen in shock, Kinsey didn't step between us. Out of the corner of my eye, I noticed Grace and Holden stumble to a stop, taking in the scene before them. Not even the driver or the guards at the gate moved. There wasn't a sound but my shaking breaths and the whispering wind, like the whole world had stilled to hear my proclamation.

"I don't know what you mean," Fitz said, forcing calm into his words despite the shock and anger I could see brimming in his eyes. Shadows swirled at the edges of my sight, and I feared he was already calling upon his magic. Maybe he'd strike me dead like the courtiers in the ballroom, before I had the chance to tell his brother and friend what he'd done.

"You murdered your sister," I hissed, pressing my blade closer, until it nicked his perfect neck. A drop of blood bloomed. "And Finley. I found his body! You killed them both."

Fitz blinked. "Finley? The messenger?"

"Cora and Finley?" Holden gasped. "Elle, what are you saying? What's happened? What would make you think Fitz would kill them? Lower your blade and tell—"

"Cordelia was strangled to death by *his* hands!" I interrupted.

Lightning slashed overhead, and wind tugged at my skirts. The electricity in the air made the hairs on the back of my neck stand on end, but I refused to be cowed by Fitz's magical display. I stared into his eyes, churning with fury and hurt, emotions that matched my own in their intensity.

"What proof do you have?" Kinsey demanded.

"He loved Cora," Holden protested in nearly the same breath, talking desperately over his friend. "You're mistaken."

"Elle," Grace murmured, a warning edging her tone. "Please put the dagger down."

"Pull back, Elle," Kinsey growled, stepping nearer. "This is out of line. Lower your weapon. Killing the crown prince will spell your own end."

"I suppose if I must die," Fitz cut in, trying and failing to appear casual, "at least it's at my own wife's lovely hands."

I ignored them both. Instead, I glared into Fitz's eyes. "You can't lie," I ground out. "Which means you *cannot deny* that your charm is a gold button, marked with tree branches and birds. Is it not?"

Fitz swallowed. "Blackford, what does this have to do with—"

"Answer the question: yes or no."

Fitz's eyes darted over my shoulder, meeting his brother's confused expression. "Yes, it's true."

"Father's coat button? Like the one we found by Cora's body?" Holden said, his words trembling. "Fitz, what is she saying?"

"And you made me trust you," I said, a single hot tear sliding down my cheek. My breath smoked in the air, swirling between us. When had it grown so cold? Thunder rumbled, low and deadly. The world tasted of electricity and salt, of ash and betrayal.

But it wasn't Fitz's lightning dancing in the air, not this time. I felt the power coursing through my blood, the current tingling through my body. This was *my* magic.

Fitz's days of training made it easy—so easy—to command it. It was an extension of my emotion, my will, my thought. Staggering back, I unleashed a cry, letting the lightning strike in a jagged line, straight for Fitz.

He snarled, lifting his arms to fight back. Another bolt of lightning flashed, colliding with mine. Clouds swirled around us, blocking off my view of the others, until it felt as if the entire world only consisted of my treacherous husband, our dark powers, and me.

I was dimly aware of Kinsey and Holden shouting, of Grace screaming.

Rain lashed at my cheeks as I reached for the lightning again, collecting the electricity in a flashing ball of gold and purple. It burned across my vision, bright and furious, hot as flame. It slammed toward his chest, but he dodged it with speed and grace.

I barely had time to cry out as he bolted forward, charging me. My dagger was out of my hand before I'd even consciously thought to throw it. It flashed silver in the growing shadows, a dimmer version of my lightning. Fitz dove to evade it, rolling across the cobblestones before springing up again, seizing my wrists.

Crying out, I flailed against him, but his grasp was firm. He swung my arms behind my back, trapping me. My lungs refused to take in air as his eyes burned into mine.

The storm died as swiftly as it had begun, leaving only a few roiling clouds overhead. Lightning continued to flash intermittently, silent yet threatening.

"I didn't kill her, Blackford," Fitz said firmly, never breaking eye contact with me.

I choked on a sob, but I couldn't tell if it stemmed from anger or sadness. Or both.

Fitz leaned in close. "I *swear* it."

Before I could make sense of anything, his gaze darted over my shoulder, eyes widening. He shoved me to the ground, my bones jarring with the impact. His body hovered over mine.

Strands of hair splayed across my face, I stared up at him in horror, but the prince wasn't attacking. His attention wasn't even on me.

I blinked up to see a ghost lurching toward us, blood streaming from its neck, its glazed eyes murderous. Kinsey whirled, throwing himself between Grace and the dead man at the same moment that he drew his sword, slicing into him. The spirit fell, landing with a thud as if he'd died all over again, though no new blood welled.

Fitz pulled away, enough that I could sit up, gaping. Night had fallen and the spirits were emerging in a whole host from the trees. Overhead, the grey clouds still loomed, flashing forked tongues of lightning.

The crown prince's gaze darted back to mine. This time, his anger seemed dimmer, replaced with a well of sadness. "Is that what you truly think of me?" he asked. "That I'm a man who would murder his own sister?"

My mind was numb with shock. "I—"

Without waiting for an answer, Fitz stood, offering me his hand. But when I took it, wrenching myself to my feet, I noticed the way his expression had shuttered. His cold mask had fallen back into place.

Tucking Grace protectively against his body, Holden cast a glance over his shoulder. "Perhaps we should retreat to the castle. We can discuss this matter there. These spirits look angry."

I shivered. "They're probably growing restless because of Fitz's magic."

Fitz's eyes cut to me. "I called off my magic," he said pointedly.

I lifted my hands, my fingers trembling and my pulse thundering in my ears, matching the rumble building in the low-swirling clouds. Flashes of lightning illuminated the shadowy forest and the countless ghosts creeping forward, drawn by my uncontrolled display. "How do I call it off?"

"Remember our lessons," Fitz said, not meeting my gaze. "Feel the way your thoughts and emotions are connected to the storm. You can command it again."

Sucking in a fortifying breath, I ignored the sounds of angry spirits stalking toward us, tuned out Kinsey and Holden's cries as they fended against them, and quieted my raging emotions. Electricity made the hairs on the back of my neck stand up, made the air taste acrid. I couldn't let my magic strike those I cared about, so I reached out, my mind guiding the lightning to lash instead at the threatening spirits, driving them back. They couldn't be killed, but they could be frightened and reminded of what it was to hurt.

At last, I forced the clouds to melt away and the thunder to quiet.

Kinsey darted toward us, Holden and a pale-faced Grace on his heels. "Back to the castle, before the ghosts return."

"Elle?" A familiar voice echoed among the trees, piercing the sudden stillness.

My heart slammed into my chest so hard it hurt. A figure stepped forward haltingly, one bad leg making his gait slow and unnatural. One arm hung limply, tucked close to his side. Blood and dirt smeared his face, and I knew the killing blow—a gash to the back of his head—was the cause of all that gore. But beneath it, his warm brown eyes and salt-dusted hair and beard were the same. His gentle, loving smile was identical to the one he'd given me so many times during his life.

"Father?" I whispered, hesitating.

Despite the awkwardness between us, Fitz noticed my uncertainty and met my gaze. "It's him."

That was all I needed to hear before I threw myself forward, winding my arms around Father and pulling him into a fierce embrace. Blood dripped from his head onto my arms, a constant, awful reminder of how he'd passed away, but it didn't keep me from holding him closely. "You're here," I choked out between sobs. "Father, I've missed you so much."

Father smoothed back my hair, cradling me with his good arm. Even in death, with his body ruined and the warmth emanating from him merely an illusion, a memory, I felt safe. "I've missed you too, my sweet girl."

I pulled back, memorizing his expression, focusing on the parts of him that remained unchanged.

Grace approached more slowly, her voice tremulous from the tears already coursing down her cheeks. She swallowed, her eyes lingering on his awful wounds. "Father?"

"It's me, child," he said, tugging her into a hug. Like me, she didn't balk at the gore, too overwhelmed to be near him again to let the morbid signs of his death stop her. "I feared so much for you, but it seems you're safe. What you've done, Elle..." Father's eyes flicked between Fitz and me. "Your magic is magnificent."

I wiped my tears, blinking as more gathered in my lashes. The pride shining in his eyes nearly broke my heart all over again.

Father's eyes darkened, like he was trying to recall something. "I've wandered for what feels like so long," he confessed, voice distant. "I'd hoped I could find and warn you." His eyes landed on my neck, tracing my throat where Fayette's gifted necklace hung. "The locket—where did you put it, Elle?"

"I gave it to Isabel."

Father frowned. "I lied to you, Elle. I'm so sorry. The locket wasn't gifted to our ancestors. I purchased it from a stranger in the underground network at Fletcher's. I didn't want you to fear about a black market piece, didn't want your mother to fret, so I told that story. As you know, I'd hoped the locket's magic would grant us great power to glamour so we could avoid the law and allow you and your sisters to keep our estate. I'd foolishly hoped to find a way out of our fae bargain, and I'm afraid in the process I became greedy for magic and power." He swallowed. "I didn't want to sell that locket, not even when Mr. Reid begged me for it. He understood our need, but he seemed desperate too."

Icy dread clawed at my chest. "Reid asked for the locket?"

Father seized my arm, his expression frantic. "I remember more now: what I needed to tell you. Stay away from him, Elle. Stay away, all of you. It happened after he and I argued about the locket—I was riding into town on business when I was killed. But it wasn't an accident. My horse didn't throw me without reason. I encountered Reid, and he startled us on purpose, charging at me with his own mount. That was why I fell. He—he murdered me."

I swayed on my feet. Our trusted friend had killed my father. All this time, I'd believed him when he offered condolences and sympathy, when he promised to protect my family in this strange place. But *he* was the reason we were here. And he must have known one of us would bring Father's locket. He'd remained close to me, perhaps biding his time until he could make *my* death look like an accident, or hoping to find a moment to steal it.

"What?" I breathed, my mind trying to comprehend Father's words.

"It wasn't an accident," Father repeated.

My eyes stung as Grace met my gaze, her own face pale with horror.

If Reid had known about the locket, that also meant he was probably the one to murder Cordelia for it. Perhaps afterward, he'd had to hide to avoid being discovered, and someone else had taken it from Cordelia's body before Reid could return. The thief, realizing it wouldn't open or respond to him, had gone on to sell it to Father. Reid must have tracked it down, or perhaps Father had shown it to Reid in confidence, hoping that a friend who'd grown up in Brytwilde could help puzzle out how to wield its magic.

But Cordelia's trust—my Father's trust—*my* trust—it had brought us all betrayal. Reid had fooled and used us.

Worst of all, I'd thrown away my growing closeness with Fitz by accusing him, and had instead chosen to rely on Reid for my family's protection. And I'd sent the locket with him.

My heart froze. "Isabel," I rasped.

CHAPTER TWENTY-SIX

My horse's hooves pounded in a swift rhythm along the narrow dirt road, chasing after Fitz's black stallion. Holden rode beside me with Grace, while Kinsey took up the rear. Each of the fae men remained alert, eyeing the forest for restless spirits. With my dress tied up so I could sit securely in the saddle, I easily kept up with Fitz's relentless pace.

Though Father's body was warm and solid behind mine, his chest never stirred with breath, a reminder that he wasn't returned to me, not truly.

"Please let them be all right," I muttered. Tears that weren't only from the cold, misty night burned my eyes.

"It's not your fault," Father reassured me, but that didn't loosen the knot of terror building in my chest as I imagined all the horrible possibilities.

His expression still distant, Fitz had, nevertheless, sprang into action immediately. He'd claimed that his magical connection to the spirits, even if it was weak, would also allow him to sense where Cordelia's locket—with her magic's powerful tie to the ghosts—was located. Anxiety clawed at my chest as I prayed and hoped that he was right.

Reid had promised he would secure Mother and my sisters in a cabin messengers used during their trips through the treacherous forest, but now I knew better than to trust his word. Based on the winding path Fitz was following, though, that might have been one of the few truths Reid had told.

A bloodied, emaciated form emerged from the darkness. With unnaturally quick movements, the spirit leapt toward the horse bearing Holden and my sister. Grace screamed, and Holden lifted a hand. The air crackled as tree roots twined around the ghost, dragging him back into the forest. Behind us, Kinsey shouted, and Holden spun in the saddle, summoning more help from the earth to push back another restless, angry soul.

Despite the mist slithering through the trees, enshrouding the dark wood in its clammy chill, sweat beaded on my forehead as I dug my heels into my gelding, urging him forward. I couldn't stop picturing other vengeful ghosts attacking my family while Reid stood by gleefully, happily waiting for my loved ones to be slaughtered and claiming the locket for himself.

Finally, a cabin emerged from the shadows. It was a simple dwelling, its windows emitting no light and giving no hint as to whether it was occupied. I couldn't see any sign of the coach they'd taken, but with the fog, it was difficult to see far beyond the building itself. Everything was quiet, like the very trees were holding their breath as they bore witness to this moment.

Fitz slowed his beast, glancing over his shoulder to meet my eyes. "Here," he announced.

He, Holden, and Kinsey reached for their blades, steel shrieking in the heavy stillness.

Without warning, an arrow sang through the air, narrowly missing Fitz. It struck the trunk behind him, its emerald and onyx feathers vivid in the darkness.

"Ravenheart," the prince snarled, his eyes alighting with feral anger.

Fitz charged his steed in the direction the arrow had come from, black clouds writhing around him. I gritted my teeth and let my magic join his, adding to the rage of the brewing storm. Lightning flashed and thunder rumbled, shattering the silence. From within the cabin, a shriek was nearly drowned out by our storm.

"Isabel!" I screamed in answer, both relieved and terrified.

Drawing my dagger, I dropped from my horse.

"Elle, wait! This is an ambush," Father warned as he dismounted. He seized my wrist, surprising me with his strength. This close to the locket Isabel wore, his figure appeared sharper, his leg and arm no longer misshapen and broken. The blood staining his face and hair—and that awful, fatal gash in the back of his head—had disappeared. Just like Cordelia, Father was looking more life-like.

I whirled to survey the clash of swords and magic as several fae emerged from the shadows, attempting to swarm Fitz and Kinsey. Fitz was locked in a fight with a Ravenheart that wielded air magic powerful enough to redirect Fitz's electricity. Lightning struck trees, setting the bark ablaze and casting the clearing in a garish, fiery glow. Smoke expanded, mingling with the mist in an otherworldly display.

Another arrow almost struck Kinsey in the shoulder. Startled, his horse reared, dropping him and leaving him vulnerable as a Ravenheart woman charged.

"No," I bit out as she leered over my friend, her palm poised above his chest as if only a touch could harm him.

Holden shouted and the earth cracked open, roots and vines tangling about the woman's legs and dragging her into the darkness. She shrieked and thrashed, attempting to use whatever power she possessed to neutralize Holden's magic, but we were in Ashwood and it was autumn. Her abilities were no match for the strength Holden possessed.

Fitz finished off the fae he'd been fighting, the stench of burnt flesh singeing the air.

"Come on," I urged, taking Father's hand and pulling him toward the cabin. "They have the Ravenhearts distracted, and Holden won't let anything happen to Grace."

"There may be more soldiers waiting for us in the cabin," Father pointed out, ever the logical planner.

But I grinned, lifting my dagger and letting my magic flow through me until electricity flared along the blade itself. For my family, I would face anything, endure anything, become anything. I'd already proven that by deceiving the fae, marrying their prince, and braving the wood and its spirits. I'd slain a phouka and survived. Between the possibility of losing another loved one or facing the darkness of this world, I would choose the darkness every time. Grief had forged me into something indomitable and unafraid of anything but the horror of grief itself.

The rush of wind and cacophony of thunder blocked out any further sounds from within the cabin as Father and I circled around to its back door. As I fumbled with the knob, my breath fogged the air, a chilly breeze kissing my temples. I repressed a shiver, wrenching the groaning door open and stumbling into a dark interior.

My heart throbbed in my throat so violently I could scarcely breathe, and in the blackness, I struggled to see more than shifting shapes and smudges. The electricity that had danced on my blade winked out, so I gritted my teeth and summoned it again, preparing myself for whatever sight awaited.

"Mother? Isabel?"

A thud. A scream. My focus on my magic wavered, but I tried again. Clouds gathered, damp and wild, swirling around me. Restless, forked tongues of lightning flashed within them, illuminating a large sitting room. One of the armchairs near the unlit hearth lay toppled on its side. Ravenheart soldiers restrained Mother, Bridget, and Maggie, whose mouths were gagged, their eyes wild. As soon as their gazes locked on me—and then on Father—they fought to speak, but only managed muffled sounds.

On a side table nearby rested a row of bottles and wineglasses, all but one filled with fae wine. My stomach churned with revulsion. It appeared the fae were eager to celebrate as soon as they finished murdering my family.

"Welcome, Princess," one of the Ravenheart men called. He was clothed all in green, setting off his olive skin and sharp black eyes that bored into my soul. "How kind of you to bring the Ashwood princes with you."

I narrowed my eyes. "You're a fool to attack us at the height of autumn."

His face twisted in an unpleasant grin. "Our powers aren't limited to summer's strength. After all, summer is all about the vitality and prime of life. We've learned how to harvest life, and that feeds our magic."

Father stepped up beside me. "Release my family," he snapped, his voice trembling with rage. In life, he'd never been intimidating; he'd loved his peaceful, slow existence, seeking knowledge and time spent with his loved ones. But now? Now his gaze was fierce, something that promised pain for anyone who threatened his wife and daughters.

But Reid and Isabel weren't anywhere to be seen, and that sent a chill through me.

"Where's Isabel?" Father asked, fear seeping into his tone.

My eyes roved over the space, settling on an open door leading into a bedroom just as Reid emerged, dragging a struggling Isabel by her hair. She kicked and writhed, doing everything in her power to pry herself from his grip. The locket still hung from her neck.

I drew a deep breath, my fears easing, if only a little. They were all alive. For now.

Reid's gaze fastened on mine, and he had the audacity to smile. "You found your magic."

I stepped forward, enunciating my words. "Release my family."

There was a blur of movement as Isabel took advantage of Reid's distraction, but she didn't try to race out of his grip. Instead, she dove for the table of wine, seizing the nearest glass of golden liquid and breaking it against his face.

He cried out in surprise as glass shattered and wine trickled down his face. It coated his lips, staining them gold. With a grimace, he wiped at his bloodied face and mouth, spitting on the floor in disgust.

Would just a small taste of fae wine be enough to affect him?

Snarling, Reid yanked Isabel against him, twisting her arms behind her back. "What gives you, the Blackfords, the right to infinite magical power?" he demanded, his expression darkening as he scanned Father's ghost. Some of the fight had left Isabel, her cheeks smeared with tears. "What need do you have of this locket, when your family already possesses the might of the Ashwood magic through marriage?"

"Tell me why you wanted Cordelia's locket," I insisted, noting the way Reid's pupils had dilated. The fae wine was taking effect, and I hoped my command would be difficult for him to ignore.

Reid's eyes flicked to the Ravenhearts gathered in the sitting room, each one unintimidated by my magical display. Each one wearing an insufferable, arrogant smirk. "For this locket, they'll grant me immortality. No more being powerless among the fae, or magicless among the strong."

"So you killed for it?" I demanded, voice rising. "Tell me everything. *Now.*"

"Yes, it's rightfully mine. I spent months seducing Cordelia for it, only for her to deny me when I asked. She claimed to love me, yet she couldn't trust me. Couldn't give up something so small so I could live forever. Everyone called her kind and generous, but I saw what she really was. Another corrupt immortal. *Selfish.*"

I repressed a shudder. Like it had done to me, the fae wine had swiftly abolished all of Reid's inhibitions, and he seemed eager to brag about his deeds.

Reid didn't stop. "Killing her was satisfying—until I was interrupted. I heard someone coming and had to hide, had to watch Finley stumble upon the body and steal her locket. I would have stopped him, but there were more footsteps. That's when the guards discovered Cordelia. I wasted time hiding from them. It took me months to track Finley down, the coward. He'd been hiding in the human world. When he couldn't open the locket, he'd decided to sell it for money, but he'd been too afraid after his theft to return to Brytwilde for a good, long while."

"You killed him too?" I asked. How had we been so deceived in this man?

Reid sneered. "Yes, and killing him was gratifying too, though he refused to tell me who'd purchased the locket. Claimed he didn't know. I left his body near where I'd killed Cordelia, because it felt right somehow, for the ones who stood in my way to die in the same place. And then..." Reid sucked in a deep breath, a vein pulsing in his neck. "I had to see your blasted father brag about his new purchase. Knowing it was *mine*. And then he refused to give me the locket, even though he pretended to be a friend. So yes, I orchestrated his death, making it look like it was an accident. But of course the day I killed him was the day he wasn't wearing his locket, and I had to wait for you to bring it to Ashwood, had to wait for a chance to take it when Fitz wouldn't find me out."

Thunder rattled the windows, and my lightning crackled dangerously. I was done with his explanations, done with hearing his awful story. All this time we had trusted him, and he had taken my father away. He'd ruined our lives, all for his greed.

My voice rose almost to a scream. *"What gives you the right to murder my family?"*

Chaos erupted. Reid drew a dagger, plunging it toward Isabel's chest. She managed to wriggle free just in time, dropping to the floor. Father lurched forward and I screamed, throwing my palm out and hurling electricity in a burning arc that missed Reid by a hair. Instead, it slammed into the wall behind him, charring wood and filling the air with acrid, blinding smoke.

As one, the Ravenhearts moved, two throwing Maggie and Mother down without care, rushing for the sister who carried the magic they craved. The third turned on Bridget, raising a hand over her heart the way the woman outside had done to Kinsey. Bridget thrashed, crying out in pain through her gag.

With my mind split in two, terrified for both my sisters, my magic snuffed out. The room was immersed in darkness.

"Elle! Go to Bridget!" Father shouted, still charging for Reid and Isabel.

Drawing a breath, I squeezed my eyes shut and imagined Fitz by the pond, advising me in the use of magic. I tasted the energy of a storm, felt the kiss of the wind, and heard the tumultuous thunder. When I opened my eyes, electricity twisted and danced around my fingers, flooding the room with sparks of light.

"Step back," I commanded, striding toward the Ravenheart man attacking my sister.

The man was too focused, too entranced in his task. Sweat beaded on Bridget's brow, and tears streaked down her cheeks as she whimpered.

I didn't hesitate. This time, my magic struck true. The man slammed backward, landing with a crash on the floor, his limbs jerking while he screamed. A metallic tang mingled with the taste of smoke in my mouth, but I refused to look away from what I'd done to protect my sister. When the man finally stilled, I released my magic, only holding onto enough to light my path toward Bridget. She swayed on her feet, wiping at her eyes and untying the gag.

"Are you all right?" I asked, my gaze sliding over her form, searching for bruises or blood.

Panting, she nodded, glancing over my shoulder toward another crashing sound. I whirled to see a woman overtaking Father, slamming a blade into his side. Even though I knew he was already dead and couldn't be wounded again, the sight made my heart twist. He stumbled away, biting back a groan. Nearby, the other fae lay in a pool of blood.

Father must have wrested Reid's blade from him. Reid himself bled from a wound in his side, but it was a shallow cut, and it didn't impede his movements as he struck at my sister. Isabel kicked and fought bravely, but she was no match for the man we'd once called friend. He knocked Isabel to the floor, his hands closing around her neck.

"Don't you dare!" I cried, my boots skidding across the floorboards as I ran. In one hand, I clutched the dagger Reid had gifted me, while in the other, I summoned more magic, until clouds and wind and rain and lightning raged around me. I was a storm. Irresistible. Unstoppable.

Just before I reached them, a form appeared at Reid's side. There was a flash of blonde hair and a pale, lovely face. Cordelia.

Though the last surviving Ravenheart shouted a warning, Reid was too engrossed in his attack, his knuckles blanching white as Isabel's face turned red. The Ravenheart lunged for Cordelia, hand reaching for her chest, perhaps hoping the memory of whatever pain she could inflict would be enough to stop the spirit. But Cordelia was unfazed. She seized Reid's shoulders and shoved him with supernatural strength, forcing him between the Ravenheart and herself.

The Ravenheart's eyes widened in shock, but apparently it was too late for whatever magic she'd called upon to be stopped. Reid's scream shredded the air, hoarse and raw and agonized. Blood blossomed across his chest, staining his navy messenger uniform. His face froze and his strangled cry cut off abruptly as a gaping hole appeared in his chest and a scarlet lump splattered to the floor.

Bile filled my mouth. *His heart.*

Reid's body crumpled, and Cordelia tossed it unceremoniously aside. She lifted her chin in defiance at the Ravenheart before her, whose face was splattered in her companion's blood, her body shaking in shock and fear and fury.

"You will not threaten my family again," Father declared, rising from where he'd fallen. Silver flashed as he lifted the dagger he'd stolen from Reid and plunged it into the final Ravenheart's chest. The woman froze for a moment, choking for breath, before she slumped to the floor in a pool of her own blood.

As suddenly as the fighting had begun, it was over.

"Isabel!" Father cried, the first to reach her and help her to her feet. Isabel sucked in air greedily.

"Oh, Father," she cried, throwing her arms around him and weeping.

My eyes snagged on Cordelia's, a wistful smile flitting over her face.

"Thank you," I breathed.

"I—I remember now," Cordelia said, studying Reid's form with a far-off look in her eyes. "James Reid was my lover. I knew Mother wouldn't be thrilled to see me with a lowly human messenger, so we'd kept it all a secret." She laughed bitterly. "I trusted him." She shook her head, wiping at her eyes. When she lifted her face to meet my stare, her expression hardened. "I'm glad I was able to stop him. I'm glad he didn't take your sister, too."

The door creaked open, and Fitz, Holden, and Kinsey charged inside, blades dripping blood and eyes wildly scanning the cabin.

"Grace, it's safe!" Holden called, and my sister crept inside. She raced to Mother and Maggie and Bridget, hugging them each in turn.

Fitz swallowed the distance between us, seizing my hands and scanning me for injuries. "Are you all right? Is your family?"

I nodded. For a moment, my guilt and uncertainty over how I'd accused and attacked him were gone, consumed by my relief that he was all right. That he still cared enough to check on me.

Then a muscle jumped in Fitz's jaw, and he released my hands, stepping back. That unreadable mask was back in place, making it impossible for me to know his thoughts. I wanted to apologize, but the words stuck in my throat. Instead, I added, "Thanks to your sister," and gestured to Cordelia.

She stood hugging herself, looking small and vulnerable as she watched her brothers.

Holden stumbled forward, tossing his blade to the floor. "Cora?"

"Are you mad at me for hiding from you?" she asked tremulously. "I'm so sorry. I was frightened and confused, and I'd forgotten so much about my life. Everything was hazy. I'm only just now beginning to remember more."

"Mad?" Holden cried. "Not at all. We've missed you."

"We could never be mad at you," Fitz affirmed. "Though I'm afraid I made you think I was when we argued. I promise you, I was only insecure and frightened of my own responsibilities. *Never* angry with you. I've only ever loved you, little sister."

With a stifled sob, Cordelia threw herself at her brothers, embracing them both in a tearful hug.

Mother took my hand, threading her fingers through mine. Her voice trembled. "Your father. Elle, you found him."

At those words, Father and Isabel turned. There were many stifled sobs and glistening eyes as he hugged each of us, murmuring about how he loved us and how glad he was that we were safe.

"We miss you," Grace said.

"We've been so lost without you," Bridget added.

Mother seemed unable to speak, too shaken with tears she couldn't stop.

Father studied us, his eyes misty and his brow furrowed. "I'm afraid I failed you. I've spent so much time thinking of all the things I wished I could say to you." He patted Grace's hand. "When your mother and I continued to have only daughters and never a son, we started to fear. We loved you dearly, but we also knew the dangers you'd be in, since my closest male relative would inherit everything we owned. My cousin has always been self-absorbed and proud, so we knew we couldn't rely upon his generosity when I died."

Father sighed. "Maybe your mother and I were proud too, to agree to a fae bargain rather than request help from our neighbors. Queen Griselda made generous promises, and your mother and I were convinced by her honeyed words. I should have fought harder to find a better way."

He bowed his head, and when I tried to speak, he lifted a hand, cutting me off. "Please, Elle. You don't know how this has weighed on me." Father turned to Grace, his eyes warm and intent. "You are kind and selfless, and I am in awe of the woman you've become. The ways in which you never swayed in your resolve to sacrifice for your family is admirable, and I am ashamed I ever felt the need to ask so much of you. I cannot tell you the thousands of times your mother and I wished we could sacrifice ourselves rather than risk seeing you suffer. It was our greatest grief and failure."

"Father—" Grace started, but he shook his head, stepping toward me and plunging on.

"Elle, your strength and care for your family is without measure. I know your mother and sisters are safe within your capable hands. You are far braver than I could have ever hoped to be, and I am so proud of you."

He approached Maggie, cradling her face in his calloused hands. "Sweet, wise child. I hope you never lose your thirst for knowledge, that you are always curious and in love with the inner workings of this world. But do not lose yourself so much in learning, as I did, that you forget to live and experience the things you read about."

Maggie blinked, brushing away a tear.

"Lydia, my love," Father murmured, pulling Mother into an embrace and whispering words meant only for her. When Mother drew back, her tears had stopped, giving way to a tremulous smile.

At last, Father turned to Isabel and Bridget, grasping their hands. "You are both so young, but I see you have much spirit and fight in you. Please continue to laugh and find the joy and lightness and humor in life. Heed your older sisters, and do not be so carefree that you forget to be cautious." He pressed a kiss to each of their foreheads.

"Father," I said as he stepped back, looking weary yet at peace. "I took Grace's place to save you." I was conscious of Fitz coming to my side, of his quick glance, but I didn't turn from my father and his relieved expression.

He stood a little taller, as if years of exhaustion and sorrow had melted away. "I'm here to find a way to bring you back."

To my surprise, Fitz reached for my hand, twining his fingers with mine. "It's...not possible." His voice was heartbreakingly tender.

I glanced between my husband and my father, a slow sense of horror and grief washing over me. The resignation on Father's face gave me a terrible feeling that he knew what Fitz meant, and that more than anything tore a hole in my chest. "What do you mean?"

"All the magic in the world cannot bring a mortal back. Necromancy only works on immortal souls who were taken before their time, because they're gifted with such long life and are imbued with magic that tethers them to the land. My magic can call to the magic that lingers in their souls."

Tears burned my eyes. "Are you saying there's no hope? Nothing at all can be done?"

"I'm so sorry." Fitz's expression was haunted, and I tore my hand from his. He flinched. "If I'd realized you knew about necromancy and had come to rescue your father, I would have explained long ago..." he continued. "But it's been such a carefully kept secret among Ashwoods for generations. As far as I know, no other fae are aware of this power. It would cause even more strife, more greed to possess our magic."

Desperation clawed at me. All my plans, all my dreams, all my hopes—they'd been for nothing. "There has to be *something*." I glanced around at my family, taking in their tear-filled eyes and expressions of grief and acceptance. No one but Grace had even known or guessed my plans. Most of them had probably never heard of necromancy, since Father and I had kept our underground dealings and illegal studies so secretive. They'd only ever expected a few more moments with Father, one last chance at goodbye.

"Elle, my child," Father said, cradling my hands in his. "It's going to be all right."

"No," I said, choking back the sob tearing at my throat. "No, Reid cannot win. His betrayal can't mean the end. It's not fair. It wasn't *your* time either. We need you. I can't live without you."

Father placed a hand against my cheek, wiping away a tear and peering intently into my eyes. "You already *are* living without me. Look at you." He glanced toward Fitz. "You're safe and happy." He looked at Holden, who'd approached Grace, wrapping his arms around her as she wept. "You are thriving, even despite my failings. You are home. And you possess powerful magic we once only dreamed about. You will never again want for anything, and there is nothing left for you to fear."

I fear a life without you, I thought, but couldn't say aloud.

I threw my arms around Father, hugging him as if my sheer willpower could hold him back from leaving for the afterlife.

"And," he added, "you will always carry your memories."

This time, I couldn't stifle my sob. "I cannot live on mere memories of love."

Father's arms tightened around me, warm and secure, just as I remembered. "Then live in the love you have found here. Hold our family together, Elle. I'll be waiting for you." Slowly, he stepped back, lifting his chin and meeting Fitz's gaze. "I am ready."

Fitz sighed. "So am I." Determination lit his gaze, and his eyes darted to Cordelia, who smiled at him. "Cora didn't die because of me, and I won't let my guilt and pain hold me back from wielding my rightful magic, not any longer. I can send you on, Mr. Blackford."

Father dipped his head. "Thank you."

I swallowed my tears as Fitz gave the command, allowing Father's soul peace in the beyond. His smile was warm as his spirit began to lose its solid appearance, growing misty about the edges, wavering for a moment, and then vanishing altogether.

He was gone. I'd lost him all over again.

CHAPTER TWENTY-SEVEN

Reid had left the coach and horses in the stables near the cabin. While Fitz climbed into the driver's seat, Holden joined my family and me inside. Meanwhile, Kinscy reined our horses together and went ahead. I'd lost sight of Cordelia after everything, and in my all-consuming sorrow, hadn't given much thought to where she'd gone.

Numb, I slumped against the seat, recalling Fitz and Holden's earlier quiet discussion. In those hazy minutes before we'd left the cabin, the brothers had stood together, talking over the possibility of war between Ashwood and Ravenheart.

"We'll send some of our warriors to clean up this cabin and search the bodies," Fitz had said, surveying the space with disgust. "See if anything hints at these Ravenhearts being more than rogues."

"I don't think the royal family was involved," Holden had pointed out. "None of them were here tonight, and this move was..."

"Ill-conceived? Foolhardy?" Fitz supplied.

"Yes," Holden said. "Why would the Ravenheart family risk all-out war at the height of autumn over a single charm?"

Fitz was quiet a moment. "If the royal family was involved, they wouldn't make it apparent. They'll claim innocence, when perhaps all along they'd secretly backed this rogue movement, hoping they'd miraculously kill off most of our family. Either way, I hope this is the end of it, though it makes me wonder what will come this summer."

Returning to the present, I sighed, glancing to the seat across from me, where Holden wrapped his arm around Grace. She leaned into him, resting her head on his shoulder. My heart ached at the sight. While we were back in the cabin, I'd been too afraid to try to reach out to Fitz, who hadn't offered his hand again after I'd pulled mine away. Surely, after my accusations and attack, he hated me. His declarations of love seemed so distant now. I'd ruined everything.

As if sensing my distress, Mother rested her hand over mine, cradling it gently. On my opposite side, Isabel and Bridget huddled together, exhausted, while Maggie, on the seat with Holden and Grace, rested against the window, her gaze distant. None of us had the energy or desire to speak, but we took comfort in one another's presence in our grief.

When we arrived at the castle, Holden escorted my mother and sisters toward their rooms, while Fitz and I paused, silent and awkward, outside the doors to our own separate quarters.

Fitz's shoulders slumped. "I—" He cleared his throat. "Do you want to be alone?"

My throat was dry, and a headache throbbed at my temples. Fitz still wasn't looking at me, and though only a foot or so separated us, the distance felt enormous. Insurmountable.

Surely he would send my family and me away after what I'd done. My accusing him of murder and attacking him was probably enough to destroy our bargain and our marriage vows. He'd send us back to the mortal world, with no home, no income, nothing to survive upon.

Or if he did not, he would become cold and indifferent toward me again. Our marriage would be bereft of his smile, his touches, his conversation. Fresh tears burned my eyes.

I hadn't realized until now, when I was on the cusp of losing it, how much Fitz's admiration had meant to me. How much *he* meant to me.

Afraid to answer his question directly and be rejected, I responded with my own. "Do *you* want to be alone?" The words came out harsher than I'd meant them.

Fitz leaned against his door, finally turning to me. His eyes searched mine, and I thought I detected fear and sadness in his expression. "No," he whispered at last. "I do not."

For a moment, I stared at him, uncertain. "I don't want to either," I confessed. A tear escaped and slid down my cheek.

Stepping forward, Fitz cupped my face in his hands and brushed my tear away with his thumb. He tipped his head toward his door. "Do you want to stay here tonight?"

Too overcome for words, I nodded.

Fitz opened the door and guided me into his quarters.

"I'm sorry," I blurted out as soon as the door clicked shut behind us. "When I saw the button, I panicked. I hoped I was wrong, but then we found Finley's body and..." I swallowed against the dryness of my throat, my excuses trailing away.

Fitz pulled me into his arms, tucking my head beneath his. "Tonight isn't the time for this conversation," he murmured. "Not when you're grieving."

"But..." I began. Wasn't he angry? Didn't he hate me?

He cut me off. "I'm here. As long as you need me." Gently, he stepped back and pulled me toward the bedroom. "You need rest. Especially after using so much magic, you have to be exhausted."

Fitz rang the bell for Lina and then started a fire himself, seating me in an armchair near the hearth. When my maid arrived, he left long enough for her to help me bathe and dress in private, thankfully not prying when she saw my tears. Perhaps she recognized the look of someone who was lost in grief that words couldn't explain. Lina settled me into bed, wrapping me in a thick blanket and leaving just as Fitz returned with a cup of tea. I managed to sip a few mouthfuls before dissolving into tears again. I was overcome, my chest aching with loss and my mind full of the words Father had said before we'd been parted for good.

Silently, Fitz climbed into bed, twining his arms around me.

I opened my mouth to speak, but he tucked my hair behind my ear and shook his head. "Tomorrow. We'll speak tomorrow."

There was much more I needed to say, but after wielding my magic and shedding so many tears, I was as weary as Fitz had expected. Tomorrow, I would find the words to tell Fitz what he meant to me, how thankful I was that he was here when he had every reason to run from me. Tomorrow, I'd beg him to forgive me.

I drifted into sleep, secure in Fitz's arms.

When I lifted my head the next morning, it pounded nearly as badly as it had after I'd been drugged with fae wine, and my eyes were gritty from the tears I'd shed. Last night, they'd seemed endless, but now, I was hollow, unable even to grieve.

I turned, seeing Fitz stirring, his arms tightening protectively around me. My heart lurched, and I felt like the most selfish person in the world as I remembered his sister. "Cordelia," I gasped. "What about her? Where is she?"

Fitz squinted against the light slipping through a gap between the curtains. "Isabel returned her locket to her."

I'd been so lost in my grief I hadn't seen, hadn't noticed what had happened between losing Father and stumbling out into the cool night to enter the coach.

"Can she be saved? Can you bring Cordelia back?" I asked.

A little bit of hope burned in my heart, the smallest ember against the chill of loss. If we could still save the princess, Reid wouldn't have won, not entirely. It wouldn't feel like I'd fought for nothing. Like a shard of redemption amidst all the other broken pieces of my life.

Fitz sat up. "I did," he said.

"What? And you're not with her right now?"

He searched my face, and for a moment I wondered if he would insist we discuss what we had avoided talking about last night. Instead, he seemed as eager to latch onto a new topic as I was. "She needed rest, and I had to be sure you were all right. Come, if you're up for it, I'd like you to meet her. *Properly*, in her living form."

At that moment, Lina knocked on the door. When Fitz called for her to come in, she strolled inside wheeling her breakfast cart and singing softly to herself. "Good morning," she said, her eyes shining when she saw Fitz and me. "I can't believe it—to see Princess Cordelia back..." Lina sniffled, blinking tears from her violet eyes. "It's wonderful."

As Fitz and I ate and Lina bustled around the room, straightening the bed, Fitz explained everything. Wearing her locket had given Cordelia even greater power, tying her to the land, her magic, and her life. She'd returned to the castle, where, as the place she'd both lived and died, necromancy had the greatest chance of working. While Lina had tended to me that night, Fitz and Holden had met with Cordelia in her old rooms. There, on Fitz's command, she had become fully corporeal, and her heart had started to beat.

"For all intents and purposes, she has a new body, one formed from the power of our land, the magic in my words, and the power in her blood. But it looks the same as her old one. *She* is the same." Fitz turned to me. "I found when the time came to focus my magic...it finally felt strong again." He exhaled, his eyes bright with hope and relief. "All this time, I was so consumed with grief and the sense that I'd failed my sister, I'd lost my tie to spirit magic. I'd ceased to believe in myself, and I couldn't access it at all. To not help the spirits move on, when generations of Ashwoods have been entrusted with that task? It was shameful. Now, I can be the crown prince my kingdom—and the mortal world—needs."

His smile was radiant, and I couldn't help but reach out to brush my hand over the stubble on his cheek, entranced by how beautiful he was when he was truly happy.

Fitz froze, drawing in a sharp breath. "Elle..." he began, and my heart leapt at the sound of my name on his lips. Hope fluttered inside me. He'd been kind to comfort me last night, but now...now I hoped he might forgive me. Might even still love me.

At that moment Lina returned from tidying the sitting room, and we jolted apart.

"I'm sorry to trouble you again," she said as she poked her head through the doorway. "But the queen has called for a grand celebration." Her eyes darted to me. "I'm to help you prepare, princess. I'll take you to your rooms, where your dress is waiting, so the prince can ready himself here and join his mother as soon as possible."

"Of course," Fitz said. He glanced at me. "I have much work to do anyway. The spirits have returned to the glade, where they belong, but that is only a semblance of the peace they deserve. Until the party, I'll need to visit the glade and begin sending those poor souls on. I'll introduce you to Cora officially at our celebration," he promised.

And I'll find the words to tell you how I feel and hope you can find it in your heart to forgive me, I silently vowed.

The celebration was held in the forest, within the same clearing where my marriage ceremony had taken place. Tiny sprites casting small globes of light fluttered among the falling crimson and gold leaves, circling in a glorious dance. Pixies danced among clusters of mushrooms, giggling and twirling like children, though I suspected some of their joy had more to do with the tiny goblets of wine in their hands. Garlands of ivy and flowers adorned the tree boughs encircling us, and long tables laden with delicacies tempted everyone.

I hesitated at the edge of the path, scanning the crowd for anyone I recognized—my family, Holden, Cordelia, or Fitz himself. At my side, Lina squeezed my arm. "You're a princess," she whispered. "Hold your head high and walk among your people like you belong. Because you *do*. The land has claimed you."

I'd explained everything that had happened as Lina had dressed me, and as soon as I'd disclosed the fact that my magic had manifested, she'd smiled smugly as if she'd known it would happen all along.

Glancing at her now, I arched a brow. Lina had clothed me in a gauzy, dusty blue dress overlaid with gold embroidery that flashed in the light and ran in patterns reminiscent of lightning bolts. She'd coiled my hair in a braided crown, adorning it with gold pins fashioned into the shapes of leaves and birds. She'd brushed my eyelids and cheekbones with gold powder. In essence, she had dressed me like an autumn princess: wearing her magic and connection to the land on full display.

"You already helped Cordelia prepare, didn't you? You were her maid before, after all."

Lina nodded, scrunching her forehead as if trying to understand where I was going with my change in topic. "She said she's willing to share me, and that I can tend to you both."

"And you ensured I was the last to arrive, didn't you?" I pressed.

Toying with one of her curls, Lina grinned deviously. Even she wore a finer dress than usual, prepared to join the celebration for the returned princess. "Of course. You must make an impression. Solidify in their minds who you are."

I stepped forward, concentrating until I felt a prickle of electricity raising the hairs on the back of my neck and making gooseflesh appear on my bare arms. Lightning flashed and twined about my fingers in a playful dance as I lifted them, letting my display of power wash me in its glow. Gasps and murmurs filled the glade as fae and humans noticed me, shuffling out of the way to create a path. Eyes full of awe and respect, love and hate, envy and pride bored into me, but I lifted my gaze until I met the gazes of the royal family gathered at the far end of the clearing.

Holden flashed me a warm, encouraging grin, and my lips twitched in response. Queen Griselda's eyes widened, burning with annoyance before her mouth curved into a begrudging smile of respect. But I only gave them cursory glances, my eyes darting to Cordelia, alive and well and laughing as she leaned on her eldest brother's arm and gestured for me to join them. Clothed in white, she was a vision, her radiant eyes and rosy cheeks making it clear she was unmistakably, miraculously alive.

My gaze lingered on Fitz, our stares locking. Though his expression was calm, bearing the usual mask he wore in public that I now knew had more to do with his reservations than his pride, I could detect the spark in his eyes. He drank in the sight of me greedily, and I nearly shivered in response.

I paused before the Ashwoods, putting out my magic and dipping my head to the queen. "I'm afraid I'm late." It was a statement, not an apology. I met her gaze unflinchingly, refusing to bow. Refusing to cower. Refusing to act contrite.

Queen Griselda studied me for a long, quiet moment. The entire clearing had gone silent, all whispers ceasing as they waited to see what their queen would do. "I suppose I have nothing to say to you, Princess," she said, gathering her skirts and dropping into a curtsey. "The land has chosen you, and I cannot go against the will of the land or its future queen. This celebration is not only for the return of my daughter, it seems, but also for you."

The crowd broke into uproarious applause, and music from unseen musicians tucked away among the trees swept on the breeze in a tantalizing, irresistible melody.

"Elle!" Cordelia cried, darting forward and leading Fitz by the arm. "It's good to see you clearly, and not from the hazy spirit world. We must join

the dance! And then I have so many things to tell you and thank you for."
She gave Fitz a mischievous smile. "That is, if my brother will share you for
a little while."

Fitz laughed. "Go on."

"I'm so sorry," Cordelia began as we stomped, clapped, and swayed to
the music, joining a large circle of courtiers. To my surprise and delight,
the motions greatly resembled a mortal dance. "I want to apologize to you
for so many things. Can we speak more freely after this dance?"

"Of course," I said.

I noticed Grace and Holden twirling nearby, and I caught my sister's eye.
She offered me a smile, even though it wobbled a little from the grief of last
night. Further down the circle, I was surprised to see Mother and Maggie
giggling alongside Isabel and Bridget, all looking fiercely hopeful despite
the dark circles beneath their eyes.

We had survived. We had seen Father and had been granted the chance
to share a goodbye. Despite our grief, we were determined to live, to soak
in our gratitude and joy that we were safe. Together.

As the dance came to an end, Cordelia drew me off to the sidelines,
under the shade of a tree. "I have so much to explain." She sighed. "In
my spirit form, everything was foggy and confusing. I couldn't remember
everything from my life, only that I had been betrayed and murdered. I was
terrified and lost, and I didn't know who to trust. I'm ashamed of how I
attacked you. I was so sure when I saw you wearing my locket that you had
been the one to kill me, and that you were conspiring against my brother.
I owe you countless apologies and all my gratitude."

"I forgive you," I blurted out, cutting the princess off before she could
continue. Her eyes glistened with tears.

"What?" she asked, startled.

"I forgive you," I said, my lips curving in a smile. "I don't know what it's
like to be a spirit, but I can understand your confusion. And if you don't
hold it against me for accusing your own brother of murdering you, I think
I can find it in myself to forgive you for your mistakes."

Cordelia's shoulders sank in relief as she loosed a laugh. "You did so
much for me. For us. Who knows what else Reid would have done or
how much more deeply his betrayals would have wounded us—and all of
Ashwood—without your help. I wouldn't even be here without you. And

Fitz...he adores you. He's told me so much about you already. It brings me so much joy to see what you've done for him."

I drew in a hopeful breath, trying to bask in Cordelia's words. Had he truly spoken so highly of me to his sister today, even after what I'd done? Surely Cordelia had to be mistaken. He couldn't still feel that way. "I haven't done anything for him," I protested. "I tried to steal from him, and I married him out of trickery. He's lost his immortality because of me. And then I accused him of murdering you! I'm sure by now he hates me."

Cordelia shook her head adamantly. "No, I explained to him how even I was confused by the button. Elle, I carried that button with me after Father died! It fell from *my* pocket when Reid murdered me. Fitz chose it as his new charm because it was so sentimental to him, and therefore especially powerful. It was his reminder of our father *and* me." She smiled sadly. "As for his immortality, he would have had to give it up anyway to ensure his human bride was his equal, powerful enough to rule alongside him. But now? With you? He is more carefree. He is more trusting and less guarded." She hesitated, her eyes dimming. "I wanted to say that I am forever grateful for the fact that you came here, but given the reason you had to move to Brytwilde, that sounds insensitive. I'm sorry for your loss, Elle. I'm sorry we couldn't bring back your father. I wish I could take away your pain the way that you took mine."

It was my turn to shake my head, tears blurring my vision. "You don't need to be sorry. It's not something you can change. He's at peace now."

It hurt to say the words, even though I knew they were true. Someday, I prayed, they would bring comfort rather than this aching chasm in my chest. Someday.

For now, I would smile and laugh and dance to numb the pain. I would live.

Cordelia and I returned to the dancing, and I took several turns with Grace, Bridget, and even my mother. At one point, Mother halted our steps to wrap her arms around me tightly, whispering in my ear. "I'm so proud of you." Overcome, I'd hugged her, dashing away my tears.

Throughout the day, I couldn't help the way my eyes wandered toward Fitz, over and over, hoping for a chance to talk to him. Each time my gaze latched onto the prince, I found him deep in conversation with various advisors and other members of the court. Now and then, Holden and Kinsey would join him, and sometimes the queen. I could only imagine the somber discussions that were taking place in the middle of our celebration, as Fitz explained the Ravenheart attack.

Though he and Holden had seemed confident that it hadn't been sanctioned by the royal family, I still knew it meant that Ashwood would have to be even more guarded come summertime. But no matter what Silverfrost, Willowbark, or Ravenheart threw against us, we would be ready. *I* would be ready to defend my kingdom and my family with my newfound magic.

One dance blurred into another, and soon I find myself spinning toward Isabel, twirling her around. "Are you all right?" I asked breathlessly, and she stopped dancing to wind her arms around me.

"Yes, thank you. Thank you for coming for me. Thank you for asking Cordelia to protect us."

"Of course," I said. "What else are older sisters for?"

I was surprised to see Isabel stifling a sob.

"I'm sorry," I went on. "I shouldn't have trusted Reid, and I should never have sent you with him."

She shook her head. "You couldn't have known. None of us could've known about what he did to father or to Princess Cordelia."

I brushed a strand of hair away from her teary face. "You were so brave, Izzy."

Isabel squeezed my hands. "I think we've had enough tears, wouldn't you agree?" She smiled. "I'm going to do as Father said, and embrace happiness with our family. For us. And for him. Let's keep dancing."

She pulled me into a new circle, and my eyes locked with Dahlia across from us. She winked. "I knew you would be a fine princess, and that the land would accept you," she called over the sounds of laughter and music. "Welcome, *officially*, to our court, Your Highness."

Hours of merriment passed, in which Cordelia helped me mingle with various courtiers, introducing me to important advisors and nobles who seemed far more inclined to greet me warmly now that I possessed magic. Even the goblins bowed deferentially. More than once, Cordelia, Holden, and Kinsey joined my family and me as we sat in the shade, sipping water to cool off from dancing and munching on sandwiches and scones, sugared berries and decadent pastries. Leaves and twigs clung to the skirts of my dress, but none of the fae seemed to mind. Many courtiers also sported leaves in their hair and dirt smudges on their clothes from lounging in the grass or sneaking into the forest to kiss their lovers in privacy. I blushed at the thought.

The day passed in a haze. As the sun began to set, vanishing behind the trees in a blaze of fiery gold and scarlet, I sat with Cordelia and my sisters. Now that Fitz was able to send the spirits on, there were no more wandering ghosts to trouble us. Today's celebration would last long into the night.

I scanned the party for Fitz, finding him already striding toward us. When he stopped in front of me, his gaze fastened on mine, intense and searching. "I'm afraid I've been far too busy with politics, when I'd much rather be celebrating with you." He extended his hand. "Would you care to dance?"

Pulse racing, I nodded, rising to accept his hand and let him lead me into the clearing, among the playful sprites and glowing twilight. The musicians began a soft song, so Fitz pulled me close, one hand resting firmly on my waist while the other clasped my hand, his calloused fingers threading through mine. For a while, neither of us spoke, and I wondered if he was savoring our nearness the way I was.

"Do you fear war with Ravenheart?" I asked, even though that wasn't what I really meant—or needed—to say.

"No," Fitz said. "We sent a messenger to them, but I expect the Ravenheart family will deny any involvement. Most likely they'll join us for a diplomatic visit in the wintertime to make amends and avoid all-out war." He smirked. "All part of the politics we engage in every year."

There was another pause as I gathered my words. "Don't you hate me?"

Fitz looked down, his brow furrowing. "Do you want me to hate you?"

I swallowed. "No. I would rather beg your forgiveness. I don't think you're the sort of man who would murder his sister. It's why I was so shocked and hurt when I confronted you. Words can't express my regret—"

Fitz's smile was grim. "From the beginning, I didn't give you much of a reason to trust me or my character."

"But you have," I insisted. "You've always kept your word and protected anyone in your care. You're honorable and sincere, and it was clear from our visit to Oakfell that your people love you. Even when I'd accused and attacked you, you defended me against that ghost. You still chose to help me save my family and then comfort me last night."

"I *was* angry at first," Fitz admitted. "But then I was hurt—terrified. I wondered if my earlier cruelties would make me lose you." He pulled away to peer into my face, reading my expression. "I would do anything for you, Elle. But I don't want you to feel obligated."

My brow scrunched in confusion. "What?"

"I understand why you married me, and why you forced yourself to be near me, even to...kiss me, when you hoped to help your father. This agreement between my mother and your parents was always unequal. The queen takes joy in preying upon the desperate, and though I had to sacrifice immortality to wed you, my circumstances are not the same as being forced into leaving your home the way you were. It might have felt like the only right choice, but I still *agreed* to this, knowing it was my responsibility. It is frowned upon to refuse to wed a mortal and risk never producing an heir, but agreeing was never necessary to my very survival."

"What are you saying?" I said again, heart beating faster.

"I'm saying I could talk to my mother. You need not stay in Ashwood." Fitz's eyes were dark and somber. "Or if she refused, I could sneak you and your family out. I have enough wealth to secure you a home in the mortal world and provide money your whole family could live upon."

My hand tightened on Fitz's shoulder, while my other trembled in his. "Is that what you want? Do you hope to send me away and be done with me?"

"Never," Fitz said fiercely. "I forgive you. I..." His throat worked. "What I want remains the same as before," he said at last. "What I want is what we agreed I shouldn't ever speak of again."

I hesitated, pausing so we were both motionless, heedless of the other couples swirling around us. Could he truly mean that? Did he really want me still?

"I think I would very much like for you to speak of it again."

Hope flared in Fitz's eyes. "I want *you*, Elle. I want your time and your smiles, your laughter and even your tears. I want your joy and your sorrow, your dreams and your nightmares." He lifted his hand from my waist to brush my cheek, sliding it back to tangle his fingers in my hair. When I didn't draw away, he leaned forward, lowering his voice to a murmur only I could hear. "I want a family with you only if *you* want one, not one built out of obligation and duty and fear of my mother's wrath. I want you as my queen, my bride, and my lover. And if I can earn it, I want every piece of your heart and soul, for you have already wholly claimed mine."

My throat was so tight with emotion I almost couldn't answer. "You have it," I whispered. "It wasn't a trick, that kiss. That's why I was so hurt when I feared...when I accused you. You already have my heart, Fitz."

Heedless of the crowd, Fitz lowered his mouth to mine, every caress of his lips tender yet consuming. When we finally pulled apart, we both laughed breathlessly, ignoring the applause from couples surrounding us. Though my grief made my heart ache with every beat, I clung to Father's parting words. *Live in the love you have found here.*

EPILOGUE

G race's footsteps sidled up softly beside me, and she laid a gentle hand on my arm. "Are you all right? Truly?"

Blinking back tears, I paused to look into her face. Mother and our other sisters had already retired to their rooms hours ago, and now, as night thickened around us, Grace and I were finally trekking back toward the castle with Cordelia, Fitz, and Holden. While the three siblings chatted together, Grace had taken the opportunity to check in with me.

"It will always hurt, losing Father," I murmured.

Grace nodded, her own eyes shimmering. Her gaze darted to Holden, Fitz, and then Cordelia before landing back on mine, a silent question in her eyes. She'd seen Fitz and me dancing and kissing earlier. She knew something was happening between us, though I probably wouldn't have a private moment with her to share everything until tomorrow.

Noticing we'd fallen behind, Fitz stopped, turning back to me.

I shot my sister a smile. "We'll talk more tomorrow," I promised.

"I suppose that's for the best," she said, stifling a yawn. "I'm sleepier than when you drugged me." She elbowed me in the side for emphasis.

Catching myself before I laughed, I thought of the nightsweet still hidden in my quarters. "I *did* agree to never drug you again."

Grace snorted. "Yes, yes, and as reassuring as that was after I cornered you about it," she said, her voice heavy with sarcasm, "I never made any promises about holding it against you."

I frowned, suddenly worried. "You said you forgave me."

Grinning wickedly, my sister nudged me again. "Yes, and I do, but that doesn't mean I can't tease and trouble you relentlessly about it for years to come."

Her laughter trailed me as I rolled my eyes and jogged ahead to catch Fitz's offered hand and stride through the castle doors. Once we'd all finished climbing the steps to our floor, I threw my sister one last look, pretending to be angry. "Goodnight, Grace," I called as she strolled down the hall toward her quarters. "Sleep deeply."

"Goodnight, Elle!" she said with a final laugh.

Cordelia kissed Fitz and Holden on the cheek, waved to Grace and me, and vanished into her own rooms. I wondered how tiring it was to experience one's first day back among the living in a real body after roaming the world as a ghost.

As Holden and Fitz exchanged quiet words about plans for political meetings for tomorrow, I hesitated outside the doors to Fitz's and my quarters. My palms had grown clammy and, despite our earlier words, I was suddenly plagued with uncertainty and nerves.

"Elle?"

I glanced up at Fitz's question, realizing we were alone save for the guards posted across the hall.

"Yes?" I asked, hoping my husband didn't notice the fear in my tone.

His eyes flicked between his door and me, reading my thoughts. "We don't have to…"

I spoke at the same time, cutting off his words. "Could I stay in your rooms tonight?"

Fitz stopped, dimple flashing. "So formal."

My cheeks flushed, but before I could try to find the words to respond, the prince had swung open his door, clasping my hand and leading me inside. As soon as the door clicked shut, my breath caught.

I spun to face Fitz anyway.

Studying my expression, he traced my cheek with gentle fingers. "You're nervous," he said, brow furrowing. "You don't need to be. I don't expect…"

"I want a proper wedding night." Again, I blurted out the words before Fitz could finish speaking. Instantly, my skin flushed hot and then cold, and I stepped back, embarrassed by my forwardness.

There was longing shimmering in Fitz's eyes, but he didn't move, remaining cautiously still. Once more, I was assaulted with doubt. He loved me, he wanted me, but maybe a part of him remained hurt and upset and wasn't ready to fully commit.

But before the swirling thoughts could grow into a storm, Fitz was there, cradling my face in his hands, trailing kisses over my cheeks and along my jaw. "Well, as my princess and future queen," he said, his voice rumbling through my own chest as he pulled me flush against him, "I suppose I must obey."

I laughed even as I shivered, relishing the warmth of his mouth as he claimed my lips. When Fitz pulled back, his gaze was full of love and need, so open and pure it made my heart swell. He planted another kiss at the corner of my mouth, and his tone turned teasing. "I am yours to command, Blackford."

THE END

Keep reading to learn more about the next book in the Fae of Brytwilde *series...*

Thank you so much for reading *Castle of Dusk and Shadows*! If you have a moment, please consider helping me out and leaving an honest review on Amazon.

A human outcast. A lone wolf shifter. And enemies bent on controlling them...
Sold to the fae, her only hope is to run.
But the cunning Silverfrost royals who seek her have never lost their prey.
Loosely inspired by Mansfield Park...
enter a Gothic reimagining of Jane Austen's story as you've never seen it before.

FORTRESS OF BLOOD AND POWER

A Fae of Brytwilde Novel

ACKNOWLEDGMENTS

Here we are, at the end of another book! As always, I have quite the list of people to thank.

Sheree, Tricia, Brittany, Kim, and Beth—thank you so much for being my alpha readers. Your feedback was integral to making *Castle* become what it is.

Emily and Rai—thank you for beta reading this book and offering additional early feedback. Your help and encouragement were invaluable.

To my friends Sheree and Malcolm for their endless support and English-major-style critique, thank you for having my back.

To my street team: Tricia, Rai, Kim, Courtney, Heidi, Meaghan, Hannah, Erin, Manda, Crissy, Lauren, and Taylor—thank you for always being there to hype up my books. And me. I appreciate you!

To my husband...thank you for bragging to others about me and my crazy fictional worlds. :)

To the One who gifted me with the ability to write: thank you for this passion that brings so much joy to myself and to others.

And finally, thank you to my readers. Whether you've been here from the beginning or this is your first book of mine, thanks for taking a chance on me and another story of my heart.

ABOUT THE AUTHOR

Rachel L. Schade was born on the first day of summer in a small town in Michigan. She attended The Ohio State University to learn how to write obnoxiously long papers, cite people who use big words, and discuss her passion: books. She has a great love for the color blue, sunshine, chocolate, and not folding her laundry. Currently she lives in Ohio with her husband and fur babies, and surrounds herself with books and coffee on a regular basis.

You can email Rachel at rachelschade@gmail.com, or find her on Facebook and Goodreads: Rachel L. Schade, and on Instagram and TikTok: @rachelschadeauthor.

www.rachelschadeauthor.com

Printed in Great Britain
by Amazon

21633416R00169